BETWEEN TWO *Fires*

TONI WILLIAMS

BETWEEN TWO FIRES

Toni Williams

1

Saturday, March 14, 2015

Bridget felt a rush of excitement as she watched him emerge through the arrivals lounge at the Elysian Island airport. He hadn't changed much - the same athletic build and rugged look. And those chiseled features - a strong jaw and firm forehead, a well-defined nose and bright, compelling eyes. *God, he looked so sexy.* She felt aroused, just by staring at him. His shoulder-length dreadlocks were jet-black and neat and he had a thin pencil-line beard and moustache.

She couldn't believe Rudy still had such a powerful effect on her. They hadn't been together for almost a year. The only thing about him that seemed different was his complexion. His fair skin had darkened slightly and now he looked almost ebony. Bridget resisted the urge to rush forward and embrace him, although it was a struggle. She could just imagine the shocked stares it would have garnered from the two customs officers hovering near the door, not to mention the three couples near her who were tossing their luggage into waiting SUVs. They had left the arrivals lounge ahead of Rudy, although their flight – a private jet - had arrived twenty minutes after Rudy's, a twin-engine Cessna. Unlike them, Rudy would have been held back at the arrivals desk for questioning and a baggage check, not least because of his dreadlocks. This was, after all, Elysian Island, the Caribbean island retreat which had become synonymous with the rarefied world of luxury; a place that counted among its residents billionaire investors, Hollywood celebrities and even members of some of the European royal families.

The three couples, all Americans, lived on Elysian Island and they were filthy rich, although looking at them no one would think so. The men wore worn-out jeans, T-shirts and sneakers and the women sported simple blouses and skirts, and worn-in walking shoes. They were Bridget's buddies and close friends of her husband, Lord Edward Henry Tennyson, 3rd Baron Alden of Castle Hill in Devonshire. Before driving off, they hugged and kissed her warmly.

Rudy stood waiting. On the ground next to him was a duffle-leather travel bag and a gym bag was slung over his shoulder. He looked so vulnerable standing there gazing all around him with curiosity, Bridget felt touched. On several occasions she'd seen similar expressions on visitors' faces as they set foot for the first time on the world's most famous paradise isle. She always got the impression that it was the airport's simplicity that surprised them. It had a two-storied, wooden aviation terminal with a central control tower and a one-lighted runway with no navigational aids. It was one of the few surviving examples of airport construction dating back to the early days of air passenger travel, and regarded by most people on the island as a cherished historical monument.

"Good day, Mr. Phillips, how are you?" said Bridget with feigned formality and a devilish glint in her eyes.

"Thrilled as ever to see you and I dare to presume that you are likewise," Rudy replied, smiling. He gazed at Bridget like a smitten teenager. She could tell he was yearning to hold her.

"Come, let's go," she said quickly and headed for the car park with Rudy in tow. "How was your flight?" she said, opening the boot of a steel-grey Hyundai SUV. "I know the weather in the U.K. has been awful."

"It was no better in Barbados. Fortunately my stopover was brief. It looks like the rain is heading this way," he said, pointing to an accumulation of dark clouds in the east.

"Did you encounter any issues with the immigration folks over here?"

"Nah! Actually those guys are cool, a bit overly-intrusive with their questions but very friendly. I had no problems."

"You mean not even males are immune to your good looks?"

"I guess you could say I'm an equal opportunity charmer."

They laughed.

"All the same, you looked quite lost back there," said Bridget.

"Actually, I was musing over how relaxed everything seems here, considering that this is Elysian Island and we're still living in a post 9-11 era. It just feels strange, after coming though all the hassles at Gatwick and Barbados."

Bridget smiled. "I know what you mean, but don't be fooled. The security here is top notch. No one gets through who isn't supposed to."

"I heard about the three paparazzi who got kicked out a few months ago, so yeah, I could believe that. But hey!" patting himself on the back. "One more addition to my resumé. I made it through the Elysian Island airport!"

Bridget eased into the driver's seat and waited for Rudy to join her. He sat down and shutting the door, he leaned forward and tried to kiss her.

"Please don't," she said firmly.

"Why, is anything wrong?"

"I've got a bone to pick with you. Until then, just relax and be a good boy."

Rudy gazed around him, frowning. "Is it just me or do you feel a sudden blast of bone-chilling air in here?"

"Very funny," Bridget retorted. She wasn't amused. Turning on the ignition, she drove out of the airport unto a two-lane road that was fairly straight. Rudy felt peeved. He was puzzled by the sudden shift in Bridget's mood. Her mobile phone rang inside her handbag tucked between the seats. She took a small clip-on headset from atop the dashboard and attached it to her right ear. "Would you mind passing me my phone, please?" she said, sounding impersonal. Rudy took the phone out of the bag and handed it to her. She launched into a spirited conversation in fluent Spanish.

Rudy gazed out the window at the immaculate white-sand beach sheltered by palm trees and lush greenery. The sea looked calm and inviting, even in the faded light of a clouded sun. The beauty of the landscape fell flat on him, especially with Bridget chatting away unintelligibly beside him, seemingly unaware of his existence.

Nevertheless, he still felt grateful to be sitting beside her. From the moment he saw her at the airport, he'd felt that powerful energy match between them, just like he'd felt when they first got to know each other. Back then, it had felt like a reunion, almost as if they'd known each other from the beginning of time. She was still as beautiful as ever; well-built with pale, supple skin, shoulder-length, dark, full-bodied hair, an oval patrician face with bewitching eyes, sumptuous lips perfectly shaped, and a cute chin. She wore a sand-colored Kurti and boot-cut trousers. She had a mystical, Moroccan look. However, beneath her charm Rudy sensed a steeliness which he hadn't perceived until now, and it surprised him. He was sure it wasn't his imagination or his ego reacting.

He could understand Bridget's delicate position; she had to watch her butt because of her husband. At sixty-seven, Lord

Edward Henry Tennyson was one of the most influential men on Elysian Island and a man well known for his eccentricities and unpredictability. Elysian Island had once been his private domain. The three square-mile Caribbean island comprising nineteen hundred acres and nestled a mile off the north-western coast of Saint Lucia, within its territorial waters, had been drawing seafarers to it like a magnet since the 19th Century. Its Edenic beauty was the main source of attraction, particularly the lush, low-lying valleys and thickly-wooded hills, the surrounding warm turquoise waters, and its golden-sand beaches, coral reefs and coves perfect for snorkeling and scuba diving.

Edward Tennyson had purchased Elysian in the early sixties from the British colonial government administering Saint Lucia at the time. It had cost him a mere fifty thousand pounds. A proud Etonian and an alumnus of Oxford and the Royal Military Academy Sandhurst, he‘d previously served with the Irish Guards during World War II. After the war he travelled extensively throughout India, North and East Africa and the West Indies.

Following the death of his father, Lord George Frederick Tennyson in 1959, Edward inherited the peerage title and the family's extensive landholdings and dairy business. After hanging around dutifully for a few months to try his hand at running the family business, he decided that the tedious mundanity of secular life was not for him. He'd grown accustomed to a privileged and carefree life of luxury, and all the years he'd spent traipsing around the world had given him an adventuresome spirit and a desire for new and exotic experiences. When he discovered that Elysian Island had been put up for sale, he saw it as a unique opportunity to satisfy his noble craving for adventure and promptly acquired it. He then formed a private company and named it the Elysian Island Company. His aim was to develop the island while preserving its pristine beauty and ecology.

Thereafter, Edward managed to seduce some of his blueblood friends and relatives into purchasing residential lots, including a few members of the European nobility and the British Royal Family.

He then commenced building the requisite infrastructure, including an airport, roads, a harbor with safe anchorage, a small desalination plant for the collection and filtration of seawater and rainwater cisterns. Telecommunications and power facilities also had to be installed. He succeeded in wooing dozens of locals from the mainland by promising them steady work at a time when the islands in the region were going through tough economic times.

He then proceeded to build an elegant home with stately pillars and a grand verandah on a hill overlooking Albion Bay, a picturesque bay on the island's leeward coast. He was the first to set roots down on his dream island. Several others followed suit and they too built chic multimillion-dollar mansions in and around Albion Bay and other parts of the island. Several of the homes were later rented out as holiday villas, fully staffed.

Edward also built a fifteen-room guest house along the coast at Albion Bay. He eventually abandoned England and settled down proudly in the land he had built with his own hands. Thenceforth, he proceeded to live the opulent life of a gilded royal.

Increasingly, new and wealthier clientele were drawn to Elysian Island's pristine beauty and the carefree lifestyle of lavish beach picnics, sunbathing and blissful idleness, not to mention its more salacious attractions - skinny-dipping, moonlight picnics with skimpily-clad male dancers, nonstop parties under the stars and late-night revelries; all done with His Lordship's blessing. As word of the new Utopia spread, the international press got wind of all the shenanigans taking place on the island. The British tabloids had a field day with it.

The natives, meanwhile, had established a village about half a mile north of Albion Bay close to the sea, with Edward's help. They called it Anse Soleil. The majority of them spoke mainly French Créole, a legacy of Saint Lucia's colonization by France in the 17th and 18th centuries before it was eventually and decisively captured by the British. By then, the French language and culture had been too deeply embedded in their psyche to be uprooted.

Ultimately, Edward sank so much of his own money into developing the island, by 1979, before he could complete all the infrastructural work, he run into financial problems and came close to depleting the Tennyson family fortune. He was forced to sell the guesthouse and a controlling interest in the Elysian Island Company to one of the homeowners, a wealthy American oil magnate, who then turned over the management of the company to his business partner and fellow American, Bill Thompson to further develop the island.

From then on, Edward's influence over Elysian Island waned. Most of the residents still continued to look up to him as a sort of patriarchal, Christopher Columbus-type symbol and he was generally held in high esteem, despite his reputation as an eccentric and a man with delusions of grandeur.

Rudy was familiar with all of this, including rumors about Edward Tennyson's flaky character. This was why he was willing to cut Bridget some slack and play along if she chose to be cautious.

Bridget took a right turn and continued past the airport towards Albion Bay. Her call had finally ended. Glancing at Rudy, she saw the frown on his face. "Please bear with me, I've got to make one more call. It's urgent. Do you mind?" she said.

Rudy shrugged, still feeling peeved. He resumed gazing sullenly out the window. His mind flashed back to the time he and Bridget first met and began having an affair. It was March, 2014 and he'd been working as a stringer for the Daily Express newspaper in London's East End, and moonlighting as an entertainment correspondent on the side. Bridget had reluctantly accompanied her husband to London to attend a theatrical production at the Royal Albert Hall put on by some distant relative of his.

An editor of one of the tabloids with whom Rudy had had a good working relationship, found out about the visit and he immediately contacted Rudy to ask him to try and get an exclusive interview with Lord Tennyson. The pay was good, the best Rudy had ever been offered. The editor knew he had familial ties to Elysian Island. He was raised by his aunt who had been one of Edwards's maids. She quit after a few years and returned to live on the mainland to take care of Rudy after his mother (a single mom) died giving birth to him. She migrated to England with him when he was nine and spent the rest of her life there until she died of cancer, three years ago.

Edward declined Rudy's request for an interview but surprised him by inviting him to dinner after learning about his roots. Rudy eagerly accepted his invitation. Ironically, the old boy had taken a liking to him and even said he was welcome to visit Elysian Island anytime, adding that he'd be happy to have him as a guest. He insisted that Rudy drop the formality and call him Edward, which Rudy gladly did.

Edward and Bridget had been scheduled to spend four days in England. The day prior to their departure, Edward introduced Rudy to his wife while dining at the Café Royal in Central London where they had been staying. Rudy was taken aback by Bridget's beauty and youthfulness. She was clearly much younger than her husband who looked well on the way to being a septuagenarian, at the very least.

The next day Rudy received a call from Bridget at his office. She invited him to her room at the hotel and it was only then he learned that Edward had already departed for the Caribbean. According to Bridget, he left in a huff because she informed him at the last minute that she'd had to schedule an urgent business appointment in London, and urged him to go on without her. She promised him she would be home in a few days. Instead, she and Rudy spent the next two weeks together and got caught up in a dizzying whirlwind romance. It was as if they were on honeymoon.

Unlike Edward who hadn't a clue what was going on, those closest to Rudy in Stockwell Park Estate in Brixton where he lived, cottoned on to his escapade with Bridget. None of them was impressed, particularly his former live-in girlfriend, Amy with whom he still had an on-again-off-again relationship. She was

British-born of Jamaican parentage. Like most of Rudy's other female friends, she constantly complained about his 'weakness for white women' and accused him of selling out his race. Some of them charged that his *shabin* (light-skinned) complexion was overrated and he took it too seriously. Rudy always rejected their assertions and reminded them of Bob Marley's Caucasian roots, stressing that he'd had no hang-ups about it; he took pleasure in rubbing it in. A couple of his chums said he was 'disrespecting Rastafari,' although they knew that his dreadlocks were more a fashion statement, albeit he sympathized with some of the Rastafarian philosophy.

He found their criticisms quite irritating. He resented anyone trying to foist their issues on him or attempting to limit him because of the color of his skin. Of the fifteen women he'd dated in the latter half of his thirty-four years, ten of them had been white. In Bridget's case, he stood firm and braved the fusillade of racially charged barbs and the denunciations of his 'adulterous' liaison, especially from Amy, and continued dating Bridget. Amy was mortified. Their unwillingness to make a clean break made it awkward for both of them. Rudy felt like he was betraying her and it bothered him. But he couldn't help it. Bridget was irresistible. Since getting to know her, he hadn't been able to get her out of his system. No other chick had ever touched him so profoundly, or caused him such emotional turmoil.

They'd become so hopelessly smitten with each other they never really got around to talking at length about Bridget's background. All Rudy knew about her was that she once lived and worked as a stockbroker in California before hooking up with Edward and moving to the Caribbean. She'd mentioned that she still dabbled in stock trading without elaborating. It wasn't that she was trying to be cagey, they were just eager to squeeze as much as they could out of the few days they had left together.

On their last day together, when Bridget realized that their tryst was coming to an end, she became very somber and despondent. Whatever was going on in her life, Rudy got the feeling that she felt trapped, although Bridget never said so outright, even when he pressed her. He sensed this from her exceedingly passionate response to his every touch when they'd made love. She'd clung to him as if she wanted to suck the life force out of him and consume him. It was as if she was afraid to let go.

He'd also sensed that same quiet desperation in the heartfelt way she thanked him for bringing some measure of happiness into her life, albeit temporarily. She was like a prisoner in solitary confinement who'd been let out so she could feel the sun on her face again, and breathe fresh air into her lungs, only to be whisked back into her cell.

She'd insisted that they keep in touch via emails and Skype, and over the phone and Rudy readily agreed. A couple of times when he pressed her, she did concede that there was tension in her marriage and she and Edward had had a strained relationship, but she refused to elaborate. Bridget then began pressing him to accept Edward's earlier invitation and come spend some time on Elysian Island. She even dangled before him the prospect of landing a cushy job at one of the three luxury hotels on the island, arguing that it would be more worth his while rather than struggling to survive as a journalist and remaining in the rut in which he had found himself – basically throwing back at him what he himself had confessed to her. Rudy had been struck by the matter-of-fact way she put it. To him it merely underscored her desperation and the length to which she was prepared to go in grappling with her demons.

For months he resisted out of pride, and because he'd felt piqued by the way Bridget had denigrated his profession. Besides, who in his right mind would venture to go live in a lion's den with the aim of stealing its mate? Bridget then came up with another brainwave. Why not take up Edward's offer and use it as an opportunity to do an in-depth travel piece on the island? That way he could kill two birds with one stone and no one would be the wiser. As she pointed out, the British press would be falling over themselves to get their hands on the story. She was right, of course.

Rudy took the bait. Bracing himself, he telephoned Edward and put the proposal to him. To his surprise, Edward said it was a 'capital idea' and readily agreed but suggested that they discuss it further. They did and eventually came to an understanding whereby Rudy would obtain two months of unpaid leave from his employer and spend that time vacationing on Elysian Island. He'd be welcome to stay at Edward's home and all his living expenses would be taken care of.

Rudy could hardly believe his luck, knowing that living on Elysian Island was way above his means. Edward also said he wished to explore other possible topics of interest related to the island's unique history. That got Rudy excited. He even took the opportunity to disclose his budding desire to research his family's ancestry, including that of his deceased aunt who used to work for Edward. Edward was all for it.

A few weeks later, and nearly a year after he and Bridget became lovers, Rudy found himself on Elysian Island, sitting next to the wife of the man who had invited him over; the woman who had had him on an emotional roller coaster, thinking constantly about her and longing to be with her, so much he'd paid Amy even less attention, and when he did, he spoke to her distractedly.

"Where has your mind gone?"

Rudy started at the sound of Bridget's voice. To his surprise, they had turned off the main road unto a hilly, tree-lined driveway. Glancing at his watch, he saw it was already quarter past twelve. "Sorry, I drifted off. I couldn't help it. At the moment, it seems the only way I can get your attention is in my imagination," he replied.

"Come off it," said Bridget, laughing. "Pretty soon you'll have my full and undivided attention." Glancing across at Rudy, she added. "I mean it."

"I can't wait," he replied. The sound of Bridget's laugh buoyed him up.

The SUV crested the hill and Bridget drove past a pair of white brick pillars with a wrought-iron sign at the top that said 'Blossom House.' She drove on into a parking lot with two Kawasaki Mule golf carts and a gray BMW i3. Next to the parking lot was a secluded courtyard with a private communal front garden laid to lawn and graced with Poinsettia Blossoms and lush-green shrub borders and a comfy-looking sitting area.

"We're home," said Bridget. They got out of the vehicle. Rudy was struck by the imposing structure confronting him. Clearly designed in the Neoclassical Greco-Roman Revivalist style, the two-storied mansion boasted an elegant high-pitched roof supported by stately pillars coupled with deeply recessed verandas, multi-paned double-hung windows and a columned entrance portico. The property offered a breathtaking view of Albion Bay dotted with palatial homes, their roofs jutting out of sheaths of greenery. Nestled along the coast was a marina, three hotels and a few beachside bars. The breeze wafting up from the sea enveloped the ridge with an airy freshness.

Bridget stared searchingly at Rudy. She could tell he was impressed and that pleased her. "A penny for your thoughts."

"Woe unto the poor bloke who aspires to winning your affection. This is going to be a hard act to follow," he replied grinning and staring at the house.

"You're not getting cold feet, are you, Mr. Phillips?"

"Nah, not as long as you're around to give me courage."

"Talking about courage, that's exactly what you'll need when I'm through with you," said Bridget with steel in her eyes.

Rudy frowned. "Now what's that supposed to mean?"

"Just remember that you've got some explaining to do but we'll get to that when you're done with Edward," Bridget replied, glaring darkly at Rudy.

A man came out onto the entrance portico. "Hi Vernon," Bridget called out to him. "Good morning," he replied, waving at her. He was brawny with a sculpted face and quite dark. Bridget turned to Rudy who was heading towards the trunk of the vehicle. "Don't worry about your luggage," she said. "Vernon will take care of it. Just come on in." She began climbing the steps. Rudy followed her.

Bridget introduced Rudy to the man on the portico. "This is Vernon Allain. He is Edward's personal assistant." The two men smiled and greeted each other. "Vernon will show you in. I will join you shortly. I've got to make a few calls," said Bridget and she went indoors ahead of them.

"Shall we go in?" said Vernon. "Edward is expecting you." His voice was slightly husky and self-assured.

"After you," Rudy replied and followed him into the house.

2

"Welcome to Elysian Island," Edward greeted Rudy warmly as he entered the living room. "I trust that you will find your stay here agreeable." Slightly over six feet tall, he was slim but looked quite lean and fresh-faced for a man of sixty-seven. He had a cherubic smile and playful eyes with a puckish glint, and a rather husky voice. He wore a simple, open-collar, white shirt and dark trousers.

"Thank you, sir. It is already way beyond what I expected," Rudy replied. They shook hands. Rudy cast a sweeping gaze at the living room. It was quite spacious with a high ceiling and simple facade with floor-to-ceiling windows that flooded the room with natural light and cool air. White linen curtains with ties at the top were draped over the windows. The walls were painted with light-colored reflective paint which contrasted nicely with the dark wood floor. The furnishings consisted of an artful juxtaposition of styles reflective of the Caribbean and the Far East and India but with a dominant British colonial theme. They included hand-woven plantation chairs, a cotton sofa placed decorously on a sisal rug, and wicker chairs with dark wood frames and light fabric palette embellished with tropical motifs. Bright, decorative vases added a vibrant burst of color to the overall texture and everything blended together to create a warm tapestry that made the room appealing to the eye and the senses. Two electric fans with rattan blades hung from the ceiling together with Hundi-and-Bell jar lanterns with hand-etched patterns, once popular in British colonial homes in India.

Despite its gracious and exotic style, to Rudy the room had an imperial air of British conquest about it and it made him slightly uncomfortable.

An elderly couple sat next to each other on the sofa. They both looked well past seventy. The man was of medium build and barrel-chested, with a slight paunch and he had a high-born air about him. The woman was short and dumpy with a pretty but somewhat weathered face and mysterious Mona Lisa eyes. Edward introduced them as Nicholas Michael Willoughby, the 13th Baron of Middleton in the County of Warwick, and his wife Lady Willoughby. They rose to acknowledge Rudy and shook hands with him.

"I am told that in addition to being a journalist, you are a poet and a painter," said Lady Willoughby.

"I write poetry and I paint." Rudy replied, wanting to kick himself. *Who, in hell, had he mentioned this to*? He wasn't sure if it was Bridget or Edward.

"You have been published, I assume."

"No, I haven't."

"Where do you exhibit your art?"

"In my living room."

Lady Willoughby blinked.

"Rudy is also an aspiring travel writer and a would-be genealogist," Edward interjected. "Are you not, Rudy?"

"Yes, I suppose you could say so."

"Rudy's aunt used to be my housekeeper before she migrated to Britain. A decent sort and very able and loyal. She was Rudy's adoptive mother. He was brought up in England ... from the age of nine, I believe?"

"Yes." Rudy replied, surprised that Edward had remembered so much about him.

"He is now on a mission of self discovery," continued Edward. "His aunt's elder brother, now deceased, lived and worked here on Elysian Island as a fisherman for many years. Rudy never got to know him and, understandably, wishes to take the opportunity while here to reconnect with his roots. Naturally, I was only too happy to assist."

Lord and Lady Willoughby seemed intrigued. They wanted to know about Rudy's life and upbringing. He indulged them and offered a brief summary of his life growing up in England along with snippets of his childhood in the nearby island of Saint Lucia, insofar as he could remember. Lady Willoughby tut-tutted at his mention of Saint Lucia.

"It is an absolutely adorable island with stunning natural beauty. The people, I dare say, are rather pleasant and hospitable but, dear me, there is so much inefficiency and official complacency. Having lived most of one's life in the UK as you have, I can only wonder how you could ever possibly adapt to this mode of existence."

"Pretty much the same as one adapts to the British weather and food, I suppose. You just do."

"Indeed," Lady Willoughby replied, still peering at Rudy with curiosity. "Are you unattached or already spoken for?"

"Unattached and available."

"Hmm, that's rather surprising."

"I'm unable to overcome my addiction to freedom," said Rudy, smiling. Lady Willoughby laughed. Edward intruded into the conversation.

"Incidentally, Rudy is also my official ghostwriter. Aside from his declared interest in travel writing and his desire to uncover his ancestral origins, I have invited him here to write my memoir."

There was a profound hush in the room followed by a look of astonishment on Lord and Lady Willoughby's faces.

"Surely, you are not serious," said Lord Willoughby.

"I have never been more serious," Edward replied.

"Does the Company know about this?" Willoughby queried, frowning.

"I couldn't care less. Besides, it is no concern of theirs."

"What will members of the Royal Family think? No doubt, this will be a source of concern to them."

"I have no doubt that Her Majesty is a stout defender of Article 10, and would surely frown upon the very notion of a British subject being denied freedom of expression."

Lady Willoughby looked quite concerned. "This is not going to be a salacious tell-all book, I hope," she said.

"I dare say this is the whole point of writing one's memoir, is it not?"

"Come now Edward, you know what I mean."

"Not a leaf shall be left unturned, I assure you, insofar as it is relevant to the subject matter."

"Why now?" Lord Willoughby demanded.

"Why not now?"

Bridget breezed into the room, a sunny smile on her face. "Lord and Lady Willoughby ... how are you?" she greeted the couple, ignoring her husband. "I was unable to join you sooner because of a pressing engagement, my apologies. Edward understands, don't you dear?"

"Naturally, my love. As always, you are forgiven. Will you join us for lunch?"

"I'm afraid I can't, dear. I promised Bill that I would pop over around two o'clock to help with the arrangements for the party this evening ... Rudy, would you like to join me? Bill and his wife are looking forward to meeting you. Bill Thompson is the CEO of the Elysian Island Company."

"Sure ... if it's okay with Edward."

"If it's okay with me, it is okay with my husband ... Isn't it darling?"

"Of course. How can I begrudge our guest the pleasure of basking in the beauty of the most desirable woman on the planet?"

Rudy caught the wry look on Edward's face, although it was fleeting. It made him uneasy.

"Lord and Lady Willoughby, do you mind?" said Bridget.

The couple exchanged glances and mumbled they didn't mind.

"Shall we go, then?" said Bridget, staring at Rudy. He excused himself without meeting Edward's eyes.

Their departure from the room was accompanied by loud silence.

3

Rudy caught up with Bridget in the entrance hall and followed her out into the courtyard. She went across to one of the Kawasaki Mules in the parking lot. Sizing up the golf cart, Rudy said, "I think you had everyone scratching their heads back there and wondering what in hell just happened."

"Who cares what you think!" Bridget snapped, eyes flashing. She tossed Rudy a key ring with two keys and pointed to the golf cart. "Think you can handle this?" she said churlishly.

"Don't see why not, it's not rocket science."

Bridget plonked herself down in the passenger seat. Rudy sat beside her. "Do you mind telling me what's eating you?" he said.

"Is it true about Edward's memoir?"

"Well ... Yeah, I guess ..."

"Quit stalling Rudy. Did Edward invite you here to write his memoir?"

"Yes, he did."

"Why didn't you tell me?"

"I figured it was his job to. He's your husband."

"Rudy, you and I have been planning how to get you over here for months. I have now discovered that you and Edward have been liaising with each other and he has asked you to write his life story. You agreed, yet not once during all this time that we have been communicating did you mention this to me ... Why, Rudy?"

"Look, Edward and I only discussed this about a month ago. I honestly didn't think it was such a big deal. Besides, I planned to tell you as soon as I got here ... which, if you recall, was just a few hours ago."

"Under what terms and conditions are you writing this book?"

"Edward will suggest an outline and I do the bulk of the writing and research, the latter with Edward's help. He has given me leeway to source a literary agent and arrange for publication."

"What about compensation?"

Again, Rudy hesitated. "Rather than a one-off payment, we have agreed to a royalty split."

"I have just one more question for you and I would appreciate a straight answer, if you don't mind."

"Okay."

"Did Edward forbid you to tell me about this book?"

Rudy took a deep breath. "Yes."

"Can we go now please?"

"Sure. Where are we heading?"

"I will direct you. It's just five minutes away."

Rudy drove the golf cart down the driveway. When they arrived near the white pillars at the entrance, Bridget said abruptly, "Turn right - in here." Rudy swung unto a gravel road lined gracefully with palm trees set in landscaped fields of colorful flowers and lush green grass. On the eastern side of the property, pencil-cedar trees stood tall like sentinels and formed natural windscreen and privacy borders. After a brief incline they came to a house set on top of a modest hill.

Rudy pulled up in front of the sprawling single-level structure with a pool in a flower garden and a private terrace with an enclosed courtyard. The exterior was a mixture of solid brickwork, pebble mosaics, local hardwoods and other natural materials, giving the house an eco-friendly look.

"This is your new home," said Bridget. Rudy gaped at her and then turned to stare at the house.

"I beg your pardon," he said.

Bridget took a key from her handbag and went and opened the door. Turning, she said, "Edward initially arranged for you to stay at Blossom House but I argued against it and suggested that this is more befitting His Lordship's biographer. It's quite pleasant and convenient and affords you all the privacy and quiet you need." Rudy just stood gazing bemusedly at the house. "Would you like me to carry you over the threshold?" said Bridget. Their eyes touched. Rudy felt relieved to see that her face had softened. She smiled and together, they laughed. The tension between them lifted, at least for the moment. "Allow me to show you around," said Bridget. Rudy followed her into the house.

The luxuriousness of the interior left him speechless. The layout of the house was quite ingenious. It was designed to create light-filled, open spaces with a grand-island hub connecting the living and entertaining areas and the dining zones. The house was positioned to provide a sweeping and unobstructed view of the outdoors, right through to Albion Bay, with the sea shimmering in the distance. A wide hallway situated away from the living and entertaining areas provided the three bedrooms complete privacy and seclusion. One was a grand master suite with a king-size four poster bed, a lavish walk-in dressing room, a bathroom with a glass-walled shower and marble bathtub, air-conditioning, an in-room safe and an outside patio with glass sliding doors. Rudy's luggage lay at the foot of the bed, to his surprise.

"Fantastic, isn't it?" said Bridget, watching Rudy's stunned reaction. "It was built four years ago by one of Edward's relatives for use as a holiday home. Unfortunately, he died unexpectedly. Since then, the house has rarely been used," Bridget explained. "All the doors and windows are fitted with Kevo electronic locks, so you'll be quite safe."

"And you said Edward agreed that I could stay here?"

"I had to persuade him. He was quite adamant that you should stay at Blossom House."

"Does he suspect what has been going on between us?"

"He probably does ... One thing you should know about my husband is that he's a very complex man and quite inscrutable. After seven years of marriage I still can't figure him out. I don't suppose the thirty-two years age difference between us helps. Deep down inside he's a sweet and loving soul. He's just very unpredictable and it's almost impossible to know what he's thinking."

"It sounds like he wanted to keep a close eye on me."

"Yes but not necessarily for the reason you think. Edward is like a chess player, and the world is his chessboard. People like you and I are the chess pieces. Trying to figure out his next move or to outplay him, could be a nightmare. To be honest, I don't know why he agreed that you could stay here instead. I just know that he decided that it would serve his purpose, whatever that is ... All the same, I know why I wanted you here."

"Well I got to be straight with you. I felt the tension between you two back there and it made me a bit uncomfortable."

"Get used to it. You have no choice."

"Actually, I do. It's just that I'm not kidding myself that good sense will prevail or that I'm going to make the right choice."

"I guess that settles it then ... I love you, Rudy. I think you know that."

"I love you too. I'm possessed by you ... By the way, aren't we supposed to be visiting some friends of yours?"

"Silly, that was a ploy to get you over here. You'll get a chance to meet them this evening at the party. I do have an engagement with them though, so sadly there will be no housewarming."

"How could you? I feel so deprived and neglected."

Bridget smiled. "Make yourself at home. The house is fully stocked. One of our maids, will be popping over to prepare you lunch when possible. Meanwhile, you have the option of dining out at the Halcyon Beach Bar & Café or the nearby Camelot Hotel or, for that matter, any of the restaurants that you prefer. The Halcyon and the Camelot are two of the most popular dining and entertainment spots on the island. The food is superb, you'll love it. Edward has authorized the Halcyon to charge your meals to his account ... Take my advice, don't argue with him."

"What about the bike?"

"Were you serious about that? You really do want to move around on a bicycle?"

"Sure. I want to get as much exercise as I can. You know I'm a fitness freak."

"Check the storage shed at the back of the house, Vernon assured me that it would have been delivered yesterday." Bridget's cell phone rang. She plucked it out of her handbag and took the call out on the terrace. She returned a few minutes later. "I'm sorry, I have to leave. Sam, the chauffeur will pick you up this evening at seven." She headed for the front door before Rudy could respond and climbed hurriedly aboard the golf cart. She waved at Rudy who stood in the doorway with a look of disappointment on his face, and quickly drove away.

Rudy watched her exit the driveway. He felt a twinge of irritation at her abrupt departure. The beauty of the house faded and everywhere grew dimmer. It was as if the soul of the place had left with Bridget. He actually had to restrain himself from asking if he could go with her. His growing attachment to Bridget, a woman he barely knew, worried him a bit, not least because he felt unable to resist it.

At the moment, his desire for her was so strong, he could barely think straight. They had so much to talk about, plus there were a few things he needed to thrash out with her. The house with its romantic air of seclusion would have been the perfect setting. He returned to the living room and flopped down into a chair. He felt fatigued all of a sudden. He suspected it was due to jet lag, which was only just starting to kick in. He also felt famished. He decided to go check out the restaurant Bridget had suggested and afterwards, stroll around a bit. That way he could kill time until the evening and the party at the Thompson guy's place, wherever that was. He headed for the bathroom.

4

The chauffeur arrived at seven o'clock sharp to pick Rudy up. He went out as soon as he heard the car engine, making it unnecessary for the driver to exit the vehicle. He peered thoughtfully at the car – a grey BMW i3. It looked spotless and well kept, and even in the soft patio light it gleamed impressively. The chauffeur gazed fixedly at him as he opened the front passenger door. The man looked gawky and a bit awkward behind the wheel, as if the car was too small for him. He had a brooding but handsome face with a broad forehead and a strong chin. Rudy noticed his surprised look as he sat next to him. He wondered if it was because he didn't look VIP enough or if perhaps it was because of his dreadlocks. He couldn't resist mocking him.

"Do you mind?" he said.

"Excuse me, what you say?" said the chauffeur.

"Could you spare me a lift? Do you think whomever you're waiting for would mind?"

The man looked puzzled. "But sir, how you mean? They send me to pick you up."

"Ah! Silly me, I should have realized that," Rudy replied, grinning. He held out his hand. "I'm Rudy."

The chauffer shook his hand with a forced smile. "My name is Samuel. Everybody call me Sam," he said.

"So where are we off to, Sam?"

"Not far, sir. To Mr. Thompson home. It's about fifteen minutes drive from here."

Rudy studied him closely. In the darkness he couldn't be sure but he could have sworn that he caught a flicker of resentment in the chap's eyes. Sam gripped the steering wheel tightly.

"Is something bothering you, Sam" said Rudy.

"No." Sam replied brusquely.

"Would you feel better if I walked? I mean, I'd hate to inconvenience you."

"It's not that sir. After this morning, I just want to be careful."

"Careful about what? What happened this morning?"

"Miss Bridget insist that is she who must go and pick you up at the airport. Since I wasn't fit to drive you then, I'm worried that maybe I'm still not good enough and I might disappoint you."

"Are you serious?"

"Of course," Sam replied with a straight face and looking straight ahead.

There was a brief silence. Rudy suddenly burst out laughing. Sam glanced at him, frowning. Rudy wiped tears from his eyes and tried to control himself. "Tell me something, Sam. Are you always that frank or does it depend on the person you're speaking to and how much he's worth?"

Sam said nothing.

"Can I ask you a question? And I would like you to give me a straight answer. Will you do that?"

"Okay."

"You don't like the idea of Lady Tennyson hanging around me, do you?"

"If you don't mind sir, it's getting late. I think we should go."

"Whatever you say, Sam. You're the boss ... And please, call me Rudy."

"Yes, sir ... Rudy." Sam turned on the ignition and drove off. The night whizzed past. In the glow of the moon the landscape was recast in a pale-grey, metallic hue.

"Were you born here, on Elysian Island?" said Rudy.

"Oh no. I come from Saint Lucia. I've been living here and working for Lord Tennyson, for ten years now."

"Where exactly in Saint Lucia are you from?"

"I from Londonderry, in Choiseul."

"No shit! Really? .... I was also born near Londonderry. I haven't been back there since I was a kid but I can vividly recall the place."

Sam glanced sharply at Rudy "You! ... Born in Saint Lucia, near Londonderry!" he exclaimed.

"Yep. I left the island for England at the age of nine."

Sam looked as if he couldn't believe what he had just heard. His eyes lit up and he smiled. Watching him, Rudy noticed that he suddenly seemed more relaxed and less hostile. He slackened his speed and turned off the main road into a driveway with thick bush on both sides and drove slowly up an incline. "Nice meeting you, Rudy. Welcome back," he said and sounded like he meant it. Rudy grinned. For the first time since entering the vehicle he felt accepted. "Thank you, my brother," he replied.

They could see lights up ahead and cars in a parking lot. Laughter and voices could be heard over the purring of the engine. Sam drove up to a wide parking area adjacent to a courtyard and deftly maneuvered the car into a vacant spot among several other vehicles. "Excuse me a minute, Ms Bridget ask me to call and let her know as soon as we reach," he said and took out a Samsung Galaxy S from his pocket. Rudy quietly took in the surroundings. The house was a villa on three levels built high on a ridge with a panoramic 360-degree view of the Caribbean Sea to the west and the Atlantic to the east. The property was surrounded by acres of night-shrouded trees and vegetation that gave it a profound air of seclusion. Landscape lighting softened the darkness and suffused the courtyard with a warm, yellow-orange glow designed to mimic a sunset. Several groups of people stood outside chatting, including a few Indian couples. Some of the women were dressed in saris.

"Ms Bridget said to tell you she coming," said Sam.

"Cool," Rudy replied. Pausing, he added, "I need a smoke, can you help?"

'It's a pity, I could have stopped to get you cigarettes at the Halcyon bar. You want me to go and get some for you?"

"Not cigarettes, ganja."

"Oh ..." Sam glanced away.

"Come on, don't tell me folks here don't smoke weed."

Sam shifted uncomfortably in his seat. "To be honest, I don't know too much about that ...," he said evasively. Fortunately for him Bridget breezed through the front door at that moment.

"See you later mate," said Rudy and he stepped out of the car.

"Hi Rudy," Bridget called out as she saw him approach. Rudy froze in his tracks and stood gaping at her. She was dressed in a black top and an ankle-length, African tie-die wrap skirt with matching head wrap. Around her neck was a beaded necklace. It was complemented by multi-stone-studded ethnic earrings. She had a courtly air about her that made her seem unearthly. At that moment, if she had asked Rudy to bow down and kiss her feet, he would have complied without hesitation. In the glare of Bridget's beauty, everything around him faded into insignificance.

"Are you all right?" said Bridget.

"Yeah ... I think so," Rudy replied, shaking his head as if to clear it. "God, you're beautiful," he whispered. Bridget laughed.

"Are you in love with me, Mr. Phillips?" she whispered back to him.

"Hopelessly."

Again, she laughed. "Bill and Jacquie are waiting. Come let me introduce you."

Rudy followed Bridget through a spacious foyer into a room that combined the living, dinning and kitchen areas into a vast and open space that seemed designed to re-create the panoramic vista outside. This desire for airy openness seemed to be a recurrent architectural theme on the island. The interior was an exotic mix of polished wooden floors, a high wood-clad ceiling, antique-style mahogany furniture and exquisite woven textiles and pebble mosaics. A flight of stairs led up to an upper level. The living room area opened onto a patio overlooking the beaches on the island's western coast.

Approximately thirty people were gathered inside, yet the room still looked somewhat bare. Some of them worked their way around two buffet tables while others gathered in groups of two or more. Their loud chatter and carefree laughter filled the room. Two waitresses hovered near the kitchen area, apparently on the lookout for new arrivals. One of them hurried across to Rudy and invited him to choose from a selection of cocktails. He settled for a Planter's Punch. Bridget introduced him to some of the guests. They were all warm and polite but there was no mistaking the curiosity on their faces when she disclosed his identity. Several of the women eyed him with interest. One of them commented on his looks. Rudy spotted two women a couple yards away whispering to each other with their eyes fixed on him and Bridget. He tried to ignore them and focus on the individuals addressing him.

A man came seemingly out of nowhere and engaged Bridget in conversation. Rudy noted the doting look on his face and felt a twinge of irritation. He wasn't close enough to hear what they were saying. The waitress returned and handed him his drink. He took it gratefully and thanked her. He barely got through the first sip when a woman held his arm and drew him aside. Rudy was immediately captivated by her classic Nubian face with its wide forehead, high cheekbones, a short fetching chin, full, lusty lips and flashing, indomitable eyes. Her mahogany skin was incredibly smooth. She wore her hair natural in an Afro-throwback style with intricate twists and turns and the sides cut short. She was wearing a beautifully tailored African tribal-print jacket with a white blouse and dark trousers. Rudy couldn't help staring at her. She passed her hand in front of his face to make sure he was still conscious. "Are you okay?' she said, quite amused.

Rudy blinked and nodded. "Yeah, I'm cool," he said.

She introduced herself. She said her name was Kadija and she was an artist. She asked Rudy if he would do her the honor of sitting for a portrait.

"Me? Why would you want to do a portrait of me?" he asked, surprised.

"I'm doing an abstract piece on the fusion of landscape and culture within a Caribbean context. There's something about you that captures the essence of that elemental synthesis."

"I'm truly flattered but could we talk about this?" Rudy replied.

"Sure, why not," said Kadija. Bridget intruded. "I hate to interrupt but I must introduce Rudy to Bill. Do you mind?"

"Not at all," said Kadija. She smiled and waved goodbye to Rudy. Bridget whisked him away to meet a man chatting with a couple in the centre of the room.

"Meet Bill Thompson. He's the CEO of the Elysian Island Company," said Bridget. The two men shook hands and exchanged pleasantries. Rudy was immediately struck by Bill Thompson's ebullience and quick-wittedness. He was a giant of man, well over six feet tall, bald-headed, thick and fleshy with an imposing presence that belied his boyish, freckled face and bubbly personality. Another man cornered Bridget and Rudy watched them melt into the gathering. Thompson reached out to a woman standing a few paces away and drew her closer.

"Meet my wife, Jacquie. Jacquie, meet Rudy," he said.

"An absolute pleasure to meet you, Mrs. Thompson," said Rudy, turning on the charm.

"Delighted to meet you," Jacquie Thompson replied with a sweet smile and a slight air of caution. She had a fixed gaze and it made Rudy uneasy. It felt as if she was trying to peer inside his soul. He actually felt naked.

"Rudy, there are a couple of friends I'd like you to meet," said Thompson. "Please, why don't you join us out on the patio? There's a buffet table out there and drinks, so rest assured you'll be well cared for."

Thompson led Rudy out unto the patio, an incredibly vast and ornate covered space alongside an outdoor terrace. It was constructed with beige-on-beige, natural marble limestone and travertine tile flooring, and furnished with a six-piece dining set, a custom-built weatherproof rattan lounger with a built-in centre table and a sixty-two inch flat screen TV. Part of it was a bar and barbecue area. The terrace was literally cut into the hillside and boasted a Jacuzzi and a huge infinity pool in a natural garden-like setting. The layout of the pool produced the visual effect of the water extending to the horizon. Next to it was a pavilion with daybeds on either side. The main house was complemented by two guest cottages and a gazebo that looked ideal for morning tea and coffee or evening cocktails. A group of four men and three women stood out on the patio munching tid bits, sipping drinks and chatting. An elderly couple sat close together on the sofa conversing with each other.

"It's an awesome house!" said Rudy, not hiding his amazement. "It's the sort of home most of us can only dream of. It must make living out here great fun."

"Glad you like it," Thompson replied with a snicker. "I guess it does no harm to be on the good side of a newsman."

Rudy laughed. Placing his hand on his heart, he said, "Tonight I'm nothing but your humble guest. Cross my heart and hope to die."

"Tell you what," said Thompson. "Why don't you refresh your drink and grab a bite, then come and join me and my friends for a chat." Patting Rudy on the back, he went across to join the couple reposing on the sofa.

Rudy headed for the buffet table, wondering what on earth could be responsible for him receiving the undivided attention of the CEO of the Elysian Island Company. He was beginning to suspect there was more to his being invited to the Thompsons' party, and it wasn't meant to be just a social call. Thompson didn't strike him as the benevolent, fatherly type who would condescend to the average Joe by humoring him with chit-chat and small talk. Was it Bridget's idea to invite him or someone else's? So far, there was no sign of Edward, and he wondered why. Shrugging, Rudy heaped food unto his plate. Satisfied he had enough, he went over to join Thompson and the couple.

"Meet Donald Jackson and his wife, Aileen," said Thompson. "Donald is a director of the Elysian Island Company. He and Aileen are very dear friends of mine." Donald was a man of considerable heft, with a ruddy face, bulging eyes and a moustache that made him look like a walrus. In contrast, his wife was almost wispy and baby-faced with bright, expressive eyes. Rudy quickly dispensed of his plate and drink unto the centre table. Donald and Aileen Jackson stood up to greet him and then resumed their seats.

Rudy settled down on one of the club chairs opposite them and next to Thompson. Aileen's name and accent caught his attention.

"You're Irish," he said.

"Yes, I am," Aileen replied. "Naturally you would notice. I am originally from Dublin. I'm told that you came over from the U.K. In which part of England do you reside?"

"Brixton."

"Oh! The heart and soul of London's African-Caribbean community. What a coincidence. It might interest you to know that I have roots in Brixton. My paternal grandfather was one of the longest operating landlords in Brixton. He once owned the Canterbury Arms. It was a community pub catering to the same patrons for forty years, most of them Irish. Did you know that Brixton had a sizeable Irish population in the past? The pub used to be a focal point of the local Irish community."

"Interesting. Have you ever lived there?"

"Unfortunately, no. I emigrated to America over thirty years ago, thanks to Donald here," said Aileen, patting her husband's knee fondly. "He's American. For the most part, we've been living between Boston, Europe and the West Indies ever since."

"So Rudy," Thompson broke in, "How do you like Elysian Island?"

"I haven't gotten around that much but from what I've seen so far, it's quite impressive – at least on the surface."

Donald Jackson placed his glass on the table, crossed his legs and peered searchingly at Rudy. "Coming over from Brixton, I imagine you would be more familiar with the inner-city life; the fast-food joints and small shops and the rundown housing, not to mention the gun and knife crimes."

"Just out of curiosity," said Thompson, "How much do you know about Elysian Island?"

"Only what I've read in the press," Rudy replied.

"In other words, not much."

"Well, I suppose it depends on your perspective. For example, from reading all the related travel articles and gossip columns, you can get a pretty clear picture of life on the island and the lavish lifestyles of its foreign residents. But no doubt, that's only half of the picture. I can't seem to find any information on the local residents. It's as if they're invisible."

"I understand," said Thompson. "But don't worry, now that you are here, feel free to move around. If you need a guide, let me know. As I've told Bridget, the Elysian Island Company would be happy to do whatever we can to make your stay enjoyable."

A waitress came over to ask if anyone cared for more drinks. Thompson and Donald Jackson requested whiskey. Rudy and Aileen declined.

Turning to Rudy, Thompson said, "It is my understanding that Edward has chosen you to ghostwrite his memoir," The matter-of-fact way he said it made it seem as if on the island, this news was already old hat. Rudy wasn't surprised. He'd been bracing himself for it. "Yes, I am," he replied.

"Are you aware," said Jackson, "that countless writers from all over the world would part with an arm and a leg to win an assignment from a man of such distinction?"

"I wouldn't doubt that. I understand how they feel," said Rudy.

"If you don't mind me asking," said Jackson, "why do you believe Edward has such confidence in you? What justifies his faith in your abilities?"

"That's a question you should probably direct to Edward. I'm just a lowly scribe."

"Well, I couldn't help wondering if his inviting you here was due to some sort of paternal sympathy on account of your origin."

"You know, Rudy," Thompson interjected, "aside from being an iconic figure, Edward is known to be a man who is very forthright and not always judicious about the views he expresses. I trust you will be able to advise him and help to steer him clear of anything potentially libelous; all the more with Bridget around to guide you. You see, one must always be alert to potential legal pitfalls in such matters, and the possibility that other players in the subject's memoir may recognize themselves and possibly sue you."

"You mean Edward is a loose cannon and you want me to rein him in."

"I wouldn't put it so harshly. Let's just say he's very impulsive and often tends to throw caution to the wind. You see, Edward is very dear to us all and we believe in looking out for him and his interests – and Bridget as well, of course. You may be wondering if I'm overreacting, and that's understandable since you don't know him the way we do."

"Actually, Edward and I still have a lot to discuss regarding the book. Remember, I only arrived this morning. All the same, thank you for alerting me to all the rocks that lie hidden beneath the waves. Even though my ship has come in, I will do my best to steer it with caution."

"Excellent! I'm glad we're on the same page."

"Incidentally, as CEO of the Elysian Island Company, I figure you must have quite a story to tell yourself. Judging by some of the news reports I came across recently in the Saint Lucia press, and in some of the other islands, there seems to be mixed feelings about the socioeconomic model that has been allowed to develop on Elysian Island. Some folks are very critical. An objective appraisal of life here could do you no harm, I imagine."

"Do I detect a sales pitch?"

"Well, if you think about it, this could be one way of putting Edward's views into perspective and balancing things out."

Thompson roared with laughter. "And it would also be a way for you to kill two suckers with one stone!" Reaching for his drink, he took a sip and peered hard at Rudy over the rim of the glass. "First of all, let's be clear. The Elysian Island Company has done some darned good work on this island, rivaling what has been achieved on the mainland. Contrary to public perception both on the mainland and in other parts of the region, the company and the residents whom we serve have done much more than build, buy and sell posh houses. We have established a full-fledged tourism industry and financed all the supporting infrastructure and facilities.

"Of course, we owe our success to the kind support of successive governments who have acknowledged our contribution to the island's economic development, and have been very helpful by way of certain tax concessions, not unlike those provided to other local tourism businesses. Our record speaks for itself and stands for all to see. We have no need to embark on a PR drive to appease certain political elements or to allay their unfounded suspicions."

All of a sudden there was a loud burst of chatter in the living room. Someone called for the gathering's attention. Thompson's wife came out unto the patio. "Bill, darling, please come. You are needed over here," she called out to her husband.

"Gentlemen, Aileen, may I be excused?" said Thompson. He got up and went to join his wife.

"I guess they're about to make the announcement," said Jackson, addressing Aileen.

"And about time too," she replied, sounding thrilled. "Come on, you two, we can't afford to miss this!"

Jackson grinned at Rudy and shrugged. "Bill's son, Trevor and his fiancé are about to announce their engagement."

"Hurry Don!" his wife urged him. Rudy followed them reluctantly. He felt like an outsider, which was somewhat unusual for him. He was normally at ease in social gatherings and mingled freely. He took pleasure in seeing people warm up to him. Now, for the first time, he felt inhibited and emotionally detached from the people around him. They made him feel inadequate, despite their cordiality. He wasn't sure if they were the problem or if it was him and this was what irritated him.

He stood near the doorway and gazed distractedly at Bill Thompson and his family as they made their announcement in the midst of 'oohs' and 'ahs' and hearty applause. Rudy's mind was on Thompson's earlier statements. He couldn't get over the way the CEO of the Elysian Island Company seemed determined to dissuade him from working with Edward on the book. Likewise his cohort, Donald Jackson, except that Jackson had been more subtle, in that the bastard had tried to question his literary abilities, even insinuating that Edward had sought to do him a favor out of pity. That had really galled him. It brought back memories of the time when some of his friends (and even some adults) had taunted him on the sly when they found out that a government minister had used his influence to get him and his aunt British visas so they could emigrate to England. He was nine years old at the time. They claimed that it was payback to his aunt for sleeping with her benefactor who, back then, had been the Minister of Foreign Affairs.

Then there was the occasion when, as a correspondent working in Brixton for the Guardian, he went to interview an elderly white couple on their experiences during the 2011 London riots. Before responding to his questions, they had wanted to know his credentials, his background and where he came from.

But all that aside, what was he to make of Thompson's promise to help him get around, although he'd made it obvious that he disapproved of this business of writing Edward's memoir?

It was the same with Bridget. Was she in cahoots with Bill Thompson to try and pressure him to turn down Edward's offer? As for Edward, if he and Thompson were so close, as Thompson had insinuated, why wasn't he at the party? His absence seemed odd, considering that both Thompson and his sidekick had given the impression that they cared very much about him and held him in high esteem.

Inside there was a burst of cheering and clapping. Someone called for a toast in honor of the soon-to-be bride and groom. Rudy spotted Bridget in the gathering. She looked as beautiful as ever. Two men had her all wrapped up in conversation. One of them was the same guy who had commandeered her earlier. Rudy quietly slipped away and went across to the patio bar for a drink. At his request, the barman whipped up a Ti Punch with consummate flair and finesse, as if he was putting on a theatrical performance. Rudy took a sip and gave him thumbs up. "Jam me, brother," he said and they bumped fists. The barman grinned proudly. Rudy returned to the same seat he had vacated and slumped back into the plush cushions. His mind drifted.

"Where has your mind gone?"

Rudy glanced up, startled. A pretty young woman was clearing away the empty glasses and smiling at him. Her full, curvaceous figure was a downright showstopper. There was no mistaking her mixed ancestry. She had a delicate, heart-shaped face, a straight nose, long-lashed eyes full of sparkle and curly, raven-black hair that hung like spools over her shoulders. Her complexion had a rich caramel hue. She was the quintessential *douglah* (mixture of African and East Indian). "I'm sorry, did I make you jump?" she said.

"Nah! I'm still sitting, aren't I?" Rudy replied, staring facetiously at his chair.

The woman laughed. "You sound like my Mum. She says that every time I scold her when she startles me," she said.

"A pleasure to meet you, I'm Rudy."

"I'm Olive Henry."

Rudy's eyes followed her hand as she wiped the table slowly, almost as if she was fondling it. He envied the table. "I don't suppose you'd care to elope with me, would you?" he said. Olive laughed, a sweet, mirthful sound that stirred him like a sensual touch.

"Be careful what you wish for. You might not be able to handle it," she warned.

"Please go ahead and put me to the test."

Again, that sensuous laugh. Rudy felt like he could listen to it all night.

"How is Edward?" said Olive.

"Quite well, the last I saw of him."

"Please give him my regards."

"I take it you two know each other well."

"My Mum works for him. She's a housekeeper." Olive strode across to the buffet table to clear away some empty dishes. Rudy eyed her legs. "Do you live around here?" he asked.

"In the village, not far from here. It's called Anse Soleil ... Are you coming to the La Rose festival?"

"La Rose! I had no idea folks here celebrated La Rose."

"Don't be silly, of course we do. This is still part of Saint Lucia."

Rudy had all but forgotten about the Feast of La Rose, a local cultural festival devoted to extolling the virtues of the rose and honouring its patron saint, Saint Rose of Lima, the 17th Century Roman Catholic ascetic. Indigenous to Saint Lucia and held annually in the rural Creole-speaking communities, the festival and its counterpart, the Feast of La Marguerite, are practiced nowhere else in the world. Rudy recalled the last time he attended a La Rose festivity he was about seven yet the memory of it still lingered vividly in his mind.

It was an elaborate and colourful celebration of pomp and pageantry with a king and queen accompanied by their royal entourage of dukes, duchesses, princes and princesses, all bedecked in the exquisite finery of British gentry. They called their sessions 'séances,' and these consisted of all-night singing and dancing in a public hall, and they also played games.

As he discovered many years later, the groups had evolved during the days of slavery and were created by the slaves to support each other in what had been for them a colossal age of terror. They were patterned after the pomp and ceremony of the Dahomeyan kingdoms of West Africa whose rulers and chieftains exercised socio-political power through ritual, drama and spectacle. Rudy further discovered that under pressure from the Church and the British Colonial overlords during the post-Emancipation period, the societies were forced to modify their festivities to make them more civilised and reflective of the gentility of Mother England.

"I thought La Rose was normally held in August. It's March," said Rudy.

"It is but a few years ago we decided to shift our festival to March so that it doesn't get overshadowed by the national festivities on the mainland. Besides, we usually go over in August to join in."

"Where is it being held and are you taking part in it?"

"In the village. I'm going to be the queen," Olive said proudly.

"Really? And who, may I ask, is the lucky guy who'll be serving as your consort?"

"Edward."

Rudy gaped at Olive. "Surely, you must be joking," he said.

"No, I'm serious. Edward is a La Rose member, has been one for years and he always supports the group financially. We asked him to be our king this year and he agreed."

"A British King of La Rose! Wouldn't the tabloids love that. I guess you guys are about to make history ... When is the festival scheduled for?"

"Next Sunday. We practice nearly every evening. How would you like to come?"

"Sure, why not."

"Come down to the dance hall on High Street in the village anytime after five in the evening. I'll look out for you ... Bye!" Olive hurried away. Rudy was itching to follow her. The chatter in the living room was still going steady and, if anything, it had gotten louder. Rudy stood up and, at the same time, he saw Sam walking briskly towards him.

"Miss Bridget send me to tell you she had to leave suddenly. She ask me to take you to her," said Sam.

Rudy was so surprised, all he could do was gape at Sam. "She's gone? Where is she?" he demanded.

"Not far. I'll wait for you outside. It's okay, no need to worry."

Rudy watched Sam walk away. Suddenly, he was in no mood to face anyone inside. He felt like sneaking out, except that it wasn't his style. He couldn't just leave and not say goodbye to his hosts. Besides, Bill Thompson's home is no place to display bad manners, he thought to himself. It would convince them that he had no class.

He found Thompson and his wife among the guests. They looked surprised that he was leaving. He didn't tell them why. He said goodbye to them and went to look for Sam.

5

Rudy found Sam sitting at the wheel waiting patiently. All throughout the fifteen-minute drive Sam remained quite taciturn. Rudy tried drawing him out but he grew cagey and kept dodging Rudy's questions about Bridget and her whereabouts. Rudy felt like strangling him! By the time they reached their destination, he was so pissed he stormed out of the vehicle and ignored Sam. The sound of waves breaking on the seashore could be heard nearby. Facing him was a beachfront bungalow with a swimming pool and an enclosed wooden sundeck. He entered the patio and rang the doorbell. Bridget opened the door almost immediately.

"Come in," she said, smiling. Rudy entered a foyer and followed her into a vast sitting room complete with a mini bar, a butler's pantry and guest washroom. It was tastefully furnished in a relaxed island-style decor with a ceramic tiled floor. Its elegance left him unmoved.

"Would you mind telling me what the hell is going on!" he demanded, scowling. "I feel like I'm caught up in a cat-and-mouse game like a character in a poorly written novel."

Bridget gazed at him with knitted brow. "What do you mean?'

"You set me up, didn't you?"

"Excuse me?"

"Why did you invite me to this party?"

"I did so on Bill's behalf."

"Bullshit! The guy doesn't even know me. Besides, I'm pretty sure he's not the sort who would invite strangers to his son's engagement party – unless he's got an ulterior motive."

Bridget gave Rudy an indulgent smile. "Don't you think you're overreacting?" she said calmly.

"The hell I am! Aside from spending half the night watching several goons drool over you while you kept your distance from me, I had to spend the rest of my time being lectured on the dangers of aiding and abetting your husband. Then, to top it off, I'm hustled away without explanation and dumped here at the behest of my puppet master - by a driver who mysteriously seems to have lost his tongue, as if he's under a gag order! Frankly, I've never had a more bizarre experience in my life!"

"Would you like a drink?"

Rudy glared furiously at Bridget and was about to excoriate her further but then checked himself. He took a deep breath. "Yeah ... Come to think of it, I could do with a drink. A scotch, please."

Bridget went across to the bar to get Rudy's drink and made herself a martini. Handing him the whisky, she said, "You sound stressed out. I'm really sorry about that. It's been a long day. You'll feel better once you've had some rest." Rudy said nothing. "Let's not forget how much you and I planned for this day," Bridget continued, "and how much we wanted to be together again."

"Ah! But there's the problem. The Bridget standing before me isn't the same one with whom I plotted and planned, and dreamed of reconnecting with."

Bridget stared calmly at Rudy. She couldn't recall ever seeing him so worked up. She actually felt a motherly tenderness towards him. "I don't understand. What do you mean?"

"Back in England I came upon this sweet, warm hearted soul, seemingly very charming and considerate but trapped in an Ice Palace, yearning to break free. I fell under her spell and she swept me off my feet, to the point where I was willing to do almost anything to free her from the cold clutches of the Ice Palace. I found a way to give her wings and for a while she managed to escape and rediscover the joy of being truly alive and free. It was like a fairy tale. I know this sounds clichéd but it's the truth. Now I'm left to wonder if her heart is frozen because of all the years she spent trapped in the Ice Palace; whether all the sweetness, warmth and sensitivity I thought I had seen have been locked up inside that frozen heart ... I know we have been reunited for only a few hours, but still you are not the same Bridget I met back in England."

Bridget went and sat on the sofa. "God, Rudy! I know you're a writer and an aspiring poet, and I'm sure you have great potential but can we come back down to earth and get real? That's the only way you and I can get what we hoped for – by cutting out the melodrama and being pragmatic and sensible ... I meant it when I said I fell in love with you. I love you now, more than ever. I know that we've taken a tremendous gamble and I know what we're up against. I also know what we *must* do in order to make things happen. You're not so clear about that and this is probably where you and I differ."

"I suppose you conspiring with Thompson to pressure me into betraying your husband is one of those things you must do."

Bridget blushed hotly. "You've been betraying my husband from the very first time you fucked me, and you continue to betray him up until this very moment. We both do. So don't you go getting self righteous on me!"

There was a pregnant pause. Rudy avoided Bridget's eyes.

"Look at me Rudy," said Bridget. Rudy glanced up. "Do you love me?"

"You know I'm crazy about you."

"Then you've got to trust me."

Rudy flopped down onto the sofa. "Incidentally, where are we?" he said, glancing around the room. "You and your husband certainly have grandiose tastes."

"This house belongs to me, not to Edward." Rudy was about to take a sip. He paused. "You seem surprised," said Bridget.

"It's a gift from him, then."

"The land on which it is built is, yes. I built the house. It's one of three that I own on the island, including the one you're living in. I purchased it from the original owner. They are all available for short or long-term lease to business visitors and vacationers."

Rudy placed his drink down on a coffee table. "I don't mean to be confrontational but why am I getting the same feeling I did back at Thompson's place; that this is not meant to be just a social call?"

Bridget stood up and walked a few paces, then turning to face Rudy, she said earnestly, "I couldn't bear the thought of the day going by without us spending some quality time together, you know that. It's obvious that this would not have been possible at Bill's place. By the same token, we also have business to discuss. Can we just focus on the fact that we're together?"

"Yeah, I guess so."

"Can we get the business part out of the way and then, hopefully get to the pleasure part afterwards? Do you mind?"

"No. It's okay with me."

"First, can I tell you about my life here since I was not as forthright with you as I should have been when we first met? Back then I couldn't bring myself to talk about these things. Emotionally, I couldn't deal with it. As you would be aware of by now, I am married to a man who happens to be one of the world's most influential and talked-about personalities. Edward counts among his closest friends several of the wealthiest and most powerful people on the planet, including members of the British Royal Family.

"As you will soon realize, over here it's the mansion or villa you own, your spending power and your social connections that matter and show who you are. The majority of the island's foreign residents are upper-class Brits, many of whom share the same values and imperial pretensions as Edward. This island was founded on a strict code of privilege and exclusivity. Trying to fit in can prove to be quite a test, especially if, like me, you're American or for that matter non-European, and if you're not in with the predominant clique. Allow me to give you some advice. Whatever you consider to be your mission here, if you want to make any serious headway you've got to gain not just Edward's acceptance, but that of all the powerbrokers."

Rudy lounged back in his seat and peered thoughtfully at Bridget. "It's about this book again, isn't it?" he said. "Do you know what is really bizarre about all this? I haven't even gotten around to discussing it fully with Edward. In any case, I just want to be sure that I'm reading you right. Both you and Thompson have been pulling out all the stops to get me to break ranks with your husband and turn down his offer. From the looks of things, I can't play along with you without upsetting him and vice versa. How can I possibly please all the powerbrokers in such a case?"

Bridget sat down next to Rudy, close enough so that she could peer deep into his eyes. "By understanding where the balance of power lies in this instance. You see, I believe – and so does Bill – Edward is not really interested in sharing his life story but rather he wants to publicly embarrass the Elysian Island Company and the mainland government by disclosing certain confidential information."

"Why would he want to do that?"

"Edward is a shareholder of the company. However, he and some of the directors don't see eye to eye on certain matters. While he is content to use you to achieve his ends, don't fool yourself into thinking that he's going to stick his neck out to save you from the repercussions of a libel suit – or possibly several that are almost certain to result from the publication of this book. Besides, what's the point of devoting so much time and energy to publishing a book that is only going to result in your earnings being consumed by lawsuits? But then, that's for you to decide.

"For me, however, whatever differences there are between Edward and the company, it is the least of my concerns. Edward has become so disillusioned with life here, he recently came to the decision to sell his remaining shares in the company and abandon the island to return to another gilded piece of paradise; Tanzania, where he once lived about sixty years ago. Can you imagine me leaving all this behind to go live in Africa, of all places, and starting life all over again from scratch?" Bridget took Rudy's glass and returned to the bar to refresh their drinks. "After living seven years on this island, it has become my world."

"What makes you think Edward would change his mind about moving if I give up on writing the book?"

"Of course, he won't. I'm not that silly. But you can help *me* avoid any attempt on his part to have me join him and stop the disaster this book could cause for many on the island, including you."

"How?"

"First, let's be clear. I'm not asking you to do me a favor. I am offering you a business proposition with guaranteed financial returns, far more than you could ever hope to make from this book."

"Don't tell me you and your associate are offering to pay me off if I agree to disappear."

"Don't be absurd. This has absolutely nothing to do with the company. Bill and I just happen to share the same views about Edward's motives. Beyond that, don't assume that we are in cahoots about anything. The business proposition that I alluded to is a totally different matter and it is my personal business."

"I'm all ears."

"I don't want Edward to change his mind about leaving but that is exactly what he'll do if you insist on giving him cause to remain here by proceeding with the book."

"You want him to leave?"

"I want what's best for him – and for me. I can no longer bear watching him wallow in his delusions of grandeur, grasping at shadows, trying to hold on in vain to the world he once knew; a world which has long since crumbled all around him. He is completely out of touch with modern-day reality. He seems to think that by returning to Tanzania he can reset the clock and recreate the past."

"But surely you can't force him to go if he ultimately chooses not to."

"He has no choice. He's almost bankrupt." Rudy stiffened. He peered at Bridget, frowning. She paused to let her words sink in. Rudy's reaction was precisely what she had expected. "You heard right," she said. "His bankers are pressing him to settle his debts and they're threatening foreclosure. At present he has no viable source of income. The only way out is to accept the company's offer to buy his remaining shares and use at least part of the proceeds to work out an acceptable deal with his creditors. He stands to gain about a million dollars from the sale ... You see, Rudy I foresaw all this from early, that's why I took the precaution of starting my own investments. In addition to the houses, I own a variety of stock holdings and assets in various parts of the world, including two properties on the mainland. I'm also an international stock market consultant. I offer stock advisory services to clients around the world. I'll go into more detail about this some other time.

"All this is being jeopardized by Edward's unpredictable and increasingly irrational tendencies and also because most of my assets were acquired while married to him. The banks could be tempted to move in on me too, to try and recoup their losses. I'm damned if I'm going to let this happen! That's why I have no intention at this stage of discouraging Edward from selling his shares in the Elysian Island Company and leaving the island. I have tried to persuade him to remain here and try to sort things out but he is adamant, and I am tired. Let him do what he wants."

"But surely, considering that he has so many wealthy friends, he should have no difficulty getting financial help."

"Obviously, you don't know Edward. He's an extremely proud man. His pride would never allow him to accept personal offers of help in any form whatsoever. If one were to suggest it to him, invariably his response would be, 'Never will I batter my dignity for handouts.' This is another one of his oddities that sorely tests my patience."

"Regarding the book, what if I can get him to agree to have a solicitor vet the manuscript? Do you think he would agree to that?"

"Not a chance. Besides, there's something else to consider, which you're overlooking. Inevitably, you will require several months to complete this book, and this poses a major problem. During that time, if I know Edward, he will stubbornly resist selling his shares in the company. The banks will almost certainly lose their patience and move to seize everything he owns, including the shares. Then my own personal assets could be at risk. I can't allow this to happen. I need to have some semblance of normalcy and stability in my life and some peace of mind. It's all I ask."

Rudy got up and began pacing back and forth, running his hands agitatedly through his locks. Turning to Bridget, he said,

"Look, I understand where you're coming from. Honestly, I do. But the problem is I can't just walk out on the guy, after all it was I who approached him in the first place. You don't shaft a guy who condescends to give you a break. It's just not my style."

"How would you like to be my business partner?"

"Excuse me?"

"I need someone who is capable, ambitious and trustworthy to manage my properties and some of my business portfolios after Edward is gone. That includes Blossom House, which has been willed to me. I also plan to increase my investments on the mainland and establish an office over there and in some of the other islands. You could help in starting things off. The job comes with a very generous income, your own personal residence here or on the mainland if you prefer, and the opportunity to travel the world and hobnob with the rich and famous. What's more, it would be good for your writing career since you would have easy access to contacts among the world's leading publishers and agents, and have no difficulty getting your work published."

"Are you serious?"

"I have never been more so."

Rudy went quiet. He looked a bit dazed.

"I need you to be honest with me, darling," said Bridget. "Aside from the fact that you're attracted to me, isn't it true that you feel dissatisfied with the level of progress you've made so far in your vocation? Isn't this a major reason why you allowed Edward to entice you into accepting the dubious job of writing his memoir? You see it as a way of jumpstarting your career and gaining recognition. Mind you, your stay here could prove to be just that, although not necessarily in the way you may have anticipated. Rather, it depends on how you play the cards that you are dealt. I think you're smart enough to realize where the source of true power lies in this world – and that to find it you've got to follow the money trail." Bridget paused to take a sip of her martini as she studied the ponderous expression on Rudy's face. It was the sort of enthralled look she had grown used to seeing on her clients' faces whenever she dangled before them prospects for enrichment that they could never have dreamed of. "With regards to my proposition," she continued, "just think about it. There's no need to make a rushed decision. We can talk about it some more when next we meet."

Rudy went quiet for a few moments and then eased back into his seat. "You know baby, there's something I've got to ask you. What became of the old maxim that a wife is supposed to support her husband for better or for worse?"

Bridget laughed scornfully. "Must I remind you once again how absurd you look standing in your tiny little glass house throwing stones? A wife who perceives that her husband is hell bent on self destruction, yet sits back and does nothing about it, certainly is not being true to him, don't you think?" With that, Bridget got up and cleared away the empty glasses with an abruptness that made it obvious that the conversation was over as far as she was concerned. Rudy wasn't done yet. He couldn't resist niggling her some more.

"I presume Edward knows that you have no intention of accompanying him if and when he goes off into oblivion."

"If he doesn't, he will sooner or later." Bridget picked up an iPhone from the countertop. She dialed a number and after a brief wait, said, "Please come over, Sam. Rudy is ready to leave." Watching Rudy, she said, "Sam is on his way. He should be here in the next ten minutes."

"Are you throwing me out?"

"Don't tempt me."

"Why are you annoyed with me? What have I done?"

"I'm not annoyed, just a bit tired, as I am sure you are too."

"How about if I stay so we can be tired together?"

Bridget smiled. "I'd love to have you in my arms tonight. God knows, I need it. But on second thoughts, maybe we shouldn't. Don't worry, it's early days yet. There'll be lots of opportunities."

Rudy got up and began pacing. Turning to Bridget, he said, "What is the point of this relationship? Where is it heading?"

"The worst thing you and I could do is get impatient and start making the wrong moves. Let's not forget I'm not single and we're having an extramarital affair. Thankfully, the people here mind their own business and we have the luxury of complete privacy, more than we could ever have hoped for elsewhere. But we must still be cautious and not overplay our hands."

"For a carefree guy like me, it's hard. I'm not used to it."

"You'll be okay, trust me. Just know that you mean the world to me and I care deeply about you." Bridget stood up and pulled Rudy to his feet. She took him in her arms. He resisted for a moment and then gave in to her. They held each other so close he could feel himself melting into the warm softness of her body and being enveloped sweetly in the unified heat of their desire. Inwardly she reached out to him with urgency and passion. In that moment, Rudy realized that Bridget truly loved him. He could feel it. They kissed long and deep and with an abandonment that left them breathless. The sound of a car engine drifted in from outside. Bridget untangled herself reluctantly from Rudy's embrace.

"When shall we meet again," he asked.

"Soon. Very soon ... Sam is here. Goodbye darling."

They stared at each other. Bridget turned and walked towards the bar as a tear began rolling down her cheek. She didn't turn around until she heard the front door click shut. Quietly, she left the living room.

6

"Please have a seat, Mr. Phillips. Bridget will be with you shortly," said the cute, waif-like receptionist. Her hot-toffee extension blended with her light-brown hair. She looked elegant in an elbow-length sleeve top, an A-line skirt and pumps, and she had an American accent.

"Thank you," said Rudy, eyeing her with interest. He could tell she was a no-nonsense type by her smooth air of professionalism; the sort of person you'd expect to be working for Bridget. It felt odd hearing her address her boss by her first name, although it wasn't surprising. He recalled when he first met Bridget, she'd been adamant that he not address her as Lady Tennyson, or even Mrs. Tennyson. She did so in Edward's presence. He'd heard her react similarly with other people.

Her office was located in a two-storied building owned by the Elysian Island Company situated in the commercial centre of Albion Bay. The name of her company was Visionary Investments. The reception area was meticulously clean and clutter free, and quite cozy-looking with contemporary design lounge furniture.

Green plants and cut flowers gave the room an atmosphere of well-being and made it aesthetically pleasing. Rudy settled into a sofa. A clock on the wall indicated eleven o'clock.

Soon after he got out of bed, Rudy got a call from Bridget. She invited him to come visit her office in Albion Bay and meet her staff. Rudy was pleasantly surprised and agreed to go.

It was almost as if Bridget had read his mind, considering that the night before, after they said goodbye, he'd spent the rest of the evening mulling over their discussion and the sobering reality that there was much more to her than he'd realized, particularly regarding her business ventures. Why on earth he had assumed her to be a housewife mostly living off the wealth of her husband, he had no idea.

As for the business proposal she'd put to him, it blew his mind. He woke up with it on the brain and was forced to take an early morning bike ride to try and calm down. Although he'd initially felt excited at the prospect of getting a first-hand look at Bridget's base of operations, as the morning wore on he began to feel slightly nervous. It dawned on him that he was venturing into the realm of the unknown insofar as Bridget was concerned. He was completely out of his depth and it was no use pretending otherwise. He was in foreign territory in every respect.

The door of Bridget's office opened and a twentyish-looking man in a white long-sleeved shirt and necktie stepped out, followed by Bill Thompson and a plain-looking young brunette and Bridget.

"Rudy!" Thompson bellowed. "Glad to see you. How's tricks?"

"So far, everything's fine," Rudy replied.

Turning to the brunette, Thompson said, "Judy, allow me to introduce Rudy, a man of letters and a pillar of the Fourth Estate." Thompson winked at Rudy and said, "Meet Judy, my secretary."

Judy bared her teeth at Rudy and the two of them shook hands.

"Tell you what," said Thompson, placing his thick, meaty arm around Rudy's shoulders. "I'd like to take you up on your assertion that there are mixed feelings in certain quarters about the 'socioeconomic model' that has developed here on the island. The Elysian Island Company is embarking on a major community-development project in the village next week. Bridget's company is also supporting the initiative. Why not come over and see some of the great things and other community stuff that we do here. Again, as you asserted, an objective appraisal of life here could do no harm. It'd be great to have you there. What do you say?"

Rudy glanced at Bridget. She smiled encouragingly at him.

"Sure, why not?" he said. "Just let me know the date, place and time."

"Wonderful!" said Thompson. "Well, so long. Look forward to seeing you." He said goodbye to Bridget and her receptionist and the man with the necktie who stood with his arms folded eyeing Rudy. Thompson and the brunette walked out the door.

Bridget introduced Rudy to the receptionist and the young man. "Meet Abigail and Adrian," she said, adding, "Adrian is a sales and trading intern and Abigail is my faithful right hand! I don't know what I'd do without them." Adrian, Abigail and Rudy all smiled and greeted each other.

"Could you please come into my office," said Bridget and she entered the office ahead of Rudy. He followed her in and shut the door.

Rudy stepped into a high-tech, luxurious space with multiple computer screens and a high-definition TV with a fifty-two inch screen. It was fitted out with wood paneling, two built-in bookshelves and a large, ornate wood desk with two brown leather armchairs. Across from the desk were two blue leather chairs and a white coffee table. A rich Persian rug was laid out on the floor. Rudy gazed around the office, bemused.

His reaction amused Bridget and she couldn't help smiling. "Please have a seat, make yourself comfortable," she said and settled down at her desk. Rudy sat gingerly in an armchair that felt unbelievably comfortable. "Have you heard from Edward?" said Bridget.

"Actually, he called me shortly before I left. We've agreed to meet next Tuesday for our first interview. It's somewhat disappointing. That's a whole week away!"

"Can't say I'm surprised. That's typical of Edward, create suspense ... Does this mean that you're going ahead with the book?"

"I guess, but that's not to say that I'm not giving serious thought to all that you've told me."

"What are your thoughts regarding all that I've said?"

"Give me some more time to think it over. I'd also like to get Edward's thoughts in terms of precisely what he's expecting of me. So far we've not had a sufficiently detailed discussion."

"You said you're meeting him on Tuesday?"

"Yeah."

Bridget went quiet and sat thinking. Glancing up, she said, smiling, "Nice to see you here anyway. Welcome to Visionary Investments, my command centre."

"Thank you, the pleasure is all mine," Rudy replied with a bow.

"I guess you're wondering what this setup is all about and what I've gotten myself into."

"That's an understatement."

"I've been involved in stock trading virtually all my working life. I started off working for a brokerage firm in San Francisco many years ago. After Edward and I got married I opted to continue in the business after moving here. It was a natural choice once I got to meet the expats living here and the island's foreign homeowners, the majority of whom are fabulously rich and always on the hunt for good financial advice or just a good deal. I realized that there was a demand for my skills so I offered them my services. The response was overwhelmingly positive and since then I've managed to create a niche for myself. No one else in the region offers the kind of specialized financial and stock-trading services that Visionary Investments provides. We've got clients not just on Elysian Island but throughout the world, including several of the islands in the West Indies. Many of them had been clients back in the days when I worked in San Francisco and I continued to serve them after I left. So there you have it. Basically this is my story and today ... here I am."

Rudy took a while to digest everything that Bridget said. He looked befuddled. He asked, frowning, "Does your husband have a stake in this business?"

"Edward has no stake in Visionary Investments. It is a limited partnership between me and two former stockbroker colleagues back in the U.S. I'm the managing general partner. We've got a subsidiary in the States and we also work with affiliates in North America and the UK. We're scheduled to open a new subsidiary in London soon. Off and on I shuttle between the U.S. and the UK and sometimes Europe. It could be very taxing but also very rewarding. I love it!"

"It's probably a naive question but is Bill Thompson one of your clients?"

"Yes, he is. We also offer stock trading advice to the Elysian Island Company. It's one of our major clients."

"Here's the part I'm not getting," said Rudy, peering quizzically at Bridget. "From what I know about stock and options trading, it's a highly stressful and brutal line of work. Everything you've said seems to indicate that you're being stretched to the limit, with your fingers in pies all over the planet! How, in God's name, can you even find time to breathe?"

Bridget rose abruptly and said, "Come with me." Rudy followed her out of the office and down a hallway where she pushed open a door to another office. It was quite spacious, stylish and sparse. A woman and three men wearing dress shirts and neckties sat at workstations with large-screen computers processing streams of data flashing ceaselessly across the monitors. They looked to be in their mid to late twenties and the woman was the only black person among them. Bridget introduced them to Rudy. "These are my loyal frontline troops," she said to Rudy. "They handle a lot of the sales and trading activities. They're well trained and highly skilled and they're all Americans." Showing him around the room, she said, "What you're looking at is basically an automated trading platform for entering trading orders using algorithms that execute pre-programmed trading instructions; for example, the details and quantities of the orders, their timing and prices. They can also manage market impact and risk and predict patterns that are likely to arise in the market over varied periods. It's all done automatically. The data is flashed to the handheld devices of traders in the New York, Chicago, San Francisco and London stock exchanges. Recently we upgraded the system and now certain trading orders can be initiated robotically, without human intervention.

"The trick is to be well organized and always have a game plan that's well coordinated. You've also got to be well informed about the markets and how they could affect your stocks, and make sure that you know the risks in every stock category. In short, you need to ensure that you have all your bases covered and a great team that's loyal and absolutely love what they do. There's no doubt it can be very hectic and stressful but it comes with the territory and for me personally, it's a price I'm willing to pay."

Rudy took it all in without uttering a word. He looked like someone who had just gone through a mind-numbing experience. He actually felt out of place standing there in his jeans, polo shirt and loafers. "Are you sure we're in the 21st Century?" he said.

Bridget laughed. "What's wrong, Mr. Phillips? You look surprised," she said teasingly.

"I feel like I'm standing on the bridge of the Starship Enterprise."

"It's not far off from that. Incidentally, we call this office Mission Control." Taking hold of Rudy's arm, Bridget ushered him to the door and waved goodbye to her four employees who waved back. Rudy didn't. He followed Bridget back to her office, looking quite subdued. Bridget returned to sit at her desk. Rudy remained standing in the middle of the room and suddenly seemed uncomfortable. "I must say today has been quite an eye opener," he said.

"In what way?"

"It woke me up. I now see things in a whole new light."

"Is that good or bad?"

"Let's just say it'll go a long way in helping me 'get real' and 'cut out the melodrama.'"

Bridget leaned forward and gave Rudy a probing stare. "You're not sulking are you?"

"Nah! Far from it."

"Aren't you happy for me?"

"Of course I am. You've achieved a hell of a lot and you should be proud."

"It would make me feel so much better if you sounded like you meant it."

"But I do, come on! It's just that it was all so unexpected. I'm still trying to recover from the shock."

Bridget gave him an indulgent smile. "I'd planned for us to do lunch but unfortunately something came up last minute and I had to schedule a conference call which starts in the next fifteen minutes. I'll give you a call after it ends and we'll arrange something. Is that oaky with you?"

"Sounds cool. Meanwhile I'll head down to the waterfront to grab a bite and explore the area a bit."

Bridget came around from behind the desk and kissed Rudy softly on the lips. "Everything is going to be okay," she said looking deeply into his eyes. "There's nothing to fear. I'm here for you. I always will be. I love you."

Rudy gave her a squeeze and kissed her on the forehead. Looking her straight in the eye, he said, "I can't bear the thought of losing you."

Bridget's eyes softened and she smiled. "You won't. I promise."

Rudy turned and walked out of the office.

7

Rudy yawned and gazed languidly at the sea. He was lounging on a wooden deck at the Halcyon Beach Bar & Café located near the beach at Albion Bay. Surrounded by swaying palm trees, it had an open-air design, a thatched roof and plenty of seating. Close to it were several thatched sunshades and loungers and piles of small flags which the bar's patrons stuck in the sand if they wished to order food or drinks from their loungers. There were lots more of them lolling out on the sand than on the deck. Rudy had just finished a delicious fish stew and felt quite full. Now he felt a strong urge for some pot.

Earlier he had been joined by a long-haired, weather-beaten Australian yachtsman named Zachary who had approached him and asked if he could join him for lunch. He said he had sailed in two days ago. Rudy had indulged him somewhat reluctantly since he wasn't exactly in the mood for talking. However, it was a good thing he had since through Zachary he found out where he could get some weed. As they chatted about the island and the challenges of life on the sea, Rudy saw signs that made him suspect that

Zachary was a heavy ganja smoker – the small burns on his right thumb and forefinger, the redness in his eyes and the sweet-and-sour odor emanating from his body. On a hunch he asked him if he knew of any weed pushers on the island. Zachary suggested a woman named Kadija, a local artist with an art studio near the village, and gave Rudy directions to her place. At first Rudy didn't recognize the name. It was only after Zachary left it clicked. He recalled the woman at Bill Thompson's party who had asked him to pose for a portrait. That perked him up immediately.

He hadn't had a smoke for several days and he knew this was one of the reasons why the urge was so strong. He also suspected that the emotional impact of the past two days, coupled with the unfamiliar surroundings had disturbed his equilibrium. He felt like the proverbial fish out of water and it annoyed him. It wasn't like him to feel small and inadequate; or at least he'd never seen himself in that light before. Incredibly, here he was being wooed by an exceptionally beautiful and wealthy woman openly declaring her love for him and offering to hand him the world on a platter, but instead of rejoicing and patting himself on the back, he kept listening to some nagging voice in the back of his head warning him to watch his ass and be wary of pretty maidens bearing gifts. So what if she happened to be the one with all the money? *Big deal.* What did he have to lose? Why was he being such a freakin' pussy?

Rudy crumpled one of the cardboard coasters on the table and flung it angrily out onto the sand.

Somehow he needed to get a spliff. That would help him keep his cool. He got up and went to the car park adjacent to the bar where he'd parked the bike he'd brought with him. He already knew the route to the village. Early in the morning while out riding, he'd spotted it in the distance from atop a hill. Rudy mounted the bike and went in search of Kadija.

He had no difficulty finding her location on the brow of the hill overlooking the village, thanks to a sign bearing the name 'Kadija's Art Studio' planted at the entrance of a narrow road adjoining the highway between Albion Bay and Anse Soleil. From there he could see clusters of huts and mid-size concrete houses spread out in the village, near the sea. He resisted the urge to go down and take a closer look and turned into the side road instead.

He found Kadija's house at the end of a brief driveway. It was quite homely-looking with two stories, a high-pitched roof and dormer, a basement and a garage. Behind the house a giant ficus tree towered majestically, the branches hovering over the structure, as if to protect it. The front yard was quite large and well tended, with banana and plantain plants and coconut trees growing on the fringes.

The basement door and windows were open. Rudy could hear movements inside. He entered a small room packed with cardboard boxes stacked on shelves and on the floor. Scattered around were paint-stained containers, unused canvases and a few tables and easels. The room was apparently being used as a storeroom. Kadija was shifting around some boxes on a shelf. She didn't hear Rudy come in.

"Hello there," he said. She spun around.

"Rudy! What a pleasant surprise," she cried.

Rudy was equally surprised by her joyous reaction. "I'm almost sorry I didn't come sooner," he replied, his eyes hungrily taking in her trim, sexy legs. The gay-colored, active-wear shorts she was wearing truly did them justice. She also had on a cute crop top with a scoop neckline and short sleeves. She had a slight Jamaican-accented ring in her voice which otherwise sounded American with a high-pitched, laid-back Brooklyn flavor.

"What brings you here and how did you find me?"

"I got directions from a new friend I met down at Halcyon Beach Bar. His name is Zachary. He's a yachtsman. I have an unbearable craving and he suggested that only you could satisfy it."

"Oooh! That sounds exciting. Tell me more."

"The walls have ears," said Rudy, glancing all around him as if to make sure no one else was listening. Leaning closer to Kadija, he whispered in her ear.

Kadija gave him a chagrined look and sucked her teeth. "What a letdown," she scoffed and cuffed him playfully on his arm.

"My suspicion tells me that thou dost have a naughty mind," Rudy quipped, grinning.

"Wait here," said Kadija. Stepping outside, she went around the side of the house. Gazing through a window Rudy saw her disappear into the bushes at the back of the house.

She returned a few minutes later with a mason jar filled with cannabis and a small packet of rolling paper and placed them on a table. "Knock yourself out," she said.

Opening the jar, Rudy sifted through the neatly balled packets of marijuana and carefully selected two dub bags. He opened and sniffed them and nodded. It was good weed, the exotic stuff. "What's the damage?" he said.

"Twenty-five dollars a pop but for you it's on the house."

Rudy began protesting but Kadija cut him off. "Please ... I insist," she said and replaced the cap over the jar. She went back outside and retraced her steps around the side of the house. While he waited, Rudy took out his wallet and plucked a business card from it. He tore a piece and formed a filter to insert into the end of the joint. He then rolled some of the weed into the rolling paper and inserted the filter at one end with practiced ease. He checked his pocket for a cigarette lighter but found none. He searched around on the tables and shelves for matches, to no avail. He cursed himself for forgetting to bring his lighter.

"What're you looking for?"

Rudy spun around, surprised to see Kadija standing in the doorway staring at him. "I was hoping you'd have matches lying around."

Kadija went across to one of the shelves, pulled out a cardboard box and took a lighter out of it. She tossed it to Rudy and stood watching him with a curious expression on her face. "I'm almost certain I know you from somewhere," she said, adding, "We've crossed paths before. I believe we were together in a previous incarnation."

"Really? ... No doubt, one encounter is more than enough for you."

"I'm serious." Kadija's eyes focused penetratingly on Rudy. "My spirit tells me that you and I were once husband and wife somewhere in the Far East."

"Let's talk about your art," Rudy said quickly to try and change the subject.

"I'm yearning to paint your portrait. Will you let me? You promised me you'd think about it."

"Sure but can't we at least get to know a little more about each other first ... in this incarnation."

Kadija went and sat on a high wooden stool. "I was born on Elysian Island. When I was thirteen I moved to Jamaica with my mom. I lived there till I was eighteen and then migrated to New York. I attended Edna Manley College of the Visual and Performing Arts where I majored in studio, visual and graphic art design. Since then I've travelled the world and lived on virtually every continent."

"What brought you back home to Elysian Island?"

Kadija's face darkened. "Someone who's nothing but a traitor and a bastard!"

"Who's that?"

"Edward Tennyson – the royal buffoon of Elysian Island!"

The venom in Kadija's voice shocked Rudy. "What did he do to you?" he asked.

"It doesn't matter. I don't want to talk about it ... Will you sit for the portrait?"

"I'd sure love to see some of your work, if you don't mind," Rudy replied, still hedging.

"Come along, I'll show you." Kadija opened an inner door and led Rudy to a room which served as her art studio. It was quite spacious, spanning the entire width of the basement. The atmospheric contrast with the other room was astounding. Rudy stepped into a burst of light, color and warmth. Sunlit windows flooded the room with natural light, which was further intensified by the white walls. The odor of oil paints and solvents hung in the air. Scattered around were a worktable, a wedging table, several shelves, a sink, a plastic-draped drying rack on wheels, a dry erase board for sketching and even equipment for ceramic art. Part of the room was closed off to form a spray booth.

Hanging on the walls were several monumental abstract canvases. They ranged from fifteen to forty feet in length. In each piece the primary colors collapsed into kaleidoscopic chaos and re-emerged as new incarnations of blue, green, yellow, red, ghostly pink and orange. The largest wall was covered with an almost mural-sized canvas seemingly depicting a dour, blue-grey sky hemorrhaging blood-red, pus-yellow, anemic white, mournful grey and funerary black, all swirling in an etheric blend of tones and textures.

Being somewhat of an art aficionado himself, Rudy detected the influence of the Chilean abstract expressionist, Roberto Matta and the Cuban, Wilfredo Lam and even Jackson Pollock known for his penchant to drip and splatter paint unto his canvas.

Kadija noted the awed look on his face. She smiled, obviously pleased. "What do you think?" she asked eagerly. Rudy told her exactly what he thought and how impressed he was with her work. She seemed surprised at the extent of his knowledge of art. "I've been influenced by quite a few painters, including all those you've mentioned," she said.

"I don't mean to cause you discomfort by returning to a subject that you're evidently not comfortable with but I've got to ask; with so much talent, why on earth did you feel the need to return and be holed up on this island?"

"Two years ago when I decided to return, I persuaded my partner to join me. Because she loved the place so much, we ended up purchasing this property. A year later we broke up and I've been here ever since. Folks here appreciate my work and for what it's worth I can live comfortably off it. That's a luxury very few artists living in the other islands can lay claim to. Virtually all of us have at some point been condemned to a life of exile in order to pursue our dreams or just to survive."

"You strike me as a free spirit, someone who thrives on discovery and adventure, and living on the edge. Has Elysian Island domesticated you or have you sold out?" Rudy caught a flash of anger in Kadija's eyes. She shrugged impatiently and said nothing. "Are you a lesbian?" he asked.

"I'm bisexual. Does that turn you off?" She gazed at him defiantly.

"It takes a hell of a lot to turn me off. In fact, I don't seem to recall ever being turned off by a beautiful woman."

Kadija smiled. "May I take this as a compliment?"

"You may."

"Guess what ,,, I'm having a party tomorrow evening. How would you like to come? You'll love it, I promise. Some of my artist friends are coming over from the States and we're going to have some wild fun."

"Sounds interesting."

"Please come."

Rudy's phone rang. Plucking it out of his pocket, he peered at the number on the display. It wasn't familiar. To his surprise, it was Olive on the other end of the line. She called to remind him of the

La Rose celebration scheduled for the upcoming weekend and to find out if he still planned to attend. He'd also promised to pop in at one of the practice sessions, she reminded him. Rudy assured her he would, and promised to pay her a visit next evening. Returning the phone to his pocket, he said, "Sorry. That was Olive Henry. I met her at Bill Thompson's party. Do you know her?"

Kadija stared coldly at Rudy and nodded.

Glancing at his watch, he said, "Did you know that she's the local La Rose queen? They're having a practice session tomorrow and I had promised her that I would attend. Unfortunately I'm going to have to decline your invitation. Sorry about that, I hope you don't mind."

"Do you have Lady Tennyson's permission?"

Rudy stiffened. "I beg your pardon?"

"Be careful Bridget doesn't get pissed off with you."

Rudy gaped at Kadija and shook his head. "It was a pleasure meeting you. Thanks for the merchandise."

"Olive Henry, Queen of La Rose. That's so absurd!"

"What's absurd about it?"

"Don't tell me you're going to be the king."

"Actually that privilege belongs to Lord Tennyson."

"What!"

"Lord Edward is going to be the Elysian Island's King of La Rose."

Kadija let out an exasperated squeal. "What a fucking moron! That man is such a clown!" Grabbing a jar of water from the worktable, she flung it against the wall, smashing it. She rounded on Rudy. "That La Rose shit is nothing but tomfoolery. Just imagine those people kowtowing to an Englishman. Locals paying homage to their former colonial master and glorifying him as their king in this day and age. It's ridiculous! How can you condone this?"

"Don't you think you're overreacting?"

"The hell I am!"

Once again, Rudy gazed at Kadija and shook his head. "You've got some serious issues," he said tautly.

"Fuck off!" she screamed at him.

Rudy walked out the door.

8

Judging by the crowd that turned up in the village at Anse Soleil for the La Rose festival, there could be no doubt that news of Edward Tennyson's participation in the event had caused quite a stir and captured everyone's attention.

All throughout the day they came, from across all class and colour lines, eager to get a glimpse of what promised to be one of the most memorable spectacles ever seen on the island.

The villagers turned out in full force for the occasion. Dozens of the resident expats and visitors also made their way to the village, if only out of courtesy or merely to view the spectacle. For several of them, it was the first time they had ever set foot in the village.

The La Rose members commenced the proceedings with a dancing procession through the streets with the royals, Edward and Olive, leading their entourage who were all dressed magnificently in the La Rose colours of red and pink. . Two attendants shielded the king and queen from the sun with large pink and red umbrellas. In addition, they were guarded by a retinue of police officers and soldiers dressed in uniforms with insignia, epaulets and gold braid, and armed with wooden rifles and swords. A band of musicians and dancers dressed in their bonny finery, followed in the rear. They included three men pounding goatskin drums strapped around their shoulders, five cuatro and tambourine players and a man shaking a *shak-shak* – a maracas made of a narrow metal cylinder filled with small pebbles. They were on their way to the village church to attend a High Mass officiated by a Catholic priest from the mainland.

After the Mass they made their way joyfully to the village dance hall, a single-storey building made of wood and cinder blocks located a short distance from the church, right next to the sea. There they were treated to coffee and sandwiches. Although it was just nine o'clock, numerous onlookers had already gathered in and outside the dance hall, including fifteen foreigners. Then something extraordinary occurred.

Some of the La Rose children came forward and presented cakes and pretty red roses to 'friends' of the society from among the upper class, namely a group of foreigners, most of them resident British expats. They graciously accepted their gifts like good sports, and they all seemed touched by the gesture.

Just before noon the society members paraded through the streets again. The first official séance was scheduled for four o'clock at the dance hall to be followed later by the *grand fete*, the biggest moment of all and the penultimate stage of the festival.

Rudy showed up at the dance hall at approximately quarter to four, much later than he'd planned. He'd forgotten that the La Rose festivities normally started early in the morning. Since Olive had only alluded to the latter part of the festival, he'd decided to sleep late and while away the rest of the morning in the hope of hooking up with Bridget for lunch, especially as she had stood him up the day before.

He'd also been looking forward to taking some choice photos of Edward in action, knowing the tabloids would be falling over themselves to get the scoop, especially if he could beat other reporters to the punch, assuming that there'd be others around, which he doubted. He figured he might as well start cashing in on any opportunities that came his way to make a few extra quid.

On realising that he'd arrived late, he felt like kicking himself. What's more he felt miffed that Bridget hadn't tried to contact him, leaving him instead to loll aimlessly on the beach. He'd tried calling her three times on her mobile phone but she didn't respond. He'd also left her a voicemail message but she didn't reply.

The dance hall was a large open space with a bare wooden floor, a stage and aluminium louver windows on both sides. On entering the hall, Rudy was struck by the number of foreigners who had showed up; at least forty, including several children, along with scores of locals, mostly from the village. They all awaited the arrival of the royals and their court with great anticipation. The hall was decorated with bright-coloured paper streamers and ornaments, bouquets of synthetic red roses pinned to the walls, red, pink and white flags and a large Union Jack mounted conspicuously on an indoor flagpole. The excitement in the air was palpable. Occasionally the foreigners and locals mingled and chatted with each other but by and large the two groups kept to themselves.

Rudy had brought his Canon EOS M2 camera. He preferred doing his own photography when covering stories and was quite skilled at it. He was about to begin taking pictures when he heard the shrill blast of whistles. Someone called for the crowd's attention. Music and singing could be heard outside. A man wearing a police uniform stood near the door. Speaking in Creole, he announced the arrival of the king and queen and instructed everyone to adhere to protocol and bow to the royals as they made their entrance. Rudy readied his camera and focussed on the door.

Edward and Olive paused inside the doorway. The camera nearly dropped from Rudy's hands as he gaped wide-eyed at Olive. She wore an elegant pink evening gown made of satin, with a long flowing train. A velvet cloak was thrown over her shoulders and a white sash was draped across her bosom. The dress was a replica of one typically worn by damsels of the British Royal Court in the

19th and early 20th centuries, in its every detail. On her head was a golden crown made of papier mâché, and cradled in the crook of her arm was a gold-painted wooden sceptre. Olive was clearly over the moon and she radiated her joy like a numinous halo. Incredibly, as if to underscore her pre-eminence, she carried a festive garland made of five-pound banknotes in her right hand. In his befuddlement, Rudy tried to estimate the total value of the notes. He figured it had to be at least five hundred pounds.

Edward was no less a spectacle. He wore a finely tailored, white suit with gold epaulets and a red sash similar to Olive's. He also wore a beautiful red rose in his buttonhole to demonstrate his loyalty to La Rose. Trailing them, their sweaty faces beaming with pride, were the dukes and princes sporting black suits embroidered in gold braid, white gloves and admirals' hats with white plumes. The two duchesses wore blush-pink evening dresses with silk lace and white hats with feather plumes.

Edward and Olive made their way to the centre of the hall amid loud fanfare. Their loyal subjects gathered dutifully around them, including a doctor, several nurses in navy-blue uniforms with snow-white aprons and caps, a magistrate, the Lord Great Chamberlain, ladies-in-waiting, the military and police. They were accompanied by a choral group led by the lead singer or *chantwelle* along with dancers and the band of musicians. There were also several child pages dressed in immaculate white First Communion suits and frocks, with toss *bulé* in their hands - spherical coloured glass used as Christmas tree ornaments. They danced and serenaded the Rose with bright-eyed alacrity and an elfin charm. They won the hearts of the audience, especially the women.

Aside from the duchesses and nurses, most of the women wore the traditional *douillette*, a floral dress girded at the waist, with a train looped over a starched petticoat or, alternatively, white blouses with a low neckline and a *jupe* – a full skirt looped over a petticoat. They all wore colourful Madras headdresses called *Tete-en-l'Aire*. The head pieces had small peaks at the front, either one peak indicating the woman was single or two peaks signifying she was married. Only three of them had head pieces with three peaks, a sign that they were widows. A couple of them wore wide-brimmed straw hats on top of their headdresses.

Nearly everyone in the audience, young and old, local and foreigner, came forward to shake the proffered royal hands. Edward smiled warmly and acknowledged all and sundry who came making obeisance. Rudy noticed that he was especially charming to the Americans in the audience, smiling and chatting graciously with them, a wily glint in his eyes.

Meanwhile, the *chantwelle* belted out another La Rose tune, and the other singers joined in. The dancers formed a circle and the other members joined in. They were preparing to dance the *Mapa,* a special dance unique to the La Rose. Round and round they went in a counter-clockwise direction with shuffling steps, shaking their hips and shoulders, their arms held up high and swaying from side to side. Edward and Olive joined in. They danced around the circuit seven times before the *chantwelle* concluded the song with a shout of "*Vive La Rose*!" The dancers echoed her cry at the top of their lungs, "*Vive La Rose*!"

The *chantwelle* then called for everyone's attention. Speaking in Creole, she said the next song was dedicated specially to their king and patron, Lord Edward Tennyson and briefly recounted all the good things he had done for La Rose and the people of Elysian Island, rich and poor alike. She repeated it in English for the sake of the foreigners. Then she broke out into a lusty chant that was promptly picked up by the other singers and backed up by the musicians. Together, they set the hall on fire with the new tune. It was as artful as it was bewildering.

"*Wa nou Edward se yon nom / Ki ni logéy / Si li chen asu logéy sa-a / Wa nou kay bwiyé La Woz'* (Edward, our King is a man / who has pride / If he keeps to this pride / Our King will shine La Woz). All along, Rudy had been snapping photos of the proceedings. The song brought him up short. He gaped incredulously at Edward. Edward smiled and nodded approvingly to his praise-singers, a look of paternalistic indulgence etched on his face. He swayed from side to side and jiggled his hips to the rhythm of the chant. Olive danced along happily beside him. Judging by her ineffable smile and the euphoric gleam in her eyes, she was clearly having an unbelievable experience. In the midst of the singing and loud chattering, someone was translating the Creole lyrics to a group of Brits and Americans in the crowd. Then the *chantwelle* launched into a new verse.

"*Misyé Edward hausé Union Jack la / Sey Béché en Langlite / Ek L'Amerique aussi / Ki vini fété la Woz*!" (Mr. Edward has hoisted the Union Jack / It is white men from England and even America / who have come to celebrate La Woz.) By then Bill Thompson and his wife who had arrived about fifteen minutes earlier, had joined them. "Thanks to King Edward, it looks like you guys have had the last laugh!" said Thompson, addressing two Englishmen and an elderly Englishwoman in a group of six, including three American men.

One of the Englishmen concurred. "And to think we beat ourselves up so much over the things that we have imparted to the rest of the world, yet the locals here are quite nice to us, aren't they?" he added to a chorus of chuckles, mostly among the Americans. The elderly Englishwoman tossed her head haughtily and said, "In the face of a woeful decline in decorum and deference, even in Britain, I say hats off to Edward for emphasising the point, if a bit crudely."

One of the Americans chimed in. "I must say this is the largest expat turnout I've seen at a La Rose festival yet, and I've been to a few of them in my time here. Seems to me Bill, the Company should consider taking a more active interest in the festivity."

"You've got a point there. At the very least, it looks like we've cottoned on to a new selling point to attract the British," said Thompson.

His wife said, with an encouraging smile, "It's a very unique cultural tradition. It would be such a shame if measures are not taken to ensure its preservation, don't you think, dear?"

Someone commented on Bridget's 'glaring absence' and another one wondered aloud why she hadn't showed up. Thompson quickly responded that he hadn't a clue and tried to change the subject. He caught sight of Rudy standing a few yards away and waved at him. Rudy waved back. Thompson excused himself and went over to join him. Patting Rudy on the back, he said, "What do you think, how're you enjoying it?"

"It's interesting," Rudy said noncommittally, avoiding Thompson's eyes.

"That's not exactly a ringing endorsement. You're a native of the island so I imagine you'd be familiar with the La Rose. What do you think of Edward's performance? How does he measure up?"

Rudy caught the mischievous twinkle in Thompson's eyes. "He's all heart. It's a good thing he doesn't have to depend on theatre or dancing for a living."

Thompson roared with laughter. Someone called out to him from the group he had just left. "See you around. Enjoy the fun," he said and left.

An outburst of laughter from among the ring of dancers caught Rudy's attention. Four La Rose police officers armed with wooden rifles had just arrested two teenage boys, one for stealing a bag of sweets dangling from the ceiling and the other for smoking without a license. Ignoring their pleas for mercy, the officers hauled them away to face the magistrate seated at a table, a chiselled-faced man with an austere bearing that was slightly overdone. He wore a forbidding black gown, a bench wig, a wing collar and bands. He proceeded to hold a mock trial of the accused thieves. Five minutes later he pronounced judgement. The culprits were each fined five dollars to be paid forthwith. No sooner they did, two of the policemen grabbed them by the seat of their pants and led them away amid a shrill chorus of laughter.

Rudy took it all in stone-faced. The drama of the court seemed to have intensified the excitement. The musicians resumed playing with gusto and this fired up the dancers. The magistrate declared the court adjourned and left the bench to join in the dancing. Edward was chatting with a group of Brits. Queen Olive danced away with her subjects while two children shimmied along behind her, holding up her train. Rudy was bewildered by it all. What confounded him the most was that he couldn't tell whether or not it was all being done in jest or if perhaps there was some sort of parodic subtext to the whole serio-comic farce. As for Edward, he seemed to be poking fun at everyone; the villagers, the Americans, British aristocracy, even himself. At that point Rudy decided he'd had enough.

Tucking his camera into the case he weaved through the crowd and out of the building. A group of people stood outside conversing. Vernon Allain, Edward's personal assistant, was among them. He and Rudy spotted each other. Walking up to Rudy, he asked, surprised, "You're leaving already?"

"I'm afraid so," Rudy replied.

"How was it? Did you enjoy yourself?"

"To be honest, I don't know whether I should laugh or cry."

"How do you mean?"

Rudy shrugged. "Never mind ... Just out of curiosity, is this typically how La Rose séances are done? I mean in terms of the slavish deference to British aristocratic values, the meticulous attention to detail that obviously went into designing the costumes; they must have cost a bloody arm and a leg! And then the tribute to Edward. Is this how you guys normally do it over here?"

Vernon chuckled. "This year it was done on a grander scale. The members of the La Rose planning committee all agreed with Edward that this time around they needed to have a festival that mirrored more closely the way it used to be done in the earlier days, way back at the beginning of the 20th century. Edward is part of the committee. He felt that over the years the quality of the festival had been allowed to deteriorate and he wanted to change this. To quote him, 'it had gone to the dogs.' They researched it at the Saint

Lucia National Archives over on the mainland. That's how they were able to come up with the designs for the outfits. As for the cost, Edward financed most of it. The people of the village are poor humble folk, they can't afford such extravagance, so everyone was happy that Edward offered to help."

"I guess there are still more activitics to come."

"Oh yes, the *Grand Fête* later this evening. There'll be a banquet and more singing and dancing, this time the quadrille and the belair and other figure dances. You're not going to miss it, are you? Edward would be disappointed."

"Would he? Do you really think so?"

"Oh yes! I'm sure."

Rudy paused, a thoughtful look on his face. Peering at Vernon, he said, "That settles it. I won't be coming ... Thank you my brother. You've just given me reason to feel good about myself for the first time today."

Vernon frowned. He looked baffled. Rudy moved closer to him and placed his arm across Vernon's shoulders. "Do you know what my greatest fear is?" he said.

"What's that?"

"Someday you and I are going to meet our African ancestors. I hope, to God, they have a sense of humour." Walking away, he added, "Have fun."

As he approached a vacant spot used as a parking area, a woman leaning against a car caught Rudy's eye. He stiffened. It was Kadija. She stared coldly at him. He became tongue-tied. Glancing away, he hurried past her, feeling embarrassed. Cursing under his breath, he continued walking towards his bike.

He thought of all the photos he had snapped of Edward in action, dancing away with Olive at his side and mingling with the commoners. He had no doubt they would fetch a tidy sum if he did an exclusive deal with one of the tabloids. But for some reason, he had lost his zeal. As he climbed onto the bike and pedalled away, he knew he would not be using the pictures. He couldn't bring himself to do it.

9

Rudy awoke from a deep sleep and sat bolt upright. He glanced at the luminous clock on the bedside table. It was 1:00 a.m. For a moment he felt disoriented. The plushness of the room, illuminated by the moonlight streaming through the windows, suddenly registered.

There was someone in the house.

He sensed the presence strongly and figured this was what had wakened him. He tiptoed across to the door and opened it slightly. He was wearing only boxer shorts. He paused a while to listen but heard nothing. Suddenly he recalled that the house was supposed to have been secured by electronic smartphone-operated Kevo locks. Before he left for Bill Thompson's party, Vernon Allain had popped in to show him how to operate them and provided him with the code. No one on the outside could get in without an iPhone equipped with the specialized app or code to unlock the doors or the windows. To do so they'd have to smash them. Nonetheless, Rudy couldn't help feeling that there was someone in the house. He decided to follow his instinct, knowing all too well that whenever he second guessed himself he ended up getting screwed.

Turning on the bedside lamp, he glanced around the room. He spotted a small wooden sculpture on top of the wardrobe. Grabbing it, he opened the door quietly and made his way stealthily down the hallway. He paused near the living room. There was no sign of anyone. He checked the dining and kitchen area but there was no one there. He shifted the drapes over the sliding glass doors to the terrace and peeked outside but saw nothing amiss. He checked the sliding doors to the patio. They were both unlocked. *Rudy froze and the hair on the nape of his neck stood on end.* He was sure he had locked and double checked both doors before going to bed. He tightened his grip on the sculpture and slowly retraced his steps back down the passageway.

He paused outside the door of the guestroom and turned the doorknob. It was locked. It shouldn't have been. He'd found the room unlocked when he moved in. It was accessible from outside through a patio with sliding doors. Unfortunately he hadn't thought to check them before going to bed. Dashing to his room, he grabbed his iPhone from the bedside table, turned on the in-built flashlight and rushed back to the other room, still armed with the sculpture. He switched on the light in the passageway. Holding the phone in his left hand, he tapped the door lock with his right index finger and a bright green halo flashed around it, followed by a click indicating the deadbolt was sprung.

He heard a dull thud inside the room. Shoving the phone into his pocket, he raised the sculpture over his head menacingly and pushed open the door, allowing the hallway light to spill into the room. There was no one inside. One of the white linen drapes over the sliding doors shifted, as if air was coming through. Rudy switched on the lights and examined the doors. One of them was not bolted and it was open slightly. He opened it wider and went out unto the patio. There was no one outside. He examined the door locks but saw no sign that they had been forced open or damaged. He locked it and searched through the room. Although it was unfamiliar he was hoping that he might still be able to detect if anything had been moved. He combed through it meticulously. Nothing looked suspicious.

He checked the living room and kitchen again but there seemed to be nothing out of place. He was now beginning to freak out and wondered if his mind was playing tricks on him. But then, what to make of the open patio doors in the bedroom? Using the iPhone he relocked the front doors and made sure they were secured. He heaved a sigh of relief. He yearned for some weed to calm his nerves. Unfortunately his stash had run out.

He shuffled resignedly back to his room and flopped down on the bed. *What the fuck's going on and what have I gotten myself into*? he thought to himself. Why would anyone want to break into the house and how did they get access to the lock code? From what he knew about these digital home security systems, you had to be a pro to hack into them. He couldn't imagine any burglar on the island with such skill using it to try and rob him, of all people. Of course, it was possible that the intruder had gained access to the lock code legitimately, which would mean it was an inside job. But if so, why? What could possibly be the motive? Evidently it wasn't a robbery since nothing was missing, at least as far as he could tell.

Rudy felt emotionally drained. He'd already been on the island for a whole week yet practically nothing had been accomplished regarding the book. He hadn't even been able to get held of Edward, all because he'd been so preoccupied with with his preparations for the La Rose festival. As for Bridget, he'd managed to have lunch with her twice and that was it. She'd been too tied up with her business affairs.

Ultimately, he was reduced to loafing on the beaches like a bum, haunting the bars, particularly the Halcyon since he could dine there without having to worry about the bill. He'd also cycled around a bit and visited the village where he discovered a quaint little bar called the Buccaneer Rum Shop & Bar, and joined a group of fishermen in a few rounds of drinks and played dominoes with them.

The rest of the time he remained indoors sleeping or surfing the net. It had been terribly frustrating. He'd felt like an animal trapped in a cage.

It was now Wednesday - three days since the La Rose festival. Two days earlier he'd been holed up indoors for the entire day because of heavy rains caused by a tropical wave that had swept over the Windward Islands, according to local meteorological reports. Being familiar with the unpredictable Caribbean weather, he wasn't surprised, just annoyed with himself for stubbornly insisting on a bicycle as his preferred mode of transport and limiting his options.

The rain finally stopped around 6:00 p.m. Earlier, around midday, Bridget had telephoned him and promised to come visiting later since, according to her, they had 'loads to discuss.' She'd raised his hopes with the assurance that it would be one of their most memorable evenings ever, thanks to the weather. Edward had gone out and was not expected to return until the following day, she further assured him.

Half an hour before their date, she called to cancel it due to an 'unexpected and urgent business engagement' and apologized profusely, making soothing noises, as if she was comforting a wounded pup. Rudy took a deep breath and pretended that he understood and then spent the rest of the evening stewing in his rage.

A couple of hours later, on a whim he decided to call his ex-girlfriend Amy in London. This proved to be a mistake. Somehow she found out that he'd travelled to the Caribbean. He hadn't told her. He decided to come clean with her. She went ballistic. For the next ten minutes he was forced to listen to her raving and ranting and going on about his shameless addiction to 'white pussy.' It didn't help that he had called her at 3:00 a.m., UK time. He eventually cut the call in exasperation.

Then around midnight, just as he was about to hit the sack, the home phone rang. It was Kadija. To his surprise, she apologized for her hostile behavior and told him she wished to make amends. Her idea of making it up to him was the two of them going out on a moonlight picnic at a secluded beach – just the two of them. Rudy accepted her apology but politely declined her offer.

An hour later, while he slept, the phone rang. Once again, it was Kadija. On realizing she had awakened him, she apologized and then proceeded to ramble on about the crushing loneliness of an artist's life and the isolation she'd had to endure in a place like Elysian Island, especially being a black woman. Then, out of the blue, she asked him about his personal life. Barely able to contain his irritation, Rudy begged off without making it seem as if he was snubbing her, and explained that he hadn't had a decent rest over the past few days.

Incredibly, Kadija called him a third time, at the break of dawn. By then he'd begun to feel as if he was being hunted. The worst part was that the strain of it all reignited his urge for some weed but with Kadija all but stalking him, he didn't relish the prospect of going up to her place.

As for Edward, Rudy's impatience with him was growing since he was eager to get started on their discussions concerning the book and arranging a schedule for the interview sessions. Although the La Rose festivities were now over, he still hadn't heard from Edward. The day before, he'd telephoned Blossom House to try and get hold of him. Vernon responded and informed Rudy that Edward was unavailable but was expected to return home later in the evening. Annoyed, Rudy told him to ensure that Edward returned his call. He didn't hide his irritation. Around 8:00 p.m. Vernon called to inform him that Edward wished to meet with him the following day at Blossom House for lunch. The lunch date was scheduled for one o'clock and Vernon arranged to pick him up at quarter to one. Rudy breathed a sigh of relief and thanked him heartfeltly.

That night he'd gone to bed feeling a bit more relaxed, only to have his sleep rudely interrupted by a supposed intruder. The last thing he needed was having to worry about his safety in a house that was pretty much isolated. He glanced at the clock. It was quarter to three. At least there was still enough time to catch a snooze, providing he could fall asleep. He toyed with the idea of taking a drink but then wondered if it might cause him to oversleep.

Fuck it. He headed for the bar and fixed himself a shot of rum and coke and returned to the bedroom. In between nursing his drink and brooding over the night's bizarre occurrence, an hour dragged by and then eventually he began dozing off. No sooner he placed the glass on the bedside table and sank down into the plush mattress, he was out like a light.

He woke up from a dreamless sleep at nine-thirty and dragged himself out of bed. He headed straight for the shower, hoping that a cold bath would revive him. With the break-in still weighing heavily on his mind, he was eager to discuss it with Bridget, provided he could get hold of her. He decided to have breakfast first since he was in no mood to have such a discussion on an empty stomach.

After his bath, while rummaging through his clothes in the closet where he had packed them away, something caught his attention. His Rasta guitar-pick necklace with the Bob Marley logo and another one with a peace sign and his name inscribed on it, were not on the top shelf where he had placed them. He treasured them deeply and always took them along when he travelled, which was why he realized immediately that they were missing. Back at home he normally tucked them away in the same spot; the upper right-hand corner of the topmost shelf in his closet. From habit he did the same thing after moving into the house. He usually wore the one with the Bob Marley logo and seldom removed it, except that he decided to the night before, although he wasn't sure why. He had placed it next to the other one. Neither was there now. On that same shelf there were a few blank CDs, two bottles of shaving cream and a few paperback novels, none of which belonged to him. He pulled everything out and pored over the shelf again, just to be sure, although he knew in his gut the necklaces were gone. He checked the rest of the closet but came up empty. Hurrying across to his travel bag near the bedside table, he searched for his camera and iPad. They were still there. His laptop was safe and sound on the night table. Apparently only the necklaces had been stolen.

This came as quite a shock; not because of the necklaces, but because it dawned on him someone had entered the room while he slept. Whoever had broken in could have done him in and he may not have lived to tell the tale. He felt a sudden flash of rage at the blatant violation of his privacy. It felt like he had been raped! He took a deep breath and tried to calm down.

Then the absurdity of the situation hit him. Why would anyone want to burglarize the place to steal two beaded necklaces? Notwithstanding they held tremendous sentimental value for him, financially they were worth very little. If anything, it was their lack of monetary value compared to the camera and iPhone or the laptop, all of which had been there for the taking, that made the burglary illogical, and made him uneasy.

Going across to the kitchen he poked through the refrigerator distractedly. There was certainly no shortage of foodstuffs. The cupboards were just as loaded, seemingly with every grocery item imaginable, and by the looks of it there was enough to feed a whole football team for several days. Under normal circumstances he would have thanked the gods for smiling on him and transforming his humdrum life into such a fantasy, albeit temporarily. Unfortunately he'd been brought back to earth by the night's strange episode. After some deliberation, he settled on coffee and a toasted egg sandwich and set about preparing them without enthusiasm.

While eating, he decided to telephone Bridget. He hoped to God she took the call and it didn't get shunted to her voicemail. She responded after the first two rings and sounded so sweet and chirpy, he felt sorry to spoil it with bad news. He told her about his ordeal. "What I can't understand," he concluded, "is how the crook was able to get in. How did he or she get access to the lock code?" There was silence on the other end of the line. Finally Bridget spoke. Rudy listened to her, frowning. "Vernon Allain!" he blurted out. "Why on earth would you want to have him of all people, come over to check the locks? Why not call the police? Don't you guys have cops here?" His frown deepened as he listened to her response. "I guess I have no choice, I'll have to settle for your man coming over. But I still think the cops should get involved?" he insisted. He asked her if she planned to come over. The scowl on his face showed his displeasure with her response. "*Tomorrow evening*? That's slow and painful torture, for God's sake! Why on earth did you want me over here if you knew you were going to be so busy? What am I going to do with myself till then?" Rudy listened to her response, his face livid. He closed his eyes and let out a sigh of frustration. "I give up. Tomorrow evening it is," he said resignedly, adding, "I finally got a date with your husband. We're meeting this afternoon at one ... God knows how much I'm longing to see you." He paused a while and suddenly looked surprised. "Edward's nephew? It's the first time I've ever heard of him. And you say he came in from the U.K. last night?" Still frowning, Rudy listened a while then just as he was about to speak, he paused and gaped wide-eyed at the phone. "She's in quite a hurry. She hung up before I could finish," he muttered, sounding puzzled.

He still had about two hours left before his rendezvous with Edward. It would be their first face-to-face meeting to discuss the book. He had really been looking forward to it. Now he was feeling apprehensive and beginning to have second thoughts; all because of Bridget's startling revelations about Edward, and Bill Thompson's warnings about the potential legal problems confronting him if he persisted with his literary ambitions. Not that he was afraid for his own skin or looking to chicken out; rather he was beginning to feel like a fly caught in a web of clashing agendas, namely that of Edward, Bridget and Bill Thompson. He would definitely have to chat with Andrew, his literary agent about the situation to get his take on it, but he could only do so after his discussions with Edward.

Regarding Bridget and Edward's marriage, it was over. That much was clear. Still, Rudy was taken aback by the intensity of Bridget's bitterness toward her husband, almost bordering on contempt. The relationship was much worse than he'd suspected. He couldn't help feeling that the age difference between them had a lot to do with it. Bridget was thirty-five - *thirty-two years* younger than the old boy, for God's sake! Rudy shook his head defeatedly. It never ceased to amaze him that so many rich old men allowed their emotions and their libido to sucker them into marrying women young enough to be their goddamn granddaughters, especially those born with perpetual golden spoons in their mouths. They seemed more prone to getting caught in such entanglements, something he always took note of from his experience working for the tabloids. Considering the dilemma facing Edward, and being a man himself, he figured he ought to feel a bit sorry for the poor bloke. But he felt nothing, no guilt nor sympathy.

He wondered how Edward would react if he took Bridget's advice and told him he'd changed his mind about the book. Not only would he risk offending the old boy, he would be pulling the rug out from under his own feet. It would make it difficult, if not impossible, for him to remain on the island and ruin his chances of producing a bestseller.

At that point Rudy realized that the last thing he wanted to do was pack up and leave. At the very least, he wanted to continue sampling the good life and prolong his escape into fantasy.

Also, he didn't want to lose Bridget. There was no point pretending that she hadn't burrowed deep into his consciousness. He would be under her spell wherever he went. Did her incredible offer to make him her business partner have anything to do with it? He wasn't sure, or perhaps he didn't want to know.

10

Within an hour of Rudy's phone conversation with Bridget, Vernon Allain showed up at the house. It was just as well since he was supposed to pick Rudy up and transport him to Blossom House for his lunch date with Edward.

"Good to see you. That was fast." Rudy ushered him in. He gave Vernon a rundown of what he'd discovered the night before. Vernon listened silently, a stolid look on his face. At the end of it, he asked, frowning, "Are you sure you locked all the doors before going to bed?"

"Absolutely."

"Did you check them – *all* of them – to be sure?"

"I checked the front and patio doors." Rudy hesitated, then added, "I forgot to double check the sliding doors in the guestroom."

"Hold on a minute." Vernon went outside to examine the exterior doors. Ten minutes later, he returned to join Rudy in the living room. "There's no sign of forced entry," he said dryly.

"Does anyone else have access to the lock code?"

"No, only you. Bridget has exclusive access to the master code, which means she's the only one, aside from you, who can access, alter or erase your pin." Peering thoughtfully at Rudy, Vernon said, "Did you actually see someone inside the house?"

"No but I heard someone."

"You mean you heard what you *thought* was someone."

"For God's sake man, I found the doors in the guest room open. How do you explain that?"

"It could have been this way before you moved in. You admit you hadn't checked them and unfortunately, neither did I ... Once again, are you sure that you ascertained for a fact that the front and patio doors were locked before you went to bed?"

"Yes, I did."

"The fact that you found them unlocked suggests otherwise."

"What are you trying to do, play devil's advocate?"

"I'm just trying to look at this objectively. Maybe the locks are flawed. These so-called smart locks have been known to malfunction. Who's to say this isn't what happened in your case? Frankly I've always been skeptical of these new-fangled devices. I cautioned Bridget against them but like so many people on this island, she's all for them."

"Listen Vernon, maybe you didn't hear me the first time; *my necklaces are missing*. Oh, wait ... don't tell me. They weren't there in the first place. I only imagined that I put them there."

"No, I believe you. If you say they were there, so be it ... When last did you set eyes on them?"

Rudy pondered a while. "Day before yesterday. I'd been wearing one of them but decided to pack it away with the other one in the closet."

"So between then and last night someone could have moved them."

"And, pray tell, who might that be?"

"Over the past few days has anyone else visited the house?"

"Just Ma Nichols, the cleaner and the chap who brought the groceries, on two occasions."

"Maybe we should have a word with both of them. Not that I'm accusing either of anything but just to be sure. I'll speak with them."

"Do you actually believe these folks would steal my stuff?"

"I won't know until I have a word with them. To be honest, from what I know of them, I don't think so but one can't always be sure. In recent times, at least two people who worked at Blossom House have been dismissed for theft. Off and on this sort of thing happens."

"Sorry mate, I beg to differ. I know beyond a shadow of a doubt what I heard and experienced last night. My instinct tells me there *was* an intruder in the house. I believe the culprit stole my necklaces, for whatever reason."

Vernon shrugged. "Suit yourself." Glancing at his watch, he added, "We better go or you'll be late for your meeting with Edward."

Rudy peered at him, frowning. "I may be wrong but you sound like you fancy yourself as the Elysian Island version of Poirot," he scoffed.

"I am a former police inspector."

"What?"

"I served in the Royal Saint Lucia Police Force for thirty years. I was also the sergeant in charge of the Elysian Island precinct for five years, up until three years ago."

"What happened, did you quit or were you put out to pasture?"

"I resigned."

"Why?"

"That's a long story. I don't care to go into it now, besides we don't have much time. Edward doesn't take kindly to being kept waiting."

"I guess it's much more lucrative serving as his Man Friday."

Vernon bore it well. "I think we should go," he said unruffled, his face deadpan. Walking past Rudy, he headed for the door. Rudy followed him.

11

As soon as he walked through the front door at Blossom House, it crossed Rudy's mind that he should tell Edward about the break-in but then he decided against it. Recalling how adamant Bridget had been that he keep it quiet and not inform the police, he figured he'd let it ride for the time being. He followed Vernon up the stairway to the second floor and into the verandah where Edward sat relaxing at a wrought iron table, part of a classical three-piece dinette set.

"Welcome." Edward got up and they shook hands. "Do make yourself at home," he said, indicating the chair opposite. Rudy did. Vernon returned inside the house. Rudy took in the breathtaking view of Albion Bay and the sea. "That's some view! It's quite spectacular," he gushed.

"Indeed. It is very satisfactory ... I trust that you have been comfortably housed and your every wish is being catered to."

"My stay has been extremely pleasant," Rudy replied, smiling. "I wish to thank you very much for your hospitality."

"Don't thank me, thank my wife. She has become quite adept at welcoming guests and making them feel cared for."

Rudy shifted uncomfortably in his seat. Edward made him a bit uneasy. A woman stepped out onto the verandah. Short, baby-faced and plump, she was dressed primly in a traditional maid's uniform; a dark, knee-length dress with a white apron and a fluffy white cap. She greeted Rudy warmly.

"This is Eleanor," said Edward and he introduced Rudy to the woman and vice versa.

"Excuse me, sir," said Eleanor, "I just want to know what Mr. Phillips prefer for lunch."

"Ah yes," said Edward, beaming cheerfully. "What're we having?"

Eleanor said they would have pumpkin soup for starters and thereafter three choices - local fish broth made with fresh tuna and green bananas, Creole shrimp in garlic and butter sauce or grilled chicken breast with a salad. Rudy settled for the Creole shrimp and so did Edward. For drinks, Rudy opted for red wine while Edward requested gin and Dubonnet.

Eleanor nodded and smiled, and went off dutifully to attend to their requests.

Turning to Edward, Rudy said, "From what I've seen of the island, it's fascinating. I would imagine you must feel quite proud of your accomplishments, and rightly so."

"As you may know, I purchased Elysian Island forty years ago. If you'd been present at that time, you would have questioned my sanity rather than consider me deserving of praise."

"Why do you say so?"

Edward leaned back, an introspective look on his face. "From the first day I set foot on the island in 1963, I all but gave in to despair and wondered what on earth had gotten into me to cause me to purchase this place. I was convinced that I had made the most frightful mistake of my life. It was all quite run down. The few available roads were terrible. The approximately two dozen natives residing here were basically squatters. They cultivated root vegetables but they were barely able to eke out a living from the land. Some of them reared free-range chickens and a few goats and sheep. I dare say they were quite disaffected. They were descendents of sharecroppers who once worked on the three sugar and cotton estates that had been functioning here back in the 1940s.

"Feral cattle and pigs roamed the land back in those days and they frequently damaged what crops and pasture there were. Worst of all, there was no electricity and a small catchment up in a hilly part of the north was the only source of water. A Great House which originally belonged to one of the estate owners was the only decent habitation on the island and even that was decrepit.

"Simply getting here was a long and tedious journey. There was no airport. The only direct flight from Britain to this part of the Caribbean was a BOAC flight to Barbados. From there I travelled aboard a seaplane to Saint Lucia and continued on to Elysian Island via a schooner.

"We landed with provisions to last about five days. When we arrived at the Great House, my wife, now deceased, told me that I was mad. The Great House had been erected on the same spot that Blossom House now occupies. Within a few months, I had to have it torn down and rebuilt." Indicating a section of the property with a sweep of his arms, Edward added, "This entire area was covered with Poinsettia Blossoms. It was absolutely delightful. The new house was eponymously named.

"Initially it was used for family holidays and to entertain friends. In 1964, soon after I arrived on the island, I formed the Elysian Island Company along with some of my relatives, and shortly thereafter we were open for business. The requisite infrastructure had to be built and utilities had to be installed. There was a lot to be done and the costs were quite considerable. I persevered, nonetheless, until my goals were achieved. Now I look upon it all with a tremendous sense of relief and self-satisfaction rather than pride."

Eleanor came out with a tray bearing their appetizers. She served Rudy and then Edward. "Hope you enjoy it," she said and walked off with her dutiful smile.

Rudy took a taste and nodded approvingly. "Tastes wonderful," he said.

Edward smiled. He seemed pleased. "Incidentally," he said, "have you had an opportunity to do some sightseeing?"

"Not as much as I would like," Rudy replied, sipping his soup. "As you could well imagine, I am more eager to begin working on your memoir."

"Indeed. I will, of course, provide relevant resource materials and other content for your perusal before we commence the interviews. However, I think you would find it helpful to familiarize yourself with the landscape and the island's topography. Elysian too has a voice and one must be attuned to it to connect with the soul of the place and factor it into the whole picture. Permit me, if I may, to explain the alignment of the various quarters." Pointing westward in the direction of Albion Bay, Edward continued, "Albion Bay, the main commercial hub, falls within the quarter of La Plaine, which encompasses a sizeable chunk of the island's leeward coast. As you can see, it is relatively flat and accessible and the sea on this side is generally calm. Further north is Grand Anse. This area too has lots of flat and fertile land. That is where three of the old sugar and cotton estates were located. It's also where the village is situated, along the coast and where the locals do most of their farming and husbandry.

"As you may have noticed, most of the villas and business places are located on the leeward coast between Albion Bay and Grand Anse. Dauphine Bay is over to the east, on the windward side. It is rather untamed and rocky and some parts are quite arid. In the centre of the island lies Mount Britannia. It rises to six hundred feet and is the highest point. I would be happy to give you a guided tour of the place whenever it is convenient."

Rudy mopped up his last bit of soup. "By all means, whenever you're ready."

As if on cue, Eleanor came out wheeling a serving trolley with their meals and drinks. Once again, she served Rudy first and then Edward, flitting back and forth with practiced efficiency and a maternal air about her.

Rudy sipped his wine and tucked in. "If you don't mind my asking, how do you spend your time? What exactly do you do?"

Edward nibbled at his shrimp. "Lately a considerable amount of my time has been spent musing over this incredibly beautiful place, wandering through it in my mind. One can't help being besotted with the landscape and all one wants to do is further enhance it. I receive about two hundred guests every year. I entertain, travel occasionally. Basically, I can do whatever I like and I have to say this gives me a great deal of satisfaction."

"I take it that you are no longer actively involved in the running of the Elysian Island Company as I presume you used to be in times past."

"Seven years ago I sold a controlling interest in the company to Ross Welch, an American oil tycoon and one of the island's homeowners. He subsequently installed Bill Thompson to take over its operations and the administration of the island. Unfortunately, we do not share the same vision for the place and he and I had a serious divergence of opinions on what the company's values and standards ought to be."

Rudy refilled his glass with wine and went to work on his salad. He was clearly enjoying his meal. "Do you care to elaborate?" he said.

Peering across at a group of figures frolicking on the beach, Edward said wistfully, "There was a time when I used to be familiar with practically everyone who resided on this island or who had merely stopped over to enjoy its natural pleasures. I knew all of them intimately, in fact. Fifty years ago when I purchased the island I had a vision of transforming it into an idyllic, self-contained world that I could then offer as a sanctuary to the sort of people who always had to be on guard from prying eyes and the intrusions of the press. A place where they could feel free to shed their inhibitions and rediscover their true selves; somewhat of a Garden of Eden, if you will. No need to burden oneself with tedious conformity to the knowledge of good and evil. Just be happy and enjoy life, without infringing on anyone's right to do likewise. You were allowed to become a resident landowner or a guest on the personal recommendations of members of the community who cared to vouch for your character - *not*, I emphasize, purely on the basis of money. This was necessary to maintain an air of wonder and mystique.

"We created a way of life here that was focused on allowing you to be whomever you wish, not on dictating who or what you can't be. We liked to be spontaneous and enjoy life. I gave them the freedom to manifest the reality they desired. Sadly, these days the notion of spontaneity and freedom has become a dangerous one."

"You sound disappointed with the way things have turned out?"

Once again Edward stared sullenly at the bathers on the beach. "Strangers ... nearly all of them are strangers to me," he said broodingly. "Most of them are here for the sun, sea and sand, the insipid gastronomic fare served up by some of the more recent bars and restaurants, and for an illusionary sense of prestige. It's all about money, no longer about breeding and character. To make money the sole deciding factor in determining who enters Elysian Island is short-sighted and irresponsible. It's a fairly recent phenomenon, you know, a classic by-product of the American contagion. Initially, when I invited Ross Welch to acquire shares in the company, I felt compelled to do so for financial reasons. Nothing is the same anymore, it has all changed."

Eleanor came to enquire if they were ready for desert. Edward declined and requested tea instead. Rudy opted for the local Piton beer. Eleanor nodded and, like a sprightly little fairy, hurried away to do their bidding.

Gazing at Rudy, Edward said, "By now you should have done some measure of research and you ought to be familiar with my heredity and the details of my early years growing up in Britain. Suffice to say I am far less interested in rehashing this relatively inconsequential part of my existence. Instead, I wish to focus on those major incidents that have had the most profound and transformative effects on my life. You will find that most of them are related to my acquisition and development of Elysian Island and latterly the ownership change at the company. One has to be here on the ground to get a feel of the world I am describing, hence the reason I insisted that you come over so that we could do the interviews face to face. Also, I think it is only fair that other persons to whom I will inevitably be making reference, be given the opportunity to provide their perspective if they so desire."

"I assume then that much of what the book deals with will be revealed publicly for the first time."

"Oh, indeed."

Rudy hesitated. Clearing his throat, he said, "I need to ask you, sir ... perhaps I should have brought it up from the start. Would you be willing to co-sign an agreement letter indemnifying me from any legal claim or action arising from the publication of the book?"

Edward smiled. "By all means, you may proceed and draft the letter."

Eleanor brought them their drinks and left.

"Also, can we agree to have a solicitor review the draft of the manuscript?"

"Let me guess. You have been warned against rushing in where angels fear to tread." Rudy glanced away. "You have not been frightened off, have you sir?" said Edward.

"Actually, having an agreement letter and involving a solicitor in the process are standard practices in the co-authorship of memoirs, as I'm sure you are aware." Rudy replied.

Edward gave him an admonishing look. "In my discussions with you thus far, I have been and continue to be candid and open. I expect no less of you."

Rudy steeled himself and met Edward's probing gaze. "There are certain individuals who are very concerned about the book," He said.

"Bill Thomson and his brood, for instance?"

"Yes."

Edward smiled indulgently. "Many years ago, prior to your birth, I promised to sell a plot of land to one of my employees. It so happened that an acquaintance of mine who was quite wealthy, expressed an interest in purchasing the same property and offered me far more than my employee could ever have afforded. Your aunt who was in my employ at the time – a wonderful lady – would have none of it. She voiced her disapproval to me quite robustly and insisted that, as a man of principle, to renege on my word for the sake of expedience would be dishonorable and a sign of weakness. Very outspoken and forthright, she was. And I dare say, very astute and persuasive." Rudy knew Edward was taking a dig at him by subtly casting doubt on his integrity. He glanced away, embarrassed. Still gazing fixedly at Rudy, Edward said, with a slight edge in his voice, "Freedom of speech and ethics are, no doubt, alien concepts to the characters whose views are of such concern to you, not least the directors of the Elysian Island Company. Not even *my* views matter, notwithstanding I am still a shareholder of the Company, and bearing in mind too that I am its founder."

Edward's remark ignited Rudy's curiosity, despite his unease. "It sounds like you and the other officials of the company don't get along," he said.

"Between us there is a significant difference of perspective. My own is based on freedom of choice and mutual consensus. It recognizes the importance of not standing in the way of the individual who wishes to discover and define their reality within the parameters of the freedoms conferred on us by natural law. It further recognizes that there is a human and spontaneous side to life. On this point, my colleagues and I have a fundamental disagreement. Presently, the company's goal is profit maximization and the commodification of virtually all aspects of life on the island. It seeks to impose its own version of reality on the residents. It dictates what is and what is not permissible, as if they are infants in need of guidelines. It is fast becoming a law unto itself." Edward's face hardened and Rudy caught the anguished look in his eyes before it vanished to be replaced by his usual equanimous smile. "I have digressed, I apologize," he said. "May we agree on a schedule for the commencement of the interviews?"

"With respect, sir you have not commented on my suggestion."

"What suggestion?"

Rudy steeled himself and tried his best to look Edward straight in the eye. "Would you agree to have a solicitor peruse the manuscript?"

"What for? Why would I want to do such a thing?"

"It would be prudent for both of us."

"You mean it would assuage Bill and Bridget's trepidation. Would this be either of their suggestion by any chance?"

"No. I assure you it isn't. I just thought it would be wise to suggest it."

"Then it is totally out of the question, I am afraid. As both you and I are aware, the memoir of Lord Edward Tennyson would be considered a prize find by many of the world's leading publishers. Assuming that your business acumen matches your literary capabilities, I expect that you would have a literary agent lying in wait for what is more than likely to be a bestseller. You ought to be prepared to do what it takes to earn this. Need I remind you that I have agreed to a seventy-five-twenty-five percent royalty split in your favor as an added incentive, rather than awarding you a pittance as ghostwriters typically earn? Additionally, let me reiterate that you will be indemnified from any legal claims arising from the publication of the book. Whether anyone dares to challenge me in court, however, remains to be seen. While I am prepared to give consideration to the views of a competent editor, I will not allow myself or you to be censored by any solicitor in the manner that you propose."

Edward's abrupt refusal caught Rudy off guard. For a moment he was lost for words. In the disconcerting silence, the distant screeching of seagulls and the persistent *pree-re-e* of peewees in nearby trees grew louder. Even the minutest of sounds became amplified and almost deafening. Rudy pretended to be occupied with adjusting the coaster under his beer.

A male voice could be heard inside. A man appeared in the doorway. Rudy and Edward glanced up at him. Edward's face lit up. "Aaron! What dragged you out of bed at such an ungodly hour?" he said.

"It's your dear wife's doing. I promised her that I would show up at the unveiling of some community project in the village sponsored by her company and the Elysian Island Company. It's scheduled for three o'clock this afternoon."

Shit! Rudy suddenly realized that he had forgotten all about the unveiling. He had given Thompson and Bridget his word that he would attend, the day he visited Bridget's office. He'd been so preoccupied with the break-in and his date with Edward, it slipped his mind.

Edward said, "Allow me to introduce you to my nephew, Aaron. He's come over on vacation."

Rudy stood up and shook hands with Aaron. "Pleased to meet you," he said.

"Same here," Aaron replied, with a broad smile. Rudy thought he bore a striking resemblance to the British newsman and CNN anchor, Richard Quest; the same elongated face, strong chin and broad forehead and the same bright, boyish smile and slightly squinting stare, down to the same gravelly voice and rectangular metal-rimmed glasses. He was about six feet tall, long-limbed and rangy and he wore a white button-down shirt, jeans and sneakers. "Welcome aboard," said Aaron. "I've heard all about you. Looks like you're in for a wild ride if Edward has his way."

Edward chuckled. "On the contrary, Rudy would argue, I'm sure, that he has found the pot of gold at the end of the rainbow, in every way imaginable."

Rudy shifted uncomfortably from one foot to the other and then hurriedly sat down and said nothing.

Staring at Edward, Aaron said, grinning, "I've been viewing photos of your coronation. I'm sorry I missed all the action."

"Rudy was there," Edward replied. "Did you enjoy the La Rose festival?" he asked, peering searchingly at Rudy.

"Aside from a small oversight, it was quite an extraordinary spectacle."

"What did we overlook?"

"You forgot to sing the British national anthem," Rudy said dryly.

"By golly, you're right! That would have been smashing, wouldn't it?"

"Don't mind him," said Aaron. "Look closely and you'll discover that he has horns and a long red tail." Turning to Edward, he said, "Would you mind terribly if I spirited Rudy away?" To

Rudy, he said, "Bridget has asked me to remind you of the unveiling. It appears that she and Bill Thompson are expecting you."

Rudy glanced uncomfortably across at Edward. "I was invited last week and I promised that I would be there. To be honest, I had forgotten about it as I was more concerned about our meeting today ... Perhaps I should contact them and explain that I'm unable to attend."

"You will do no such thing!" Edward said firmly. "Far be it from me to deny Bridget and Bill the pleasure of your company. You must do the honorable thing and attend. Besides, this is the perfect opportunity for you and Aaron to get acquainted."

"Certainly, if you insist. When will we meet again?"

"Once more, I must beg your indulgence. I need at the very least a few days to collate certain source materials that I wish to share with you, and sort through some other pending matters. I'm afraid I've been rather delinquent, mostly as a result of my preoccupation with the festival. I suggest we meet again a week from today – Wednesday, to be precise - here at the same time, for our first interview. We will then agree on a schedule for further sessions. Is that agreeable to you?"

"I guess it's okay," said Rudy, reluctantly and clearly disappointed with the delay. He rose to his feet. "Thanks for lunch. It was wonderful," he added. He and Edward shook hands.

"The pleasure is all mine."

"Off we go," said Aaron, heading for the door. "See you later," he said, waving at Edward. Rudy followed him downstairs.

12

Rudy and Aaron arrived in the village at three and found a gathering of about forty already there. The new community and literacy centre turned out to be a two-storied structure in the heart of the village, near a primary school and a health centre. The ground floor was the literacy centre, a modest-sized space equipped with a children's library and an internet cafe. While chatting with Aaron on the way up, Rudy learnt that it was Bridget who originally came up with the idea for the project and she sought the support of the Elysian Island Company. Visionary Investments financed part of the construction and the computers. The company footed the bill for the remainder of the construction and the bulk of the furnishings. The local internet service provider was brought on board as a cosponsor.

The unveiling was a simple affair held under a tent. Bill Thompson and Bridget were present along with other representatives of their respective companies and about fifteen VIP guests, including two of the island's wealthiest homeowners. Dozens of people from the village were there, including several schoolchildren. Olive was also there, to Rudy's delight. There were also a photographer and a videographer, both locals.

The event lasted half an hour and amounted to little more than a chorus of brief speeches delivered by a beaming Thompson and two rather acquiescent-looking government officials. They all touted the 'crucial importance' of the new facilities and the immense good they would do for the village, especially the children. The audience listened with dutiful attentiveness, and on cue they rewarded each speaker with a round of applause.

Afterwards, Thompson and Bridget hung around for about fifteen minutes fraternizing with the VIPs before they begged off and made their departure. The VIPs also took their leave. A table laden with snacks had been set up under a smaller tent. Two women, evidently serving as hostesses, urged the villagers to come and enjoy the treats and not to allow them to go to waste. They were more than happy to oblige. They descended on the table and began sampling the delicacies, laughing and chatting away.

Rudy declined while Aaron went over to help himself. The only foreigner among the group milling around the table, he stood out like a sore thumb. He joined in their chatter and even traded quips with some of the men. One of them asked him how his Creole was coming along. Aaron promptly gave him a demonstration that had the men in stitches. They couldn't stop laughing. One of them wiped tears from his eyes. It was almost as if Aaron was playing to the gallery and taking perverse pleasure in his obvious popularity. Studying him, Rudy detected traces of Edward's satiric wit, and he seemed to have a penchant for burlesque theatrics. He also saw signs that Aaron was a bit of a weirdo.

The eldest son of Edward's sister, he, like his uncle, was born to wealth and blessed with a trust fund, so he had no need to earn a living. He was thirty-seven. As he'd disclosed candidly to Rudy, he'd adamantly resisted his parents' attempts to marry him off and to have him play his part in managing the family country estate. They had also tried to involve him in national politics in the House of Lords, but he rebuffed them, opting instead to pursue a freewheeling life touring Europe. He subsequently returned home with the customary objets d'art that supposedly attested to the cultural and artistic superiority of the classical Greco-Roman civilizations. He took pleasure in exploring exotic parts of the Third World. When in Britain, he spent much of his time entertaining, and during winters he usually went hunting with hounds and shooting game birds. Most summers he went romping through the Caribbean. He'd been visiting Elysian Island since his early teens. Over the years he'd made a number of investments, several of them on the advice of Bridget, and for the most part they had paid off. They included varied stock options and the acquisition of a vacation home in East Hampton, New York, a duplex apartment in western Paris and a seaside bungalow on Elysian Island. He popped into Elysian Island this time around to attend some private parties to which he'd been invited. An avid mountain climber, he also planned on doing some mountain climbing in the rainforests of Soufriere on the mainland. Notwithstanding his oddball streak, Rudy felt reasonably comfortable with him and even managed to overlook, among other things, his sometimes flippant response to questions and his devil-may-care outlook on life.

Rudy spotted Olive milling around in the crowd. When they first met at Bill Thompson's party, he'd assumed she was a servant since she'd been waiting on tables. He'd since discovered that she was a preschool teacher and had merely been helping out at the party. She seemed to be quite popular among the villagers. She interacted with them uninhibitedly and they responded warmly to her. Even Aaron seemed to have a soft spot for her. He surprised her with a gift. She was so excited, she couldn't resist opening it. It was a bottle of Can Can by Paris Hilton au de parfum. She was positively thrilled. Aaron looked pleased with himself. "It's guaranteed not to drive a man away," he said.

All along, Olive had been conscious of Rudy's presence and he could sense it. She eventually managed to disengage from the others and hurried across to him. She told him how happy she was to see him at the unveiling. Rudy thought she looked quite lovely in a maroon skirt and white long-sleeved shirt, with black mid-heel pumps. They spent the next few minutes chatting and laughing. Rudy found her joy infectious and he had fun monkeying around with her. He asked if he could take some photos of her with his iPhone. She readily agreed on condition that they took some together. Rudy signaled Aaron to come over. Aaron explained that he and Olive knew each from way back when she was in primary school.

"Would you mind doing us the honors," said Rudy, handing him the phone.

"Not at all, my pleasure," Aaron replied cheerfully.

One of the men from the village took offence at Rudy's friendliness towards Olive and the way he'd been frolicking with her. He was tall, lean and craggy-faced with a mop of thick woolly hair that resembled candy floss. It looked like it hadn't been combed in months. He had a strange, bug-eyed look and etched into his face were the indelible lines and fissures wrought by a hard life lived without much joy or hope. His name was Oscar. He glared darkly at Rudy and deliberately stepped into Aaron's field of vision before he could snap the photo. Neither Olive nor Aaron seemed surprised by his antics. They tried to reason with him in a bid to keep him from interfering but Oscar was having none of it. Turning to Aaron, he said with a reproachful look, "Mr. Aaron, how you could allow Miss Olive, our angel – our queen - to take picture with a old Rasta drugsman? That not right sah!" He glowered at Rudy.

Rudy gaped at Oscar in disbelief. He shook his head and tried to keep his cool but deep inside he was seething. Aaron drew Oscar aside and placing an arm across his shoulders, he tried reasoning with him again. This time he succeeded and got Oscar to promise that he wouldn't intervene. "I think he's got it," he said, winking at Rudy and Olive. Once again, he directed them to stand close to each other. He snapped two shots, then as he was about to snap a third, Oscar who had been sitting sullenly on a tree stump, jumped to his feet and stepped in front of the camera. "Wait, Mr. Aaron!" he exclaimed. Pointing to his jeans trousers, he said, "You see these jeans, sah? Is a present from Miss Olive. She bring them for me the other day when she come from Martinique. Please sah, these jeans is special to me. Miss Olive I beg you, please let me take a picture with you in them."

Some of the villagers realized what was going on. Several of them excoriated Oscar and demanded that he 'leave the people alone.' One of the men asked Aaron if he wanted him to drag Oscar away. Aaron chuckled and politely declined his offer. Meanwhile, Oscar gently drew Olive away from Rudy and stood next to her. Rudy took a whiff of alcohol on his breath. In a fit of rage he shoved him away roughly. Oscar careened into a tent pole and tripped, crashing into the chairs.

Olive grabbed Rudy's arm to try and restrain him. "Come on, Rudy don't get carried away, that's not called for," she said.

"Carried away!" Rudy snapped. "Why don't you try restraining this nut!" he said indignantly.

"Please Rudy, take it easy and keep your voice down," said Olive calmly. She patiently explained to Rudy that his violent reaction was childish. Rudy took offence and began arguing with her. Aaron moved quickly between them and gently drew Rudy away.

"What the hell is this guy's problem?" Rudy demanded, fuming.

"It's okay, don't let him get under your skin," said Olive soothingly. Placing her hand comfortingly on his shoulder, she said, "Everyone in the village knows Oscar is a pest and sometimes he could really get on your nerves. We try our best to put up with him. He's a bit slow mentally, and he has a bit of a drinking problem ... He also has a crush on me ever since I was a teenager. I've learned to put up with it. He's really quite harmless," Olive explained.

"If you ask me, he needs to be kept on a leash," Rudy retorted.

Meanwhile, Aaron managed to coax Oscar into a more agreeable mood. He began laughing and joking and even offered to give Aaron Creole lessons free of charge. Aaron signaled Olive and Rudy to come over and persuaded Oscar to take a photo with them. He called two women and two men to come and join in, took a few steps back and began snapping photos of the group. Oscar beamed with pride.

"Okay mate, it's your turn," Aaron said to Rudy. Rudy obliged grudgingly. Using the iPhone once again, he took several photos of the group with Oscar fidgeting and shifting irritatingly, either to improve his posture or to edge closer to Olive. Secretly, and despite Aaron's attempt to broach a rapprochement between him and Oscar, Rudy felt a smoldering resentment towards the rural misfit for embarrassing him in the presence of so many people. The mere sight of him fawning over Olive and making a spectacle of himself, made Rudy sick to his stomach.

When they were through taking photos, Olive said it was getting late and she had to go check on her mother who was sick in bed with the flu. The other people gradually dispersed with the exception of Oscar who hung around watching Rudy and Olive like a hawk. Rudy promised to call her later since she insisted that he did. "My birthday is coming up soon and I'm planning a party," said Olive, adding, "Both you and Aaron are invited! I'll tell you all about it." Then she gave Rudy a peck on the cheek and said goodbye to him and Aaron. Oscar sucked his teeth and stormed away.

Walking up to Rudy, Aaron said, "I dare say, a stiff drink would do you well after this episode."

"My hands around this moron's throat would do me a lot better," Rudy replied.

Reaching into his pocket, Aaron pulled out a gold pocketwatch. Glancing at it, he said, "From here I'll be heading off to the beach for a moonlight party hosted by a German friend. You're welcome to tag along if you wish."

"Thanks but I couldn't impose on you."

"Bollocks! I insist. I guarantee you it will be fun. You'll find the ladies quite entertaining, including Shernel and Shenele, twin sisters and both Jamaicans. They arrived here as guests aboard a yacht belonging to my German friend. I'm rather partial to Shenele. She's a girl with a wonderful one-track mind."

Rudy gaped at Aaron in mock surprise. "You're proving to be quite a dirty old man, even in your youth," he said teasingly. Aaron let loose a loud guffaw. Together, they headed towards Aaron's Land Rover.

13

Bridget lolled in a chaise lounge beside the pool, clutching a book to her bosom. She was about to begin reading when she paused. Gazing at the cover photo of Diana, Princess of Wales, she frowned. It occurred to her that this would be her third time re-reading *Diana: Her True Story in Her Own Words,* the tell-all tale of Princess Di's life and disastrous royal marriage. She slammed the book shut and tossed it aside.

Each time she returned to it, it was for the same reason; the stress of her marriage was becoming unbearable and she felt at the end of her tether. It wasn't that she felt a personal kinship with Diana but rather she could identify with the emotions of a woman in the prime of her life being sucked into a world for which she had been totally unprepared. It was as if in Diana's plight she found some sort of validation for her feeling of being wronged. She also felt a bit less inclined to beat up on herself for her naiveté and inability to perceive, until it was too late, that she and Edward were products of different species from two different dimensions.

Even after she came to realize this, for a while she stubbornly persisted in believing that somehow they would find a way to work things out between them, and everything would return to how it used to be in the beginning of their relationship, when it was all love and bliss.

What an ass she'd been!

The inevitable question came to mind and, for the umpteenth time she reflected on it, as if to console herself; 'What young woman could have resisted being seduced by a real-life nobleman, especially one as charming and rich as Lord Edward Henry Tennyson, the owner of an island in the Caribbean, one of the world's most exclusive and luxurious retreats?

An only child, Bridget grew up in the U.S. Mid-Western state of Wisconsin. She was thirteen when her father died. A year prior to his death he had been diagnosed with prostate cancer.

She recalled the way she and Edward first met. It was quite weird. She'd gone to England to attend her Aunt Margaret's funeral – her mother's older sister. Incredibly, Margaret – Lady James Erskin, as she was formally known – had married into one of Britain's grandest families, real-life Downton Abbey types, and spent her life virtually exiled in England. Bridget recalled that she'd met her aunt only once, when she was six years old. She had come to America for a few days to visit her family. After she left, she never returned and since then there had been almost no contact between the respective families. Bridget came to suspect that there had been some degree of estrangement between her mother and her aunt, although she'd never been sure why since at home, the matter was never discussed.

It turned out that her aunt's husband and Edward were second cousins, so naturally Edward attended the funeral along with other members of his family. Afterwards, Bridget and Edward were introduced to each other. They immediately hit it off.

Bridget smiled ruefully as she recalled how taken aback Edward had seemed when he discovered that she was a stockbroker.

At the time she was unattached, and had been employed with a brokerage firm in San Francisco for almost six years. She got into stock trading after leaving university where she majored in accounting, finance and business administration. California proved to be the ideal place to work as a stockbroker because of the abundant job opportunities and plenty of wealthy residents and institutions constantly looking for investment advisors to manage their money and assets. She was pretty much at the top of her game when Edward drifted into her life. She was rated among the firm's top performers thanks to her uncanny economic forecasting skills, plus she was servicing a sizeable pool of clients. Within the first two years, commissions were rolling in and her losses were minimal and few and far between.

All this came at a high cost. From the start, she badly underestimated the amount of time and energy she would have to devote to the job, and the demands it would place on her personal life. It was not unusual to work fourteen-hour days for months on end. She suffered through four broken relationships as a result of the pressures of the job. In the fourth one she was engaged to be married and wedding plans had been well on the way when she and her fiancé called it quits. The breakup was acrimonious. Like his predecessors, he accused her of being overly ambitious, ego-driven and much too obsessed with money.

The first time Edward visited her in America, that same week she'd been to see a psychotherapist. She didn't tell him. It was her third visit. She'd also been on antidepressants. Never before in her life had she felt so lonely and lost. Edward walked into her life at a point when she was vulnerable and needed someone to help her maintain her sanity. Notwithstanding that he was nearly twice her age, she'd found him to be quite charming and considerate, a brilliant conversationalist with a devilish sense of humor and he was the perfect gentleman. He was also quite dashing in his own way, and good looking too. She'd also found him to be generous to a fault and she loved the way he wooed her with flowers and exotic candle-lit dinners, the old-fashioned way, and very British. It had all been so romantic. In him she found a dear friend and, in time, a good lover, as well as a father figure.

Edward had been a widower back then, his wife having died three years earlier. They'd lived apart for seven years. He also had a son and daughter and they were about ten years older than Bridget. Edward was clearly besotted with her and he pursued her determinedly, shuttling between the Caribbean and California, sometimes twice a month. Bridget thought it best not to tell her mother and so kept the truth from her for as long as she could.

Meantime, she was losing her zeal for her job. It wasn't like she'd been losing interest in stock trading. Far from it. She relished the cut and thrust and the high-risk nature of her work, and the challenge of living on the edge. It was invigorating and it gave her a rush of adrenaline. She found that the more she worked, the more fun she had. She'd also felt a strong sense of commitment to her clients who trusted her and depended on her guidance and advice. Ultimately it was her growing exasperation with having to put up with the persistent condescension and biasness of some of her male colleagues and managers towards the few female brokers in the firm that caused her to feel demotivated.

In the latter stage of her employment, she'd felt that she and the other women were increasingly being assigned inferior accounts and getting less support than their male colleagues, despite their generally solid performance. Even more infuriating was the fact that the brokers were all being paid strictly by commissions rather than on the basis of performance. Since the managers couldn't change the commission-based system, it meant there was no possibility of the brokers getting pay hikes. And since the female brokers were being assigned fewer and often lower-level accounts than their male colleagues, it meant there was a glaring disparity in their pay. In the end, Bridget got so dispirited she found that she had to force herself to show up at the office. Having to cope with the stress and repeated failure of her personal relationships, made it worse.

Edward saw an opening. He very subtly set about trying to influence her to quit her job and start life afresh – with him in his island paradise. She could even help him manage his finances and business affairs, he suggested. That was six months after they met. "Please do come," he'd urged her. "I have a fantastic surprise for you."

Bridget succumbed and decided to accept his invitation to visit Elysian Island. She'd been all too aware that moving to Elysian would mean that her client portfolios would have to be reassigned to the firm's other brokers, predominantly the males no doubt, because of their so-called 'greater ability to make sales,' compared to the women. The very thought of it had enraged her! All the same, her mind was made up. She packed up and took off with Edward but made it clear to him that she wasn't going to stay, just for a visit.

On arriving in Elysian Island, she was completely bowled over by what she encountered there. Up until then she'd known very little about the Caribbean and even less about the tiny island that had become a retreat for the super-rich. Edward had remarked, somewhat condescendingly, that he wasn't surprised since Americans know almost nothing of the world beyond their borders.

Bridget instantly fell in love with the island. She found it easy to adapt since in some ways it smacked of the San Francisco Bay Area in terms of the warm, sunny weather throughout much of the year, and even the occasional mist and low-lying stratus clouds at higher elevations, which reminded her of the frequent San Francisco fog. Moreover, she was astute enough to realize that there were potentially rich pickings to be had given her business acumen and her skills as a broker, plus the fact that the island was frequented by multimillionaires and celebrities.

At Blossom House she'd felt reasonably comfortable and at home. Edward professed his love for her at every opportunity and begged her hand in marriage. He offered her the world and seemed willing to prostrate himself at her feet. He was also an excellent host and entertained his guests with exceeding generosity. He considered it his duty and recoiled from the thought of not doing it properly, even regarded it as contemptible and a source of disgrace.

Furthermore, from all indications, he'd appeared to be a genuinely caring person. He also had a hilarious sense of humor.

All in all, Bridget felt that she couldn't have asked for a more pleasant change of circumstances. Her credulity was such that she even found Edward's obvious eccentricities and veiled contempt for modernity intriguing.

Surprisingly, she'd not felt intimidated or discomfited in any way by Edward's aristocratic background. She actually found it appealing in a detached sort of way. However, it was not something that she dwelt on; probably because, being an American, she was not used to it.

Two days after she arrived on the island, Edward did something incredible. Coincidentally, it happened to be her birthday. He took her to a scenic spot overlooking Albion Bay and informed her that the land she was standing on was her birthday gift from him, offered with his heartfelt love and appreciation. The parcel consisted of five acres. She was so stunned, he could have knocked her over with a feather. She took a while to recover. Later she was wined and dined at the nearby Camelot Hotel late into the night.

Before returning to America, she agreed to marry Edward. When Bridget broke the news to her mother, she was shocked and devastated. She'd begged Bridget not to rush into marriage. Bridget recalled her asking with tears in her eyes, "Do you want to end up like your aunt, Maggie, isolated and cut off from your family?" She said her sister died forlorn and miserable, regretting the course she had taken in life. It was the first time that her mother had admitted this and it shook Bridget. Despite that, in her heart, she revolted against what seemed like an attempt by her mother to constrain her and dictate to her how to live her life. Her mom had also tried to discourage her from pursuing a career in stock trading, insisting that she remain in Wisconsin and try getting into banking instead. Bridget could tell that she was mostly worried about prestige, the sort that stock trading couldn't confer, as far as she was concerned.

It was for this same reason she had refrained from telling her about the problems she'd been having at her workplace; she didn't want to have to put up with the usual, 'I told you so' refrain. None of this diminished her love for her mother. It was just that over time, she had learnt how to keep that love from making her feel guilty for rejecting her mom's never-ending attempts to protect her 'little girl.'

In the end, she stood by her decision to marry Edward. The wedding was held at Blossom House and it was quite a lavish affair. Thankfully, her mother relented and attended. She'd mingled and chatted, said all the right things and tried to look accepting, although Bridget could tell that she was just putting up a brave front, and her feelings about the marriage hadn't changed.

Very little of the wedding had reflected her tastes or preferences, and the majority of the guests had been strangers to her. She gritted her teeth and bore it. Several of Edward's relatives came over from England. His mother had been unable to make it as she had been ailing. His son and daughter stayed away.

After the wedding, everything went as well as could be expected of a matrimonial union birthed in a fairy tale world. They honeymooned in the Maldives.

It took a while before Bridget realized that there wasn't going to be a happily-ever-after ending. Increasingly, she noticed that Edward was adopting a condescending attitude towards her. This was the first real cause of friction between them.

She also discovered that he took pleasure in toying with her emotions and played mind games with her. It had started with him suddenly insisting that she accompany him to places on the island that he knew made her very uncomfortable, such as climbing Mount Britannia in the island's interior, knowing full well that she was terrified of heights.

Sometimes, for no apparent reason, he'd press her to accompany him when he went visiting certain friends of his, although he knew she didn't care to or, in some cases, disliked them.

Another of his disturbing practices was pointedly complimenting other women in her presence when they entertained guests at home or went out partying. Conversely, there were occasions when he deliberately refrained from commending her on her looks and attire as she expected. This she'd found hard to take, since she loved being told how good she looked, especially by Edward.

What she'd found particularly disturbing and bizarre were those times when Edward arranged dates for her with other men. The first time he did this she humored him by obliging, considering that the man she was supposed to go out with was a middle-aged English bachelor named Preston who owned a chandlery at the marina; a guy who was usually gracious and kind to her. In his usual artful manner, Edward had sought to persuade her that it was nothing more than a way of helping her to adapt and feel more comfortable with the idiosyncrasies of folks on the island. Preston took her out to dinner at the Camelot. Although it had felt odd, it wasn't an unpleasant experience. After she returned home, Edward sat her down, offered her a drink and casually questioned her about the evening. She responded reluctantly, feeling foolish.

He asked her to go out a second time, with another man. Her instinctive reaction was to rebel but for some reason she'd held back; perhaps because her marriage was still young and she didn't want to cause a rift between them so early. She agreed to go.

When she returned, his reaction was the same; he waited till she was settled, and then questioned her about her rendezvous, trying his utmost to do so as inoffensively as possible, and all the while observing her closely. It was as if he'd regarded her as some sort of scientific specimen and he was conducting an experiment to observe her reaction. She'd hated it, and she was angry at herself! When she complained, he made light of it, and in a brazen display of twisted logic he chided her for her seeming lack of self-confidence and wondered aloud if her reluctance was proof of her inability to be faithful to him. He seemed to be deliberately goading her to test her strength and will power, yet at the same time it was hard to tell because he went about it with an incredible air of serenity and composure.

Thereafter she put her foot down and refused to play along with him anymore.

Even then he would devise other ways to toy with her feelings in between the times when he reverted to the sweet, charming, lovable Edward she initially befriended and married wholeheartedly.

Then she had to deal with his temper tantrums, which erupted every now and again, without warning.

From the start, Bridget realized that she had gotten herself entangled with a larger-than-life character. However, it soon became clear that she hadn't realized the half of it. Nevertheless, although most people on Elysian Island considered Edward eccentric, they all gave him due recognition as the one who almost single-handedly transformed it from a mosquito-infested islet into an Edenic retreat, coveted by world-famous socialites and the filthy rich. Some of them fondly referred to him as the Emperor of Elysian Island. The locals thought the world of him – most of them at least. Edward, in turn, treated them almost like family, the same as he treated the domestic staff at Blossom House.

Initially, he assisted many of those who had migrated from the mainland by offering them free cash and building materials to help with the construction of their homes and the village. Located just outside of the village, near the beach, was a small, pleasantly ramshackle fish market where several of the fishermen plied their daily catch of fresh fish, lobsters and crabs. Edward had financed its construction and, through the years, he contributed to its upkeep. In the villagers' eyes, he could do no wrong. And Edward was brilliant at charming them.

All the fawning over the Emperor of Elysian Island, especially by the domestic staff at Blossom House, irritated Bridget. It also made her jealous. Altogether, there were eight of them; three housekeepers, a cook, two gardeners, a chauffeur and Edward's personal assistant, Vernon Allain. While they were always courteous to her, they tended to be cautious when dealing with her, in stark contrast to the way they interacted with Edward. Bridget sensed that they could tell whenever there was friction between her and Edward. They were not used to this sort of tension in the house, so naturally they would assume that she must be the cause of it. It was rumored that Edward's former wife also had difficulty coping with his 'weirdness' but she bore it well, and like a true lady who understood the virtue of keeping up appearances, she learned how to paper over the cracks in their marriage while they lived together at Blossom House.

Regarding his finances, Bridget soon discovered, to her great shock, that Edward was only rich on paper and he was being kept afloat by the sufferance of his creditors. Even before they began courting, Edward had been having financial problems. His luxurious lifestyle was being sustained mainly by loans and a hefty overdraft. The only assets he had left were Blossom House and a fifteen-thousand square-foot plot of land in Grand Anse, up in the north of the island.

In spite of that, when it came to throwing a bash, no one on the island could outdo him. Up until recently, he held a beach picnic or luncheon almost every week, although from what she'd been told this was far fewer than he used to in the earlier years when it was done on an even more lavish scale. Some of his gossipier chums were happy to regale her with tales of all-night parties of unbridled revelry at Blossom House and beach picnics hosted almost daily by Edward, where nude sunbathing and skinny dipping were de rigueur. The guests feasted on lobster, caviar and champagne served by butlers on fine china and silverware. She'd been taken aback to learn that among the invitees were several members of the British, French and German nobility.

Moreover, Edward was an incurable philanthropist. Over the years he had, among other things, footed the medical bills of some of his household staff and also provided scholarships and bursaries to the children of several of them, including Olive Henry whose mother worked as a housekeeper. Edward had grown so fond of Olive he financed her education through secondary school and A Level College and treated her as if she was his daughter.

To top it off, he hated accounting and seldom kept track of his expenses. Such behavior was anathema to Bridget and it had been the cause of quite a few spats between them. Invariably, Edward dismissed her concerns about money as a 'typical working-class obsession,' and with his characteristic air of nonchalance, he tried to give the impression that money was the least of his concerns. But she wasn't fooled. A couple of times he let his guard down and inadvertently exposed his chagrin in all its nakedness. He became the proverbial emperor with no clothes.

On one of those occasions they were having breakfast when, out of the blue, Edward confessed to Bridget how distressed he felt at what he suspected was his creditors' loss of confidence in him and their thinly-veiled attempts to rein him in. He went quiet for a while then told her about all the difficulties he'd endured in the early days when he was developing the island and putting in the required infrastructure, even housing for the workers and their families, all of which he paid for out of his own pocket. This time, as he recounted it, his dejection was palpable.

"I tried to introduce service charges to defray some of the costs but many of the homeowners flatly refused to pay. I found it all rather tedious," he'd confessed to her. He said in the end he'd had to borrow money and sell a considerable amount of his assets, locally and in England, and some of his personal possessions, including several family heirlooms. "Back then, there was a lot of goodwill from many, but not much else. I fear it is the same now ... I don't regret anything about Elysian Island, it must be said," he added.

Recalling his words brought tears to Bridget's eyes. In all fairness, she had to concede that their relationship hadn't been all bad, and to some extent she felt rotten for having dwelt mostly on their conflicts and disagreements. She recalled that their first few months together as husband and wife were spent travelling in Europe and pretty much just having fun. They seemed to find so much to do together in those days. Then gradually, as Edward's friends and neighbors on the island began to grow more accepting of her, she started making new friends, both males and females, and they'd socialize and have fun together. This continued in the succeeding years. "God, how I miss it all!" Bridget whispered softly.

Her rapport with Edward's relatives was another issue she'd had to grapple with. Initially, Edward had sought to prepare her for the repercussions of his failure to meet his family's expectations, since they had expected him to 'marry well' by blending his bloodline with that of another grand family or at the very least, with someone of immense wealth, if not sufficiently high pedigree. Hence it came as no surprise that getting to know his relatives didn't turn out to be an altogether pleasant experience.

Nonetheless, she got the opportunity to vacation in a vast, elegant 18th century country house with a hunting lodge and a farm belonging to Edward's eighty-five year old paternal uncle. Its high-priced decor coupled with its extraordinary grandeur and the presence of twenty domestic servants made the experience quite astounding and infused it with a dreamlike quality. She also got to spend a romantic week together with Edward at a nearby country estate in a luxurious six-room rented cottage with lots of antique furniture.

Ultimately, her introduction to the world of Britain's upper crust proved to be a bit trying, yet at times quite revealing insofar as she was able to perceive their world view from close up and their thought processes vis-à-vis that of ordinary people like herself. Each time she travelled to England with Edward she got to meet and socialize with his blueblood friends and relatives; people, for the most part, with inherited wealth and who were defined by their titles. Some of them came from Britain's oldest families. She also got the opportunity to go horseback riding, play polo, go shooting and fishing and even fox hunting. Although she'd found it fascinating, it was hard to connect with the surreal grandeur of it all. What confounded her even more were the raised eyebrows and cold silence she encountered each time she alluded to their posh lifestyle. Edward later informed her, to her great embarrassment, that among the upper classes it is unfashionable to be characterized as 'posh.' "From personal experience, anyone who publicly identifies himself as posh is by definition, not," he added. Bridget found it all a bit much.

Among the older toffs, including Edward's octogenarian mother and some members of his extended family, she encountered an air of aloofness and studied curiosity that seemed to indicate what was expected of her; namely, that she know her place and consider herself fortunate for having been availed of the privilege of sporting an elegant title in front of her name.

She had felt more comfortable among those closer to her age or younger, although some of them were not exactly warm or approachable. Being an open and outgoing person, inclined to laugh and talk with strangers on the street – and in that regard, very American – Bridget found the courtly world of British aristocracy a bit stifling. A few of the kids amused her, though. They were fascinated with her American background and seemed to find it 'cool' that she had been based in California, the home state of Hollywood.

For some of the men, her beauty was more than enough to speed up the process of acceptance, and she figured she could have had more than a few of them eating out of her hand if she tried hard enough. Their interest perked up all the more when she informed them that she was a stockbroker. That was when she came to realize that the elite have just as keen an interest in hard cash as the average Joe on the street. One aging duke confirmed this when he whispered to her in his plummy voice that the aristocracy were often asset rich but cash poor. Edward, himself, personified that truth. Her acquaintanceship with some of her male admirers blossomed into friendship and, over time, opened doors to very useful business and social connections, even among some of the City of London's most powerful organizations, such as the Worshipful Company of Mercers, of which Edward was a member. Ultimately, this would prove to be very beneficial to her financially in that she was able to make good use of her stock-trading skills, knowledge and experience.

She was also able to develop close friendships and business connections with several expatriates and homeowners on the island, including the directors of the Elysian Island Company, and Bill Thompson and his wife, Jacquie. Thankfully, they came from varied national and cultural backgrounds, albeit more than half of them were British. She also enjoyed the social life centered on private intimate gatherings frequently held outdoors under the stars. Best of all, living on Elysian Island helped her re-establish her connection with the sea, which she had all but lost while working in the jungle of U.S stock trading.

During her childhood and teenage years, Bridget spent many summers sailing with her grandparents who came from Portland, Maine. Her late grandfather was a former U.S. Coast Guard officer and a diehard seaman and he had owned a yacht and a sailboat. She used to accompany him when he participated in the Bermuda Race, a grueling six-hundred and thirty-five mile yachting race from Newport, Rhode Island to the island of Bermuda. She became quite adept at handling yachts and sailboats. Her grandfather also taught her quite a lot about boatbuilding.

She was thrilled to discover that Elysian Island had a vibrant yachting culture, which, along with her love for Edward, was a major reason she had felt impelled to move to the Caribbean. Besides Bill Thompson and his wife, she had a group of close friends that she socialized with regularly. They were mostly American women living on Elysian Island and they had been there longer than she had. Their camaraderie was all too often a source of comfort to her, especially when she and Edward were at loggerheads or when he became distant and irascible, which was becoming more frequent, especially in recent months. His latest gripe was with the Elysian Island Company and its development plans for the island.

Since selling his controlling interest in the company, his power and influence had waned, and he found this hard to accept, even though he wouldn't admit it. The directors' recent decision to sell more house lots enraged him. Edward was convinced the island was becoming overcrowded and, according to him, he feared it would soon be overrun by undesirables, including white-collar criminals, drug barons and the 'seedy, scheming Wall Street types.' He fulminated against the property sales, denouncing them as cheap commercialization at its worst.

Bridget smiled ruefully as she recalled how Edward had reserved the worst part of his vitriol for her. He'd had it in for her once he realized that she and Bill Thompson had become close buddies and they were developing a good business relationship. Bill and several of the directors consulted her regularly on financial and stock-trading matters – unlike Edward, her own husband. No matter how much she tried to offer him advice on managing his finances and inheritance, he refused to accept it. The bizarre part of it all was that she was forced to sit back helplessly and watch Edward's financial status deteriorate, even as her own personal finances and assets grew thanks to a series of shrewd investments she'd made over the years. To make matters worse, he consistently turned her down each time she offered to loan him money.

To some extent, this was in keeping with his nature and his tendency to remain stoical and unmoved under pressure, like several of the Brits she knew who were of his generation. However, she didn't believe his refusal to accept help was merely about pride or embarrassment. Despite everything, she cared deeply about him and he knew it. He also knew how much not being able to help him was hurting her. That was one of the main reasons why he was so obstinate in his refusal. She had no doubt about it. It was a power play on his part, another one of his mind games. It was the same with the book he planned to have published. He knew all too well that the very thought of him putting out a tell-all book would have many people on the island on edge, even panicky. His friends in England and elsewhere, including some in royal circles would also have reason to be concerned. It was as if he was able to extract power and energy from everyone's fear, so he cunningly stirred it up and feasted on it. It more than made up for his waning influence and the realization that his financial demise was imminent.

His latest offensive was to announce his plans to sell Blossom House, pack up and move to Tanzania. She indulged him by listening attentively as he 'enlightened' her on the logic of such a move. In the end she said she understood and thought it was probably the best thing for him. It was not the response he had expected. For a while he seemed confused, and for Edward that was a rarity. For once, the centre of power had shifted. At that very moment it struck Bridget that she had meant it when she said it was the right decision. She had lied though, when she said it was right for *him.* Rather, it was right for her! She wanted him gone. She wanted to be free.

Prior to meeting Rudy she would not have had the heart to entertain such thoughts. She would have come up with a million and one reasons why she should be grateful to Edward for all he had done for her. She would have had to struggle alone with the thought that all her romantic relationships were doomed to end in disaster, and it had been a mistake to leave California to marry Edward. After several months of agonizing over the calamitous turn her marriage had taken, she was forced to concede that the turning point came when it dawned on her that with Edward, she never felt needed. She found no reason to believe that she had brought into his life any element without which he could not feel fulfilled or complete. Although he continued to tell how much he loved and needed her in his life, despite all their problems, if it was true, she couldn't feel it. To her they were mere words. She honestly believed that if Edward was forced to do without his two cherished 18th-century Chinese Imperial vases, he would feel a greater sense of loss.

With Rudy, it was different. She knew that he was crazy about her and unlike Edward he was the sort of person that could be honed and molded. Not that he was a pushover or had no mind of his own. Far from it. He was actually quite strong willed, a bit feisty and street smart. What she particularly loved about him was his earthy simplicity and warmheartedness. The mere fact that she hadn't been able to get him out of her system and longed so much to be with him - and Rudy likewise - although they'd had no more than a brief fling back in England, said a lot about the chemistry at work between them.

She couldn't help feeling that their liaison had not been coincidental, perhaps Divine Providence, notwithstanding she had been two-timing Edward. She recalled the turmoil she'd been going through at the time because of the increasing tension between her and Edward. She had felt at her wits end. She needed someone to open up to and unburden her heart. Rudy came on the scene at the right time. He became a source of comfort to her, even though just for a while. When he eventually made love to her, it was the most beautiful experience she'd ever had.

On the other hand, Rudy came across as easygoing, almost to the point of being happy-go-lucky, plus he had a roving eye. *That* she found troubling, especially with his handsome looks. He also limited himself career-wise, as well as economically and socially, and unlike her, he wasn't very objective in his reasoning. He couldn't see the wood for the trees. He needed to be guided, and that she was perfectly capable of doing. He also needed her to help him see the big picture. They complemented each other in this regard, certainly far more than was the case with Edward. Unlike Edward, Rudy needed her; and she too needed him to reawaken the matriarchal side of her once again, and to help her feel more secure and in control in a relationship, as she had grown used to feeling when handling business matters. She wanted to be able to love wholeheartedly and passionately, and without restraint. And God knows, she could do without the fucking mind games and emotional blackmail!

"Excuse me, Miss Bridget."

Bridget glanced up, startled. Looking down at her was a buxomy woman with a plump, cheerful face. She looked slightly squelched in her dainty little snow-white blouse and black skirt coupled with black leather shoes that were so neatly polished, they gleamed in the sunlight. "Sorry to make you jump," she said quickly.

"That's okay, Meredith," said Bridget with a wan smile.

"I just come to let you know that it almost three o'clock. I remember you said you have an appointment and I know you don't like to be late."

"Damn! Is it already?" Bridget shot up from the chaise lounge. "Be a darling and run my bath, please. I'll be in shortly."

"Yes, Miss," Meredith hurried back to the house.

If it hadn't been for Meredith, she would have been late for her lunch date with Carolyn and Blessing, two of her closest friends. The past few weeks had been exceptionally hectic, stretching her to the limit, so she felt grateful to be able to take the weekend off. She wasn't really in the mood to meet with the girls. Off and on they met for lunch and chitchat. This time they had agreed to meet at the Grand Yacht Haven Marina in Albion Bay.

The night before, she and Edward had gotten into another heated argument over her involvement with the Elysian Island Company. It upset her so badly, she woke up next morning in one of her darkest moods ever. The only reason she hadn't telephoned her friends to request that the date be postponed was because she damned well didn't care to hang around house or be anywhere near Edward. Furthermore, she had a date with Rudy later in the day and she figured she might as well kill some time with the girls until then. She had taken the precaution to keep the weekend free of business appointments. It bothered her that during the two weeks Rudy had been on the island, they hadn't been able to spend any quality time together. Now she intended to make up for that.

She headed back into the house.

14

Among Elysian Island's scenic treasures, the Grand Yacht Haven Marina was considered by many to be the pearl in the oyster. Located in a sheltered breakwater cove that provided natural protection from the trade winds and the sea, the marina was set against a backdrop of calm aquamarine waters and an overarching vault of celestial blue laced with drifting bales of fleecy whiteness. It was a sight to behold. It was equipped with sixty-three berths and specialised deepwater slips for mega-yachts, and a vast boatyard. It also had a sprawling recreational area with a mini shopping centre comprising of retail stores and luxury boutiques, a supermarket, a duty-free chandlery, and a swimming pool. Across from the shopping centre were three exotic restaurants offering a panoply of menus from a wide cross-section of world cultures, including Mexican, Asian, Caribbean and European. There were also an on-site customs and immigration office, a duty-free gas station for outgoing boats and a bank. The marina's grandeur and lavishness were such that it was almost as if it occupied a unique dimensional space in the socioeconomic fabric of Elysian Island.

Bridget and two other women sat comfortably in reclining chairs under a colourful patio umbrella outside the Mi Casa Mexicana restaurant. Bridget looked quite relaxed in a navy-blue tank top and jeans. Lunch had gone well and she felt reasonably satisfied except for the fact that the blonde sitting across from her had gotten into her talkative mood. She was trying hard not to lose her patience with the woman as she droned on in that preachy tone that Bridget often found infuriating. Her name was Carolyn and she was full-bosomed and a bit on the chubby side, and quite attractive. Seated next to her was Blessing, an easygoing but sober-headed brunette with an astute mind and a sympathetic disposition. A short distance away, the two women's husbands were playing in the pool with their children.

Bridget sighed and shifted irritably in her seat. The blonde kept prattling on and on about some dream she'd had the night before. Bridget and Blessing exchanged knowing glances. Blessing smiled. "So Bridget, have you been embarking on any naughty adventures lately?" she said in an obvious attempt to shut Carolyn up.

"Well Blessing, I'm surprised at your curiosity after Martin's solemn vow to keep you well clear of Edward's 'bacchanalian trysts.'"

Blessing laughed. "Don't mind Martin, you know what a prude he is."

Carolyn promptly lost interest in her dream. Her eyes lit up.

"Edward's rock-themed party, God wasn't it the bomb! Those gorgeous young village guys dressed up as glam rockers with their outrageous outfits, makeup and sole-platform boots and corny wigs. No one throws a party like your husband! What on earth will he think of next?"

Blessing laughed. "The high point for me was the group that showed up in the nude wearing sporrans. I think that's what did it for Martin. Being Scottish, he took great offence."

Listening to the two women, Bridget recalled the luncheon Edward had organised in a tented pavilion three weeks ago, followed immediately after by the late-night glam-rock party that went on way into the wee hours of the morning. Edward had warned her that the party was going to be 'awfully naughty and original,' and it turned out to be exactly that. Never mind that it had wreaked havoc on his wallet, he had no regrets about wining and dining people who, in the main, were far better off than him financially. "You know how it is with Edward. With every party he tries to outdo himself, and come hell or high water he will have his way," she said ruefully.

"Is everything okay?" said Blessing, with a concerned look. She noticed Bridget's frown and the faraway look in her eyes.

"Oh, I'm fine ...," said Bridget. "By the way, how is Sherrie-Ann?"

"She's fine. Lately she's been busy dreaming up plans for her upcoming birthday party. She turns six next month. Which brings me to my latest announcement ... Sherrie-Ann is soon going to have company." Blessing glanced down at her tummy and rubbed it gently.

"You kidding!" Carolyn exclaimed.

"Blessing, congratulations!" said Bridget. "But I don't understand. How is it possible?"

"Artificial insemination. Martin and I arranged it five months ago in the States. We decided to keep it to ourselves until we were sure it was successful."

"When did you find out that you were pregnant?" said Bridget.

"Three days ago. Doctor Hardy confirmed it."

"Martin must be over the moon!" said Carolyn.

"Oh, he's thrilled, naturally. In fact he's still afraid to believe it's actually true."

"I'm not surprised," said Bridget. "How long have you two been trying?"

"Ten years. To be honest we had all but given up and as recently as two months ago we were considering adopting another child."

"Sorry if I sound rude," said Carolyn, an inquisitive gleam in her eyes. "I've been meaning to ask, which of you are responsible for your inability to conceive naturally?"

"Martin."

"Did you know before you got married?"

"No, I didn't."

"If you had," said Bridget, "would you have married him?"

Blessing pondered for a moment. "I married Martin because I love him so, yes, I guess I would have," she replied.

"Artificial insemination," said Bridget musingly. "Kind of makes you realise that marriage has become somewhat anachronistic, don't you think?"

"What do you mean?" said Blessing, frowning.

"We persist in making men the focal point of our lives even when we can afford to do otherwise and still live financially secure and comfortably."

"Come on, Bridget, the sperm has to come from somewhere for those of us who can't do without children and long to have a family," Blessing countered.

"I agree it has to come from a man but he doesn't have to be a husband. You've just proved it."

"Gee, I don't know but single parenthood has never appealed to me."

"It's not about kids or parenthood, it's about men's persistent failure to live up to our expectations, even as impregnators!"

Carolyn chuckled. "It's funny you should say that. I actually lay in bed last night pondering over this issue of expectations and the importance of a male presence in a woman's life, and started asking myself whether I had not allowed Stephen to become a bad habit that I can't seem to shake. Sort of like an addiction you've resigned yourself to living with."

Bridget smiled. "Have you ever tried stepping out of your life and looking down on it from a distance? You should try it if you haven't. When I do, it's like I'm looking down at a world that is completely alien to me and sometimes I can't even tell where Edward fits in."

Blessing gave a wry grin. "I guess I better not try it then. I usually discard anything that doesn't fit."

"Do you think there's any chance that some day the laws will be amended so that wives could be allowed to make husbands redundant?" said Carolyn. They all laughed. "For one thing it would probably be less stressful than a divorce and cheaper in the end," she added.

"Then they'd ask for the right to join a union," said Blessing.

"Actually, Stephen is not bad. He tries to please me, he still sweet talks me, and he's great with the kids," said Carolyn.

"Martin loves me and he's committed to our marriage, and he can change a diaper," Blessing chipped in.

Bridget had no comment. Her silence resounded.

"How're things with you and Edward? Not getting any better, I suppose," said Blessing.

"It's bad enough," Bridget replied. She told them about Edward's latest plans to publish his memoir.

"Bill told Martin and me about it," said Blessing. "It seems to be a hot topic among folks at the Company. Some individuals are worried and I imagine a few of them may be quaking in their shoes."

"That Rudy guy, the writer," said Carolyn, beaming. "He's quite a hunk! Resisting the temptation must be quite a chore."

Bridget smiled. "I'm sure it is ... for Rudy."

"Honestly though, doesn't he turn you on?"

Bridget laughed.

"I'm wondering," said Blessing. "Is he aware that his coming here has caused a stir?"

"He came at Edward's invitation. I'm not sure he was aware that he was walking into a hornet's nest."

"A hornet's nest. What do you mean?"

"Never mind ... I think Martin is trying to get your attention."

Blessing and Carolyn glanced in the direction of Blessing's husband, a tall dark-haired man wearing only Bermuda shorts. He stood on the far side of the pool holding unto his daughter who was propped up playfully on his back. They both waved at Blessing. She waved back at them.

"That's it girls, I'm afraid I must go now," she said apologetically.

"So long darling! Make sure you guard that bulge jealously," said Carolyn.

"I will, thanks!"

"Bye Blessing," said Bridget, sounding somewhat unenthusiastic. Unlike Carolyn, she hadn't waved at Martin.

"That hubby of mine must have sneaked off to the pub," said Carolyn, scanning the dockside suspiciously. "I'm probably going to have to pry him loose from a double martini. I don't fancy having to prop him up on the way home."

"As for me, I've got an appointment," Bridget interjected quickly. She'd had her fill of Carolyn's chatter. Ordinarily she would have indulged her, except that at the moment she was feeling a bit cranky and distracted. Rudy was supposed to meet her alongside the dock at three, which was in the next fifteen minutes. She reached for her handbag on the table. Both women got up simultaneously and exchanged goodbyes. Bridget took off briskly down a wide concrete walkway in search of Rudy.

15

It was ten minutes past four when Bridget arrived at the berth. It comprised of neatly designed piers fitted with walkways for the deepwater slips, each with a dock box. More than half the slips were occupied by yachts of varied lengths, ranging from forty feet to two-hundred and eighty-five feet super-yachts, and a few speedboats. Bridget spotted Rudy pacing to and fro near a bench a few yards from the water's edge. He was dressed in a T-shirt, jeans and Gucci 'Brooklyn' sneakers. His locks hung free, as usual. A plump fortyish-looking man named Charley who worked as a deckhand, was apparently trying to humor him. It was so like Charley to try and relieve Rudy of his discomfort by regaling him with old seamen's jokes, no doubt. Bridget grinned.

Earlier she had instructed Sam to pick Rudy up and drop him off at the marina. That was after she telephoned Rudy and insisted that he join her. At first he was reluctant because he'd been invited to Olive Henry's birthday party, scheduled for the same day and hosted by none other than Edward. Edward had apparently gotten so carried away by the thrill of his coronation he couldn't resist another opportunity to make a spectacle of himself, and so condescended to honor his 'queen' by making a big to-do of her birthday.

Rudy had sounded quite eager to go, much to Bridget's surprise. But then it flashed through her mind that she'd spotted him chatting up Olive, first at the engagement party for Bill Thompson's son and subsequently just before the commencement of the unveiling of the community and literacy centre in the village. At Blossom House, she'd overheard Olive's mother, Estelle, Edward's favorite among the maids, speaking to him glowingly about Rudy. He'd apparently been visiting them and spending time with Olive. Also, Aaron had told her about Rudy's tussle with the well-known village simpleton, Oscar over Olive, after the unveiling ceremony! At that point the nickel dropped.

Rudy had claimed that he'd promised to accompany Aaron to the birthday party and he didn't want to disappoint him but Bridget didn't buy it. Her instinct told her that he'd promised *Olive* that he would attend and was reluctant to disappoint her. She told him it was imperative that they meet because they had urgent matters to discuss. She warned him not to disappoint her. Rudy eventually backed down and agreed to come.

"Hi, Rudy," she said walking up to him and smiling sweetly. "Charley, so nice of you to keep Rudy company. I'd hate him to feel lonely."

"Miss Bridget, how're you? It's so nice to see you," Charley gushed. "You know you can always count on me to look after your guest," he added, beaming proudly.

"Hello, Miss Bridget," said Rudy. "Now that I have dutifully obeyed you, I am eager to know what good things lie in store for the needy."

Turning to Charley, Bridget said, "Have you prepared Summer Breeze?"

"Yes Miss, of course," he replied. Pointing to a yacht moored to the pier a few yards away, he added, "She well wash down and ready to go. Whenever you ready." The vessel was a forty-foot Sea Ray Sundancer with a fairly wide foredeck and high guard rails. An inflatable rubber dinghy was tied to the stern. Figures moved around on the decks of two other nearby yachts.

Bridget gave Rudy an impish smile. "Have you ever piloted a yacht before?" she asked.

"A yacht? ... No, I haven't," he replied.

"How'd you like to learn?"

Rudy peered at the vessel. "Are we going sailing?"

"Naturally."

"Okay ... Where's the skipper?"

"At your service, sir," Bridget replied with a smirk. "Come on Charley, let's get started." Charley hurried on ahead of them and climbed onto the deck. He went down into the companionway and soon re-emerged with a duffel bag and two inflatable life vests. From inside the bag he extracted a small electronic device; a wireless Yacht Controller. Placing the life vests and the device in the cockpit, he jumped back down unto thc dock. He stood ready to untie the boat's docking lines as soon as Bridget gave the word.

Bridget climbed on deck and Rudy followed her. She ushered him aboard with a dazzling smile and a flourish that indicated how proud she felt. Rudy looked quite befuddled, as if he was struggling to come to terms with something he considered inconceivable. "Does this belong to you?" he asked quietly.

"Yes, it does ... Come on, let me show you around." Bridget proceeded to give him a guided tour of the vessel, starting with the cockpit. It was adorned with pearly-white leather upholstery that made it look sleek and luxurious. It was quite a large area with bench seating, a portside bar with a faucet and an ice maker, a U-shaped lounge with white, vinyl-covered seats, a detachable table and a rotating helm seat. The cockpit could easily be converted into a sun pad and accommodate up to nine guests. The burl-wood dash was arranged in three tiers, with an impressive array of instruments and electronics, including a color chart plotter, a marine radio and a custom-built stereo, all close-fitted and easily accessible. Aft of the cockpit was a transom door that led to a swim platform.

Bridget then took Rudy to the mid-cabin below the helm. It was quite elegant with a curved sofa and a fiberglass table, a TV set and DVD player. It was also equipped with air conditioning and central heating, making it perfect for dining and relaxation. The upholstery was a plush mix of fabric and leather complemented by vinyl paneling. The space could convert into a double-settee berth and private stateroom.

From there they went into the adjacent master stateroom. It had a pedestal bed and hanging closets made of cedar, as well as port and starboard vanities fitted with cabinets that provided copious storage, a VacuFlush toilet and a stand-up fiberglass shower.

Finally they checked out the galley. It was adorned with stainless-steel sinks in granite countertops, a refrigerator-freezer, a three-burner electric stove and microwave, plus a coffeemaker and blender, and plenty of storage above and below. Large skylights and side windows with opening portholes allowed the interior of the vessel to be flooded with natural light. The Summer Breeze was custom-built so that it could transform into a single-masted Gunter-rigged sloop with either a single foresail of the jib type, or a spinnaker, and a mainsail.

The tour concluded, Bridget and Rudy went back up on deck. Rudy looked dazed. He walked quietly over to the helm and just stood gazing around the cockpit and passing his hands wistfully over the instruments on the dash.

"Well .... What do you think?" said Bridget, eager to hear his reaction.

"I'm almost afraid to think ... This is beyond words. You never cease to amaze me."

Bridget laughed. Aside from wanting to impress Rudy, she'd wanted to make him feel really special. "This is my home away from home. Enjoy it, that's why you're here." She instructed Charley to loosen the docking lines. Handing Rudy one of the life vests, she put the other one on. Down on the pier, Charley had finished loosening the lines. He flung them onto the deck as the engines started up. Bridget was poised at the helm surveying the position of the bow and stern vis-à-vis the dock and the other boats on the port and starboard sides. She resembled a sea nymph poised stoutly in the wind as it blew across the deck. The Yacht Controller dangled from a cord around her neck.

Lately she had taken to using it to navigate the yacht when she went cruising 'short-handed' or, on rare occasions, if she went out alone. The wireless remote-control device, the size of a smartphone, fit easily in the palm of her hand. She could use it to control the yacht's electronic systems and easily maneuver it from any point on the vessel. She fiddled with the switches and, as if by magic, the engines and aft thrusters groaned and the boat began inching backwards, away from the dock. Bridget positioned it carefully to avoid coming into contact with the pier and the boats moored next to it. Back on shore, Charley nodded his approval and gave them the thumbs up.

Bridget kept the boat in reverse gear until she was satisfied that it was clear of the dock, and then she let it idle for a moment. Using the throttle and shift, she put one engine in forward, and the other in reverse with expert precision. This caused the yacht to pivot three-hundred and sixty degrees on its axis. It was an awesome sight. She then set the controls to manual mode. Taking the wheel, she eased the throttle forward and the boat sliced smoothly through the water. The dinghy slid placidly along behind like a calf trailing a heifer. Rudy joined her at the helm.

"Where on earth did you learn to handle a yacht like this?" he demanded.

"My grandparents were avid yachties from Portland, Maine. As a child, whenever I went visiting during summer vacation, they often took me along on boating trips. It was great fun! I learnt a lot from them. It's really not that difficult to handle a yacht if you set your heart to it and you can think logically."

Rudy watched the shoreline recede into the distance. "Where are we heading," he asked.

Bridget swung the boat gently to starboard, then straightened up and steered downwind, holding a course due west. It surged forward, gliding through the swells like a giant sea creature. She maintained a cruising speed of thirteen knots, allowing Rudy to feel the yacht's awesome power beneath his feet.

"We're going to hold this course for a while and then turn east and head further down the coast," she called out to him through the wind.

"Okay," he shouted, moving closer to her. "I imagine the two of us out here like this must be quite a sight. Aren't you worried what your friends might think?"

"Are you afraid to be alone out here with me?"

"Actually, I'm enjoying it."

"So am I ... Let's not spoil it worrying about what others think." Bridget eased back the throttle and cut the boat's speed. "Look over there!" she shouted pointing towards the port side. A school of bluenose dolphins had emerged literally out of the deep blue and swam ahead of them, streaking through the water at amazing speeds, as if daring Bridget and Rudy to keep up with them. They watched in awe as the dolphins continued their frolicking. After a few more minutes of showboating, they headed out to open sea and disappeared beneath the surface.

Bridget let the yacht glide further out and then cut the engine. "Now we're going to do some sailing," she said and went to work raising the sails. Both the sails and reefing lines were connected to a two-speed electric winch located in the cockpit. Unfurling and raising the sails was simply a matter of releasing the cam cleats that secured the ropes, turning the winch and pushing a button on the dash. Bridget pulled the mainsail up using wire halyards and then locked the halyards down. With Rudy's help she used the winch to trim the sails. Standing with her back to the wind, she tried to determine which direction it was coming from so she could adjust the sail. She had a clear view of the bow and stern.

"This is where your crash course begins," she called out to Rudy. "Pay attention because in a while our lives will be in your hands."

"Oh no!" Rudy protested. "You can't be serious. No way!"

"You dare to defy the orders of your captain?"

"Bridget! Come on now."

"Over the next few hours you're going to help with the sails and the steering. At this very moment we're sailing directly into the wind. If we don't adjust the sail we're heading for trouble!"

As if on cue a stiff squall blew seemingly out of nowhere and nudged the boat on the starboard side, causing it to keel slightly.

"Why didn't you bring your deckhand along," Rudy moaned.

"Stop wasting time, Rudy."

Rudy knew all too well that when Bridget got into her stubborn mood, she was unshakeable. Nothing he did or said could dissuade her. The buildings in the marina resembled toys in the distance. He tried reasoning with Bridget once more, to no avail. Exasperated, he gave up. Like a chastened schoolboy resigned to his fate, he allowed Bridget to go ahead and instruct him in the art of sailing.

Using a patient, almost motherly approach, she explained to him how to adjust the boat's mainsail by tacking and jibing and how to turn the bow and stern through the wind between the positions of ten o'clock and two o'clock, depending on whether they were sailing upwind or downwind. She also taught him the rules of steering.

Despite his bristling ego, Rudy got caught up in the exercise and soon began to warm up to the challenge. It took him almost an hour and a half to get the hang of the various maneuvers, especially how to tack and jibe. He did his best to memorize the different nautical terms. He actually found Bridget to be a very skilful tutor and quite knowledgeable about sailing. He was also fascinated by the way she seemed to come alive out on the ocean. She flitted to and fro over the side decks with amazing agility and exuded energy and confidence. She was in an incredibly light-hearted mood and virtually everything was a source of amusement for her, particularly when Rudy made mistakes, some of which caused him to end up flat on his ass.

At one point Bridget was demonstrating how to swing the mainsail across the boat in order to switch it from the port to starboard side, and yelled out to him, "Prepare to tack!" He yelled back, "Okay, I'm ready!" just as she had instructed him. Unfortunately he got in the way of the boom as it swung across the boat and he forgot to duck. It hit him with a solid thud on the side of his head and swept him off his feet. He hit the deck flat on his belly like a landed fish.

"Are you all right!" Bridget yelled anxiously.

"Yeah ... I think so," Rudy mumbled. Bridget tried to keep a contrite face, without success. She cracked up and couldn't stop laughing. Rudy chuckled in between grimaces. Bridget went up to him and rubbed his head and kissed it. Rudy let out a contented sigh.

It was turning out to be the most exciting and hilarious excursion he ever had. Sailing on the high seas, Bridget was clearly in her element. Rudy had no idea that she had such a deep love for the sea. It seemed to have brought out a whole new side of her; one that was tender, warm and cheerful. It was as if she had become a little girl all over again and her exuberance was infectious.

She seemed pleased with Rudy's performance and that made him feel good. After the first two hours, she made him do the tack and jibe drill over and over again for another forty minutes to make sure he got the hang of it. She was rigorous and relentless but Rudy realized that each time it got easier, and the wind was cooperating. He became so preoccupied with trying to master the sails, he lost track of time and didn't realize that the light had faded. The sun had burnt down to a flaming orange and was bowing out over the horizon. Standing close behind Bridget, Rudy took the smell of herbal essence in her hair. He breathed it in deeply. Quietly, they watched the sun ignite the horizon and turn it fiery crimson. Then it settled majestically on the sea line and flashed a glimmery light across the sea towards the yacht, as if it was rolling out the red carpet for Bridget and Rudy. "Oh my God, look!" Bridget exclaimed and stared in awe at the enchanting solar display.

"It certainly is mind blowing, I'll grant you that!" said Rudy. "It's getting late. Shouldn't we be heading back?" The sea had all but swallowed the sun. An orange sliver, like a splotch of blood, remained on the surface. The dusk was ageing rapidly into night and the air had grown cooler. All around, colors were fading. Overhead, in the east a full moon began rising expectantly in anticipation of the demise of its nemesis.

Bridget decided to change course but rather than head back to the marina, she said they'd head south. She said she wanted to enjoy a few hours of moonlight sailing before returning home. "We'll sail south for about one and a half nautical miles then head east towards the coast. There's a private cove with very good anchorage where we can pause for a while and get romantic. It's quite beautiful."

Rudy wasn't comfortable with the idea of prolonging their trip. Aside from the risk of the two of them being out alone in open waters at night, what if word of this got around on the island? Doing this sort of thing on the sly was one thing; however, frolicking openly with the wife of your host who happened to be a British noble was quite another matter. He voiced his concerns to Bridget.

"You do have an option. You're free to jump overboard and swim back to the marina to save your reputation," she retorted.

"Doesn't it bother you at all?"

"Quit worrying. No one can see us. Just try to live in the moment." Placing her arms around Rudy's neck, Bridget drew him closer and hugged him tightly. They kissed sensuously and with slow, tender deliberation. Suddenly Bridget drew away. She told Rudy to get ready to tack as they would be sailing upwind. The moon seemed to have ballooned to several times its normal size. It hung so low over the horizon it was almost as if you could reach out and touch it. The sea lit up with a blue neon glow and shone with equal luminosity. Dark shadows hovered but the neon glow held them at bay. Bridget and Rudy had no difficulty seeing their way around. Together they swung the mainsail across the boat to try and turn the bow and work their way to the port side and into an upwind area. Bridget urged him to hurry across to the cockpit and use the wheel to operate the tiller and align the rudder with the sail. She warned him not to pull the tiller too sharply to avoid stalling or slowing the boat down, and reminded him for the umpteenth time to move the tiller in the direction opposite to the movement of the bow. "Okay! Gothcha!" Rudy yelled back, waiting for Bridget to pull the sail. The boat's bow began turning through the wind, causing the mainsail to switch to the port side. They kept the yacht turning until the sail stopped flapping. It was quite a smooth turn. This put them on a close-haul course towards ten o'clock.

"Straighten the tiller! We're now on a new course," said Bridget. Carefully judging the direction of the wind, she adjusted the mainsail some more to allow the wind to flow around the curved sail and thereby give the boat forward thrust. The yacht surged forward. She continued adjusting the sails to keep it moving in a straight line. In between checking the sails, she moved around tidying up the ropes strewn out on the deck while Rudy manned the helm. Her agility and the seeming masculine strength she displayed in handling the sails held Rudy transfixed. He couldn't take his eyes off her. In the soft glow of the moon she looked even more enchanting. She called out to him and it was only then he realized he had forgotten that he was supposed to be steering. Bridget joined him in the cockpit and checked to ensure that he kept the rudder straight. They were now heading inland towards the coast. The yacht held a fairly straight course for another fifteen minutes and then Bridget took over the helm. She let the boat continue its push towards the shore. About eight-hundred yards offshore she said it was time to furl the sail and prepare for anchoring. Using an electronic mainsail furling system in the cockpit she was able to wrap the mainsail from the boom and lock the boom in place.

"I need to pop down below deck. Please take over the steering," said Bridget, and hurrying down the port-side deck, she disappeared down the companionway. A few minutes later she came back up on deck with a device which resembled a laptop. "This is a GPS chartplotter," she explained. "It helps you plot the boat's position on a nautical chart so you can see where you are vis-à-vis the coast and various points on land, and detect potential hazards." She sat down cross-legged on the deck and fiddled with the device.

Alone at the helm, Rudy gripped the wheel and glanced around him apprehensively. Bridget came and joined him at the helm. Handing him the GPS chartplotter, she strode over to the bow of the vessel to visually check the anchor and make sure the line was free to run through the bow roller. She had already gauged the water depth with the chartplotter. Once again, she rejoined Rudy at the helm and relieved him of the wheel. She started the engines and gently eased the throttle forward, allowing the yacht to slide slowly over the moonlit waves, all the while keeping an eye on the chartplotter. She could feel a strong current in the area and it seemed to be affecting their drift more than the wind. She decided to head into the current since it was stronger. A stray cloud drifted across the moon. Bridget slowed the boat further and allowed it to coast. It came to a stop as the moon broke free from the cloud and reemerged in full glory.

At that point Bridget decided to drop the anchor. She opted to activate the anchor windlass from the cockpit rather than doing it manually from the bow because she wanted to involve Rudy and get him familiar with the procedure. She explained the process and when she was satisfied that he understood, she pressed a button on the switch panel. Immediately there was a whirring sound and the anchor began to drop. Allowing Rudy to take over, she took a torchlight from a locker near the helm seat and went to the bow to monitor the anchor's descent. She made sure the line was running smoothly through the bow roller and monitored the drop until the anchor touched the seabed. She checked the tautness in the line. The reduced strain on it told her it had reached the bottom. "Turn off the windlass!" she shouted at Rudy. The whirring sound stopped and it was all quiet again. The wind and the currents seemed to have died down. The boat bobbed up and down in the waves. Bridget told Rudy to put the engine in reverse. "Be careful, not too fast!" she warned. "Back it up slowly." Meanwhile, she wrapped the anchor line around the bow cleat and allowed Rudy to reverse until the line became taut, and then told him to stop. She was satisfied that the anchor was set firmly in the bottom. Making her way back to the cockpit, she said, "How has it been so far?"

"Like nothing I've ever experienced. I still can't believe I actually allowed you to coax me into doing this."

"Would you do it again if you got the chance?"

"Let's not get ahead of ourselves. Let's wait and make sure we survive then I'll be happy to take your question."

Bridget laughed. Rudy loved the sound, it had such a ring of jollity. Bridget pressed up against him and looked straight into his eyes. "Hungry?" she asked.

"Yeah ... in more ways than one."

"I just thought of the perfect way to end the day. We could do some moonlight bathing."

Rudy's arms encircled her waist and he drew her closer. "Out here? Okay, don't tell me – we're gonna get kinky and you're going to make me walk the plank."

Bridget giggled. "Don't be silly. Let's go across on the beach."

"Are you kidding?" said Rudy peering through the darkness at the shrouded shoreline

"We can use the dinghy. Come on! Be a darling and get us a couple of towels, some drinks and stuff from the blue cooler in the bar. No alcohol, of course." Before Rudy could respond, Bridget grabbed the torch near the dash and headed for the transom door in the stern. She opened it and stepped out onto the swim platform. The dinghy was moored across the stern. She shone the torchlight inside of it to ascertain that Charley had packed the oars and a pump. Rudy returned with two towels, a plastic bag containing a few canned drinks and biscuits.

"At least we've got life jackets. I guess there's hope." he said.

"Relax, your life is safe in my hands." said Bridget as she boarded the dinghy. Rudy followed her.

16

Skimming smoothly over the surface with the sea breeze in their faces, Rudy and Bridget peered through the darkness at a concrete bulwark about two-hundred feet offshore, evidently built to reduce the intensity of wave action inshore and provide safe harborage. Five minutes later they reached the beach.

Bridget tilted the outboard and killed the engine. Fortunately there were no swells or breaking waves and this made beaching easy. Rudy jumped into the water and pulled the dinghy up to the sand. Following Bridget's instructions, he hauled it way above the water line, close to an almond tree and tied it to the trunk. The surf rolled in so softly, it was barely audible, as if it was fearful of disturbing the intruders. The moonlight revealed a fairly ample beach extending a couple hundred yards and hemmed in by a horseshoe-shaped cove. Set against a cliff, it looked as if the mountain had cupped its bouldered arms to create a gigantic puddle. Peering at its craggy face, Rudy made out handrails and a flight of steps cut into the hillside. Spaced out on the sand were four hexagonal wooden gazebos and five beach umbrellas with loungers. A structure caught his eye at the southern end of the beach. It looked like a small beach-volleyball court.

"Are we on someone's property?" he asked.

"You could say that," Bridget replied, hugging him from behind. "Those steps lead up to a villa overlooking the bay. It belongs to Curt Mann, the founder of a leading German software company."

"This is one hell of an isolated spot."

"It's meant to be. It's a private retreat for nudist bathing."

"Really?"

"Only a select few have access to it ... including yours truly." Bridget let go of Rudy. "Do you know what this means?"

"What?"

Slowly, Bridget stripped off her lifejacket and blouse. She wasn't wearing a bra. Her breasts were full and firm with prominent areolas and small tits that protruded tantalizingly. Rudy's eyes feasted on them. She unbuttoned her jeans and pulled down the zipper. Arching forward, she wriggled out of them. She had no panties on. She tossed the trousers aside and stood naked. Rudy's eyes popped out of his head. Bridget had the most beautiful and shapely female figure he'd ever seen, and in the moonlight it looked more enticing than ever. She had strong shoulders, slightly broader than her hips, a small waist and lean, statuesque limbs. Rudy's eyes devoured her toned stomach and voluptuous thighs and her titillating vagina. Watching him, Bridget caressed her body provocatively and smiled. She clearly felt confident and in control.

"I'm going for a swim ... Are you coming?" she said. The dazed look on Rudy's face made her laugh. Walking up to him, she tugged at his shorts. "Don't just stand there, get these off," she said. Rudy didn't need any more encouragement. He pulled off his life jacket and tee shirt, hurriedly took off his pants and stood in his underwear. "Don't you dare!" said Bridget, grabbing the underwear. "Come on, get rid of it." She pulled the underwear all the way down to Rudy's ankles. He kicked it away. Bridget took hold of his penis and squeezed it tenderly. It stiffened. Rudy took her in his arms. Bridget pressed against him. He hugged her tighter and they kissed deeply. Suddenly she pulled away and ran towards the sea. She waded several feet into the water and dived beneath the surface.

Rudy followed her, wading into the gently rolling surf until the water reached up to his waist and then he slid beneath the surface. They resurfaced simultaneously. For the next fifteen minutes they swam around and frolicked, all the while laughing and teasing each other like children. A stiff breeze intruded and joined in ruffling the sea. It lingered a while voyeuristically before retreating back into anonymity.

"Time to head back to shore," said Bridget. "Come on!"

"Sure thing," Rudy agreed, sounding a bit overeager.

They swam back together with Rudy switching from freestyle to backstrokes and showing off his swimming skills. When they reached near the shore, he took her hand and helped her up. He couldn't resist eyeing her as she stepped out of the water. Running across to one of the beach umbrellas, he grabbed hold of two loungers and dragged them under a gazebo, placing them close together. He then hurried across to the almond tree where they had left the towels and handed one to Bridget as she approached. They took turns wiping each other. Rudy leaned over and took her left nipple in his mouth. He relished its salty sweetness. Rolling his tongue over it, he toyed with it. Bridget gasped. She pressed Rudy's head against her breasts and all but suffocated him. Grabbing her waist, he thrust against her, causing her to lose her balance and topple over. She landed on a towel which lay partially spread out on the sand.

"Oh Rudy ...." she sighed. Rudy's lips found hers and they kissed ferociously. Her ardor was so intense, Bridget felt like she was going up in flames. She lost touch with time and surrendered completely to the heat of her passion. Edward's face flashed in her mind and suddenly made her realize how much pleasure she got from being unfaithful to him. The flames of her desire were burning out years of marital frustration. "Give it to me ... *yes!*" she pleaded, willing Rudy to make her revenge sweeter. In between her screams of pleasure, tears streamed down her face.

"Bridget! Oh my God!" Rudy yelled as he pumped into her. Bridget opened up to receive him. He humped away furiously, taking this moment of control to unleash his Black virility and subdue her. It was not often that he had her in a position of powerlessness. The more she moaned, the harder and deeper he thrust into her. At one point she screamed and Rudy felt her nails digging into his flesh as she kneaded his back. Never before had he gotten such pleasure from inflicting pain. Inhaling her humidity and panting hard, he ploughed into her from all angles. Bridget moaned and whimpered like a wounded animal. In the conflagration there was a fusion of pleasure and pain and they melted into each other. Time stood still and the world was no more. There was neither sound nor silence, no awareness of anything but an all-consuming, transcendent bliss that was beyond words. At that moment they felt a spiritual connection and love for each other. Their souls became one and detonated, unleashing a powerful orgasmic explosion. Bridget's scream echoed across the bay as she came. In the nearby trees there was a loud flapping of wings followed by irritated squawks.

Rudy rolled over onto his back, totally spent. Bridget snuggled up to him. He held her close. Quietly, they gazed up at the almost cloud-free expanse. The moon seemed unusually bright, as if it had been trying to expose something below. It repainted the bay in an even more silvery glow. A wayward wind wafted across the cove, stirring up the briny smell of the surf. Up on the hillside there was nonstop whispering among the ruffled trees. Rudy and Bridget embraced each other tighter, oblivious to the tiny sand crabs flitting in and out of holes, all around them.

Bridget eventually disentangled from Rudy's arms and sat facing him. Her moonlit breasts jutted out temptingly. Staring

Rudy straight in the eye, she said, "I need you to be absolutely straight and honest with me."

"Okay, shoot."

"Are you seeing anyone else right now?"

"No."

"Have you been screwing around? And I don't mean here on Elysian Island."

"What kind of question is that?"

"Have you?"

"No ... No I haven't"

"No need to be cagey, I'm not trying to entrap you or anything. I just need you to be straight up with me."

Rudy hesitated. "I've had a few flings but nothing serious. Up until recently I had been in a relationship, which you knew about. That's all but done now."

"*All but* done?"

"It's over. We're through," Rudy surprised himself by weathering Bridget's probing stare and skeptical mien. He had a feeling she wasn't buying it. Bearing up, he said, "After you left England, I often reflected on the time we spent together. To be honest, there were times when I almost wished we had never met."

"Why?"

"You've become an obsession. From the moment I let you into my heart, I knew there could be no turning back. I suspect Edward would understand perfectly what I mean."

"Do you love me?"

"I'm almost afraid to think about it."

"Please do. I need to know."

"For God's sake, Bridget, you're a married woman! I'm fooling around with another man's wife; a man who has not only been good to me, he has opened up a door of opportunity for me."

"Dear Rudy has a conscience after all."

"No need to be sarcastic," Rudy snapped.

"I don't want to talk about Edward right now. Let's talk about me and you."

"What do I have of value to offer you? *Nothing.* We both know that, so let's not kid ourselves."

"Tell me, Rudy, what do you think I expect from you?"

"A lifelong commitment and all that entails."

"What do you think it entails?"

"With you, it's difficult to say."

"Am I supposed to take this as a compliment?"

"It's just the truth, at least from my perspective."

"You know, Edward has his faults but if there's one thing I admire about him, he knows what he wants and he's not afraid to go after it."

"And you can't say the same about me, I suppose."

"To be honest, no, I can't. I don't doubt for one minute that you love me or that you care about me. I also know that deep down inside, you crave other things – just like the rest of us. An opportunity to hit the big time, money, the good life. Let's be honest, isn't that part of the reason why you're here? And why not, there's nothing wrong with that. What's sad is not having the honesty or the guts to face up to the reality of what you *must* do in order to get what you want. The two are interdependent; you can't separate one from the other. If you do, you may as well forget it ... I love you Rudy. I need you in my life and I'm prepared to do whatever it takes ... What about you? Are you willing to do the same? Do you care about me that much?"

Rudy glanced away and said nothing. Bridget stood up and walked to the edge of the waterline. She stooped down and began doodling in the sand with her fingers. Rudy gazed wistfully at her beautifully arched back against the glittering sea. She resembled one of the Nereides depicted in ancient Grecian art. Although he hadn't admitted it, Bridget's words hit him below the belt and touched a raw spot in the very core of his being. Considering all the dead-end relationships he'd had in the past, mostly with clingy, insecure chicks from East London's housing estates, all financially hard-up like him and caught up on the nine-to-five treadmill or on welfare, it was hard to believe that his luck had changed so dramatically he was now living it up in one of the world's most exclusive destinations and being sought after by a beautiful woman of means. Unlike his former babes, Bridget was of a different caliber, not just because of her wealth or, for that matter, because she was white.

Among the things he'd come to appreciate about her were her genuine frankness and honesty, and her courage and determination. She was quintessentially Aries; spontaneous, energetic, brazen, adventurous and very open and straight-forward. Conversely, he discovered early that she could be quite impatient and impetuous, and lately he was beginning to suspect she had a calculating and ruthless streak. It was her fiercely independent spirit, however, that he found most disconcerting. In her presence, he kept feeling like he constantly had to prove himself and make sure that he knew what he was about, even during ordinary conversations with her. Trying to bullshit her was no easy task, and well neigh impossible.

Now that he was getting a clearer picture of the extent of Bridget's personal wealth and influence, it was making Rudy feel more uneasy – even intimidated. Oddly, it didn't seem to matter as much when he thought of her merely as the wife of a millionaire. In any case, it was one thing to fool around with a married woman who had wealth and money to her name; it was quite another matter to be involved with one who had a healthy dose of ambition to go along with her wealth. To make matters worse, Rudy now found himself caught between Bridget's ambitions and the machinations of her husband. He couldn't have found himself in a more fucked up position.

At the same time, Bridget was an incredibly desirable woman, not to mention a good lay, and he was genuinely attracted to her. For the first time ever, he was actually beginning to think of himself as 'falling in love,' whatever the hell that meant. Until now, the thought of having a serious and committed relationship had never crossed his mind, and that said a lot. Bridget was having a mind-blowing effect on him. Watching her skip playfully in the limpid waves, he felt a fervid rush of affection for her. He went over and took her in his arms. She returned his embrace with unabashed gratitude. They kissed passionately. It was Rudy who eventually broke the spell.

"It's getting late, shouldn't we go now?" he said.

"Yes, I think we should."

Together, arm in arm and giggling, they returned to the gazebo and put their clothes back on. Rudy retrieved the towels and the bag of refreshments, which remained untouched, and they headed for the dinghy. He untied it and pulled it down to the water's edge.

"No need to fret, this time we'll forego sailing,' said Bridget, reading Rudy's mind. "We'll use the engines."

Rudy breathed a mock sigh of relief and feigned wiping sweat off his brow. "I declare, great are thy tender mercies." They climbed aboard the dinghy laughing.

Aboard the yacht, Bridget took over the helm. Within twenty minutes the vessel powered away and they headed back to the marina.

17

Albion Bay was in a surly mood. Its face darkened at the sight of rain clouds rolling in over the horizon. They hovered menacingly over the sea and dampened the distant hills. The sea was dotted with sailboats and the occasional jet ski.

Rudy stood in the surf shaking his locks and squeezing the seawater out of them. He wore tight-fitting Speedo swimming trunks that exposed his firm, masculine body – the sinewy chest and thighs, and rippling torso – complemented by his flowing black mane. He cut a dashing picture. He pushed through the waves with leonine strides and headed for a secluded spot under an almond tree away from a group of bathers playing in the water. He pulled his knapsack down from a low-hanging branch and took out his iPhone to check whether he'd received any emails or text messages from Bridget. There was an expectant look on his face as he scrolled through the unread emails. None was from Bridget and there were no new text messages. His heart fell. He'd been checking since early in the morning and this was the fourth time.

She'd left for New York Sunday evening, the day after their sensational boating trip. From there she was due to travel to London before returning home. It was supposed to be a business trip involving some investment deals that she needed to wrap up; at least so she claimed. Rudy wasn't sure if to believe her, especially recalling the stunt she had pulled on Edward back in England so they could spend time together. This was her second overseas trip in *five days* and he found this a bit odd. He wondered if it was a harbinger of things to come.

Two days prior to her latest trip she'd left for Martinique by private air charter and returned the same day in the evening. Exactly what that trip entailed, Rudy hadn't a clue other than it was 'business.' As for her talk about client confidentiality, it didn't wash with him. It seemed to be just an excuse.

He found Bridget's attitude condescending and he felt belittled and disrespected. Yet although he resented being treated like some glorified poodle, he didn't press her to be straight with him. He felt that he shouldn't have to; she ought to have been more discerning and not take him for granted. Unless, of course, it was deliberate and she was hiding something from him. The way he saw it, no man should have to put up with such treatment from a woman. And to think that Bridget had actually tried to coax him into becoming her business partner! Business ornament was probably what she meant.

All of this, coupled with the fact that he seemed to be getting nowhere with Edward, was seriously getting on Rudy's nerves. It was now Saturday, a full week after his tryst with Bridget. His appointment with Edward had come and gone yet they still hadn't been able to meet. It had been scheduled for Wednesday but the day prior to that, Vernon called to inform him that Edward had to attend an urgent business meeting on the mainland, the same day of the interview, and apologized on Edward's behalf. The interview had to be postponed again! The following evening Bridget telephoned Rudy. When he told her about the postponement of the session with Edward, she disclosed that Edward had had to attend a meeting with his bankers.

Rudy found all this quite disturbing, to say the least. To make matters worse, Bridget was convinced that the delay was also deliberate and meant to taunt her. She came to this conclusion because of the way Edward kept reminding her condescendingly about 'the virtue of patience' when they were together and she seemed irritated. While his words had seemed casual and innocuous, she had lived with him long enough to know that they were anything but. Despite her suspicions, Rudy couldn't shake the feeling that both of them were playing him, and it annoyed him. However, Bridget certainly wasn't kidding when she described Edward as eccentric, he thought; if anything, she'd put it mildly. Edward was, to say the least, bizarre, and it was virtually impossible to tell what was going through his mind or what to expect from him. As a result, Rudy was beginning to feel uneasy around him.

The recent incident at the Halcyon Beach Bar was a case in point. He'd met Edward there with a grey-haired man and two elderly women. Edward introduced him to them and then turning to Rudy, he said, "With Bridget gone, I hope you don't feel neglected." To the others, he said, "Rudy and Bridget get along swimmingly, it must be said. They go off cavorting regularly and Bridget has now become his yachting instructor ... I do hope you're having a jolly good time," he added pleasantly, all the while flashing his disarming smile and exuding a benevolent calm that was almost beatific. Rudy recalled the grey-haired man peering at him over his spectacles and chuckling, and the two women glancing knowingly at each other.

The sound of barking woke him up from his reverie. A poodle stood a couple of feet away from him. It had curly black-and-white fur, dark, inquisitive eyes and long shaggy ears that made it look as if it had just been to the hairstylist. It cocked its head to one side and peered circumspectly at him. A short distance away a woman and a little girl pranced around playfully in the waves. It was still overcast and the rain, though delayed, still seemed imminent. Rudy rose up from the sand. The dog backed away warily and resumed barking querulously at him. The woman called out to it and it drew away reluctantly, growling. She waved cheerfully at Rudy and he waved back at her. A brunette with copper-toned hair and a dazzling smile, she was quite pretty. Rudy fixated on her near-nude body. She wore a skin-tight micro-bikini made of a pink, silk-like fabric. The seawater caused it to fuse with her svelte, evenly-tanned skin. Her drippy, shoulder-length hair hung free. Rudy felt sorry that she called the dog away, making it unnecessary for her to come closer. She came out of the water to get the dog. He eyed the dark mound of her vagina, which was clearly visible through the near-transparent fabric. Then she turned to pick up the dog and exposed the bare cheeks of her ass. The bikini-string in her butt-crack, although barely visible, made her derrière even more enticing.

"Damn!" said Rudy, eyes popping. He was about to go introduce himself to try his luck when his phone rang. "Shit!" he blurted out and went reluctantly to pick it up. Olive's cell phone number appeared on the screen. "Hi, Olive," he said. *Help me, please!* said Olive in a feverish whisper. She sounded terrified. "Olive! What's wrong?" said Rudy, alarmed. Again, she whispered, *Help me!* and the line went dead. Rudy dialed her number but the line was engaged. He tried three more times but each time he got her voicemail. He couldn't call her home since she had no landline. Rudy hurriedly put on his T-shirt and sandals and ran towards the spot near the road where he'd parked his bicycle, unaware that the brunette was gaping at him. He completely forgot his knapsack.

His immediate impulse was to head for Olive's home in the village but he had no idea if she was there or where else she might be. He figured she wouldn't be at her school since the last time they spoke she said it was due to close for mid-term break the following day. He telephoned the school nevertheless. Fortunately a woman answered the phone almost immediately but just as he thought, Olive was not at work. She said she didn't know her whereabouts. Olive's plea for help reverberated in Rudy's head. He had a sick feeling in the pit of his stomach. For a moment he was paralyzed, unsure what to do.

Jumping unto the bike, he took off in the direction of Blossom House. It occurred to him that riding all the way to the village would take at least fifteen minutes – much too long. Blossom House was just a five-minute ride away and there he could ask for permission to use one of the vehicles.

He took off in a panicked dash, pedaling furiously and garnering curious stares from a couple passersby. Coming round the first bend, he had to veer sharply to his left to avoid colliding with a car. The driver came to a screeching halt and glared at Rudy in disbelief. Ignoring him, Rudy negotiated two more curves with a daringness bordering on recklessness, then turned into the driveway leading to Blossom House.

Out in the courtyard, Sam was busy polishing the BMW. Rudy felt relieved to see him. He slowed to a halt and dismounted the bicycle. "Hey Sam, I need your help! I need to borrow the car!" he exclaimed, panting.

"What?"

"I need to borrow the car. Olive is in danger! I've got to get to her."

Sam gaped at Rudy as if he was some strange object that had just dropped from the sky. "Borrow which car?" he replied, as if he couldn't believe his ears.

"Listen man, just hand me the keys. I'll explain later. Olive is in danger ... I'm serious!"

"Hand you which keys? Is either you mad or you been smoking something that too strong for you," Sam retorted.

Rudy took a deep breath and tried to control himself. "Okay, if you won't let me have the car, would you mind driving me over to the village?"

"If Mr. Edward or Miss Bridget say I can take you, fine. But you'll have to ask one of them first."

"Where's Edward, is he here?"

"No, he down by the marina."

Rudy was trying hard not to strangle Sam. He spotted the car keys in the ignition. Suddenly he placed his hand over his trouser pocket and paused. Glancing up at Sam, he said, "My phone ... It's vibrating." He pulled out the phone to take the call. "Bridget!" he exclaimed. "How are you?" He paused a while, then said, "Sam? Yes, he's still here ... He was supposed to pick you up at the airport two hours ago? Good God! He's right here happily polishing the car." Rudy gave Sam a look as if to say *you're in deep shit.*

"She reach already!" Sam cried out, looking shocked. "But I thought she said her flight is tomorrow morning."

Nodding, Rudy said, "I'll certainly tell him that for you. See you soon." Tucking away the phone, he said "She wants to speak to you. She's going to call you on the landline in the house."

"Oh shit!" Sam dashed across the courtyard and ran up the steps to the house. Rudy jumped into the driver's seat and hurriedly turned on the ignition. Sam was about to enter the house when he heard the sound of the engine. He spun around. "Hey!" he shouted but Rudy was already heading down the driveway. "Hey you! Stop! Stop there!" Sam yelled. The look on his face was one of utter disbelief.

"Up yours, sucker!" said Rudy, peering in the rear-view mirror. He pulled out of the driveway unto the highway and took off, tires screeching. The landscape was overwhelmed by a sodden bleakness and the moistened hills had turned anemic. A stiff wind was blowing forcefully out of the east, a sure sign that rain was on the way and coming fast. Rudy turned the power windows up and drove through a white sheet of rain. He turned on the windscreen wipers and the air conditioner. Rain poured down clatteringly on the roof and windshield and made it difficult to see the road clearly.

Elysian's evergreen face was recast in a deathly grey. So far, Rudy hadn't encountered any vehicles along the road. He nearly drove past the junction leading to the village. He spotted it in the nick of time and braked carefully to avoid skidding. Reversing the car, he turned into the high street.

He drove down a lane and tried his best to avoid potholes filled with water. Across the road he could see curtains shifting in the windows of some of the houses and eyes peering out of inquisitive faces. He turned into another lane that led to a dead end. Eight small wooden houses lay in close proximity to each other. Closer to the end of the lane was a two-storied wood-and-wall structure, bigger than all the others. It belonged to Olive's older brother who, according to her, worked on a cruise ship. It partially obscured her home, which was built at the end of a cul-de-sac.

Rudy parked the car and dashed through the rain towards Olive's home. He rapped three times on the door and waited anxiously. Nothing happened. He pounded on it harder but there was still no response. The wind whipped up the rain, causing it to attack him. He hunched up against the door, all drenched. He turned the doorknob and the door swung open. Stepping in, he shut it quickly.

"Hello, Olive!" There was no answer. The interior of the house was somewhat clunky with a living room leading to a cramped dining room with a table and six chairs, two cabinets and a dining buffet. Just beyond was the kitchen. There was no sign of anyone. A narrow corridor separated two bedrooms from the living and dining rooms. This part of the house was dark and gloomy due to insufficient light. Rudy tried to figure out which of the two bedrooms was Olive's. He knocked on one door and then the other. No response. Slowly he opened the one to his left and froze.

A figure lay on a bed in a corner of the room. The windows were shut and curtains were drawn over them, making the teal-colored room dull and stuffy. It contained a wardrobe and a dresser, and on the floor was a colorful bedroom rug. Rudy peered at the figure on the bed. The person was covered with a dark-blue blanket and only their head and the lower part of their left leg were visible, the latter sticking out from under the blanket and touching the floor. Rudy took a while to accept that he was staring at Olive. He forced himself to move closer to the bed, his heart pounding. "Olive?" he whispered, his voice quavering. She lay with the left side of her face against the pillow, as if she had dozed off. Both of her eyes were open. A faint odor of Ambergis perfume hung in the air, Olive's favorite. Rudy dashed across to the windows and wrenched open the curtains to let in the light and rushed back to the bed. He gazed at Olive's face, focusing on her eyes. They stared blankly past him.

"Oh my God!" His first thought was that Olive had suffered a stroke or a heart attack but then he noticed a couple of bruises on her neck. Looking further down he saw a moist patch on the blanket's dark-blue fabric, near her breasts. There was no mistaking its red tinge. Slowly, Rudy lifted the blanket, his hand trembling. He reared back in horror.

On Olive's left side, about half an inch from her abdomen, was a gaping hole. The wound and part of the mattress were soaked with blood. It was obvious that she had been stabbed with brutal force, judging by the depth of the wound. A shiny black handle jutted out from under the blanket. Rudy didn't need to look closer to know it was a knife. Rudy shut his eyes and took a deep breath. He was trying hard not to hyperventilate. He wasn't sure what made him reach out and take hold of the blanket again. Steeling himself, he whipped it off the body. Olive lay on her back, her legs spread wide open. She had no panties on. Her T-shirt had ridden up to her navel. Between her thighs was a broomstick. The handle had apparently been rammed up her vagina.

Bile rose in Rudy's throat and he vomited. Rushing out of the room, he stumbled into the living room and collapsed into a chair. He felt weak and his mind was reeling. He could barely think. Reaching for his phone, he dialed 911, his hand trembling. Even as he did so it occurred to him that he had no knowledge of the level of police presence on the island. He'd never enquired. The phone on the other end of the line rang three times before someone answered. Rudy took a deep breath and blurted out what he'd just witnessed. The voice asked for his name and location. He explained as best he could and ended the call, unsure if he'd completed it or just gave up. On impulse he called Vernon Allain. He wasn't sure why. Vernon responded promptly.

"Hey Vernon, it's Rudy ... Olive is dead! She's been murdered. You've got to come!" Rudy blurted out. He told Vernon where to find him. Vernon began questioning him but Rudy shut him up. "Quit wasting time, damn it, and get the fuck over here!" he shouted and terminated the call.

He sat all alone with the memory of Olive's mutilated body. Outside, the rain pounded the corrugated-iron roof without let up, drowning out all other sounds. He would have left the house if it hadn't been for the downpour.

Strangely, the predominating thought on his mind was not who murdered Olive but could he have gotten there sooner to save her. For whatever reason, he was the one she reached out to when she was in danger and he had failed her. If Sam hadn't procrastinated when he asked to borrow the car, might he have gotten there in time to prevent Olive's death?

The questions just kept on coming and each one was like a dagger piercing his heart. Tears filled his eyes. He tried to hold them back but he couldn't.

When the police eventually came, they found him sitting with his head in his hands, weeping.

18

Rudy had been waiting for barely five minutes in the police interrogation room but in his anxiety it felt like five days. The room was little more than a cubbyhole with a desk, three chairs and a filing cabinet. The Mediterranean-blue walls and bare wooden floor, and the poor lighting accentuated its smallness and he felt like the walls were closing in on him. It seemed like it was meant to cause great discomfort to suspects. The police officer who had ushered him in, assured him that the inspector would be with him shortly but the bloke seemed to be taking his jolly time.

It came as no surprise when he found out that the police had deemed him to be a person of interest. That was to be expected considering that he was the one who had alerted them after discovering Olive's body. Initially, four police officers turned up at the house and they proceeded to cordon off and inspect the crime scene. He'd noted that three of them were relatively young, seemingly in their mid-twenties. He'd since discovered that they were part of a complement of six officers stationed at a police station in Albion Bay, and a separate precinct of the mainland

Royal St. Lucia Police Force. After one of the officers finished questioning him, Rudy was informed that they would still need to speak to him at a later date. The casual way the cop said it had made it seem like it was just routine and no big deal.

However, when he responded to a knock on his door early next morning and discovered that it was a police officer bearing a letter requesting that he come to the police station to be interviewed, Rudy knew it was going to be anything but casual.

He immediately thought of calling Bridget but then reluctantly decided against it since she still hadn't returned from London. The disappointment he felt at her absence was palpable; further proof of his growing attachment to her. He turned to Vernon and Edward for help instead. He had no choice. While both of them agreed that he should accede to the police request, they strongly cautioned him against waiving his right to have an attorney present during the interview, which he'd made clear he intended to do.

"I have nothing to fear. I've not done anything wrong," Rudy had insisted stubbornly. Nevertheless, Edward informed him with the sufferance of a parent overriding his recalcitrant son that he would arrange for legal representation on his behalf, perchance it was needed. Olive's death hit Edward hard. That was obvious from his forlorn expression and the sometimes distant look in his eyes, which was unusual.

After conferring with Edward and Vernon, Rudy received a call from Bridget. Vernon had contacted her to inform her about the murder. From her panicked response, Rudy could tell that she was in a state of shock. However, she'd seemed more concerned about him than about Olive or her family. In a way, Rudy felt soothed by that and it made him feel a bit more reassured. He'd felt ashamed to have to admit it to himself, but it was the truth. Bridget promised to return home within forty-eight hours.

Rudy recalled Vernon's exasperation with him because of his insistence on going it alone instead of waiting for Edward to arrange legal help, especially as it was being offered free of charge.

The casualness of the investigating officers at the crime scene and their generally unassuming manner had made him feel they were the sort of guys he could handle, notwithstanding his anxiety.

He got his first surprise when the inspector entered the room. A burley six-footer with a strong, intrepid face, he gazed fixedly at Rudy. Not only had he never seen the chap before, Rudy couldn't recall seeing any police officer remotely resembling him at the crime scene.

"Mr. Phillips, how do you do? I'm Inspector Leroy Butcher," he greeted Rudy in a distinct East London Cockney accent. He noticed Rudy's puzzled expression. "Is anything wrong?" he said.

"Were you at the crime scene?"

"Yes but I came over from the mainland. You had already left when I arrived."

"And you are a member of the local police force?"

"Yes. I have been for the past five years." Turning to a police officer who had followed him into the room, Butcher added, "This is Officer Jason Alfred."

Rudy nodded at the man who stared woodenly back at him and stood quietly by the door. Rudy vaguely recalled seeing someone like him at Olive's place. At the moment his mind was a bit woozy, so he figured he could be mistaken.

"You're far away from home ... I hear you're from London," said Butcher as he sat at the desk. He was carrying a CD tape recorder and a CD case. He placed them down on the desk and pushed the tape recorder slightly closer to Rudy.

"Yes, I am," Rudy replied. "So are you, obviously, but I don't suppose that's going to win me any points with you."

Butcher laughed. "I'm afraid not ... all the same, thanks for agreeing to this interview and for helping us with our investigation ... Do you mind if I address you by your first name?"

"No, that's fine with me."

"Splendid ... Before we begin, gentlemen, could you please switch off all cell phones and any other electronic devices you may have on your person."

Rudy took out his iPhone, switched it off and replaced it in his pocket. Butcher reached across and tore the cellophane wrapper from the CD case. He extracted the CD and inserted it in the recorder. "Do you have any objections to this interview being recorded?" he asked.

"No, it's fine with me."

Butcher switched the recorder on and stated the place of the interview, the date and time, his name and position. He signaled to the other officer to come forward and state his name and rank. He then directed Rudy to state his full name, address, date of birth and his National Insurance number. Rudy complied. "I must first caution you, just to be clear, that you're not under arrest and you are free to leave if you wish," said Butcher, adding, "You also have the right to consult with a solicitor during the course of this interview. Do you understand this caution?"

"Understood. Please proceed," Rudy replied, his eyes moving studiously from Butcher's stolid face to that of his sidekick, which was as expressive as the wall.

"It is my understanding that you are the one who first telephoned the police station to report the death of Miss Olive Henry. Is that correct?"

"Yes."

"How did you come to be at her residence on the day that you purportedly discovered her body?"

Rudy took a deep breath and steeled himself. He gave Butcher a detailed account of what had transpired between the time he received the call from Olive and the moment that he found her body.

Butcher listened with rapt attention. Afterwards, he pondered a moment and peered through narrowed slits at Rudy. "Did you say you received a cell phone call from Ms Henry?" he asked.

"Yes."

"That's odd ... No cell phone was recovered at the crime scene?"

That gave Rudy a jolt. "That can't be. I assure you, she did call me and she sounded terrified!" he said, looking puzzled.

"Do you recall seeing a cell phone when you entered her room?"

Thinking back, it dawned on Rudy that he hadn't, and until now this hadn't even occurred to him. "No I didn't," he said softly, sounding disturbed.

"All the same, it must have been quite an ordeal for you ... How did you feel when you discovered the body of the deceased?"

"Oh God! I can't explain ... It was horrible."

"What did you do?"

"I'm not sure ... All I remember is running out of the room and throwing up."

"Did you run outside of the house?"

"I don't think so ... No, I didn't, it was raining. I remained in the living room until the police arrived."

"Were you alone with the body all that time?"

"Yes."

"Were you an acquaintance of the deceased?"

"We were friends?"

"How long had the two of you been friends?"

"I met her soon after I arrived here three weeks ago."

"Did the two of you go out and socialize, and have fun together?"

"No, not really."

"Did you have a romantic relationship with her?"

"No! Like I said, we were just friends."

"On the day of the unveiling of the new community centre in Anse Soleil, were you present and did you and Olive have an altercation?"

The question caught Rudy off guard. He faltered and for a moment, lost his trend of thought. Butcher watched him closely.

"Well ... sort of. We had a brief argument but it wasn't anything serious. It was over some guy called Oscar from the village who kept interfering while Olive and I were having our photos taken. What does that have to do with anything?"

"You know what the Good Book says about not letting the sun set on one's anger. Sage advice, wouldn't you say? Who knows what could happen if that anger erupts again? It could get out of control and turn deadly."

"Now just a minute! What the hell are you insinuating?"

"Two of Olive's neighbors reported to the police that they heard the sound of raised voices coming from the direction of her home prior to the discovery of her body. On the day of Olive Henry's death, when you visited her home, were the two of you involved in an altercation?"

"The hell we were!"

"Is that a yes or a no?"

"No! She was already dead when I got there. I've told you that."

"Aside from Olive, was there anyone else present during the time that you were in the house?"

"No! A thousand times, no!"

"So only you know what transpired. Is that a fair statement?"

"Transpired? Nothing transpired! She was dead, God damn it! I found her dead!"

Butcher glanced at the other officer and nodded. The man opened the door and stuck his head out. He whispered to someone and hurriedly shut the door. Butcher sat quietly peering at the CD recorder as if trying to decide whether or not he should turn it off. Rudy gazed questioningly at both of them. The door opened slightly and the other officer reached out and took a small wooden box from someone, and quietly closed the door. He went across and placed it on the desk and returned to stand by the door.

Still gazing at the recorder, Butcher stated clearly what the box contained, adding that the items were evidential material obtained at the scene of the homicide. He uncovered the box, pushed it closer to Rudy and invited him to take a look inside.

Rudy did and then sat dead still, an apoplectic look on his face. Inside the box were his guitar pick necklace with the Bob Marley logo and the other one with the peace sign; the same necklaces that had been stolen from the house a few days after he moved in. So much had happened since then, he'd actually forgotten about them. He gaped at Butcher. "Where did you get these?"

"Before proceeding further, I must caution you that your responses to my following questions regarding the contents of this box or your failure to respond, could be used as evidence against you in any subsequent criminal proceedings ... Do you recognize the items in this box before you?"

"They belong to me, yes."

"Both necklaces were found on the bed where the body of the deceased was discovered, the same day of the homicide. They were beneath the bed sheets. Do you know how they got there?"

"God in heaven! I have no idea. These necklaces were stolen from the house where I live!" Rudy went on to explain how he woke up to find that the house had been burglarized and the necklaces were missing.

"Did you report the theft to the police?"

"No ... I didn't."

"Why not?"

"I was going to but ..." Rudy checked himself. He was about to say that Bridget had advised him against it. "I decided that it was no big deal, it wasn't necessary."

"Didn't it disturb you that someone broke into your home, violated your privacy, endangered your life and stole your necklaces? You didn't think this was serious enough to warrant a report to the police?"

"No, damn it! I didn't! I mean how often do you get homes broken into here? Hardly ever, from what I'm told. I decided to leave it alone. It's not as if the necklaces are valuable. They're just tokens."

"Tokens that were found at the scene of a homicide. Tokens that belong to you - that you have not satisfactorily explained how they came to be in the home of the deceased, under her bed sheet!"

"Good God! I can't believe this is happening. Can't you see? I've been framed! Somebody is trying to set me up!"

"And who might that be, Mr. Phillips? Why would anyone want to frame you?"

"For God's sake, I don't know! Listen, do you seriously believe I would murder Olive and leave my necklaces where they could easily be found? ... I imagine that to the learned Inspector, this constitutes the perfect crime. I sneak in, murder Olive and happily leave my belongings on her bed since our esteemed police wouldn't ever think of searching there for clues, nor would they be able to trace the necklaces back to me."

Butcher stiffened. His lips tightened. "All I'm trying to understand is how and why two necklaces belonging to you turned up at the scene of the crime; items which, by virtue of where they were found, suggest the owner's possible involvement in a criminal offence."

"That's it! I'm not answering any more questions. I wish to consult with my attorney. Until then, I refuse to answer any more of your questions."

Butcher nodded. "I understand. You've made a wise decision."

"Am I free to go?"

Butcher gave him an indulgent smile. "Certainly ... but with the understanding that you're still a person of interest, and that we may require your further assistance pending the full outcome of our investigation. On that score, I trust that you don't intend to leave Elysian Island any time soon and that it won't be necessary for the police to restrict your movements."

As the full import of Butcher's words sank in, Rudy's body turned cold and, once again, he felt a sick feeling in the pit of his stomach, just like he'd felt the day he discovered Olive's body. Butcher was obviously not a man to be taken lightly or underestimated. Despite his attempt to project an air of reasonableness and professionalism, it was clear that he had Rudy in his sights and intended to make sure that he didn't leave the island. Rudy's heart sank as he watched Butcher close the box with his necklaces and hand it quietly to the other police officer, who in turn stepped out of the room with it and returned within seconds.

"That's the end of the interview. I'm now going to switch off the recorder," said Butcher and he turned off the device. He then sealed and labeled it and signed it. He asked Rudy and the other cop to sign it as well. "Thanks for your cooperation," said Butcher, flashing a smile that didn't quite reach his eyes. Rudy said nothing. He stood up and walked past the stone-faced officer and out the door.

19

Rudy woke up abruptly, startled by the explosive sound of gunfire. A second shot rang out, followed by two more. He sprang from the bed and hit the floor in panic. Another sharp crack rang out, followed by the hissing sound of a bullet whizzing by. He covered his head and curled up on the floor. The shooter was coming to get him. He was sure of it. He waited but nothing happened. He lay still and waited some more. Everywhere was quiet except for the sloshing sound of the sea beneath him. He gazed apprehensively around the room. The house was a private beachfront bungalow and part of it was perched directly over the sea.

Rudy got up slowly and went to peep into the living room. There was no one there. The house belonged to Aaron. He was supposed to have left three days ago for the mainland to go mountain climbing in the rainforests deep inside the island's interior. Realizing that Rudy had found himself in a jam following Olive's murder, he'd had no hesitation letting him stay at the house when Rudy told him he needed to be alone for a while, and didn't want anyone to know his whereabouts unless it was absolutely necessary. Rudy was reluctant to return to the house at Albion Bay after his ordeal four days ago at the police station. As if the grilling from Butcher hadn't been bad enough, the next day two cops showed up at the house with a search warrant. Ignoring his protests, they proceeded to virtually ransack the house searching for evidence to further implicate him - *the motherfuckers.* They came up empty handed.

Rudy glanced at a clock on the living room wall. It was 6:00 a.m. He could hear someone moving around outside in the yard. His heart was pounding. He recalled seeing a machete somewhere in the kitchen. He dashed across and found it in one of the drawers in the kitchen cupboard. Grabbing it, he rushed back to the living room and held it at the ready. The house was in a relatively isolated area and for the past few days there hadn't been a soul in sight. He couldn't figure out who in hell would want to invade the place and shoot him. The cops flashed in his mind and, for a moment, he wondered if they had come to get him, perhaps worried that he might try to sneak out of the island. He quickly dismissed the thought as silly and irrational. Could it be Olive's killer? *Stop it, damn it!* he scolded himself.

The waves lapped at the underbelly of the house. Edging closer to a window, Rudy gently pushed aside the curtain and peeked outside. His jaw drooped. He couldn't believe his eyes. For a while he just stood there, then his face darkened. He pulled open the door and stormed out.

20

Aaron stood a few yards from the house holding a Winchester rifle. He was so preoccupied he didn't see Rudy. He swung the gun lever down and forward to extract and eject the fired case. He then pulled the lever back and up to the starting position.

"Aaron ... What on earth are you doing!" Rudy snapped.

"Hello, how are you, mate?" Aaron replied cheerily.

"For goodness sake! What the fuck are you trying to do, give me a heart attack? ... Besides, what are you doing here? I thought you were supposed to be out mountain climbing."

Aaron walked across with the rifle cradled in the crook of his arm. "Did I scare you? How thoughtless of me, I apologize." He seemed genuinely concerned. Rudy still looked flabbergasted. Aaron said, with a smirk, "Can we agree to lay down our arms?"

"What?"

Aaron stared pointedly at the machete in Rudy's hand. Rudy glanced down at it, looked up at him and shook his head despairingly.

"My trip had to be postponed for tomorrow," Aaron explained. "I forgot that I had to attend a birthday party for Sir Paul Scoon, an old family friend. The poor chap is ill and ageing. While there, lo and behold, he takes me aside and presents me with this absolutely incredible gift!" He held up the rifle. "A genuine Winchester 1873. He's had it for more than sixty years. Knowing me to be an avid gun collector, he insisted that I have it. He thought it would make the perfect addition to my collection. He is right, of course. I dutifully refused but he would have none of it, thankfully." Aaron passed his hand lovingly over the gun barrel. It had an oil-finish walnut stock, a classic blue crescent buttplate and a twenty-inch barrel. Engraved distinctively on the barrel were the words 'Manufactured by the Winchester Repeating Arms Co.', underscoring the gun's authenticity. "Classic Americana," said Aaron, proudly. "I couldn't resist testing it, so I woke up bright and early and drove out here. I didn't want to risk scaring Sir Paul's neighbors half to death, which I seem to have done to you. Over here there are no houses close by."

"Are you kidding? By the sound of this thing, you'd have to be as far away as the North Pole not to hear it going off."

"All the same, my good sir, I hereby bestow on you the privilege of guarding it with your life, if need be, until my return. Follow me, if you please." Aaron walked past Rudy into the house. Rudy followed him. Before closing the door, he paused to look around the yard. The sound of the gunshots had been so powerful, he couldn't help wondering who else might have heard them and that made him uneasy. The last thing he needed was the police showing up because of someone's complaint, especially with him in the house. Typically, Aaron couldn't give a damn.

All was calm and quiet outside. Aaron's Land Rover was parked a few yards away amidst an oasis of palm trees growing defiantly out of the dry sandy soil. Rudy went in and shut the door.

Aaron had apparently gone to his room. Rudy returned to the bedroom and changed into a pair of navy blue workout shorts and white tee-shirt, brushed his teeth and returned to the living room. It was quite vast with a bar and furnished with a five-piece hand-painted Italian sofa set. The bungalow was expertly crafted with a high-pitched timber roof designed in the palapa style, without the thatch. The living room gave access to an open deck with a panoramic view of the Caribbean Sea. It was designed with a glass-bottom floor that afforded a clear view of the shimmery water and the seabed adorned with variegated coral, undulating seaweed and the occasional fish flitting to and fro. The northern tip of the island was visible in the distance. The frontal part of the house cantilevered over the seabank on concrete columns constructed about fifteen feet above sea level, high enough to withstand sea surges. The interior consisted of polished hardwood floors and walls and shuttered windows made of mahogany and teak. The three double bedrooms were adorned with handcrafted furnishings, a full bathroom with warm shower and solar-powered electricity and cable TV. Rudy's room had rattan furnishings and a king-size bed, and a thirty-two inch desktop computer with high-speed internet connection. In spite of its artful design and lavish furnishings, the house had the air of a bachelor pad and lacked a lived-in feel.

Rudy went to the kitchen and turned on the coffeemaker. He returned to the living room and flopped down on the sofa. He liked the room's outdoorsy openness with the sea breeze blowing through the house. He found it soothing. At the same time he found it hard not to feel a bit envious, even resentful, on seeing the way Aaron treated it all with bored indifference, like a kid who had grown tired of a once cherished toy. During the two months that he spent annually on the island, Aaron seldom stayed in the house more than two weeks at a time. The rest of the year it was put up for lease. Rudy thought ruefully of his one-bedroom council flat back in Brixton and the possibility that it might no longer be available when he returned. He had allowed a friend to move in temporarily to take care of it in his absence but apparently he had been pissing off the neighbors with his loud music. One of them had emailed him to complain.

Mulling over all this, Rudy was forced to be honest with himself. The lavish lifestyle he'd been enjoying on Elysian Island was a welcome relief from having to worry about whether or not he'd be able to pay his council flat rent or utility bills, or if he should settle for sandwiches or warmed-up, pre-packaged meals rather than dining out and risk putting a hole in his wallet. So far not a cent had come from his pocket to cover the cost of lodging and meals, except the occasional drinks and snacks he'd had at a couple of the less pricey joints, including the village bar. It was amazing to realize how easily one could get used to the good life. It was almost beginning to feel normal, despite his being on the island for such a short time. Yet the likes of Aaron who was born to wealth, all too often seemed to treat it so frivolously. This, Rudy found vexing.

"Have you received any word yet on the status of the investigation?" said Aaron as he entered the living room.

"Not yet. That Inspector Butcher guy is probably still working overtime to try and pin the murder on me."

"I wouldn't bother about it if I were you. It's been four days now. Surely they would have moved in by now if they had any concrete evidence implicating you."

"Yeah, I've been thinking the same thing ... Has there been any reaction to the murder from the local press? Since moving here I've pretty much unplugged from the outside world."

"Local press indeed," Aaron snorted. "I can't say that I've seen any enthusiasm for covering the story from that lot beyond the airing of a carefully worded press release from the police on a couple of the local radio and TV stations. I'm told there were also brief reports in two of the newspapers, including one citing rumors and hearsay but nothing conveying the true horror of the crime."

"That's odd," said Rudy, frowning.

"Not necessarily – that is, if one understands the way 'stuff works' over here, as the Americans would say. No doubt, Leroy Butcher and his brood are being tight-lipped with the press, and offering the usual excuse of not wishing to jeopardize the investigation, and your media colleagues seem to have bought it hook, line and sinker. To their credit, two local reporters turned up on the island yesterday but got no further than the offices of the Elysian Island Company where they were politely turned away empty handed and weren't allowed to speak to the folks in the village.

"That said, one of the government ministers has announced his resignation, reportedly over some scandal. Believe it or not, the announcement was made on the same day of the murder! Rather unfortunate for dear Olive. Presently, this bit of political theatre is all the rage over on the mainland. It has proved to be rather propitious for the Elysian Island Company, I imagine. Let's not forget the island practically belongs to the consortium of landowners who form the company and they've got their pristine image to worry about."

Shaking his head, Rudy let out a weighty sigh. "This whole shit is just surreal," he muttered dejectedly.

Aaron grabbed a cushion from one of the chairs and dropped it on the floor in the middle of the room. He sat on it cross legged with his shoulders slightly hunched, like a yogi. He had changed into a faded pair of jeans and sneakers and a rather colorful Hawaiian shirt which he left unbuttoned. His nude, flame-haired chest caught Rudy's attention. Gazing at him, Rudy recalled a red-haired Okapi chimpanzee he had once seen in the Los Angeles Zoo.

"You know, the birthday bash for Sir Paul was quite a do," said Aaron, grinning. "I drank myself to within inches of being well and truly arseholed. It's a bloody miracle I managed to get out of bed and drive all the way out here."

"Care for something to eat?" said Rudy.

"No thank you. I'm so stuffed, I doubt I'd be able to hold it down. No disrespect to you, of course. A drink would do nicely ... On second thoughts, don't bother, allow me." Aaron pounced agilely to his feet and headed for the bar. "What'll you have?"

"Coffee, please. Thanks."

Aaron went to the kitchen to prepare the coffee and took it across to Rudy. "How has it been so far? What have you been up to?" he asked.

"Mostly feeling sorry for myself and wondering how the devil I could have been so insane as to land myself in such a mess by coming to this island."

Aaron paused as he was about to open the refrigerator. "Really? Why, is it because of Olive's death?"

"No. It's because of my own idiocy. And herein lies the problem. How does one escape from one's own stupidity?"

Aaron ejected a few ice cubes from the icemaker, popped them into a glass and helped himself to a copious shot of Vermouth. He then added a touch of strong rum, orange bitters, pineapple juice, vodka, tomato juice and a little milk and stirred it thoroughly. Satisfied, he returned to sit on the floor. Rudy gaped at his glass. "What on earth are you drinking?"

"I call it the Mojito Bonfire. It aids with blood circulation .... On the question of your declared 'stupidity,' do you care to be more explicit?"

Rudy hesitated, then shrugged. He told Aaron for the first time about his ghost-writing deal with Edward and the terms under which he'd agreed to stay on Elysian Island. He also spoke about how difficult the past few weeks had been for him, openly showing his frustration at not being able to start working on the book because of Edward's constant procrastination. He put the blame for his entanglement in Olive's murder squarely on Edward's head. Finally, he told Aaron what he thought of his uncle's unpredictability and odd behavior. He didn't mince his words.

"Believe me, your uncle is the weirdest bloke I've ever come across, and trust me, as one who has dabbled in entertainment journalism, I've crossed paths with some pretty bizarre characters in my time."

Aaron chuckled. "He is unorthodox, I'll grant you that. The old boy is anything but ordinary and he does have some radical views on life. I'm not sure I would characterize him as bizarre."

"Oh yeah ... I forgot that we view life from opposite sides of the fence. What's bizarre to me is ordinary and mundane to folks like you and vice versa."

"You're not going to play the class-warfare game with me, are you?"

"Nah ... I get grumpy whenever my beauty sleep is ruined, albeit by the master's kin."

Aaron grabbed a cushion from the sofa and flung it at Rudy. "Get stuffed!" he said and returned to the bar for another dose of his cherished potion. He went back and sat on the chair cross legged. He didn't bother to remove his shoes. Around the soles were caked with mud. "Tell you what," he said. "Why don't we do a litmus test to determine if Edward is truly bizarre as you claim?"

"A litmus test, what do you mean?"

"It's quite simple. I ask you a question and you give me an honest answer. How you respond will help us decide who's barmy, you or Edward."

"Okay, shoot."

"Are you fucking Bridget?"

Rudy shot up off the chair as if he'd been stung. He turned pale, as if he'd seen a ghost. "What did you say?"

"How long have you been screwing my uncle's wife?"

"Okay, that's it! This conversation is over."

Aaron gave a dastardly chuckle. "Don't be upset. In fact, you don't have to respond if you don't care to. Let's make believe, for a moment, that you *are* fucking Bridget. One would think that you'd thank your lucky stars that you're here living the good life rather than six feet under with a bullet in your skull ... Don't you agree? In such a case, one would have to deduce that the only thing that spares you from the latter fate is Edward's 'bizarreness'; the fact that he does not think or reason the ordinary way like the rest of us."

Rudy avoided Aaron's probing stare. He slumped back into the chair and gazed blankly at the floor. After a while he glanced up. "You're as creepy as your uncle."

Aaron got up and sat on the floor. He began doing floor exercises. "That's more or less what my family says, including my mother. I can't, for the life of me, figure out why."

"Have you ever thought to check out the side effects of those concoctions that you seem to relish?"

"What for? That would take the mystery out of it. The beauty of life is discovery."

"Right ... Maybe I should get something to eat. I'm going to need it to keep up with you." Rudy headed for the kitchen.

"Hey Rudy!"

Rudy turned around. Aaron sat with his back against the chair. "Take my advice. Relax, soak in some sun, sea and sand and quit worrying. Enjoy your vacation and don't look a gift horse in the mouth."

Rudy was about to counter with a wisecrack when they heard a vehicle pull up outside. The two men stared at each other.

"Expecting anyone?" said Aaron.

"No way, are you kidding?"

"Hmm, wonder who it might be. Let's find out." Aaron went and looked through the window. Turning to Rudy, he said, "I'm afraid you've got visitors."

Rudy stiffened. "Who?"

"Lady Macbeth and her trusted valet."

"How did they know I was here? Did you tell them?"

"Of course not."

"So how did they know?"

Aaron shrugged. "Lucky guess. Or perhaps someone spotted you."

"No way, I never left the house until this morning."

"Maybe you were spotted from the sea by someone on a yacht. Were you out on the deck?"

"Yes, I was ... and come to think of it, a couple of speed boats did pass by."

Outside, two vehicle doors slammed shut.

"Ah well, I may as well effect my departure. I'm going to have a marvelous time roughing it in the great outdoors. I shall be back over the weekend. Cheerio." With that, he was out the door.

21

The sound of chatter drifted in from outside. Rudy turned on the coffeemaker and was about to pop two slices of bread in the toaster when the door opened. Bridget stepped in, followed by Vernon. She looked so stunning, Rudy momentarily forgot all his worries. She wore dark-grey, high waist trousers with a flared cut and a belt, along with a buttoned-down shirt and a blazer. She was the picture of Parisian chic. It was obvious that she'd popped in on the way to her office as her get up was more suited for work. Rudy wasn't sure if to feel flattered or concerned since only a crisis could drag Bridget away from her work, and he figured she would be none too pleased at having to divert from her normal route to travel this far just to see him.

"Hi Rudy," she said in a soft, stirring tone.

"Hello." Rudy fumbled with the bread slices and, for some reason, he had difficulty fitting them inside the toaster slots. The coffeemaker went off. He turned it back on then checked himself and turned it off again.

"We thought you had absconded. Why did you suddenly disappear?" Bridget's voice had suddenly turned frosty.

"I just needed to be alone for a while." Rudy avoided her eyes. He and Vernon exchanged glances.

"How you doing?" said Vernon.

"I'm cool."

Bridget sat on the sofa. Vernon remained standing. Rudy remained in the kitchen. "How did the two of you find me?" he said.

"What are you afraid of?" Bridget demanded, ignoring his question.

"Who says I'm afraid? Like I said, I needed some peace and quiet to reflect and do some soul searching."

"You could have just said so, out of courtesy rather than running off like that. Besides, why couldn't you do your soul searching back at the house?"

Rudy went and sat opposite Bridget. "Maybe it's because I'm growing tired of feeling that I have to account for my actions and whereabouts, even my thoughts."

Bridget crossed her legs and lounged back in the chair. Rudy eyed her thighs as her skirt rode up exposing their smooth texture.

"I don't mean to sound critical," said Bridget, "but we are looking out for you and working in your best interests – including Vernon. I do hope you appreciate that."

Rudy said nothing.

"You now have a lawyer representing you." Bridget fixed him with her characteristically probing stare. "Edward has retained the services of Clifford Allen. He's a British-born lawyer based on the mainland in Castries, and one of the best. It was obviously a mistake not to have him present when you were being questioned by the police."

"Words cannot express how beholden I am to you and His Lordship for your gracious kindness. What can I possibly do to repay you?"

Vernon lowered his head and gave a surreptitious little smirk.

Rudy stood up. "Can I offer you guys anything?" he said, braving Bridget's withering stare. Both she and Vernon declined his offer.

"Okay, look, I admit I was wrong to face the cops without a solicitor. But, hell, how was I to know that someone was looking to frame me?"

"You mean the necklaces," said Vernon. "No need to worry about that now. Bridget and I had a chat with the Inspector. You should have told him that we advised you not to report the theft to the police."

"Growing up, I learned not to rat on my friends. They've got nothing on me. There's no way they can link me to Olive's murder."

"You're going to have to explain that to a jury if you insist on playing your hermit game all the way out here," Bridget retorted. "Let's hope you can be more convincing than you were with the cops."

"What are you driving at?"

"Clifford is coming in tomorrow and expects you to be available for a consultation. He's already had a chat with the police. From here on, if you fail to show up when required, you're going to be on your own. Edward is not pleased about your little vanishing act. You should at least have tried to keep in touch with him."

"This solicitor guy, how does he feel about the investigation so far?"

"Ask Vernon, he was on a conference call that Clifford had with him and Edward."

Rudy turned to Vernon. Vernon spotted an ottoman stool near the sofa. He took it and placed it in a neutral spot between Rudy and Bridget.

"The police have received the autopsy report. It indicates that the cause of death was a stab wound to the left side of the back, resulting in the perforation of the left lung and a hemothorax - the accumulation of blood in the pleural cavity. They were also able to determine the time of Olive's death. Clifford Allen was able to obtain from the telephone company by subpoena, a record of your mobile phone calls on the day of the murder, as well as statements from witnesses verifying your whereabouts; for example, Samuel and Amanda. Clifford determined that you couldn't possibly have been at Olive's house around the time the murder took place. As a result, he was able to stave off your arrest, for the time being at least. He was also able to convince Butcher that you're not a flight risk."

"You said statements from Samuel and Amanda. Who's Amanda?"

"An exceedingly pretty brunette who happened to have been close enough to you at Beulah Beach," Bridget butted in. Rudy noted the telltale tapping of her foot. "She was kind enough to vouch for your whereabouts at the time in question," she added.

"Really? Why did she do that? Who asked her to?"

"This is a tiny island, word gets around. She found out about you and volunteered the information, initially to Edward," Vernon explained. "Incidentally, you forgot your knapsack on the beach. She turned it over to Edward."

"Blimey! That was quick work. This lawyer guy is good."

"Clifford is one of the best criminal lawyers you can find anywhere. He's also very costly," Bridget said emphatically.

Rudy heaved a sigh and went quiet for a moment. "I must be honest with you," he said, staring earnestly at Bridget. "I feel like a huge weight just came off my shoulders. I'm grateful ... I mean it."

Bridget smiled. Her face softened. "Everything is going to be fine. There's no need to worry."

"There's only one problem," said Rudy.

"What's that?"

"How do I clear my name?"

"Excuse me?"

"By now it must be all over the place that my necklaces were found at the scene of the murder. What do you think most people are going to conclude?"

"Oh, come on," said Bridget. "Do you seriously believe the police would publicly disclose such evidentiary information? Not even the press has been privy to much of the details of the murder."

"Are you kidding me? Forget the press; we're talking about my personal image and reputation. Folks know that I was called in for questioning and, frankly, having seen the performance of some of the officers who showed up when I called to report the murder – their casual, almost lackadaisical attitude – I wouldn't bet on them keeping this business about my necklaces close to their chest ... Go on Vernon, tell us what you think and be honest. As an ex-cop, can thc island's police be trusted to keep such matters confidential?"

"I think they're aware that the presumption of innocence could be undermined if they were to indiscriminately release evidence that enables members of the public to know why a person was suspected in the first place. Or at least they should know. In any case, Leroy Butcher is leading the investigation and he's known to be a no-nonsense guy."

"You're evading the question. Can you or anyone else guarantee that details of the investigation won't be leaked?"

"Of course not, and that applies to every police force."

"From your knowledge and experience, has it ever happened before, whether here on this island or back on the mainland?"

"Yes, it has."

"End of story."

"Aren't you overreacting?" said Bridget.

"My instinct tells me I'm not ... Besides, you heard the man. And let's not forget something else. There's a killer out there who tried to frame me. Don't you think he or she would be eager to let the world know that my possessions were found right next to Olive's body? Surely, that was the aim in the first place; to implicate me publicly."

"Agreed," said Bridget. "But at the moment you have not been arrested and you are not a suspect. As far as the police are concerned, you are only assisting with the investigation."

"In the court of public opinion I will be considered a suspect. I can already hear folks whispering behind my back everywhere I go on this island, especially in the village. To be honest, right now I'm very reluctant to go over there. That's the way it's going to be until the murderer is found."

"Is this why you came hiding out here?"

"Initially, no but after four days of reflection and soul searching, the reality hit me. I had nothing to do with Olive's death, yet people are going to think that I did and that's eating away at my soul."

"So what do you intend to do about it?" said Bridget, frowning.

"Find the murderer."

"What!"

"All I've got to do is find out who broke into the house at Albion Bay and stole my necklaces. Find the person who did it and we find the killer."

"Are you out of your mind? That would be tampering with a police investigation. Now you're really asking to be locked up!"

Vernon seemed taken aback. Frowning, he said, "That's not a good idea. Leave it to Leroy Butcher. He's a good investigator, one of the best ... Trust me."

"*Trust you*?" Rudy snapped, an incredulous look on his face. "I seem to recall that what landed me in this mess in the first place was the advice from both of you against reporting my stolen necklaces to the cops."

Vernon's frown deepened. "I can't help getting the feeling that you're looking down on our local police. In fact, worse than that, I think your condescending attitude is directed not merely at them but at the country of your birth."

"What in God's name are you talking about?"

"Would it make you happier if the case was being investigated solely by British officers?"

Rudy gaped at Vernon, lost for words. For a moment there was an uncomfortable silence.

"You seem to be taking this rather personally," said Rudy. "I know that you're an ex-police officer but nevertheless ..."

"Guys!" Bridget butted in. Staring at Vernon, she said, "Would you mind giving Rudy and me a few minutes, please?"

"Sure." Vernon got up and walked out of the house, ignoring Rudy.

"Have you had breakfast," said Bridget.

"Not yet." Rudy gazed at the clock. It was quarter to ten. "It's still early. Can I get you anything?"

"No, I'm fine, thanks." Bridget hesitated. "How long do you intend to remain on this island?"

"At the moment, that's up to the cops. Left to Butcher, it won't be anytime soon."

"Between Clifford and Edward, they're going to handle the police regarding your freedom of movement, so on that score you have nothing to fear ... Strangely, Edward seems genuinely concerned about you. Until we discovered your whereabouts, he was actually fretting. I've never known Edward to fret about anything."

"I'm relieved that he doesn't think I had anything to do with Olive's death. I know how deeply he cared about her. What's ironic is that, more than anyone else, I blame myself for her death. She begged for my help and I couldn't save her."

"Come on, Rudy don't think of it this way. You did your best. That's the most you could have done. Olive would never hold it against you."

Rudy rose abruptly and went out onto the deck. He stood facing the sea. Bridget followed him outside. She saw him wipe a tear from his eye. She took him in her arms and hugged him. Unable to hold back anymore, he cried. He wept like a baby.

"Go on, let it all out," said Bridget soothingly and cradled him in her arms. She held him for while, then gently lifted his head off her shoulder and gave him a peck on the nose. He held her tight. The gentle rippling of the sea was quite relaxing and made them feel at peace. The sound of a speedboat engine rose up in the distance and immediately they saw it curl around the headland toward the north. Instinctively, they drew away from each other.

"Shall I get you a drink?" said Bridget.

"Yes please. Ice-cold lemonade. There's a batch in the fridge."

Rudy sat down on the glass floor and gazed absently into the water. Bridget returned with the lemonade and a bowl full of biscuits. Handing him the glass, she placed the bowl on a glass-topped table and sat on one of three chairs. A flock of seagulls flew across the sky and three of them plunged into the sea in search of fish

"You've been through quite an ordeal. I think you need a break from this island for a while," said Bridget.

"What do you mean?"

"You're obviously very upset. I believe Olive's death is going to haunt you for quite some time and prevent you from thinking rationally. You need a break."

"And what do you suggest?"

"Ideally, it would be good if you could return to England for about a month or so."

"You must be joking!"

"I'm serious. I think you should take a break from here."

"I'm sure the cops will be thrilled to hear that."

"As I've said, Clifford will take care of it. He's confident that he can persuade Leroy Butcher to drop any objections he may have to you travelling."

"Look, I've been here for over three weeks and I'm still not able to get started on what I came here to do. All I've been doing is loafing around, waiting for your husband to make up his mind. This whole situation is not only frustrating, it's ludicrous! And as if I haven't been through enough, you're now suggesting that I procrastinate further and prolong the agony. At this stage, even if it was possible for me to leave, I'm not even sure that I would want to return."

"Okay, forget England. You could go someplace else that would be convenient for both of us."

Rudy gaped incredulously at Bridget. "Where else can I go? Besides, sweetheart, I hope you're not suggesting that I take off with a leash around my neck so that you can pull me in anytime, from anywhere, are you? Because that's what it sounds like to me."

"No darling, what I'm suggesting is that, if you are fed up of waiting on Edward to make up his mind, mark my words, the wait has only just begun. Considering the grim mood that Edward has been in since Olive's death, don't expect him to pay any attention to this book in the near future, which is by no means a bad thing. You're going to be in limbo for the next few months, at the very least ... Mind you, that is assuming he'll be able to continue his financial generosity that long."

"I thought you wanted me to be here on Elysian Island so that you and I could be closer to each other. That's one of the main reasons I came out here, isn't it? I thought you couldn't bear me being away from you for too long. See how you reacted earlier this morning, all because I stayed away for a few days. Was this for real or was it just my imagination?"

"Don't be silly, nothing between us has changed. I long to have you near me all the time."

"Assuming that I'm allowed to leave, anywhere I go will be hundreds if not thousands of miles away from you, if I'm not mistaken ... And please don't say you could hop on a plane anytime and we could be together again."

"I'm concerned about you. I hate to say it but Olive's death has changed everything. It has even changed you. I think you meant it when you said you want to find the killer. I'm sorry but you're not thinking rationally and if you keep on this way, you're heading for trouble. I love you Rudy. I don't want you hurt, or for that matter in jail. You're quite pigheaded and emotional. That's why I think you need a break from here, just for a while. It doesn't have to be England. Why not spend some time over on the mainland? It's ten minutes away. We could meet there privately. It's your homeland isn't it? Go relax, meet old friends and thereafter take it from there."

"You don't understand. I would be leaving here with a cloud over my head. People will continually be speculating whether or not I was involved in the murder. It's going to be that way until Olive's killer is found. Somebody deliberately tried to frame me and make me look like a vicious murderer and the reality of this is just eating away at me."

"But you're assuming that people know about the necklaces. How do you know that? You're allowing yourself to become a prisoner of your fears."

"How do I know? Because I am a native of this country and it's not as if I have been away so long that I can't remember the cultural dynamics that are at work here. If there's one thing I do know, it is that on the island a lie has no legs but it has wings."

"What about Edward's book?"

"I need to have a talk with him once and for all. I'm going to give him an ultimatum and insist that he takes a firm decision whether or not we go ahead with this book. To be honest, it's going to be difficult for me to focus on it or even maintain my enthusiasm ... On the other hand, perhaps if I'm away from here for a bit, I could probably function better and be more focused. So, yeah, maybe you've got a point."

"My point was certainly not to make it easier for you to continue with this so-called book. Let's be very clear about that."

"I know. I have no illusions about that. I know that's one of the reasons you would like to keep me as far away from Edward as possible." Winking, Rudy added, "Damn that pesky thing called technology!"

Bridget stood up and took Rudy's glass which still had some ice cubes. She calmly tugged the waistband of his shorts and poured the ice cubes into his crotch.

"Oow!" Rudy jumped to his feet and shook the ice out of his pants. "You shouldn't have done that, now downstairs is in need of heating to drive away the cold," he added with an impish grin.

"Don't you dare!" Bridget barely made it to the living room before Rudy grabbed hold of her. Pulling her hard against him, he pressed his face into the side of her neck and pretended to bite into it like a vampire. Giggling, Bridget tried to push him away. Rudy tightened his grip and kissed her neck, tickling it with his tongue. Bridget inhaled his warm masculine odor and felt herself capitulating to the force of his desire. His locks brushed against her neck and tickled it sweetly.

"No, Rudy, we can't ... not here." His lips found hers and she opened up to receive his tongue. They kissed furiously and deeply, rubbing and melding into each other until they became one incandescent flame. Their passion blazed and Bridget felt her soul being consumed. She moaned with pleasure. Someone coughed outside. Reality intruded, forcing them to draw away from each other reluctantly. Bridget went to retrieve her handbag. "I must go. When will I see you again? You can't stay here indefinitely," she said.

"After Aaron returns. He's due back this weekend."

"Clifford needs to speak with you. He won't wait forever."

"I will go. I promise."

Bridget walked up to Rudy and kissed him softly on the cheek. Heading for the door, she paused with her hand on the doorknob. "Your cell phone ... please leave it on."

Rudy nodded. He didn't see her out. Two doors slammed shut and a vehicle drove off, leaving him alone with the wind-ruffled stillness and the restless billowing of the sea, seemingly mirroring his restive spirit.

The prospect of returning to square one to reap the harvest of his own mercenary ambitions darkened his mood once again. Although no one had yet broached the subject, there was one cross that he still had to bear; Olive's funeral. He wasn't even sure of the date and he was apprehensive about contacting her mother or any of her friends to enquire. Could Bridget be right? Was he allowing himself to become a prisoner of his fears? Or worse, his guilty conscience. He sighed and ran his fingers agitatedly through his locks.

He headed for the bedroom and returned with a joint already lit. He switched on the hi-fi system. The Bob Marley CD he'd been listening to for the past two days was still in the CD player. He turned it on and Marley's soulful voice filled the room with his heart-stirring tune, 'Them Belly Full But We Hungry.' Rudy stretched out on the sofa and drew hard on his spliff. Smoke swirled around his head and the pungent grassy odor of ganja slowly permeated the room. He sang along in between puffs.

"Forget your troubles and dance!

"Forget your sorrows and dance!"

22

Everyone in the village seemed to have turned out for Olive's funeral. The cemetery was right next to the church and they all assembled their after the service. It was an uneven grassy plot of land with a few mango trees growing on the fringes. Rudy stood alone under one of the trees, dressed in a dark pinstripe suit and black shirt with no tie. Prior to the commencement of the church service, hardly anyone paid him any attention, although occasionally he could feel eyes staring at him.

Afterwards, members of Olive's family (mostly cousins who came over from the mainland) joined the pallbearers to escort the coffin to the gravesite. Someone began wailing as it was being wheeled out of the church. Two women broke down and soon the air was filled with sobbing and weeping. An elderly lady collapsed and had to be helped up. Tears welled up in Rudy's eyes as he watched the scene and he was forced to look away. He'd had to fight hard to resist the urge to leave.

In the forefront of the pallbearers was a somber-faced Edward accompanied by Vernon. Rudy had noted that Edward was not the only white person present at the funeral. Twenty others attended, including Bill Thompson and his wife, two ageing British aristocratic couples and a couple of well-known multimillionaires. Rudy knew that their attendance, coupled with the presence of scores of villagers, made Olive's funeral one of the most notable events in the history of Anse Soleil. Bridget was nowhere to be seen.

Olive's mother had stood briefly outside the church entrance speaking to friends and relatives and thanking them for attending the service. Rudy had approached her apprehensively. She took his hand and patted it gently and gave him a kindly smile. Soon after, a few people approached him and chatted with him briefly. It was almost as if they had taken the cue from Olive's mother. He'd felt relieved.

The sound of singing drifted mournfully across from the graveside as the grave diggers prepared to lower the casket into the tomb. A woman screamed and fainted. A little girl squealed and had to be restrained from going too close to the tomb.

Rudy decided to leave. He couldn't bear it any more.

"Hello."

Rudy spun around. He looked surprised. "Hi," he replied gazing at the woman standing before him. She was the same one he had encountered on the beach the day of Olive's murder.

"Did I startle you? I'm sorry," she said apologetically.

"No ... it's okay. I bet you get jumpy in graveyards too."

"Indeed," she said, amused. She had a Bostonian accent. "I'm Amanda." She extended her hand. She was dressed sedately in a navy blue pants suit, a dark blouse and a hat.

"Pleased to meet you, I'm Rudy."

"I know ... Being here must be hard for you."

Her words made Rudy uneasy. "It's very hard ... But I had to come." Looking her straight in the eye, he added, "Thanks for what you did ... I had nothing to do with her death."

People began moving away from the grave. The gravediggers were fitting the covering over the tomb.

Rudy and Amanda exited the cemetery together.

"My Rolls Royce is parked over there," said Rudy, pointing to the bicycle propped up by the kickstand in a graveled parking area near the church.

"Surely, you didn't cycle all the way here?"

"I did. It's how I get around. You should try it. Works wonders for your health."

"I've got a pickup truck. Would you like a lift? You might as well, aren't we heading in the same direction? Your bike can fit in the back."

"Thanks, I appreciate it and so will the old hooves." Rudy hoisted the bike onto the truck and joined Amanda in the cab. Other people were entering their vehicles. As Amanda drove off, Rudy noted with interest that most of the vehicle owners were foreigners.

23

"That was quite a moving service, don't you think? The turnout was also very impressive," said Amanda as they approached the highway junction.

"I'm not surprised. Olive was very popular. The turnout was clearly meant to be a show of solidarity ... I take it that you and her were friends."

"Not really. I ran into her occasionally in Albion Bay. I attended the funeral to provide moral support to Edward, bless him. They were very close and he has taken her death very hard."

"Yes, I know."

"When he told me about the murder and the police investigation, and how they had been questioning you, I recalled seeing you on the beach and the way you suddenly fled as if you'd seen a ghost after receiving a phone call ... or was it a text message? I was also aware of the time. I realized then that I had to make a statement to the police."

"I assure you that my grandchildren and great grandchildren will be told all about you and your mission of mercy."

Amanda laughed. "Let's hope you're a good granddad, otherwise they'll never forgive me."

Rudy smiled. "Seriously though ... thanks."

"Are the police still bothering you?"

"Not really. Since my last interview with them, they haven't contacted me."

"Edward also told me about your necklaces and how they were found at the scene of the murder."

Rudy glanced sharply at Amanda. "They were planted there. I had nothing to do with Olive's death," he reiterated defensively.

"Edward is convinced of that and I know him well enough to trust his word."

Rudy relaxed and let out an inaudible sigh. He told Amanda about the burglary.

"How do you suppose the thief got in?" she said, adding, "From what I know, these electronic door locks are supposed to be very secure."

"That's what I can't figure out. Edward and his wife, as well as Vernon, keep insisting that I must have left a window unlocked or turned off the lock system inadvertently, or it may have been a system failure. My instinct tells me otherwise. Unfortunately, I don't know enough about these techno gadgets to disprove them."

"My son, Amin would know. He's quite a technology whiz. Perhaps you can ask him."

"Sure, I'd love to. How can I meet him?"

Albion Bay lay straight ahead. Amanda changed gear and eased her speed. "Why don't you come over for lunch? My home is less than five minutes away."

"Sure. I'd love to."

"Fine. Off we go."

Amanda turned unto a dirt track and drove up a rocky incline. Gradually, it leveled out into a more even surface. She continued along a paved driveway and into a vegetative tunnel composed of intertwining trees with dense canopies, many of them leaning forward as if to whisper conspiratorially to one another. They came to a ridge overlooking Albion Bay. Amanda's home loomed ahead.

Rudy noted that it was relatively modest compared to those he'd seen in that part of the island. It was a two-storied wood-and-concrete structure with a balcony and patio and an eco-friendly feel. Surrounding it were flowers and fruit trees, including mangoes, grapefruits, avocados and bananas. The area offered a spectacular view of the coastline and the Caribbean Sea. The ghostly outline of Martinique was visible on the horizon.

"The view is magnificent, it just blows me away," said Rudy. "And your home is lovely!"

"It is wonderful, isn't it? I don't own the property, however. I lease it for two months every year. I've been doing so for the past five years ... It's such a beautiful day, do you mind having lunch out on the patio or would you prefer to go indoors?"

"Out here is perfect."

"I'm going over to alert Martha, the maid. Would you like a drink?"

"Yes please, a beer or rum punch would do nicely."

"Great! Make yourself comfortable, I'll be back."

There was a cheerful bounce in Amanda's step as she made her way into the house.

Gazing all around him, Rudy pondered over Amanda. He noticed that she wasn't wearing a wedding ring and this made him curious. He recalled the day when he first saw her she'd had a little girl with her. There was something bewitching about her. He found her company invigorating and refreshing. He remembered how incredibly sexy she'd looked that day on the beach and the way it had set his hormones on fire. She struck him as the sort of woman who knew how to modulate her charm to suit the occasion, like an angel dimming its brilliance so as not to be unduly dazzling.

A woman came hurrying towards him with a drink on a tray. It was Martha, the maid. She was short and quite rotund, with a friendly, girlish face.

"Good afternoon, sir," she said courteously and served him a flamboyant glass of rum punch.

"Thank you," Rudy replied and took a sip. "Whoo! That's first class ... I mean it."

"Thank you." Martha looked surprised. She smiled. "If you want more, just let me know."

"I certainly will."

"Lunch for today is chicken and tomato stew. That's okay with you?"

"Sounds great."

Notwithstanding her smile, Rudy detected the woman's curiosity, evident in her focused stare. She walked away just as Amanda came outside with a poodle in tow, the same one that had surprised Rudy on the beach. Amanda conversed briefly with Martha and then went to join Rudy. She had changed into a pebble laki Hawaiian dress and it was charmingly colorful. The dog walked up to Rudy and sniffed him a few times but apparently decided he wasn't worth the bother. Turning away, it went exploring in the bushes.

"Come on, let's go cool out," said Amanda. Together, they walked across to the patio, a spacious area built with a combination of slate and stone. It was furnished with a seven-piece, black-bronze dining set made of genuine cast aluminum. The patio was surrounded by garden plants and they filled the air with the commingled fragrances of lavender, mint and scented gardenias growing in terracotta pots and wooden planters. Amanda and Rudy sat close to each other. "Lunch won't be long," she said, adding, "Amin will be coming out to meet you in a while. He's all wrapped up in one of his video games."

"Only three of you live here?"

"Four of us. Amin, who's fifteen, my five-year old adopted daughter Petal, Martha and I. You could call us a family."

"You're obviously American. Which part of the U.S. are you from?"

"We live in Boston. This house is our summer home. Martha lives in the village but stays here whenever we're home. Amin's father and I are divorced. I'm a consulting psychologist. I now work mainly from home and mostly part time. I gave up working full time seven years ago so I could devote more time to taking care of Amin. He suffers from Asperger's Syndrome. It's a milder form of autism. He's incredibly bright and gifted, despite his condition. He's been deemed to have an exceptionally high IQ. He has a passion for computers and computer programming and is very knowledgeable about anything to do with ICT. If you could see him in action, it would amaze you."

"How does the condition affect him then?"

"For one thing, he has difficulty reading and understanding people and their motives. This makes him easy prey for those who try to take advantage of him, including kids. Some of them could be quite cruel. At school they make him do some very odd things, just for the fun of it. He's currently in high school. He has few friends his age. He also has a bit of a problem with his motor skills. Ordinarily he doesn't talk much, except when he's in a good mood or if you engage him in technical topics, particularly about computers. Dear God, he can go on and on in a virtual nonstop monologue! He's extremely creative and very methodical in everything he does. According to the doctors, these are all traits of kids who suffer with Asperger's Syndrome. Growing up, he needed specialized care and lots of love and still does. He's my life and I love him dearly."

"He sounds like a fascinating kid. Did he naturally gravitate to computers or did you have something to do with it?"

"That was more his father's doing. He's a software engineer. He owns and runs a software firm in Silicon Valley."

Amanda and Rudy glanced toward the house as Martha came out wheeling a three-tier serving trolley packed with dishes.

"Martha is somewhat of a culinary expert. She previously worked as a kitchen assistant at one of the restaurants in the marina, for many years. I'm lucky to have her," said Amanda, smiling at Martha.

"Oh no, Miss Amanda, *I'm* the lucky one," Martha replied, smiling and served Amanda first with a chicken and tomato stew over white rice and two slices of avocado. She followed it up with a side dish of black beans and mango slices with basil leaves sliced into slivers and ginger dressing. She offered Rudy the same. "Enjoy it!" she said and placed the remainder of the meal on the table along with plates, cutlery and glasses and two bottles of wine in an ice bucket. She then wheeled the trolley back to the house.

"I understand that you have Caribbean and British roots?" said Amanda as she tucked into her meal.

"I was born in Saint Lucia but I've lived in England most of my life. As for my roots, they've been watered by the rivers of Africa and God knows where else, as you could probably tell."

"Interesting ... Oh, here comes Amin."

Rudy's fork froze halfway to his mouth. He gaped at the youth ambling across the yard. The boy was slightly darker than him with jet black hair, and he was so slim and lanky, he resembled a string bean. He seemed to be dragging his left leg, although it was barely noticeable. He wore a DC Boys black T-shirt, baggy jeans and sneakers. "Hello," he greeted Rudy in a soft-spoken, adenoidal voice.

"How are you?" Rudy couldn't take his eyes off the youth.

"Amin, this is Rudy. He's a journalist and he's visiting the island. We spoke about him some time ago, remember?"

"Yeah, I think so," he replied, avoiding Rudy's eyes. He seemed shy.

"Amin's dad is Pakistani," said Bridget, as if reading Rudy's mind. A little girl came running across the yard toward the patio. She looked about five, and had bright hazel eyes and a cute, heartwarming face. "This is Petal. Sweetheart, say hello to Rudy."

"Hello," said Petal, her eyes beaming with curiosity. "Are you a Rastafarian?" she asked in a cute singsong voice.

"Not really. I just look like one."

Petal stared at Rudy as if to say, I thought so, and looked even more curious. Tilting her head, she peered circumspectly at his hair. "Does that mean that your locks are fake?"

"No ..." Rudy glanced at Amanda who looked quite amused. He bent forward with his head close to Petal. "Would you like to feel them to make sure?" he asked.

"Sure." She reached out and squeezed a tuft of Rudy's hair then gently rolled it in her tiny hand, as if testing it to make sure his locks were real. Glancing at Amin, she nodded and said, with a disappointed look on her face, "Yep, they are dreadlocks."

"Told you so," he replied smugly. "That means you owe me your desert next time we go out to lunch."

Smiling, Amanda said, "Cheer up sweetheart, come have lunch with me."

Rudy reached into his jacket pocket and took out a small leather-and-stone 'Thai Karma' bracelet. He'd bought it at a flea market in Covent Garden a year ago. He'd been wearing the same jacket and had tucked the bracelet into one of the pockets, and forgot all about it. He only realized this after he'd gotten dressed and left for the funeral. "Tell you what," he said holding it out to

Petal, "I'd like to give you this as a special gift to make up for your loss. What do you say?"

"Wow! Can I Mom? ... Please!" she asked pleadingly.

"Well ..." Amanda sounded hesitant. "I'm not so sure ..."

"Please," Rudy interjected. "Consider it as a token of appreciation to you as well. Who knows, at this very moment I could have been dining alone in far more unpleasant circumstances were it not for you."

Amanda turned to Petal. "Okay, darling. You may accept it – providing you eat your veggies today."

"Oh, I will!" Petal replied and poked her tongue out at Amin. Hoisting herself up onto a chair, she placed the bracelet on the table. Amanda passed empty plates to Petal and Amin and served them lunch. There was a familial air of fun and gaiety as they dined and chatted away on topics ranging from Amanda's family life in Boston and the two kids' experiences in school, to Rudy recounting what life was like for him as a West Indian growing up in Britain. He regaled them with hilarious anecdotes that had Amanda in stitches and the children laughing heartily. Occasionally, even the dog joined in, barking excitedly as if to show its amusement.

This continued after Martha served a second course of oven-baked sweet plantain. Much of the time, Rudy held the floor. He had the two children captivated and this gave him great pleasure. Amin loosened up and became quite animated.

Martha rounded out the meal with coconut cake and ice cream. The desert upstaged Rudy, as far as Petal was concerned. She lost interest in him and began feasting on it. After gobbling it up, she left the table and went to play with the dog.

Seated in the company of Amanda and her family, Rudy couldn't remember ever feeling more at peace, especially with the unspoiled, blue-green splendor of his surroundings. The property's awesome elevation gave you the ethereal feeling of being suspended in midair. It felt like a dream. He had to force his attention back to the people sitting before him.

"So Amin, your mom tells me that you're the go-to guy for anything to do with computers," Rudy said, smiling.

"Technology fascinates me, all kinds, but especially internet and mobile communication technologies. It is the key to decoding life."

"Hmm, that tells me a lot. I'm ashamed to say that I'm a complete dunce when it comes to ICT, so you're light years ahead of me, no doubt. In fact, if you hear the sound of coughing, that's me biting your dust."

Amin laughed. Rudy paused a moment to think. "Would you, by any chance, know anything about electronic home security systems and how they work?"

"Yes."

Rudy told him about the smart locks at the house in Albion Bay and the robbery. "The thing is, I feel pretty sure that all the doors and windows were locked that night and I had never shared my pin code with anyone. There were absolutely no signs of forced entry yet someone was able to compromise the system, which is supposed to be basically foolproof from what I was led to believe. What do you think?"

"A foolproof security system?" Amin frowned as if he found the idea strange. "There's no such thing."

"What do you mean?"

"Connecting anything to the internet makes it vulnerable to attack. If you know what to do, you can hack into almost any network system and gain access to people's passwords and security codes, their personal files and more."

"But how easy or difficult is it?"

"That depends on you. The first thing you need to be aware of is that when you're using a wireless router, if it isn't configured properly, it could pose a security risk. If your wireless network is open or unsecured, an intruder can easily gain access to your internal network without you even realizing it. Once they've done that, they can use it for a whole lot of illegal activities, such as stealing your Internet bandwidth, using your network to download unlawful content or infect computers with viruses or spyware and send spam and spyware to other computers.

"There are many different ways someone can gain unauthorized access to your network, including using software and hacking tools, many of which are available on the internet. You can use them to hack into network systems and devices – like your front-door lock or smartphone or an IP camera. The hacker can then gain access to your passwords and security codes and even alter them. They can also access your files and emails and much more and do it from practically anywhere in the world once they have an internet connection. What's more, all the companies in the electronic door lock business rely on the built-in protective features of Bluetooth SMART, which is not foolproof. Practically all these systems have potential weaknesses that can be exploited by someone who knows how and is determined."

Rudy was quite taken aback by Amin's level of knowledge. He couldn't help being impressed. "Okay, understood. But let's think about this. I wouldn't be surprised if this island has more millionaires per square mile than anywhere else. I can hardly imagine Bill Thompson and the Elysian Island Company would support the use of a security system in homes on the island that is not top notch and tamper proof, considering how much is at stake."

"It can be done! Why are you doubting me? I know what I'm saying," Amin retorted. All of a sudden he seemed agitated. His left leg began trembling.

"Darling, Rudy believes you. He just wants you to help him understand better how it could be done," Amanda interjected quickly and gave Rudy a cautionary stare.

"I'm sorry Amin, I didn't mean to offend you. I apologize." Rudy tried to sound as contrite as he could. "Your mum's right. Like I told you, I'm a complete ignoramous when it comes to these matters, so please bear with me." He offered to bump fists with Amin. "What say you, are we friends?" Amin hesitated, then gave a lopsided smile.

"We're friends," he conceded magnanimously. They bumped fists. Amin reiterated his views on the vulnerabilities of electronic network-based systems and in a virtually unbroken monologue, he went on to cite several examples of smart locks being successfully hacked in homes and hotels, and assured Rudy that they had all been reported in the global mainstream media. He even offered to email him links to the stories.

Once again, Rudy was flabbergasted by the depth of his knowledge and how well read he seemed to be. Nodding at Amanda, he said, "No doubt about it, he knows his stuff." Gazing at Amin, he said, "Nuff respect!"

Amin smirked.

Turning again to Amanda, Rudy said, "Do you have a smart lock system?"

"Sure, I imagine many homeowners here do."

"Who manages the system?"

"The company has contracted a local firm to manage home security on the island. It's based on the mainland and it's actually a subsidiary of a foreign-owned company. But having said that, the home owners here do have the impression that the security system on the island is extremely reliable, and in fairness to the company, burglaries are extremely rare. There are none that I am aware of since we've been vacationing here."

"Now comes the million-dollar question," said Rudy, gazing at Amin. "Do you think there is anyone here on the island – not counting you, of course – who is technically savvy enough to hack into electronic door locks? To begin with, I think we can safely rule out the likelihood of the culprit being from the village. Most of the people there don't even own computers and only a few of them have an internet connection. If you ask me, there's not much chance the presumed hacker is on the other side of the world either, or even outside of Saint Lucia. That leaves the expatriate community on Elysian Island."

"The breach could have occurred from within the security firm. What if the person who broke into your house works for the company?" said Amin.

Rudy's eyes lit up. Gazing at Amanda, he asked, "Are there any employees of the home-security provider based here?"

"I'm not sure. I do know that there are occasions when their technicians are required to be on the ground here but I don't know why specifically."

"Have you checked the video footage on your IP camera?" said Amin.

"IP camera? ... There isn't one at the house."

"Yes, there is, isn't there Mom?"

"I believe so. I seem to recall Edward telling us that his wife had IP cameras installed on their properties, including Blossom House, after the murder – or suicide, depending on who you believe – that occurred some years ago at the house higher up from the one where you live. Edward is not exactly a fan of IP cameras and only agreed to them being installed at Blossom House at Bridget's insistence. According to him, he values his privacy and resents the idea of being under the perpetual surveillance of an electronic all-seeing eye. Those where you live should still be there, I imagine."

Rudy was so stunned, all he could do was gape at Amanda and Amin. "But there's no sign of any surveillance cameras at the house."

"That's probably because they installed a covert security camera, like one hidden in a clock for example," Amin suggested.

"No one ever told me this. I know absolutely nothing about any of the things you've just said."

"Another thing," Amin continued, "Cybercriminals can use IP cameras as a jump-off point to infiltrate and compromise virtually any electronic device in your home that is connected to the internet. I won't go into too much detail, you'd find it too complex. Basically IP cameras operate on a LINUX-based System-on-Chip that is known to be vulnerable to attack."

Rudy was no longer focusing on what Amin was saying, he was thinking of Bridget and Vernon. Why did neither of them mention anything about a surveillance camera at the house when he told them about the robbery? What could possibly be their motive for withholding such vital information? To compound the matter, Bridget had tried her damndest to dissuade him from reporting the break-in to the police. *A suicide or murder on Elysian Island next door to the house where he lived*?

"Rudy ... are you okay?" said Amanda, intruding into his thoughts. She sounded concerned.

"Huh? ... yes ... Did you say there was a murder in a house close to where I live?"

"Yes, about four years ago – the year after the kids and I came visiting Elysian Island for the first time. From what I was told, a glamorous German heiress was found shot to death in her £30,000-a-month villa. Ultimately her death was ruled a suicide, except that it later emerged that it had been determined that the bullet which killed her did not match the gun that was found next to her body. No killer was ever found nor was there any convincing motive established for what several people believed was murder, so life on the island simply went back to normal. Her distraught family have alleged that the murder investigation was botched and purposely obstructed and the details hushed up to protect Elysian Island's image. That's as much as I know. To date, no light has been shed on the killing and it still remains a mystery."

Rudy went quiet for a while, lost in thought. Glancing up, he said, "It's been a wonderful lunch and I enjoyed every minute with you guys. Do you mind if I leave? There's something I've got to do. It's urgent."

"That's fine, we understand," Amanda replied. "Come on, I'll drive you into town."

"Tell you what, why don't we exchange email addresses and phone numbers and keep in touch? Amin, feel free to shoot me links to some of the stuff you've been telling me about. I sure need to be educated."

Amin promptly reached into his pocket and brought up a slip of paper and a pen. He tore the paper in half and each of them wrote down their respective cell phone numbers and email addresses. Rudy took one of the bits of paper and tucked it into his pocket. They all stood up. Rudy gave Amin a bear hug. "Thanks, bro. You've been a great help. Let's keep in touch, what do you say?"

"Sure."

Neither Petal nor the dog was anywhere to be seen. Rudy followed Amanda to the pickup truck.

24

To his surprise, Rudy found the Buccaneer Rum Shop & Bar closed when he turned up there for his rendezvous with Vernon Allain. Two hours earlier he'd called Vernon and they agreed to meet at the bar. Prior to that, he'd tried telephoning Bridget several times, without success, much to his irritation. He left her voicemail but she was yet to respond.

Two windows were open in the pool-room section of the bar but the door was shut. There was no sign of anyone on the beach across the road. A hut where some of the fishermen stored their equipment was shut. The sea breeze was fairly strong as was the fishy smell of the surf. Off and on the silence was ruptured by the breaking of the waves. Rudy felt disappointed, and wondered what could have held Vernon back. He'd been under the impression that the bar remained open throughout the day and into the night. It was just five o'clock.

Since Vernon lived nearby, he decided to go check if he was in. As he turned the bike around, he heard the sound of laughter at the back of the building. He propped the bike against a breadfruit tree and went to take a look. Vernon and three men sat in a backyard sharing a bottle of rum. One of them was Toussaint Emile, the proprietor of the bar. He wore a wide-brimmed Panama hat with the elastic band tucked beneath his chin, and a black T-shirt with a Christmas snowman emblazoned across the front. The other two men, both middle-aged, wore black shirts and grey trousers. Rudy got the feeling that they had come there straight from the funeral. "Good day gentlemen," he greeted them.

"Rudy! How're you?" Toussaint Emile replied. The two men who looked like they were in mourning nodded brusquely. Vernon excused himself and steered Rudy out of the yard. "Let's go inside," he said and pushed open the door to the bar. They sat at one of the tables. "Sorry for not waiting outside. I got so caught up in the conversation with the guys, I lost track of the time."

"Why is the place so deserted, is today their Sabbath?"

"It's been like that most of the day out of respect for Olive. Since today was the funeral, Toussaint decided he would open this evening at six. So what's up? You sounded like you were desperate to see me."

"Oh Vernon, you have no idea! 'Desperate' is putting it mildly. It's to do with the break-in at the house. Wait till you hear the brilliant idea I came up with to solve this puzzle. I thought to myself, *silly guy, why didn't it occur to you to simply check the video footage in the security cameras at the house.* Then I thought, *dumb ass, what're you talking about? There are no IP cameras installed there. If there were, my dear friends, Bridget and Vernon would most certainly have told me so …* Or would they? What do you say, Vernon? Would they?"

Vernon looked taken aback. He gazed out the window at the sea, a thoughtful look on his face. He seemed to be weighing his response carefully. "It's not my duty to inform you about security arrangements at the house," he replied.

"So there *are* IP cameras installed there! Did Bridget instruct you not to inform me about them?"

"No."

"Why do you think she said nothing about it even after the robbery?"

"Perhaps you should ask her."

"Come on Vernon, quit holding out. Where exactly are the cameras and have they been functioning all this time? You can at least tell me that."

Vernon avoided his eyes. "One is hidden in the porch light. The other one is disguised as a smoke detector. It's in the living room. Who told you about them?"

"Never mind who told me, that's not the point. Both you and Bridget misled and deceived me, that is the issue! How can I trust either of you now? For that matter, how do I know it wasn't you who broke into the house and set me up? How do I know that you're not Olive's killer?"

Vernon shot up from his seat, eyes blazing, his face taut with rage. He looked like he was about to lunge at Rudy. Somehow he managed to control himself. "Watch your mouth!" he snapped and sat down.

"Someone's playing me, Vernon and like it or not, you're a part of it. For God's sake man, you should know better, you're an ex-cop!" Rudy got up and began pacing. "I need to check the video footage from the camera. Where is it?"

"I'm not the one you should be speaking to about this. You need to speak to Bridget or Edward."

Rudy paused a while to think. It suddenly occurred to him that he was letting his emotions run away with him and using the wrong approach. It was putting Vernon on the defensive and alienating him. He decided to change tack. "Listen, you and I know that I'm not out of the woods as far as this murder is concerned. Whoever is trying to frame me, picked on me for a reason. *Why me,* out of the hundreds of people on this island? And the killer is still out there, free to get away if they wish. We can't allow this to happen. You're an ex-cop, think about it."

"I understand how you feel. I'm not trying to implicate you in anything. Neither is Bridget, in all fairness to her. She probably didn't even remember the IP cameras, and for good reason. Several months ago it was discovered that there was a bug in the camera software. It allowed anyone with the camera IP address to view both the live and recorded video footage by simply pressing 'OK' in the dialogue box when prompted for a username and password. It was decided to turn them off along with all the other electrical appliances until a fix could be found. Before you moved in, the house remained unoccupied for several months and I'm almost certain that with Bridget always being so busy, this matter was placed on the back burner and remained forgotten all this time. Could the cameras have been turned on by Jim, the cleaner before you moved in? I don't know but I guess it's possible. Bridget trusts him and he's allowed to do that. At the time, I never gave it a thought. But we should have double checked, I'll grant you that. I'll inform Bridget and have it checked as soon as possible."

"That's fair enough. How soon can we do that?"

"I'll get back to you by tomorrow."

"What if I told you that the door lock was hacked and that's how the intruder got in?"

"How do you know that?"

"I got an expert opinion from someone who knows a lot about these things. He has no doubt that's how the crook got in and I'm convinced he's right. I understand there's a local security firm that is responsible for providing security services to many of the foreign homeowners on the island. My source believes that there is a strong possibility the firm's network system may have been compromised and that's how the hacker was able to access the locks. In other words, the intruder may be an employee of the firm."

"That sounds like a whole lot of speculation to me."

"But it's plausible and worth looking into."

"How do you plan on doing that?"

"First we need to check the IP camera for video footage. We also need to find out who the firm's IT technicians are, including any who are based here. The Elysian Island Company and the homeowners need to be alerted that the security network system may have been compromised and this puts them all at risk. Considering how folks here are so obsessed with privacy, I would imagine this would be of great concern to them."

"Whoa! Hold your horses, you're moving way too fast. Inform the company? You can't be making those kinds of allegations to the company without any proof. They'll just laugh at you!"

"What if I can prove that what I've said is true?"

"Go ahead and prove it. But let me warn you, even though you are able to, it won't make a difference. There's no way the Elysian Island Company or the security firm, ICTS Services is going to provide you with internal information about their business. You should know that."

"What about Clifford Allen, the lawyer? He can serve them with a subpoena."

"My dear young man, Mr. Allen was hired to defend you against possible police charges stemming from Olive's murder, not to help you play detective and solve matters that should be left to the police. There's a big difference between being an investigative reporter and a crime investigator."

"That's just the cop in you talking. I say let's put it to Bridget and see what she says."

"You might as well suggest to her that you go storming into the company's offices, guns blazing," Vernon sneered. "I wish you luck."

"Well, she and Thompson are good buddies. I should think that if there's a likelihood that the safety of the company's shareholders and homeowner clients is in jeopardy, she would be eager to alert him and urge him to address the problem."

"Yes, by keeping it hush-hush and making sure folks like you don't go around spreading unsubstantiated claims and getting people all worked up."

"Hey, I'm not the problem here. I'm the victim of a situation for which they are both responsible."

"Why do you think Bridget wants you to leave here all of a sudden?"

"What do you mean?"

"Didn't she suggest that you take some time off and go hang out somewhere else?"

"Yeah."

"Give me a minute, I'll be back. I'm going over to my car. It's parked at the back." Vernon stood up and headed for the door.

He returned a few minutes later with a newspaper and dropped it on the table in front of Rudy. "Go ahead, take a look."

It was a copy of the Guardian newspaper from London. Rudy picked it up. Olive's photo jumped out at him. It was accompanied by a story about a 'brutal murder on Elysian Island, the exclusive island paradise.' Rudy's heart skipped a beat when he saw his name. The article cited him as the person who had discovered Olive's body. It noted that he was being questioned by the police, adding that attempts to contact him for comment had been unsuccessful.

"Right now, you're a liability," said Vernon, watching him closely. "Bridget may have been heartbroken at your sudden disappearance but not so much that she couldn't see that it was a damn lucky thing you were out of sight for a while. You must understand that this island thrives on maintaining the image of a tropical paradise offering peace and tranquility – a Garden of Eden where there are no economic or social problems and no crime, and everyone is happy and safe. Bridget is a business woman, and a very successful one at that. She too has a stake in promoting this image.

"You, my dear friend are a cat among the pigeons, all the more considering why you're here, plus the fact that you're a journalist. To make matters worse, because of what you're now planning to do, you're starting to look like the serpent in Eden. From the start, Mr. Thompson and several people in the company were not happy about you coming here, just as they're not happy about the book that you're planning to write. So ... do you still think Bill Thompson and Bridget would want to entertain you?"

"So what are you suggesting, that I shut up and behave?"

"As much as it pains me to side with Bridget, I think she's right, you should make yourself inconspicuous for a while."

"Why do I get the feeling that you dislike Bridget?"

There was an awkward silence. Rudy shoved the newspaper away. "There's one more thing. I've been told that some time ago someone was either killed or committed suicide in the house next to where I live. Is that true?"

"Yes." Vernon lowered his head but not before Rudy caught the pained look in his eyes. "I'd rather not speak about this now. Maybe some other time." Looking up, he said, "Take my advice; enjoy your stay here as best you can but don't try and swim against the tide. Don't make the same mistake as Edward. If you think you have credible evidence about the robbery, pass it on to the police and let them handle it."

Two vehicles pulled up outside the building followed by the sound of chattering and laughter. Toussaint entered the bar and hurriedly opened the windows that were still shut. Dusk was already settling in. He turned on the lights and then began dusting the countertop with an air of expectancy. In a backroom kitchen the clanking of cutlery and plates signaled preparations were underway for taking meal orders. A group of about twenty men streamed in and most of them headed for the bar. The rest fanned out among the tables.

"They just came from the wake at Olive's place," Vernon explained as he and Rudy watched the boisterous takeover of Toussaint's bar. "They came over here to round things off."

Some of the men came over and greeted Vernon and Rudy, and one offered them a drink. Rudy recognized him as Charley, the deckhand he'd met at the marina. "This one is on me," said Rudy. "What'll you have?"

Charley patted him on the back approvingly and called out to Toussaint for a shot of white rum. Vernon opted for whiskey. Rudy went to place the orders. The gathering at the bar had increased considerably as more patrons filed in. There were a few women among them. Rudy managed to catch Toussaint's attention over the loud chatter and was about to order the drinks when someone bumped into him and threw him off balance. He collided with a man and accidentally knocked his drink out of his hand. The glass fell to the floor and shattered.

The man gaped at Rudy and then at the broken glass in disbelief. It was Rudy's adversary, Oscar.

"What de hell! What's de meaning of this?" Oscar demanded, scowling. His speech was a bit slurred.

"My apologies, it was an accident," Rudy replied apologetically.

"Accident! What you mean accident? And who invite you here? You eh cause enough trouble already? Olive dead and is all because of you!"

The shock of Oscar's words sent a chill through Rudy. He felt so numb, he could barely speak. Everyone in the bar went deathly quiet.

"I don't want any trouble with you," said Rudy. Turning to Toussaint, he added, "Please, can I pay for the brother's drink? And give him another one, whatever he wants. I'll also pay for the glass."

"No!" Oscar yelled. "I want nothing from this fake – this baldhead Rasta. He have no right coming here to drink on Olive head!"

"Take it easy, Oscar," said Toussaint, frowning.

"Yes man, Oscar take it easy and cool out yourself," said someone in the gathering. Rudy turned away and headed back to the table to rejoin Vernon.

"Hey you! Don' turn your back on me when am talking to you!" Oscar shouted threateningly. Rushing up to Rudy, he pushed him hard and sent him sprawling across the table. As Rudy straightened up, Oscar grabbed him by his collar. Immediately several men surrounded Oscar. Grabbing hold of him, they shoved him away and forced him out of the bar. Outside, the men began remonstrating with him loudly. From inside, Rudy could hear Oscar shouting his name and cursing.

"That's it! I'm out of here," he said, visibly distressed. "What on earth is this guy's problem? What have I ever done to him?" he demanded, staring plaintively at Vernon.

Vernon shrugged. "I guess he had too much to drink before coming here. It loosened his tongue. He's just a wayward little pest, don't bother with him," he said consolingly.

Rudy returned to the counter and paid for the drinks he had originally ordered plus extra for refills. Returning to the table, he said, "Guess I'll be heading back to Albion Bay. Thanks for coming over." He walked away before Vernon could respond. All eyes were on him as he plodded out of the bar without a word to anyone.

The men who had forced Oscar out had all re-entered the bar. There was no sign of Oscar outside. A couple of hanging lights in the verandah cast a pallid glow that barely ruffled the darkness. Rudy walked across to the breadfruit tree where he had left the bicycle. He checked his watch. It was quarter to eight. He had a twenty-minute ride ahead of him but he wasn't worried. At this time, traffic along the road would be low to non-existent. Besides, he figured he needed the physical exertion and fresh sea breeze to clear his head and cool the rage smoldering inside him.

A figure emerged from the shadows among a cluster of bushes and lunged at him. Rudy heard the rustling of leaves and spun around but by then a hand had already grabbed his throat. He and the figure crashed to the ground in a heap, knocking over the bicycle. The stench of white rum and stale sweat emanated from the person's body and made Rudy feel like vomiting.

"I'll teach you to fuck around with me, baldhead Rasta!" Oscar hissed. Somehow, Rudy managed to push him off and quickly rose to his feet. Oscar got up and stood facing him, his body hunched forward in a menacing, ape-like posture. Rudy could now see him clearly as they had moved closer to the light emanating from the verandah. Oscar was holding an empty rum bottle.

"No man, stop! Don't do it! I don't want any trouble with you," said Rudy pleadingly.

"Too late, you already in trouble with me," Oscar retorted. "Remember, is you who hit me first! Since then I been wantin' to teach you a lesson. Now your ass is mine!"

Rudy backed away, all the while keeping his eye on the bottle in Oscar's hand. He noticed Oscar was a bit unsteady on his feet and realized he could bring him down with an American football-style tackle. Physically, Oscar was no match for him. Still, he hesitated; he wasn't sure why. He decided to try reasoning with him instead.

"Listen to me! I want you to look me in the eye like a man and tell me what exactly it is you have against me. Why do you want to hurt me?"

"Olive would have marry me if it wasn' for you. We woulda been together but you had to come and interfere. Now see what happen. Look she dead and is your fault. You cause it! You and your friends." Suddenly Oscar began sobbing and sniveling like a baby. Rudy gaped at him dumfounded.

"Come on, Oscar, you know that's not true. *Me and my friends*? What are you talking about? I know how you felt about Olive but she wasn't interested in you, you know that. Long before I arrived here she's been telling you that. Isn't that right? ... You know it is! There was nothing going on between Olive and me. I'm sure you know that too. Ask anybody in the village."

"Liar! You liar!" Oscar sobbed. "People here take me for a fool. You too. I know Olive had love me. But all of you was fighting against me because of y'all jealousy!"

"Come on Oscar, that's not true."

"Shut up! Even the police against me. You know what really hurt me? They come and question me. *Me Oscar* of all people. As if I could ever do anything to hurt a woman I love so much. May God punish those *salopes*!" Oscar wiped tears from his eyes but continued to hold the bottle up threateningly. "You had no right to come and interfere. I'll teach you a lesson, motherfucker!"

Two men came out of the bar. "What's going on over there!' one of them shouted in Creole.

"It's Oscar!" the other one yelled. "Look he going to kill the Rastaman!"

Rudy glanced at them. At the same time Oscar rushed at him. He barely noticed it out of the corner of his eye. He instinctively moved a full step closer to him and counterattacked by grabbing Oscar's waist as their bodies collided and whipping his pivotal foot from under him with his right leg. Oscar crashed to the ground with a mighty thud. The bottle flew out of his hand. A loud "Whooo!" went up from a group that had gathered outside. They felt Oscar's pain. They all rushed forward to gape at Oscar moaning and wriggling like a worm on the ground. They were quite animated. Two men helped Oscar up. Rudy moved away from him and, picking up the bottle, he tossed it in the bushes. One of the men shouted, "Hey Ras! It look like Bruce Lee is your father." Vernon broke away from the gathering and hurried across to Rudy.

"What happened?" he said.

Pointing to the bushes, Rudy replied, "He was hiding in there. He jumped me just as I was about to leave."

"I know that move – a spring-hip counter technique. Where did you learn that?"

"I've done some basic judo. It came in handy. I'm a bit rusty but fortunately he's drunk so that made it easy for me."

"Did he hurt you?"

"Nah, I'm cool."

Somebody retched and began vomiting. It was Oscar. Rudy and Vernon watched as two men all but dragged him towards the back of the building.

"I should be pissed off with this guy but to be honest, I feel sorry for him," said Rudy, a grim look on his face.

"You want a ride home?"

"Nah, it's okay. This is one time I could do with the sky over my head and the wind in my face. See you." Rudy picked up the bike from where it had fallen.

"Hey Rudy," said Vernon. Rudy paused. "I'm not authorized to access the footage in the IP cameras but you can. The username and password are stored on the desktop computer in the guest bedroom. You probably won't even need them if the bug is still in the system." Both men stared at each other. "Who knows, the gods may be in your favor," Vernon added and he turned and walked back towards the bar.

25

Rudy paced back and forth, unable to keep still. The night before, he had barely slept. When he got back from the village, he immediately checked the computer in the spare room as Vernon had suggested. To his delight, he managed to locate the username and password for the IP camera after searching through the files on the hard drive. Fortunately the files were not password protected.

Since he knew where to look for the IP cameras, he was able to find them without difficulty. Recalling what Vernon had said about them being switched off, he'd been afraid to keep his hopes up but then he got the surprise of his life. The camera hidden in the smoke detector inside the living room had been switched off but the one hidden in the patio light was functioning! He almost screamed with jubilation. Using his laptop he was able to access the archived footage with the username and password. It had taken him several hours to scroll through the footage before he finally got what he was searching for; a male figure wearing a black hooded sweatshirt walking across the front yard and into the patio out of the view of the camera and then coming into view briefly before disappearing around the side of the house. The whole episode lasted about three minutes.

After scrolling through the video for another twenty minutes, he found more footage showing the same figure taking off in a panicked dash across the front yard and disappearing into the bushes. That bit lasted about one minute.

However, his initial joy was tempered by the realization that the video was very blurred and grainy. Being familiar with video cameras, he suspected the problem was either software related or due to insufficient outside lighting; or perhaps it had to do with the network configuration.

His disappointment was palpable. He'd considered surfing the net in search of discussion boards and online forums where similar issues were being discussed, and then he thought of Amin. He decided to run it by him.

By then it was almost midnight. Rather than call Amin so late, he sent him a text message instead, hoping he was still up, and asked if he was online. The reply came back almost instantly, stating simply 'yes'.

Rudy promptly fired off an email explaining the problem to Amin and gave him the IP camera internet address, username and password. Ten minutes later Amin responded with his diagnosis; inadequate lighting had caused the poor image quality. He offered to try and fix it with specialized software, warning that at best it would take a few hours. It was almost twelve thirty. Reluctantly, Rudy urged Amin to go to bed and leave it till the morning. He ended his email hoping aloud that Amanda didn't find out he had kept Amin up so late, and praying that the youth took the hint. 'Don't worry,' Amin wrote back. *Good boy*, Rudy whispered.

As much as it had pained him to have to wait so long, Rudy's instinct warned him not to push his luck. Aside from not wanting to take advantage of the youth, he didn't want to risk running afoul of his Mum perchance she found out that he had kept her son up late.

No sooner he woke up next morning, he patiently settled down to wait.

Come ten o'clock he was still waiting. At quarter past ten his phone rang. It was Amanda. Despite his anxiety, Rudy warmed up to the sound of her voice. It was even more soothing over the phone. She'd merely called to say hello and see how he was doing. After a brief chat, she told him she and the kids were due to go on a lunch date within half an hour. Rudy stiffened. "Is Amin going?" he asked, barely able to conceal his anxiety. Amanda said he was supposed to but he was all wrapped up in some project on his computer and he'd asked to be excused. Rudy exhaled. "Oh dear, I wonder what could have him so pre-occupied?" he said, oozing innocence.

"It's best not to probe. When he's this wrapped up in something, he doesn't take kindly to being disturbed." Amanda then asked Rudy if he had made any headway in resolving the issue of the break-in. He said he hadn't as yet. On a hunch, he asked if she would approve of him asking Amin to try and use his technological skills to access the house electronic lock system to prove whether or not it could be done. He deliberately avoided using the word 'hacking.' Amanda put her foot down and said no. "There is no way I'm going to allow Amin to do this without Edward or his wife's consent," she added. Rudy felt like kicking himself. He immediately apologized and told her to forget he asked. The conversation ended on a lighter note with Amanda sounding her normal self.

Bridget loomed in Rudy's thoughts as soon as the call ended. It happened so abruptly, it felt like an intrusion meant to ward off an unwelcome presence. If anything, it underscored the fact that Bridget was no longer calling to check up on him like she used to in the beginning, even when she was out of the island.

It was four days since he moved back to the house from Aaron's place and during that time they had only spoken to each other twice, and that was before the funeral. On both occasions it was he who reached out to her. Thereafter she became unreachable. Each time he phoned her he got her voicemail. He didn't even bother to leave a message.

For the life of him, he couldn't figure out what on earth could have Bridget so damned preoccupied and secretive, notwithstanding the pressures of her work. Each time he thought about it, logic intervened to remind him that falling for a married woman was risky business. His heart countered by arousing his affection for her; an amorous crush that he knew he could never experience with any other woman.

Despite his growing frustration with Bridget, he'd felt somewhat irritated when he realized Vernon didn't think much of her, even though he hadn't admitted it outright. Nevertheless, Vernon's suggestion that Bridget wanted him out of the way had resonated with him, not least because a few days earlier she had urged him to consider moving to the mainland or even back to the U.K..

No matter how he tried, he couldn't figure out what was on her mind, any more than he could deduce Edward's motives.

At the moment he wasn't sure what to believe about either of them.

An email alert on his phone caught his attention. Glancing at it, he perked up. It was an email from Amin. Hurrying across to his laptop, he opened the email, which had two video attachments and a message from Amin. He said he'd managed to enhance the quality of the video using a video editor and several artistic and professional filters. Rudy downloaded and opened the first file. He was taken aback at the clarity and crispness of the images compared to the originals. There was only one hitch; the intruder's face was obscured by a black hoodie.

Even worse, the man approached the house with his shoulders hunched, his hands tucked inside his pockets and his head lowered as if he was conscious of the presence of a surveillance camera or perhaps just being cautious. For a fleeting moment his nose and chin became visible as he exited the patio and went around the side of the house, evidently towards the guestroom with the sliding doors.

Rudy checked the other video clip but it was pretty much the same. The chap's face was obscured by the hood.

"Shit!" he blurted out, angrily. Using Photoshop he spent the next hour panning and zooming the images to see if he could get a clearer view of the character's face but it was no use. He slammed his fist down on the desk in a rage. Not satisfied, he stood up and kicked the chair. He walked towards the door, then turned and glared at the laptop screen. Still unwilling to give up, he went back and peered again at the monitor. Suddenly he stiffened. Moving closer to the screen, he gazed at it with a thoughtful look on his face.

Straightening the chair, he sat down again and began zooming in the second video to get a closer look at it. It showed the crook running away. As the image zoomed in closer, Rudy focused on a patch with thick red-colored stitching in the shape of a horseshoe on one of the back pockets of the man's jeans. He was positive he had seen it somewhere before. The only problem was he couldn't recall where.

He spent the next five minutes wracking his brain and continued focusing on the image.

Suddenly he grabbed his mobile phone and searched through a series of photos he had saved in it. He selected four of them and, using a photo app, he uploaded them into the cloud via Dropbox. He then switched over to the laptop to get a better view of them. They were all photographs he had taken of Olive and Aaron and some other people from the village during the unveiling of the village community and literacy centre. He focused on one of the pictures of Olive and three men from the village and expanded it.

"Son of a bitch!" he exclaimed as he gaped at the horseshoe patch with the same red stitching he had seen in the video. It was on the front pocket of one of the men's trousers.

The man was none other than Oscar.

26

Bridget curled up in the cushiony softness of a canopied bed, watching rain pounding against the windows. The room's exotic layout and its white, yellow and earth tones gave it a cheerful and relaxing feel. It was quite spacious with a small sitting area and a loveseat and coffee table. Edward lay next to Bridget snoring softly and with his arm stretched limply across her naked breasts. His nude body pressed warmly against hers. Throughout her body, from her scalp to the tips of her fingers and toes, she felt an unbelievably sweet, tingly sensation. This was not unusual, it always happened after she had an orgasm. But this time it was different. It lasted for about fifteen minutes, although it felt like hours. She felt supremely relaxed and glowed with feline contentment. It was as if a lifetime of stress had drained out of her.

This was how it used to be in the early days of her relationship with Edward, especially during the honeymoon phase of their marriage. The connection she'd felt with him back then, which had since waned, suddenly felt renewed, and this she found perplexing. It made no sense because their relationship could not have been more strained, particularly with all that had transpired in recent weeks, more so since Rudy's arrival on the scene.

Was she still in love with Edward? Deep inside, was she still hoping that somehow things would improve between them, in spite of everything? What about Rudy? Could she be in love with both men at the same time? Was it possible?

She recalled reading somewhere that a woman could fall for two different men, and even more, and love each one differently. Was this the case with her?

Edward stirred and snuggled up closer to her. Bridget could tell that he was still asleep. She gently lifted his arm off her breasts and eased it down on the bed. She got up softly and went and stood in front of one of several arched windows spanning the length and breadth of the room. Hugging herself, she gazed through rain-splattered panes at the distorted, overcast landscape. A hazy cloud of whiteness had all but obliterated parts of Albion Bay.

Financially, she didn't need Edward. She was now at a stage where, if push came to shove, she could walk away from her life on the island and not suffer any serious economic dislocation. She had carefully seen to that.

Lately, much of her travels and business engagements were devoted to ensuring that her finances and assets were safeguarded and in good shape. She didn't believe in leaving anything to chance, least of all her future financial security. She had come too far and endured too much to allow all the gains she'd made to be undone.

She knew her frequent absences and globetrotting angered both Edward and Rudy but she was not willing to appease them by giving ground on that issue. For her own sake and that of Edward himself, and even Rudy - her dearly beloved, short-sighted, unambitious Rudy - she had to stand firm.

Given the choice, would she break up with Edward? Did she really want to? Could she do without a steady man in her life? This last thought rankled every time it popped into her head. The very fact that she constantly felt the urge to ponder this question, seemed to her a subconscious acknowledgement that the 'need' for a man had been well and truly ingrained in her; otherwise why would she feel compelled to grapple with it? Why else would the prospect of her marriage ending in divorce upset her so? Likewise the thought of losing her hold on Rudy.

Sometimes she dreaded being alone with her thoughts. Who knows, perhaps this was another reason why she felt the need to be continuously on the move. But then it was also invigorating, all the wheeling and dealing and the travelling to and fro, and it brought her such relief. It felt like she inhabited two separate worlds, one giving her a momentary respite from the other.

"I had all but forgotten how enchanting you look in the nude, especially in early morning twilight." Edward's voice had a husky ring. He lay with his head propped up on his hand, eyeing Bridget.

Bridget turned around. She watched him with her arms folded across her chest. Poised in the window arch against the light, she resembled a portrait of a nude model set in a picture frame. "You were wonderful," she said, her smile warm and inviting.

"If only life could be made to stand still."

"What if it could?"

Edward sat on the edge of the bed, stark naked. At sixty-seven, his body was surprisingly firm and lean, and strikingly pale. "Hopefully the age gap between us would cease to matter and I could continue to revel in it as a vindication of my virility."

Bridget would have laughed except that she realized Edward meant it. She frowned. "Darling ... in all our years of marriage, that's the first time you ever brought up our age difference."

"Does it shock you?"

"Coming from you, yes it does."

"I am a wanderer lost in the wilderness, trying to find my way to your heart. Over time, one grows weary and begins to despair."

Bridget walked up to Edward, cupped his face in her hands and kissed him tenderly on the lips. "It used to be so wonderful in the beginning," she whispered. "Do you remember the time we stayed at that beautiful 19th century cottage in Devonshire, and the time we went skiing in the Swiss Alps and stayed at that beautiful Alpine chalet? It was so wonderful! We had such fun and did so many things together. It seemed like we could have achieved so much working as a team and accomplishing great things on this island. Then all of a sudden everything changed. Yesterday we had a great time together and last night was out of this world! It was truly as if we managed to turn back the clock."

"Yes ... We might as well try to make the most of our time here and have fun while we may. The sun is setting on what's left of it."

"What do you mean?"

Edward stood up and walked toward the window. It was still raining. He gazed outside for a while then turned to face Bridget. "I have received word from my solicitors. My application for an Individual Voluntary Agreement in respect of my loan payments has been rejected by the banks. I am now officially bankrupt."

Bridget gaped at Edward, shocked. She hurried across to the walk-in closet and put on a knit robe. Although this had been expected, hearing Edward say it hit her hard and touched her deeply.

By the time she returned, Edward had already put on his housecoat. "Darling, I'm so sorry. I wasn't aware. When did this happen?" she said.

"Five days ago."

"Why didn't you tell me then?"

"Because you were unavailable, as always."

"I'm sorry, I've had to negotiate some very important deals and it's been so unbelievably hectic for me ... What are you going to do?"

"Geoff informs me that a couple of his clients are interested in purchasing Blossom House. Somehow or other something will be worked out. I have little choice but to bow to the inevitable."

"But you don't have to. I keep telling you, why not allow me to work something out with the banks on your behalf? On *our* behalf."

"God knows how many times I've had to endure a reversal of fortunes. If I must do so once more, so be it."

"Stiff upper lip ... soldier on like a jolly good fellow."

"Now that it has come to this, I intend to leave Elysian Island. Dare I presume that you will join me?"

Bridget went and sat on the loveseat near the foot of the bed. "Where will you go?"

"That I am yet to decide but go I shall."

"It's so like you to be mysterious. Have you forgotten that we have other properties here?"

"You do. I don't."

"Edward, this is absurd. How many times do we have to go over this? If you prefer, I can arrange to purchase Blossom House ... That way nothing changes and everything is back to normal."

Edward laughed.

"I rather doubt things would return to normal, not if I persist in annoying you and the company by refusing to let myself be blinded by the dazzling light on your gold-plated road to Damascus; not to mention if I persist with my literary ambitions, which I intend to do."

"Why did you marry me?"

"Because I fell in love with you. I still love you very much."

"You're just not the man I thought I had married. I woke up this morning thinking, maybe it was wrong to keep thinking this way but it seems we are back to square one. Once again, you've become a stranger. You are an enigma. I just can't understand you. I don't think anyone can. It's as if you like it this way."

"Why do you refuse to consider the possibility that it is you who have changed since coming here and falling under the influence of your new business associates and becoming 'liberated' and 'empowered'? I unashamedly admit that in the battle to win your affection, I have lost miserably to the likes of Bill Thompson and all the rest of them."

"Please Edward, not again! Don't keep blaming my friends and my career for the problems in our marriage. For God's sake, if you need a scapegoat, let us both look in the mirror."

Edward began pacing, a grim look on his face. He paused in front of the window and gazed unseeingly through the rain-splashed panes.

Bridget sat with her arms and legs crossed, watching him. "Can you really turn your back on this island, a place you practically built from the ground up?"

Edward gazed thoughtfully at the floor and said, "I feel sorry to have to leave such a treasure behind. When I got word of the banks' decision, it nearly killed me. But there is no shame in facing the inevitable, I suppose."

They both went quiet, and in the silence they felt a sense of discomfiture. Bridget tried to think of something to say but nothing came to mind.

Edward broke into her thoughts. "I expect Rudy to join me when I leave."

"What?"

"Whether or not he realizes it – or even deserves it, for that matter – taking him along with me would be an act of mercy on my part. It would prevent him from throwing his life away and making an utter ass of himself. His dear aunt, bless her, would have expected no less of me."

"Really? ... How incredibly chivalrous of you, My Lord," Bridget scoffed, her face red, her eyes flashing.

"Furthermore," Edward continued, unmoved, "Now that I will be less preoccupied and have fewer distractions, I will be able to devote more time to telling the incredible tale of my life on Elysian Island. Initially, I had balked at Rudy's suggestion based on the advice of a prospective literary agent that I consider selling the movie rights to the book. On second thoughts, I think it is worth considering, don't you?"

"For once, you don't sound convincing," said Bridget, wryly amused. "What makes you think Rudy would want to follow you around like the hired help?"

"It would be in your interest if he did, for the time being at least. He has made some interesting discoveries that should concern you."

"What discoveries?"

"Vernon has informed me that he has discovered the identity of the thief who broke into the house. He also seems to believe that the break-in was the result of someone deliberately tampering with the electronic locks. Needless to say, if he is correct this has implications for the security of other people on the island."

"How did he discover the person's identity?"

"From one of the surveillance cameras."

"That's impossible!" Bridget sprung to her feet. "Both cameras were turned off months ago due to some technical issues. Vernon knows about it."

"Not so, I'm afraid. According to Vernon, the one overlooking the front courtyard is functional. He has confirmed that it was innocently turned on by the caretaker prior to Rudy moving in."

"Why wasn't I informed of this? Why hasn't Rudy said anything to me?"

"He would first have to locate you, I imagine. And as you know all too well, that's not exactly an easy feat to accomplish. Frankly, I fail to comprehend why you have not given this matter more urgent attention, particularly after Olive's murder. At the very least, considering how you fought desperately to have Rudy stay at your house rather than at Blossom House, as was originally planned, one would have thought that his safety would have been of paramount importance to you. You never even reported the break-in to the police!"

"That's irrelevant! It's my house, I have a right to know what he's up to and he should have informed me about all of this. Who broke into the house?"

"I have no idea, nor does Vernon. Rudy is keeping it close to his chest. Evidently, he wants to personally confront the culprit."

"What!"

"Vernon promised to try and get hold of him in an effort to dissuade him. Whether or not he has succeeded, I haven't the slightest idea."

"What is he thinking? Is he out of his mind?"

"Ah, my dear, journalists are like that. A curious sort, I dare say."

"We've got to stop him!"

"In that case you must inform the police and allow them to handle the matter as you ought to have done from the start. Would you like me to discuss it with Inspector Butcher?"

"No! Leave the police out of it. I will handle it myself."

"Surely you're not contemplating putting your business interests ahead of the security of the homeowners on the island, are you?"

"Don't be silly, you're overreacting. At the very least, I would like to discuss this with Bill first."

"There is a murderer on the loose, for God's sake! Besides, what about the issue of the break-in and how the burglar was able to circumvent the security system? To this day, it has not been addressed. Why the procrastination? Rudy has continued to insist that it was not due to negligence or an oversight on his part. Many of the homeowners, including me, foolishly allowed ourselves to be swayed by your recommendations, supported by Bill Thompson, and placed our trust and confidence in these new fangled devices, which you claimed are the ultimate in home security. Increasingly, the world seems to be waking up to the reality that this is not the case."

"So what are you suggesting?"

"The police must be given the opportunity to fully investigate these matters. We owe it to Olive. It may hold the key to determining who was responsible for her death. Hopefully, this will help to guard against such a horrific crime recurring on the island."

"You, as well as I, know that in the past fifty years there has only ever been one other case of unnatural death on this island and that was a suicide many years ago."

"Suicide indeed! Don't you dare bring up the issue of Elsa Bergman's death. You and I know the company fought desperately to sweep this incident under the carpet, and even seemed willing to go as far as interfering with the police investigation. Never again, not as long as there is breath in my body!"

"You're being rather melodramatic. It is not like you."

"Will you speak to Leroy Butcher or shall I?"

"I would like to discuss it with Rudy first and then with Bill. I think it is only fair that Bill be involved since you insist on dragging the company into this matter."

"Very well, my dear. I await the outcome with bated breath."

"So long Edward, I'm heading for a bath," Bridget said coldly and stormed out of the room.

27

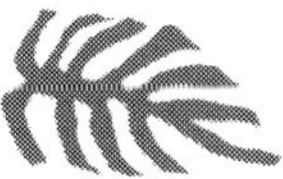

Rudy felt so grateful to see that the sky had cleared he almost went down on his knees in thanksgiving. After raining almost nonstop for over twenty-four hours, finally the showers eased up around 11:30 a.m.

After his shocking discovery, he'd felt so excited, when he went to bed he barely slept. Earlier, he'd telephoned Vernon to give him the news. He couldn't help it! He even blurted out that he was going after the culprit. That was a mistake.

Vernon immediately warned him not to do anything foolish. Rudy had expected that, coming from an ex-cop. He didn't disclose the intruder's identity, although Vernon asked him repeatedly. He didn't want him to interfere. He was determined to have a showdown with Oscar and he'd be damned if he'd let Vernon talk him out of it. He hung up with Vernon protesting stridently.

Now that the rain was over, Rudy was all set to head to the village and he was eager to do so before Vernon alerted Edward or Bridget, as he expected him to. He would have to use the bike since he had no other option. He wished to God he could have borrowed one of the vehicles at Blossom House but he knew there was no chance of that, certainly not if Sam had anything to do with it.

He hurriedly finished off his breakfast and went to get dressed. Ten minutes later he re-emerged in a polo shirt, jeans and sneakers and with his knapsack on his back. Inside of it was an iPad, a notebook, a few pens and two printouts of the video images. At the last minute, he decided to bring along his USB voice recorder, just to be on the safe side. The device, which resembled an ordinary memory stick, doubled up as a covert voice recorder and he sometimes used it for news assignments. With 4GB of memory capable of storing up to five hours of voice recordings and capturing a clear voice over a five-meter radius, he figured it was the perfect tool to have in his arsenal when he confronted Oscar. He dashed back to the room to get it.

His mobile phone rang as he was about to walk out the front door. He took it out of his pocket irritably and glanced at the display. It was Aaron calling. "Damn, what does he want?" Rudy muttered. Reluctantly, he took the call.

"I say, old chap, what are you doing out of the slammer?" Aaron greeted him.

Rudy took a deep breath. It was a good thing Aaron was not standing in front of him. "What do you want?" he demanded curtly. Aaron said he'd just come from visiting Blossom House and Edward had told him that Rudy had discovered the burglar's identity. Rudy said he had and listened impatiently to Aaron trying to coax him into disclosing more details. He rebuffed him and didn't even try to do it politely. Aaron then said something that took him completely by surprise.

"I'd be more than happy to go with you to round up the bastard." He even offered to come and pick Rudy up in his Land Rover. "Surely, you're not planning to take off on this miserable contraption you keep punishing yourself with, are you?" he added.

Despite Rudy's reservations, Aaron had him thinking. His offer of support was clearly genuine and proffered with no apparent strings attached. Rudy was surprised that Aaron hadn't tried to warn him off or lecture him, like Vernon. He perceived in that a measure of acceptance on Aaron's part, bordering on an overture of camaraderie. His penchant for adventure, no doubt, also played a part.

Aaron cautioned him about the weather and then, as if to sway him further, he gave Rudy another warning. "Trust me mate, you'll need all the help you can get. Right at this moment, Lady Macbeth is baying for your blood!"

Lady Macbeth. Aaron's pet name for Bridget. Rudy reflected for a moment, then he gave in and agreed that Aaron could go along with him, providing he didn't tell anyone, especially Bridget, and he came over immediately. Aaron agreed and promptly took off.

28

Aaron pulled up near the village fish market. Initially he'd seemed surprised when Rudy told him that it was Oscar who had broken into the house and he voiced his doubts.

"I know the bugger is a bit of a nuisance with a weakness for the bottle, and he's been involved in a few petty acts of praedial larceny in the past, but housebreaking? Doesn't quite sound like Oscar to me," he said. He became even more skeptical when Rudy admitted that the crook's face was not visible on the video. When Rudy told him about the stitched design on the intruder's jeans, and that it looked exactly like the one he had recently seen Oscar wearing, Aaron still wasn't impressed.

"You may as well issue a public notice urging everyone on the island to bring their jeans to have them inspected to make sure there aren't other suspects," Aaron sneered. Rudy shot him a rueful glance then demanded that he stop the vehicle so he could see the evidence for himself. Aaron obliged and parked briefly at the side of the road. After viewing the videos and the photograph of Oscar, he eventually conceded that Rudy could be on to something.

After discussing it some more, however, they both agreed that it was highly unlikely, if not impossible, that a man like Oscar could ever be able to hack into electronic locks.

"I can't imagine the poor chap has ever switched on a computer in his life, far less hack into a smart lock. It would surprise me if he even owns a mobile phone," said Aaron. Nevertheless, they agreed Oscar must surely know the hacker. "I know where he lives," said Aaron. "It's a short distance from here, in an isolated spot high up on a ridge, between the village and Mount Britannia. That area is called Auberge. Oscar lives with his grandfather and goes crab hunting in the same area. He pretty much survives on crab hunting. He traps them in the wooded areas and sells them by the roadside or at the fish market,"

With that they drove off.

29

Auberge was a mere fifteen-minute drive away. Oscar and his grandfather lived in one of the more elevated parts of Elysian Island, on a plateau overlooking the island's central-ridge forest reserve. Fortunately, Aaron was able to negotiate almost the entire length of the dirt track leading up to their home. The remainder of the climb took about five minutes of walking.

Dark clouds rolled in ominously from the east as they approached Oscar's home, a small, solitary wooden hut. An old man sat on the steps grating a dried coconut, evidently to make coconut oil. A few chickens hovered around him, clucking hopefully. The hut was little more than a rectangular wooden box with a narrow door that resembled the open mouth of a corpse, and two windows that looked like eyeless sockets. It seemed to barely have enough space for two. The few sheets of galvanized iron roofing were disfigured by rust that was so thick it resembled scabs on a sore. The weather-beaten walls resembled tanned animal hide and had obviously never been touched by a coat of paint. Even with the door and windows open, inside looked dark and gloomy.

The old man was mainly skin and bones and quite dark. He wore a ragged pair of shorts and no shirt and he was barefooted. He appeared to have once been very tall, except that now his shoulders were hunched and he had a slight stoop, which was visible even as he sat. He had a hardy face with a strong chin, a square jaw and a broad forehead, and his eyes shone brightly. It was a face full of character. It had surprisingly few wrinkles and, unlike the rest of him, seemed to have held up well against the onslaught of time. His waning power and vitality seemed to have centered in that strong, indomitable face, as if to make a last stand against his imminent demise.

Rudy gaped at him and the hut, speechless. It struck him that the house looked more like a lair than a home. He was quite taken aback.

"Bonjour messieurs," the old man greeted them in a croaky voice.

"Comment ça va?" Aaron replied cheerily. "Oops, sorry to disturb your admirers," he added, alluding to the chickens as they scurried away, squawking in protest. He asked after the old man's health, speaking in a mixture of Creole and English that made him sound clownish.

Still gazing at the old man and the surroundings, Rudy felt like he had gone back in time about a hundred years. He had to remind himself that he was still in the fairy-tale land of ineffable beauty and the home of the super-rich. It made him feel extremely uncomfortable, even embarrassed. Although his Creole was only marginally better than Aaron's, he tried piloting the conversation and started off by introducing himself. The old man said his name was Guillaume but he was also known as Akajou Gwan Bwa after the age-old trees high up in the nearby forests. He confirmed that Oscar was his grandson and asked if he had found himself in trouble again. Even before Rudy could respond, the old man made the sign of the cross and begged God to forgive him for having played a part in bringing such a worthless vagabond into the world to 'cause people so much headache.'

"No sir, we just want to have a chat with him," Rudy said quickly in Creole. The old man breathed a sigh of relief and crossed himself again. He said Oscar was not far away. Putting away the coconut, he hobbled down the steps and signaled Rudy and Aaron to follow him. He led them towards a wooded area behind the house. On the ground were two bamboo-tube traps, each close to a crab burrow. "Wait here," said Guillaume, "Otherwise the mud will dirty your clothes. I will go in the bush to look for him." He hobbled along ahead of them and disappeared amongst the trees.

Aaron took hold of one of the traps and lifted it carefully. "Here, take a look at this," he said. The trap was made from the nodal section of a bamboo stem. At the upper front end of it was a trapdoor-hole fitted with a bowstring braced by a wooden spindle, and at the rear was a small trigger hole. The trigger was baited with bits of ripe banana to entice the crab with the expectation that once it brushed against the trigger, this would immediately cause the trapdoor to slam shut. "Fascinating, isn't it?" Aaron gushed.

"It looks quite neat. Haven't seen one of these since my boyhood days."

"Neat?" Aaron frowned. "It's a bloody work of art! It looks even finer than the two I've got amid the tropical art collection in my grand salon back home in England."

"You got bamboo traps in your drawing room?"

"Naturally. They are quite visionary pieces, don't you think?"

"You bloody well bet I don't! Surely, you must be joking."

"Here, take a good look." Aaron held the trap up close to Rudy. It smelt of rancid coconut and decayed matter. "It's the ultimate symbol of desire and entrapment – the fall of man; the current theme of our earthly existence captured in an ancient native artefact, the crab-hunting bamboo trap. Absolutely brilliant! That's why I can't help returning to this place time and again." The foul odor from the trap wafted up in the breeze. Rudy reached out and took it from Aaron. "Let's return it to its rightful place, shall we, for the good of posterity," he said wryly and replaced the trap next to the crab hole. Suddenly they heard voices accompanied by the rustling of bushes. Guillaume and Oscar emerged from amongst the trees.

Oscar stiffened at the sight of Rudy. In one hand he carried a bunch of wriggling crabs tied up with thick vines, and he had a bamboo tube on his shoulder. He wore a pair of cut-off jeans stained with mud and a torn-up shirt. Guillaume was also carrying a bunch of crabs. Their legs and claws were carefully tied to their bodies. A proud, gummy smile lit up the old man's face.

"By Jove, you've bagged quite a trophy, well done!" said Aaron in English. "You must be proud of yourself."

"Yes, boss. Today was a good day," Oscar replied, eyeing Rudy coldly. He dropped the bundle of crabs on the ground and lifting the bamboo off his shoulder, he placed it next to them. Sticking his hand inside the bamboo, he pulled out six young crabs. He carried them about ten yards away and released them, then returned to join the other two men. "Whenever I catch small ones I does let them go so they can grow bigger," he explained to Aaron. "The female ones too. Those that have eggs in their belly, so that we can get more crabs later."

"How can you tell the males from the females?" Aaron enquired.

"The female ones have a round, wide flap on their belly. The males' own more narrow and it pointed," Oscar replied.

Moving closer to Oscar, Aaron placed his arm across his shoulders. "Do you mind if we wait here while you and your granddad put away the crabs? We need your help to solve a little matter."

"My help, boss?"

"Yes, yes. It's okay, no need to be nervous. It won't take long. Run along, we'll be waiting here for you."

"Relax brother, we just want to talk," Rudy chipped in gently, trying not to spook Oscar. He could tell Oscar was very uneasy, although he wasn't sure if it was because of his presence or for some other reason. He picked up the bundle of crabs Oscar had dropped on the ground and handed it to him. Oscar took it quietly and avoided Rudy's eyes. He swung the empty trap back unto his shoulder and together, he and his grandfather made their way back to the hut.

Rudy run his hands feverishly through his hair. "Right at this very moment I should be pissed off and relishing the opportunity to nail this guy but believe it or not, I'm actually wishing I didn't have to .... Crazy, isn't it?"

"I know of game hunters in Africa who felt the same way when they were on the verge of making their first kill. They are all women."

"Have these two guys been living here all their lives?"

"In Oscar's case, yes, of course. Right on this very spot. Guillaume originally came from the mainland. Oscar's mother died when he was very young and he was left in his grandfather's care. He never knew his father."

"How does it make you feel coming here all these years and seeing them live under these conditions?"

"Do you pity the old boy? If Guillaume were to suspect this, he would feel terribly insulted."

"What's that supposed to mean?"

"He's a proud old man; a direct descendent of the *Neg Djiné.*"

"The who?"

Aaron frowned. Tut-tutting, he said, "You do need to brush up on your local history. The *Neg Djiné* are a group of people from a rural community in the north of Saint Lucia who are said to be descendents of a group of free Africans who arrived on the island around the mid 19th century, during the post-Emancipation period. They practice an animistic religion called *Kelé* and Guillaume is said to have been a *Kelé* priest back in his home community. He's always been content to live by the little he earns and accepts handouts from no one, which of course can't be said of Oscar. As he constantly says, 'What God keeps for the poor, no man can destroy.' He considers Oscar a cross that he has to bear. Edward sold him the tiny spot he lives on for ten quid some fifty years ago. If you were to try relocating him from here, it would kill him instantly."

Rudy and Aaron turned around at the sound of footsteps sloshing through mud. Oscar was heading towards them. Rudy spotted a rickety bench with a backrest under a golden apple tree, seemingly out of earshot of the hut. He suggested to Aaron that they go sit over there, and signaled Oscar to join them. Aaron allowed him and Oscar to sit while he remained standing.

Oscar sat about three feet away from Rudy. The scowl on his face and his frosty silence underscored his determination to have nothing whatsoever to do with Rudy.

Rudy took his iPad out of the knapsack and placed it down on the bench. The device immediately caught Oscar's attention. While he fixated on it, Rudy fiddled with the USB voice recorder in his pocket. He wasted no time in getting down to business. He told Oscar about the break-in and the theft of his necklaces, all the while watching his reaction closely. Oscar sat motionless listening to him with a deadpan expression.

"Do you know anything about this robbery?" Rudy asked him quietly. Oscar reared back as if he had been electrocuted and gaped at Rudy, shocked. "Me!" he squealed. "How is me you askin'? I don't know nothing about robbery!"

"Take it easy, all I want from you is the truth."

Oscar sprang to his feet. His popping eyes and drooping jaw emphasized his outrage, which was executed with theatrical perfection. "So what, now you calling me a liar? First you call me a t'ief, now you calling me a liar!" he exclaimed.

Rudy switched on the iPad and located the video clips. "Have a look at this," he said and pushed the device closer to Oscar so he could get a clear view of it. Oscar's gaze was transfixed on the video. Rudy's years of experience as a journalist had taught him how to keep a close eye on the body language of whomever he was interviewing. He was watching Oscar's clenched fists and he also caught a flicker of fear in his eyes. He zoomed in the image of the burglar's jeans pocket with the red stitching and paused it. He then took out a large color printout of the photo of Oscar wearing the lookalike jeans and held both images up, side by side. "Here's what I'm going to do," he said. "First I'm going to show this to your grandfather, then to the police if you don't cooperate with me."

Aaron walked up to Oscar and placed his arm around his shoulders. "How do you think Guillaume is going to feel if he sees that?" he asked Oscar gently. "He's a straight and honest man ... If I know him he's going to be terribly angry; so angry he might haul you down to the police himself."

Oscar drew away and sat abruptly on the bench. "No! Don't tell Guillaume, please," he pleaded. The mention of his grandfather's name seemed to have struck terror in his heart. Rudy was taken aback by the sudden change in his reaction. He frowned questioningly at Aaron.

"It's okay," Aaron said soothingly to Oscar. "There'll be no need to tell Guillaume anything if we can sort this little matter out between us, what do you say? All you need to do is tell Rudy the truth. Now ... strictly between us, did you break and enter his home and steal his necklaces?"

Oscar hesitated. His eyes darted furtively from Rudy to Aaron. He slumped against the backrest, his shoulders drooped. "Is not my fault, he make me do it," he moaned, sounding like he was on the verge of tears. "Things was rough. I had no money, that's why I do it. He tell me he just wanted to play a little joke on you, so he ask me to break into the house and take something of yours for him. He tell me you wouldn' be there and nobody would be in the house. I not a t'ief. I didn't want to steal your things. I thought it was a joke and he was your friend."

"Who the hell is 'he'? Who are you talking about?" Rudy demanded.

"Is not my fault, honest."

Rudy rounded on Oscar. "Who the fuck is 'he'? What on earth are you talking about?" he shouted.

Aaron stepped in between them. "Easy, take it easy," he said, placing his hand on Rudy's shoulder. Turning to Oscar, he said, "Tell me, how were you able to get into the house? The doors and windows have electronic locks and they can only be unlocked with a special code. None of the locks was damaged, which means the intruder did not force his way in. How did you get in?"

"Electric locks?" Oscar looked puzzled. "I don't know nothing about electric lock. When I reach there, the house was unlock ... I swear! I pass through the sliding door in the bedroom rather than the front door so nobody would see me. I didn't have to do nothing to unlock it. They had already tell me I would find it open. I don't know nothing about electric locks."

Aaron and Rudy looked at each other.

"Do you know what a computer hacker is, Oscar?" said Aaron.

"What?"

"A computer hacker."

"No. What's that?" Oscar was now quite confused and even looked frightened.

"Who did you give my necklaces to?" said Rudy.

"I thought he was your friend. He tell me he's your friend."

"Okay, fine. Just tell me who 'he' is. What is his name? That's all I need to know."

"No, please ... I can't tell you that."

"What the f---. Listen Oscar, somebody killed Olive and the murderer tried to frame me by planting my necklaces near her body. The same necklaces you stole! How do we know it wasn't you who murdered Olive and tried to set me up?"

"Me! ... Kill Olive?" Oscar gaped in horror at Rudy. "Ahh Rastaman, how can you say such a thing? Me, of all people, kill Olive? A woman I did love so much." Tears welled up in Oscar's eyes. He held his head and began to cry.

Rudy's face was a portrait of exasperation. He was trying hard not to physically attack Oscar. He began pacing in the mud and running his hands agitatedly though his locks. Aaron stepped in once again. Edging closer to Oscar, he said, "Remember old chap, we had a deal. Rudy and I promised not to spill the beans to your grandfather but in return you've got to be more helpful. Rudy is an innocent man in trouble with the law, all because of you and your friend. Guillaume is not going to be very happy with you when he finds out. So who would you rather us protect, you or your friend?"

"Okay! Okay! I will tell you. but not here, please. Let me go and change my dirty clothes and we'll go down by the road and then I'll tell you."

Aaron peered thoughtfully at Oscar. "Fair enough. Run along and make it snappy, we're waiting."

"Yes boss ... I coming just now." Oscar turned and walked away dejectedly toward the hut. Each step clearly felt like a punishment.

Rudy watched him in dismay. He switched off the USB voice recorder in his pocket and said, "Is this guy for real? And why is he so uptight about his grandfather?"

Aaron chuckled. "As I mentioned earlier, Guillaume used to be a *Kelé* priest. Among the villagers, it is believed that he has mystical powers; a seer of sorts or a *gardeur* to use the Creole parlance, and that's another reason why he is highly respected, in some cases even feared. No one fears him more than Oscar. He wouldn't dare lie to the old man since Guillaume can reportedly use his so-called powers to discover if he'd been fibbing or to *démenti* him as they say. Oscar would then be in even worse trouble. No doubt that's why the poor bastard is so terrified. Such is the nature of the simpleminded illiterate."

"Oh shit! ... Look!" Rudy pointed over Aaron's shoulder. Aaron spun around just in time to see Oscar dashing toward the bushes on the edge of the plateau. He ran down the slope and disappeared amongst the trees.

"He's trying to escape!" Rudy yelled. "Come on!" Together he and Aaron bolted towards the area where they had spotted Oscar. It was densely wooded and carpeted with thick bush and giant ferns. There was no sign of Oscar. "Damn! Looks like we've lost him," said Rudy ruefully as he paused to look around. The terrain varied from a moderate incline to a steep drop further down. "This place looks quite risky," said Rudy.

"You're right. He may not have gone far and could well be trying to outfox us."

"How?"

"Come along," said Aaron as he retraced his steps back up to the plateau. "I suspect that he has doubled back to the area east of where we saw him disappear in the bushes. That's where he does his crab hunting. That section is quite rugged and steep but he's probably hoping we'll focus our attention there while he slips away and hides somewhere else. I've been here before and I have a good recollection of the topography. I suggest you wait up here to make sure he doesn't double back again and make fools of us. I will head across to the slope to look for him."

"Are you kidding? You could be down there searching for hours."

"Not necessarily. I would have you know that I am an able mountain climber with fairly good tracking skills. Besides, once he's within earshot I need only remind him of Guillaume and tell him that you've gone to see the old man," Aaron said, sniggering. Pausing at the edge of the plateau, he said, "If you hear a sharp whistle, that's me letting you know that I've found him." he continued down the slope, amongst the trees.

Rudy resumed pacing. Fortunately, he didn't have to wait long. A sharp whistle pierced the silence. It came from an easterly direction, deep inside the bushes. Rudy scrambled down the slope, trying to follow the same route as Aaron. Aaron issued another sharp whistle. Rudy pushed through the bushes faster as he tried to determine where the whistle came from. Thick brush flayed his face and body at every turn. His legs got entangled in creepers and the slippery ground made it difficult for him to stay on his feet. Twice he slipped and landed on his ass. He pressed on undaunted, working his way deeper into the bush. "Over here!" Aaron shouted somewhere to his right. He sounded closer than Rudy had expected. A few minutes later they spotted each other.

"Be careful," Aaron shouted. "There's a precipice ahead."

Rudy reached him panting. "Where is he?" he blurted out. Aaron pointed to a deep gorge.

"He's down there dangling from the jutting root of a tree, barely hanging on for dear life."

"What happened?"

"Evidently he heard me coming and tried to give me the slip but lost his footing and went over the edge."

Rudy went closer to the edge of the cliff and looked down. Oscar was literally dangling from a tree root jutting out of the cliff face, about six feet down. Somehow he'd managed to grab hold of it as he fell. The only other thing holding him up was a small rock embedded in the cliff on which he'd managed to place his left foot for support. Below him was a gaping chasm that seemed to plunge into oblivion.

"Help me, please!" Oscar screamed.

Rudy turned to Aaron. "He's barely hanging on! What are we going to do?"

"I can try reaching him but we need a rope to pull him up. I'm afraid I must ask you to return to the plateau. I've got some climbing gear in the Land Rover, including a rope bag. Would you mind bringing the bag? It's in the boot. Meanwhile, I will try to comfort our dear friend."

Rudy rushed back up the hill while Aaron stood on the edge of the cliff urging Oscar to hang on.

Rudy returned with the bag slung over his shoulder and tried his best not to lose his footing on the slippery slope. He handed it to Aaron. Aaron opened it and pulled out a twenty-foot length of rope, a harness and a hunting knife. He strapped on the harness and selected a tree with a modest girth about four feet from the cliff edge where Oscar was suspended. Curling one end of the rope around the tree trunk, he formed a fixed loop and fastened it with a double overhand knot. "That's called a double bowline," he explained, working swiftly. "It's also known as a nautical line and works just as well for boating, as for mountain climbing." At the other end of the rope he made another loop and created double bowline knots.

Reaching into the bag, he pulled out another rope and forming another loop with double bowline knots, he tied one end to the stem of another tree that was slightly out of alignment with the point where Oscar was suspended. He attached the other end to the harness.

"What're you up to?" said Rudy with an impatient note in his voice.

"I'm going to lower myself over the edge and take the other rope with me so I can fit Oscar's foot into the loop. With the other end of it tied firmly to the tree, he's going to hold on to the rope once his foot is secure in the loop and then it will be your job to pull him up. He's fairly lightweight and you're tough enough.

Meanwhile, I'm going to pull myself back up and help you pull him to safety."

"Are you sure this is going to work?"

"Don't see why not. It would be rather unfortunate for us both if it doesn't." Leaning forward, Aaron looked over the edge at Oscar who was now barely hanging onto the tree root. Aaron turned to face the tree and held on to both ropes, including the one tied to the harness. Gradually he stepped backwards over the edge and began the descent, taking care to place his feet in crevices and on rocks that were firmly embedded in the side of the cliff. As he usually did on a risky climb, he mentally blocked out his surroundings and tried to avoid rationalizing so as not to lose his nerve.

Oscar watched him with terror-filled eyes. The root he was clinging to was gradually coming loose from the soil and causing chunks of mud and rocks to plunge down into the gorge. "Easy, don't panic," Aaron urged him as he carefully lodged his feet into a wide crevice. As he drew abreast with Oscar, he shouted at Rudy, "Shift the rope as close to Oscar's body as you can!" Rudy followed his instructions. Gripping the rope attached to the harness with his right hand, Aaron used his free hand to draw the other rope closer to Oscar's legs. "Stick your foot in the loop then hold on to the rope with both hands ... Now!" he bellowed at Oscar. Oscar gazed at the rope and hesitated. "Do it, damn it!" Aaron barked. Oscar tried and missed. He tried again, then a third time, to no avail. He trembled horribly. On the fourth attempt he managed to get his right foot into the loop. "Now grab the rope with both hands ... *quickly*!" Aaron yelled. Oscar grabbed hold of the rope. His weight caused it to drop a few inches and then it grew taut and held.

Up on the ledge, Rudy glanced at the tree. He couldn't believe the knots had held. He glanced back down at the cliff. Aaron was already pulling himself back up. Oscar was left alone, clinging for dear life to the rope. He glanced down into the gaping, bottomless gorge and quickly averted his eyes. Together, Rudy and Aaron began pulling him up. Rudy stood closer to the cliff edge while

Aaron stood behind him taking in the slack and helping to pull Oscar up. As Oscar's head appeared over the edge, Rudy glanced behind at Aaron and yelled, "Wait! Hang on a minute!" They both paused and drew the rope tight. Holding on to it with his left hand, Rudy reached into his back pocket and pulled out Aaron's hunting knife. Still gripping the rope tightly, he placed the knife blade against the rope and glared malevolently at Oscar.

"Now, this is your last chance!" he hissed. "Tell me who helped you break into the house. Tell me now or I'm going to cut this fucking rope!"

"Rudy, what the devil are you doing?" Aaron snapped.

"Either he talks or he gets a one-way ticket to hell!"

The rope began inching back down due to their loss of momentum.

"Oh God! My foot, it squeezing! The rope cutting my foot!" Oscar squealed.

"Goodbye Oscar," said Rudy and he pressed the knife against the rope.

"Wait! No, please! Larry Thompson. He's the one, he make me do it! He ask me to break and enter your house!"

"Larry Thompson? Who the fuck is that?"

"He was by the beach in a car that had black tint all around. He was driving and I think there had somebody else in the car but their window was up and I didn't see who. He barely open his window and I give him the necklaces. Please believe me, is the truth! Have mercy on me, please," Oscar moaned. He and Rudy stared at each other. Fear clashed with suspicion.

"How did my necklaces end up on Olive's bed? Did you put them there?" Rudy demanded.

"No, it wasn't me! I swear!"

Rudy pressed the knife harder into the rope, slicing some of the filaments. "Talk, damn it! Who put them there?"

"I don't know, is not me! I bring both of them for Larry but I don't know what he do with them. *I swear* - on my mother grave! Oh, God, please believe me!" Oscar pleaded.

Rudy dropped the knife and resumed pulling the rope while Aaron backed him up. Within a few seconds, Oscar's torso was up unto the ledge. Leaning forward, Rudy grabbed him by the seat of his pants and pulled him all the way up with one huge tug and dragged him along the ground close to the tree.

Oscar sat up quickly and pulled the rope gingerly from his foot. It left a dark welt across the mid-foot and it bled slightly. Rudy ignored him and looked questioningly at Aaron. "Who's Larry Thompson?" he asked.

Aaron said nothing and began untying the ropes from the trees. There was no mistaking the alarmed look on his face. Rudy noticed it. This was the first time he saw Aaron looking disturbed.

Oscar gently massaged his foot. Gaping at Rudy, he said, "Oh Lord, Rastaman! You mean you woulda have the heart to kill me? A man life in danger and you want to kill him? Jah will punish you, Rastaman!" He continued massaging his foot, tears in his eyes. "You wicked Rastaman," he sobbed. "You have the heart of a criminal. Jah will smite you!"

"Not as much as he's going to smite you for Olive's death, you bastard!" Rudy retorted. Oscar flinched and drew away.

"Easy gentlemen," said Aaron quietly as he coiled up the ropes and placed them in the bag along with the knife and harness. Oscar struggled up from the ground and limped away, ahead of Rudy and Aaron, looking quite sullen. Aaron slung the bag over his shoulders and gazed up through the tree branches at the overcast sky. "We better get going before the rain comes down," he said.

"Not so fast. Who's this Larry guy?" Rudy demanded.

"Bill Thompson's son."

"What?"

"You heard correctly. The son of the CEO of the Elysian Island Company ... Come on, let's go." Aaron began climbing the hill.

30

Bridget and Bill Thompson were already there waiting when Rudy walked into the restaurant at the Camelot Hotel at midday. He could tell by their expressions that they were not pleased at being kept waiting. He was nearly half an hour late and frankly, he didn't give a damn.

He only came at Bridget's insistence. The day before they'd had quite a stormy spat. He'd gone looking for her at Blossom House bright and early, in an agitated state. He was surprised to find her at home. Straight off the bat, Bridget demanded an explanation as to why he had not kept her abreast of all that had been going on over the past few days.

Rudy managed to control his anger. He told her about Oscar and how he had discovered that he was the one who had broken into the house. He was careful not to drag Amanda and Amin into it for fear it made Bridget suspicious of both him and Amanda, especially with the mood she was in.

It got worse when he told her about the incident with Oscar and Oscar's allegations about Bill Thompson's son. Bridget excoriated him for taking matters into his own hands and not seeking her advice beforehand. She tried to discourage him from reporting the matter to the police, which didn't surprise him. According to her, since Bill Thompson's son had been implicated, it was only fair that the matter be discussed with him and his wife first.

Their argument became so heated, two of the maids came near the living room entrance, eavesdropping. Rudy knew they were there because he didn't hear their footsteps continue down the hallway. Before long, Edward wandered into the room and got involved in the exchange. He became quite livid when he found out that Bridget had insisted that Rudy not inform the police of what he'd discovered until she discussed it with Bill Thompson. He turned to Rudy and said, "Need I remind you that you are in my employ, and that I bear responsibility for you? I demand that you report the matter to the police ... Now, what is your decision?" Rudy gaped from one to the other, tongue-tied.

Bridget stepped in. "Rudy is my guest," she calmly rebuked Edward, adding, "This so-called 'incident' that you refer to occurred at *my* house. Need I remind you of that?"

Edward flounced out of the room.

Bridget then hustled him out of the house and into the courtyard where they continued arguing. Without realizing it, she had made him more defiant and resentful because of the subtle way she'd kept hinting at his dependency while reminding him of Edward's financial limitations, as usual.

Rudy finally agreed to a meeting with Bill Thompson out of sheer exhaustion and to try and get Bridget off his back. He figured he couldn't possibly get himself in a more screwed-up position, even if he tried. He couldn't think of leaving the island. With Leroy Butcher still on his case, the cops would almost certainly move to stop him if he tried. Despite Bridget's assurance that the lawyer was confident that Butcher could be persuaded to allow him to travel freely, so far Rudy hadn't seen any indication of that.

He didn't even feel he could trust the cops, including Leroy Butcher. For all he knew, the son of a bitch could be itching to throw the book at him. Butcher had made his feelings towards him quite plain when they ran into each other near the Halcyon Beach Bar, the day after his interview at the police station. Although it was early days yet, Rudy couldn't resist quizzing Butcher about the investigation to try and get a sense of the extent to which he was being viewed as a suspect. Butcher had merely smiled and gave him evasive answers. "Cheer up and look on the bright side," he said. "You couldn't have picked a better place to end up in hot water." When Rudy asked him what he meant by that, he replied, "You've got to admit, Elysian Island has got some of the prettiest and richest snow-white angels this side of heaven. For any playboy on the hunt, this is the closest thing to the Promised Land, don't you think?"

With that he gave Rudy a friendly pat on the back and took off. Rudy stared darts and arrows at him and secretly prayed for the bastard to be struck by a bolt of lightning!

More than ever, he felt cornered and trapped; which was why he didn't give a shit as he walked in late for his meeting with Bridget and her sidekick. There were less than a dozen diners in the restaurant. Bridget and Thompson had chosen a corner table isolated from the others with a striking view of the beach and sail boats criss-crossing the shimmering waters. As usual, the mere sight of Bridget sent Rudy's blood rushing. She wore a button-up blouse and knee-length skirt that clung to her curves and accentuated her figure, yet was conservative enough to make her look classy and chic. She accessorized with pointy-toed, leather pumps, a simple black bag and a choker. She wore her hair pulled back, artfully detailing around her neckline.

"Rudy, how are?" Thompson greeted Rudy in his booming voice but minus the hail-and-hearty gusto he had displayed the previous times they'd met.

"Fine, thank you," Rudy replied, adding, "Good day, Bridget." Bridget stared at him while she fiddled with a salt shaker and said nothing. A young male waiter brought them menus and hung around to take their orders. Bridget suggested callaloo soup, banana salad and seafood pasta and both Rudy and Thompson agreed. Rudy also ordered a beer. The waiter smiled dutifully and went to place the orders.

"I'm very sorry to learn that your brief stay here has been somewhat of a baptism by fire," said Thompson with a grave face and furrowed brow. He looked genuinely disturbed. "That damned robbery, followed by Olive's tragic murder, and now this latest revelation from Bridget concerning Oscar, it's all downright insane! I can hardly believe this is happening here."

"That's quite understandable, especially if it involves incidents outside your normal areas of concern, I would imagine." Rudy replied.

"What's the status of the police investigation? Have they been in touch with you?"

"Not officially."

"What does that mean?"

"Leroy Butcher and I have crossed paths since my last interview with him. He gave no indication whether they had made any progress with the investigation. It leaves me pretty much in limbo."

"I see. Let's cut to the chase, as you Brits would say. Where does my son fit into all this mess?"

The waiter brought them their appetizers and Rudy's beer, smiled sweetly at Rudy and left. Bridget avoided eye contact with Rudy and focused instead on her drink, toying with the swizzle and cheery.

Rudy told Thompson about the break-in and recounted all the related incidents that had transpired since. Thompson listened attentively, his countenance darkening with every detail Rudy rained down on him. The bit about Oscar on the cliff touched him. Turning to Bridget, he said, "I want to thank you guys for informing me of this. Goodness knows how I'm going to break this news to Jacquie. It's going to break her heart."

"Tell that to Rudy, he thought it was the wrong thing to do."

Thompson frowned at Rudy. "Why?"

"I initially got into trouble with the law for not reporting the break-in as I should have. I don't want to find myself in the same jam again."

"No! No! No! This isn't Britain, or for that matter over on the mainland. This is Elysian Island. We have our way of sorting things out here ... all perfectly within the law of course ... Do you have children, Rudy?"

"No."

"When I say I am grateful for you coming first to inform me of this, I speak as a father, not as the CEO of the Elysian Island Company. No father on the face of this earth ever wants to deal with an allegation such as the one you have just made. It is like someone driving a stake into your heart. That is not to say that I believe there is any truth to Oscar's accusation. I totally reject it. However, I will not sit here and pretend that my son is an angel. Far from it, he's downright wayward and a fucking pain in the ass! That boy has been the cause of much pain to both me and my wife. As a father, I've tried to figure out where I could have gone wrong but ... Never mind. What proof have you got other than Oscar's word that Larry tampered with your locks to enable Oscar to get in?"

"I have no concrete proof yet, just Oscar's word."

"But according to you, all Oscar said was that he was told to go to the house and he would find it unlocked. Everyone on the island knows that Oscar is an intellectually and mentally challenged youth. He doesn't know shit about sophisticated electronic systems. He probably doesn't even know how to turn a light bulb on. He never said the system had been hacked nor did he say anyone had told him so, am I right?"

"I agree he didn't but I think you and I can safely assume that's how he got in."

"You assumed that. I don't, not unless it's proven. At present, Larry is not even on Elysian Island. To my knowledge, he's been fooling around in Soufriere on the mainland and galavanting aimlessly between Saint Lucia and Jamaica over the past few months. In any case, even though it was proven that the lock system had been hacked to allow Oscar to get in, that's not to say that Larry was the one who actually tampered with the locks to let him in. Furthermore, what could possibly be his motive for being directly involved or, God forbid, in perpetrating such a heinous crime on a young woman he is not known to have been involved with in any way or form? ... Can you see where I'm going with this?"

"Very much so. It's Oscar's word against the son of one of the richest men in the world."

"Regardless of how he has turned out, Larry is my son! What sort of father would I be if I am not prepared to defend him to the death until he is proven to be guilty of what you accused him of? Granted, I am also doing it because I cannot accept the implications of your allegation, because to do so I would have to believe that my son had a hand in the brutal murder of an innocent young woman. My heart, my very soul cannot accept this!"

There was heavy silence around the table.

Rudy gazed at his drink, which up to that point he had not touched. "Mr. Thompson, what you don't seem to understand is that your refusal to accept the clear possibility of your son's involvement in the crime has dire implications for me personally. Presently, I'm the fall guy. The police have their sights set on me and it's only a matter of time before they swoop in ... What I'm trying to say to you is that the only way to keep the heat off your son is by me continuing to serve as the sacrificial lamb."

"Nonsense! The police have nothing on you. If they had, you would have been in the slammer a long time ago. Don't overestimate Leroy Butcher. Sure, he's bright and he's smart but the fact that he came to an understanding with Clifford Allen and held off laying charges against you means that he's aware that the cards, as they currently stand, are stacked against him and he doesn't think he can make a charge stick. He's got nothing on you, plain and simple."

"Put yourself in my position. What do you suggest I do?"

"I think Butcher should be encouraged to change his plans to keep you cooped up here. This investigation needs to come to a conclusion, one way or the other. Elysian Island is a mere three and a half square miles, for God's sake! The murder took place in a village of less than two hundred people. Why the hell should a murder investigation there take so long? It's ridiculous!"

Rudy frowned. "What about the expatriate community? Why should they be above suspicion?"

"My point is that the population of this island is too damn small to warrant a long, drawn out murder investigation, which has clearly been going nowhere. Thank God, so far we've not had to deal with a barrage of media bloodhounds."

"I have mentioned to Rudy that he should consider leaving the island, at least for the mainland," Bridget interjected. "I don't think the police here would have a problem with that, Elysian Island is part of Saint Lucia. Granted, the police over there may still opt to maintain travel restrictions on him but even that is better than being cooped up here. Besides, that's where he was born, it's his homeland."

Rudy leaned forward and stared at Bridget. "What about Olive's killer? If everything plays out the way you suggest, does it mean we simply turn a blind eye and allow the murderer to go free? Doesn't that bother you?"

"Leave that to Leroy Butcher and his men, Rudy, that's their job. It's what they're being paid to do!" There was an exasperated ring in Bridget's voice. "You've got a life to live. The important thing is you're innocent and the police need to concede that they have nothing on you. You need to move on and get on with your life."

"I can't move on, not until there's justice for Olive."

Bridget and Rudy glared at each other. Neither of them blinked.

Thompson intervened smoothly. "Listen Rudy, I understand that you feel awful about Olive's death but why are you taking it so personally? Why have you suddenly become her avenger?"

"I guess at some point in life one has to stand up for something."

"Sure, provided you're doing it on your own time and money," Bridget sneered.

Rudy gazed down at the table in silence. After a while he looked up and said, "You're right. I've overstayed my welcome. That was a mistake – even bigger than the one I made by agreeing to come here in the first place."

Thompson cleared his throat in an obvious attempt to break the tension. Peering at Rudy, he said, "What about your plan to write Edward's memoir? What's become of that?"

"I have no idea. I'm not sure Edward does either."

"Why am I not surprised? As you yourself have just insinuated, you screwed up when you decided to put your life on hold to go in search of the pot of gold at the end of the rainbow. If there is one thing I have learned after many years in business, it's watch your ass and always count the cost."

"We all make mistakes and miscalculations," Rudy said ruefully. Staring pointedly at Bridget, he added, "Especially when you naively allow others to goad you into doing what's convenient for them rather than for you."

"You want to know something else I've learned?" Thompson watched Rudy straight in the eye. "Mistrust the obvious ... always mistrust the obvious. Mind you, that's one bit of advice I never thought I'd have to give to a journalist."

Rudy stood up. "It's been nice chatting with you both." He pushed back his chair.

"Wait a minute, where are you going? What about lunch?" Thompson looked taken aback.

"Actually I decided to have it somewhere else, on my own time and money."

"Oh come on, Rudy. Don't be so sensitive," said Bridget.

Rudy was already a couple yards across the room when he turned and said, "I'm going to find out who killed Olive, one way or the other. You can bet on it ... Let the chips fall where they may."

The waiter was on his way with the second course. "Sir!" he called out to Rudy. "Lunch is ready."

Rudy ignored him and walked out of the restaurant.

31

Rudy stormed through the living room, fuming, and almost tripped over a cushion on the floor. He kicked it savagely, propelling it across the room. The memory of Bridget's stunning beauty lingered and intensified his rage, yet at the same time, it ignited a flaming lust inside him. If only he could have gotten hold of her; he swore to God, he would rough her up and abuse her right there on the floor; punish her until she yelled and screamed for mercy. He sat abruptly on the floor and leaned wearily against a chair. The more incensed he became with Bridget, the more he felt attached to her. It was a strange masochistic obsession that puzzled him. Even more perplexing was how he'd felt when Bridget suggested that he leave the island. Automatically the thought came to him, *will I lose her?*

Although he couldn't stop thinking of Olive and despite his determination to seek justice for her, if only for the sake of his conscience, Rudy realized that every step he took in that direction put him at odds with Bridget, and it was putting a strain on their relationship. Her sycophantic attachment to Bill Thompson was another problem. It was the main reason he had walked out on them.

Sitting in their presence, knowing how sympathetic Bridget was to Thompson and his son, had really pissed him off, considering that it was his ass on the line; the same one who had been there for her, consoling and comforting her back in England when they first met. The same Rudy Phillips she had encouraged to put his life on hold to come and be with her. Never in his life had he met such a complex woman like Bridget. She seemed to grow more baffling by the day.

Rudy pushed off the chair and stood up. His mind returned to the real reason he'd returned to the house from the beach where he'd spent the last half hour trying to cool off his head after leaving the restaurant. He was expecting an email from Amin. Earlier in the morning, before he left, he'd emailed Amin to update him on Oscar's revelations. He had also telephoned Amanda to inform her as well but more so to hear the sound of her voice. Their conversation was brief because she had been on the way out but she promised to call him later.

Rudy had also asked Amin if he could help him establish the veracity of Oscar's claims by tracing the supposed hacker to see if it linked back directly to Larry Thompson. He also wanted to know how much Amin knew about Larry and whether they were friends. For some reason, Aaron had been reluctant to talk about him and merely told Rudy that growing up, Larry had always been a problem kid with a rebellious streak. According to him, of late he'd had some problems with substance abuse but he didn't go into details. Aaron's reticence had annoyed Rudy but, at the same time, he deduced that he and the Thompsons were close, and he sensed that Aaron didn't want to seem disloyal. He decided not to press him further.

He went to his room and turned on his laptop to check his emails. There was none yet from Amin. He felt slightly disappointed. On impulse, he decided to check his other email accounts. He glanced over the Facebook notifications which were piling up in his Yahoo inbox. He had only checked them twice since arriving on the island. He simply hadn't the time or the inclination. As he was about to scroll past the notifications, one caught his eye. It was a message from Facebook informing him that he had recently changed his password. He pondered over this for a moment. He couldn't recall changing his password, certainly not in the past year. He frowned as he read the rest of the email, which cautioned him that he may have been the victim of a phishing scam and directed him to click on a link to regain control of his account. He immediately tried to log into his account with his original password but he couldn't get in. He tried again twice, to no avail. He followed the Facebook instructions to change the password and in five minutes he was able to regain access to his account.

He returned to scrolling through his other Facebook messages. One of them caught his attention. It was a personal message from a friend named Jenny based in England. It said, 'What the fuck were you thinking posting this, are you nuts!' It was sent twenty-four hours ago. He hadn't posted anything on Facebook in over two months. He resumed scrolling up the page and then he froze.

Uploaded unto it was a large glossy photo of Olive's body. It wasn't covered with the sheet as he'd found her. She lay with the lower half of her body from the waist down, naked and exposed, and her legs spread-eagled. The stab wound in the side of her back was clearly visible and etched with blood. Mercifully, the image didn't reveal the most revolting part; the broomstick shoved up her vagina, evidently because it had been inserted at some point after she died. The picture had been posted in his name. Beneath it was the caption 'Courtesy Google Nexus 5.'

Rudy felt a sick churning in the pit of his stomach. Bile rose in his throat and he felt like he was going to puke. He lurched out of the chair, knocking it over and rushed to the bathroom. He barely made it through the door when he began throwing up. He collapsed unto his knees and retched violently. He almost passed out. For about five minutes he remained on all fours emptying his guts. Eventually he tried to get up off the floor and careened across the bathroom. He managed to sit on the edge of the bathtub. It took a few more minutes for him to get his wind back. Struggling to his feet, he walked shakily to the broom closet and forced himself to clean up the foul-smelling mess.

Slowly, as his mind cleared, the terrifying thought hit him that some, if not all, of his Facebook friends would have already seen the picture. It galvanized him into action.

Stumbling back to the bedroom, he faced his laptop, trembling, as if the thought of touching it horrified him. He had to muster all his strength and willpower to look at the photo again. He focused on the date of the posting. It had been uploaded two days ago. He gazed further down at the comments and got another shock. There was an outpouring of rage on the page as many of the commenters voiced their shock and outrage at the photo. Several of them asked Rudy how he could have had the heart to post it on Facebook. Two of them attacked him with a barrage of expletives. Another wondered if his brain had been fried by the Caribbean sun.

Rudy quickly deleted the photo, his hand trembling. Forcing himself to concentrate, he posted a note apologizing for the image and explained that his Facebook account had been hacked. He logged out quickly on realizing that three of his friends were logged in. The last thing he needed was to have them question him about the photo. He hurriedly checked his Linkedin, Twitter and other email accounts, hoping to God that that they hadn't also been hacked. There was nothing amiss. He breathed a sigh of relief.

How and by whom was the picture taken? In his desperation to get rid of it, Rudy never gave a thought to its origin.

Its source was as obvious as it was revolting.

After butchering Olive, the murderer had cold bloodedly taken a snapshot of the body with the malicious intent of further demeaning Olive and to taunt him.

And the caption beneath the photo; *Courtesy Google Nexus 5.*

Olive had owned a Google Nexus 5 smartphone given to her by her brother who worked on the cruise ship. It had been, for her, a source of pride and joy. From what Rudy's lawyer had told him the last time they spoke, after he left Aaron's home, the police had not found any trace of the phone. Could Olive's body have been photographed with the very same phone? If so, it could mean only one thing; the phone was quite likely still in the killer's possession.

As he sat gazing at the computer and mulling over his thoughts, Rudy noticed something strange. The cursor was moving to and fro across the screen, seemingly with a life of its own, although his hand was nowhere near the mouse. Suddenly the CD drive opened. Within seconds, the three web browsers he had opened closed one after the other. After that, nothing else happened and everything seemed normal. Rudy immediately realized that someone had hacked into his computer and was playing around with him.

He shut his eyes and, once again, he felt a wave of nausea. This time he managed to control it.

A slow-burning rage erupted inside him.

He never felt so violated and demeaned. It made him feel helpless and vulnerable because he had no way of retaliating or fighting back. He was at the mercy of a faceless, sadistic coward – someone who was obviously out to humiliate and destroy him, for whatever reason. The more he thought about it, the more enraged he became.

The doorbell rang.

Rudy was so upset, it took two more rings before it registered that there was someone at the door. He went to open it, scowling. "Amin!" he said, surprised. "I wasn't expecting you."

"I thought I'd take a chance and pop over instead of emailing you. I hope it's okay."

"Sure!" Rudy opened the door wider. "Please come in."

Amin entered and stood in the middle of the room looking a bit uncomfortable. He wore a dark, short-sleeve button-down shirt, slim-fit jeans and high lace-up boots, and he had a haversack on his back, which gave him a nerdy look. He looked slimmer and frailer than Rudy remembered him.

"Can I get you anything?"

"No thank you. I won't be long. I've got to join Mom and Petal at the marina in the next hour and a half." Amin peered curiously at Rudy. "You look strange, as if you've just seen a ghost. Are you alright?"

"I guess so ... Well actually, not quite." Rudy flopped down wearily on a chair. He told Amin about the photo he had just found on his Facebook page and the remote interference in his computer. "It's not surprising to me that someone would hack into my Facebook account. I know this happens to lots of people. But I imagine you'd have to be fairly knowledgeable about the victim to correctly answer Facebook's security questions and have them send you a code to change the person's password, which I know is how it's usually done."

Amin gave Rudy a condescending smile like a father amused at his son's naïveté. "Hacking into Facebook accounts has become a sport. There are tons of websites that show you how it's done and how to hack Facebbook passwords, including one that advertises itself as the 'Number One place for Facebook password hacking.' It even offers video demonstrations. That's kids' stuff. Once the hacker knows your email address, which I'm sure is not difficult to find with you being a journalist, and through your other online profiles, they have a good shot at guessing your answers to the security questions.

"As for hacking into your computer, I can do it easily by installing a Remote Access Trojan or RAT and using it to gain access any time. It will listen on a UDP or TCP port and wait for you to connect and go online. Once you're connected, I have full access to your computer and I can access files, programs, even your webcam."

Rudy shook his head defeatedly. "The more I learn about all this stuff, the more I realize that we are truly caught up in a matrix that disempowers us and makes us vulnerable in so many ways."

"It's not as bad as it looks. All you need to do is try and understand the ins and outs of the matrix and how it works. The problem is most of us couldn't be bothered."

"It's one thing to worry about being hacked, but it's a hell of a thing when it actually happens to you. It's like being raped. I've never felt more violated in my life!"

"Can I have a look at your computer?" said Amin.

"Sure, come on."

Amin followed Rudy into the bedroom. Tossing his haversack on the bed, he pulled the chair and settled in front of the laptop, studying it carefully.

"Ha!" he exclaimed and laughed. "The hacker is still connected. In order to track him I'm going to download a program from the net and save it to your hard drive. It's called TCPView. It'll help me see the hacker's IP address and their approximate geographic location. If I'm lucky, I might even be able to get the login names from their computer and clues from their host names."

Rudy watched in amazement as Amin set about tracking the intruder. He went through the process nimbly, working at astounding speed and with intense concentration. Rudy actually felt relieved watching him, and for the first time in weeks he sensed that he was getting somewhere.

He quietly drew away and sat on the bed brooding over the day's events and all that had transpired over the past few days.

Time slid by.

"I've got him!" Amin shouted. He startled Rudy who had been lost in thought. Rudy sprang up from the bed and rushed to peer over Amin's shoulder. "It took me less than fifteen minutes," Amin said proudly. "It looks like your suspicions were right. Larry Thompson is the hacker or at least whoever it is, is using his computer and IP address. The person's location is Saint Lucia. My guess is on the mainland. It turned out to be a bit easier than I expected. Larry didn't try very hard to conceal his identity or maybe he doesn't know how. All the clues point to him."

"Son of a bitch!" Rudy let out a squeal of delight. He practically hoisted Amin from the chair and gave him a huge bear hug. Amin grinned sheepishly and bore it.

"Thank you, little brother!" Rudy gushed. "I thank you from the bottom of my heart. You're a Godsend. Finally I seem to be making headway and it's all thanks to you."

"I'm going to save the information but not on your laptop. I'll email it to myself and later store it in the cloud. That way you can access it from anywhere. You can then make a report to the internet service provider and also the cops." Amin returned to the computer to email the information.

As soon as he was finished, his phone rang. He glanced at the number on the screen. "Hi Mom," he said and turned off the laptop. "I won't be late. I'm on my way." turning to Rudy, he said, "Got to go now."

Rudy thanked him again and escorted him to the door. They exchanged a high five and Amin took off on a bike, which he had come with.

Back indoors, Rudy collapsed unto the sofa and quietly savored what seemed like a small flicker of hope in what was turning out to be a bruising rite of passage. His moment of exhilaration didn't last long however, as he was soon back to brooding over his predicament and trying to determine his next course of action.

For some reason he felt extremely tense and he was having difficulty thinking clearly. He knew he was prone to panic attacks when under serious pressure and it was happening to him again. He resisted the urge to swear. He needed a spliff. Whenever his nerves started acting up, weed usually helped.

He got up and went to the bedroom to get some. As he opened the door he blurted out "Oh fuck!" He suddenly recalled he had smoked the last bit the night before. "When it fucking rains, it pours," he muttered in frustration.

To get some more cannabis he'd have to go all the way to Kadija's place, which he didn't relish doing. With his nerves so frayed, the last thing he needed was a rendezvous with a kook like Kadija, or to get into an emotional tussle with her. He was in no mood for it. But he had no choice; he desperately needed a smoke. This was one time he couldn't do without it.

Shrugging, he went to the bathroom to freshen up and to get ready to leave.

32

No sooner he reached Kadija's home, Rudy's heart sank. Her vehicle was not in the garage and her studio was shut. He found this odd since it was Thursday and Kadija had told him that she normally took Wednesday and Thursday off to relax at home and find inspiration and reconnect with her inner self. Except for the euphonious trilling of the birds, everywhere was quiet. The giant ficus tree still hovered over the house and seemed to embrace it even tighter in its branches, as if it was guarding Kadija's home jealously and was fearful of being replaced by a rival. Not even the wind seemed able to penetrate its canopy. Around the yard fruit trees bowed in its awesome presence, and the birds flitted playfully amongst its branches, tweeting and chirping, as if showing off.

Rudy parked the bike and climbed the steps, unwilling to accept that he had wasted his time and energy travelling nearly two miles for nothing. Glancing around the verandah, he noticed that all the jalousie windows were shut. He called out but no one answered. He checked the door. It was unlocked. Pushing it open, he stepped in. The living room was painted a bright shade of blue, reminiscent of the sea, and it looked reasonably spacious. The decor was cool and relaxing, and reflective of the Caribbean predilection for a mixture of furnishing styles in a single room. Campeche chairs and a wicker chaise lounge were coupled with a coffee table with ornate carvings, a bookcase and a white couch decorated with throw pillows sporting hibiscus, seashell and starfish motifs. Jute rugs lay under the chairs. A mixture of abstract and landscape paintings hung on the walls and green plants flourished in pots all around the room.

Rudy heard the sound of someone sobbing. It sounded like a woman and it was coming from one of the rooms lower down the corridor. He listened carefully but couldn't distinguish the voice. He speculated that it might be one of Kadija's girlfriends since she had admitted to being bisexual the last time he visited her home. He figured he should withdraw and respect the person's privacy but his curiosity got the better of him.

He rapped his knuckles against the wooden partition and called out again, this time louder. The crying stopped. A tense silence ensued. A door opened at the end of the corridor and a woman stepped out. She was slim with full breasts, broad hips and shapely legs. Short, beige-blonde hair framed her diamond-shaped face. She had radiant blue-grey eyes, kissable Greta Garbo lips and a cute cleft chin that made her look quite captivating. She wore a sheer white blouse and brief shorts and she was barefooted. She gaped at Rudy, surprised.

"Hello," he said, ogling the woman's body.

"Hello," she replied in a fruity voice, so soft it was barely audible.

"I'm sorry to disturb you," Rudy said apologetically, adding, "You look familiar. Have we met before?" The words were barely out of his mouth when he recalled they'd met briefly at the beach picnic he had attended with Aaron. She'd been clinging to a hatchet-faced German dude twice her age who owned a massive luxury yacht. "Ah! I remember, you're Alina."

The woman walked past him without responding. Rudy followed her into the living room. She sat on the chaise lounge and bent low with her elbows on her knees and her hands covering her face.

"Is there anything I can do to help?" said Rudy, sounding concerned.

The woman uncovered her face and fixed him with her bright, absorbing eyes. "Yes," she replied. "Marry me."

Rudy blinked. He sat beside her on the chair. "Actually what I meant was to help ease your burden, not make it more unbearable."

Alina's eyes softened and she gave him a worn smile. "I don't think so," she said, adding, "I remember you ... Aaron's friend." Her English was passable and tinged with a heavy Russian accent.

"If I recall correctly, you are Russian?"

"Yes but I am from Ukraine ... You are from this island, no?"

"Yes, over on the mainland but I was raised in England."

"And you are Rudy."

"Yes ... now that we've got the introductions out of the way, what's the matter? What's troubling you?"

"I saw my mother last night. She came to visit me and beg me to look after Alexei and Anna, my younger brother and sister."

"Where are they and where is your mother?"

"My mother ... she died nine years ago while I was still in school. She visited me last night for the third time. She look so sad."

"What about your brother and sister?"

"I don't know. Seven years ago I left them back in Ukraine. Now I have lost touch with them. I did not mean to. Life was very hard. I wanted to take care of them. In seven years I have not seen or heard of them. I don't even know where they are."

"How old are they?"

"Alexei is twelve and Anna is ten."

"Why haven't you returned to check up on them?"

Once more, Alina burst into tears. "I can't! ... God forgive me but I can't."

"What do you mean you can't? ... Why?"

"I just can't," she sobbed. Jumping out of the chair, she ran across the room and stood in front of an open window overlooking the side of the house.

Rudy went over and placed his hands consolingly over her shoulders. "Don't be upset, things will work out somehow. You must be strong for the children." Gently, he drew her away from the window and back to the couch. Placing his index finger under her chin, he gazed deep into her blue-grey eyes. "Russian women are supposed to be strong. They would enter a house on fire," he whispered softly. His words ignited a spark in Alina and the cloud hanging over her lifted ever so slightly. She managed a partial smile. "Sometimes we are strong in showing our weakness," she said.

"Aside from the children, would you like to tell me exactly what's bothering you?"

"I would just like to wake up some day and feel safe and know that I am free to go wherever I want and do whatever I please ... just for once in my life."

"Why do you feel that you can't?"

"You would not understand."

"Go on, try me."

"Can I rest my head on your shoulder?"

"By all means." Rudy shifted closer to Alina and curled his arm around her. She rested her head against his chest. "I feel safe sitting close to you," she said.

Resting his head against hers, Rudy quietly savored the soothing warmth of her body. He couldn't take his eyes off her legs and her lily-white skin, so smooth and supple it looked like porcelain. Her feet were slightly arched and slender with beautifully tapered toes. They looked incredibly sexy. He had to restrain himself from bending down to kiss them. Alina snuggled up closer and closed her eyes, surrendering completely to the moment.

The front door opened and Kadija walked in. Rudy only realized she was in the house after she shut the door. Alina quickly straightened up and drew away from Rudy.

"What have we here?" said Kadija, staring at both of them.

"Hi," said Rudy. "Sorry, I didn't hear you come in. I hope you don't mind the intrusion."

Kadija ignored him and stood glaring at Alina. "What is the meaning of this?" she demanded. "What do you think you're playing at?"

"I'm sorry, Kadija. Forgive me," said Alina, imploringly. There was fear in her eyes. Kadija's sudden appearance seemed to have traumatized her. Kadija flung her handbag onto the floor and walked up to Alina.

"Do you find Rudy attractive? Do you have the hots for him?"

"Hey! Cool it, Kadija," said Rudy. Once again, Kadija ignored him.

"Answer me, Alina! Would you like to have Rudy fuck you?"

Rudy jumped to his feet. "Come on, cut it out!" he said, grabbing Kadija's arm. "That's enough. What do you think you're doing?"

"Shut the fuck up!" Kadija snapped and shook his arm off. Reaching out, she grabbed hold of Alina's flimsy blouse and ripped it off her, leaving her breasts exposed. "Come on, bitch! Get it all off. What, are you shy? Don't you want to screw a Rastaman!" Kadija took another swipe at Alina and grabbed hold of her shorts.

She pulled hard, and tore open the zipper. Alina screamed and tried to fend her off. Kadija lunged at her and they both landed on the floor. She managed to get a grip on Alina's shorts again and began pulling them off her. Rudy stepped in and yanked her off Alina. Kadija tried pushing past him to get at Alina but Rudy pushed her roughly unto the couch. Alina pulled up her shorts and rushed out of the room into the corridor. She entered one of the bedrooms and slammed the door.

"Start packing your stuff, bitch! You're out of here!" Kadija screamed.

Rudy gaped at her in shock and disbelief. "Are you insane? What on earth has come over you?" He was so angry, his hands were trembling.

Kadija stared at him and laughed. "You've got some nerve! What do you think my home is, a fucking brothel?"

"I came in and found Alina crying. I just wanted to console her, I didn't mean anything by it."

Kadija went to pick up her handbag. She took out a bunch of keys and flung the bag on the couch irritably. "What do you want anyway?" she demanded, glaring at him.

"I need some weed, especially after all that drama."

Kadija walked past him and went to open two louver windows at the front of the house to let in some fresh air. "Follow me," she said curtly and opened the door. Rudy followed her down to her art studio. Unlocking the door, she said, "Can you open up the windows, please?" She went around the side of the house towards the back. Rudy worked his way through the heady smell of spray fixative, oils and paint and around easels, canvases and opened all the louvers. Light flooded the room and transformed it into a canvas of jumbled artistry. A backdoor opened and Kadija emerged carrying a mason jar filled with packets of cannabis and placed it on a work bench. "Knock yourself out," she said and settled into a worn-out drafting chair, her eyes fixed on Rudy.

Rudy sifted through the neatly balled-up packets of weed. He carefully selected two dub bags, opened and sniffed them. He nodded, satisfied. Since he was already familiar with Kadija's prices, he didn't bother to ask. He took out a U.S. fifty-dollar bill from his wallet and placed it under the jar. Tucking the weed into his pocket, he said, "Thanks, I need that."

"Quite desperately too, by the looks of you."

Rudy let it ride. He opened his mouth to say something then paused. He pondered his words carefully then asked, "What's going to become of Alina?"

"What's that got to do with you?"

Looking her straight in the eye, he said, "I'm extremely worried about her safety after seeing the way you treated her."

Kadija laughed. "Wasn't this exactly what got you into trouble? Worrying about the 'safety' of a woman, in this case Olive, and trying to protect her. Haven't you learned your lesson?"

"I beg your pardon? What the hell is that supposed to mean?"

"Never mind. Forget it."

There was a silent moment of tension.

"I guess I'll be heading off," said Rudy.

"So soon, what's the hurry?"

"I wouldn't want to overstay my welcome."

"By the way, how have you been keeping? Is worrying about Olive still keeping you up at night?"

Rudy peered thoughtfully at Kadija. "As a matter of fact, yes it has."

"Are you still a suspect?"

"What kind of a question is that?"

"Just a question ... Are you?"

"I had nothing to do with Olive's death."

"But you're not off the hook yet, are you?" Kadija's focused stare made Rudy uneasy for some reason.

"Does that disappoint you?"

"On the contrary, I can't figure out why you and everybody else are still so grief stricken about that woman's death."

"That's an awful thing to say."

Kadija shrugged. "It's just my opinion ... Do you think the killer will be caught?"

"By God, I hope so! I'll tell you something else. I intend to do whatever it takes to help bring the murderer to justice."

"That's if the killer lets you."

"At least I know whom not to count on if I need words of encouragement." Glancing at his watch, Rudy added, "I better leave, it's getting late."

"Hey Rudy! ..." Rudy paused near the door. Kadija got off the chair and walked up to him. "I hear you're now on Larry Thompson's case. Is that true?"

Rudy glanced sharply at Kadija. She gazed back at him defiantly. "Who told you that?" he demanded.

"I have my sources."

"Is he your friend?"

"What if he is?"

"Is he!"

"Yes."

"Your good friend?"

"Just friends."

"Do you know where he is?"

"Who knows, he's all over the damn place. Why?"

"We have a score to settle."

"A score to settle? With Larry?"

"Yeah."

"Why, what did he do?"

"I thought you had sources. If so, by now they should already have told you."

"Darling, are you sure you know what you're getting yourself into?"

"How do you mean?"

"Larry is not the sort of person you want to fool around with. The same applies to his father."

"Correction, I'm the one who's being fooled around with by your friend ... What exactly are you trying to tell me?"

"I know we don't get along. I also know you despise me. Maybe it's my fault you feel this way about me. I probably deserve it. Still, I'm human, and I'm a woman. It hurts to be rejected. Despite all that, I'd hate to see you get hurt. I wish you'd go. Just pack up and leave this island. Quit letting that Bridget woman and her husband use you. You're being played Rudy. Wake up, open your eyes! Do yourself a favor and get the hell away from these people."

"You wouldn't be telling me this at the behest of your friend, would you?"

"No! Just look into my eyes, look into my soul and you'll know I mean it. I don't want to see you hurt."

"Who's going to hurt me?"

"I have nothing more to say ... It's your life."

"Wow! Aren't we mysterious ... I appreciate your concern but I've said my piece and I stand by it. I want justice for Olive."

Kadija stormed out of the studio, knocking a chair out of the way. She climbed the steps and entered the house without even glancing back.

Outside, Rudy gaped bemusedly at the house, and then slowly made his way to the bike parked at the bottom of the steps. He wasn't quite sure what to make of his exchange with Kadija, particularly her allusion to the Thompsons and her own admitted friendship with Larry Thompson.

What really struck him, although he'd tried not to show it, was when she said she'd heard he was 'now on Larry's case.' Thinking of this so disturbed him, he forgot to mount the bicycle and wheeled it away distractedly.

He regretted not pressing Kadija further. He had let his anger and contempt for her get the better of him. Her outrageous treatment of Alina had really got to him, further exacerbating his growing intolerance of her.

How on earth could she have known that he was unto Larry Thompson? It was only about four hours ago that he'd met with Bridget and Bill Thompson to discuss this. He later discussed it with Amin. He hadn't spoken about it with anyone else since then. His instinct told him the leak could not have come from Amin. He felt certain of that. He paused at the end of the driveway pondering his next step.

He finally came to a decision. It was time to pay Leroy Butcher a visit and lay all his cards on the table, including the taped recording of Oscar's confession. Oscar would inevitably end up in hot water. Rudy felt a twinge of conscience but not enough to make him change his mind.

Following the robbery, he ended up making a fool of himself by letting Bridget dissuade him from reporting it to the police. No way he was going to allow this to happen again, even if she raised hell. Furthermore, no one was going to turn him into a sacrificial lamb to cover some wayward rich kid's ass!

Whatever happened, he had to keep Amin out of it. He was even prepared to lie to the cops if necessary, to ensure that the youth was not dragged into the whole affair. It wasn't just because he wanted to protect Amin; he valued his friendship with Amanda and he didn't want to do anything to jeopardize it. He was all too aware that she had saved him from being detained by the cops when she vouched for his whereabouts on the day of Olive's murder; and that was before they even knew each other. For as long as he lived, he would never forget what she had done for him.

Rudy glanced at his watch. It was half past five. He figured he'd better grab a bite but first he'd have to drop off his weed at the house. Considering all he'd been through, plus the fact that Kadija gave him the creeps, he wasn't prepared to take any chances.

His friend, Zachary, the Australian yachtie who had initially given him directions to Kadija's house, came to mind. If anyone could give him some helpful leads about Larry Thompson's whereabouts, it would be him. They had since met a couple of times for drinks and to shoot the breeze. Zachary was a man with an ear to the ground, and he'd seemed to know quite a lot about the goings-on of Elysian Island's jetsetters.

Rudy mounted the bike and pushed off down the road to Albion Bay.

33

Rudy downed his sixth beer after struggling to finish off his dinner. Halfway through the meal he'd lost his appetite, through no fault of the chef's. He just wasn't in the mood for it. There were several people at the Halcyon Beach Bar and judging by the rising wave of chatter, they were increasing in number. A hi-fi music system was playing reggae in the background. Off and on an emcee intruded to extol Elysian Island's 'amazing beauty and pleasures' in a faux American accent, in a bid to further excite the crowd. Rudy tuned out and ignored the people milling around. His mind was on a telephone conversation he'd had with Zachary earlier.

The yachtie had spent the day out sailing and he was just edging into the harbor when he received Rudy's call. He promised to return the call and did so fifteen minutes later. Rudy gave him a quick rundown of all he had gone through since their last rendezvous, including his latest discovery about Larry Thompson and the youth's father's reaction. "Poor Bill, he's certainly had to put up with a hell of a lot from this kid," Zachary replied, his voice sounding grim.

He said, from what he'd learned about Larry Thompson, he'd gotten himself entangled with some shady elements, including some suspected Columbian drug traffickers with a base somewhere in the town of Soufriere on the island's south-western coast. It was also rumored that they were involved in money laundering, gun running, human trafficking and even internet scams. But then it got worse. Zachary said that back home in America Larry had chalked up a string of fines for speeding, driving under the influence and without a license, even assaulting a police officer. On at least one occasion he was arrested for possession of drugs. "It is my understanding that he has a heroin addiction problem and Bill and Jacquie, bless them, have had to ship him off to rehab several times. They're at their wits end with the lad," Zachary further explained. The eldest of Bill Thompson's three children, his mother was Bill's first wife. He was bounced back and forth between both parents for much of his adolescent years. Zachary was convinced that this had contributed to Larry's rebellious and deviant nature. Word on the ground, according to Zachary, was that lately, he'd been spending more time in Saint Lucia and popped in occasionally to see his family and some of his friends.

At the end of their conversation, Rudy was fuming. He decided he'd have to make a report to the police and confer with Leroy Butcher. At this stage, he didn't have much choice. After all what he'd been through, the thought of sitting back and doing nothing with Larry Thompson cooling out his heels next door in Soufriere, made him sick to his stomach!

He intercepted the same waiter who had served him earlier, and asked him for the bill. He waited impatiently for him to return and left without tipping him.

***

Out in the parking lot Rudy heard someone calling out to him. Turning, he saw Leroy Butcher walking briskly towards him.

He was dressed in plain clothes and carrying what looked like a takeaway meal.

"It's been a while since we've crossed paths. How're you doing?" said Butcher, smiling.

"I'm cool. What a coincidence, I was just thinking about popping in to see you."

"Is that right? What's up?"

"I wish to make a report regarding certain matters that have come up concerning Olive's murder."

"Now that's what I call a dream suspect." Butcher grinned and patted Rudy on the back. "Just kidding ... Why don't we take the weight off our feet," he said, gesturing to his car parked a few yards away. Rudy followed Butcher to the vehicle. He settled in the passenger seat.

"I'm all ears," said Butcher, easing back comfortably.

"I know who broke into the house and stole my necklaces and I've discovered how it was done ... A guy named Oscar is the culprit. He's from the village."

"I know Oscar." Butcher shifted in his seat to stare at Rudy. "How do you know that?"

Rudy told him about the secret IP camera and how he found out that it had been operational all along. Once again, he kept Amin and Amanda out of it. "I've got the video footage of him breaking into the house and I'd like to turn it over to you."

"That's funny, I specifically asked Mrs. Tennyson on the day she informed me about the break-in, whether the house has surveillance cameras. She said it doesn't."

"As I explained a moment ago, I wasn't aware of it until a few days ago. I can't speak for Bridget but I imagine she was being honest if she had assumed at the time that the system was deactivated, which it had apparently been for some time up until I arrived." Rudy could tell Butcher wasn't buying it by the skeptical frown on his face.

"Is Oscar clearly visible in the video?" he asked.

"I was able to identify him by the markings on the trousers he was wearing."

"What?"

"There's red stitching in the shape of a horse on one of the back pockets of the thief's jeans. Oscar has a pair of jeans with identical markings. I've got a photo of him wearing them."

"You must be joking. That's all you've got?"

"I confronted him and he admitted it was him."

Butcher gaped incredulously at Rudy. "Since when have you become a police investigator?" he said, his voice hardening.

"Oscar disclosed the identity of the person who helped him break into the house by hacking into the smart locks," Rudy added, ignoring Butcher's sarcasm.

"And who, pray tell, is that?"

"Larry Thompson ... Bill Thompson's son."

Butcher sat bolt upright. "What are you saying?" he demanded.

"Oscar breaks into the house, he steals my necklaces and these same necklaces end up at the scene of the murder. Larry Thompson starts it off by helping him gain entry into the house. Oscar snatches the necklaces and he says he turned them over to Larry. According to him, that was the last he saw of them."

A duel of stares ensued between Rudy and Butcher. Butcher was the first to break eye contact. Frowning, he pondered for a moment. "That's all very interesting," he said. "There's only one problem?"

"What's that?"

"All I've got is your word for it."

"On the contrary, I have a taped recording of Oscar's confession ... I also have proof that Larry Thompson not only hacked into the security system, he has also been hacking into my personal computer and my email accounts. Today I discovered that someone had remotely posted a gruesome photo of Olive's body to my Facebook page – can you believe it? *My Facebook page*, for God's sake, where all my friends could see it! There was also a caption at the bottom of the photo – 'Courtesy of Google Nexus 5.' Olive's phone was the same model, a clear indication to me that her own phone had been used to take a snapshot of the body. I've been able to trace the hacker and I have the data that connects Larry Thompson to all of these hacking incidents. I would like to turn it over to you along with Oscar's recorded confession."

"My! My! My! You certainly have been busy, Mr. Phillips."

"When would you like me to turn over the evidence?"

"Where is it?"

"At the house."

"There's no point in waiting, then. Let's go over to your place, shall we?"

"Sure."

Both men fastened their seatbelts and Butcher quietly drove off.

34

Back at the house the two men settled down in the quiet comfort of the living room. Butcher had declined Rudy's offer of a drink. He quietly watched as Rudy inserted a USB flash drive into one of the ports on his laptop. "This is a 4GB covert voice recorder and combined memory stick. You can store up to five hours of voice recordings on it," Rudy explained, a tad condescendingly. Butcher said nothing. He spoilt it for Rudy by not looking impressed. Rudy played the recording of Oscar's confession and they listened in rapt silence to Oscar spilling his guts, at some points practically screaming out the details of how Larry Thompson had persuaded him to break into Rudy's home and steal 'something small' belonging to him. There was no mistaking the terror in his voice. Butcher seemed taken aback. He gazed suspiciously at Rudy.

"What the hell did you do to this guy? He sounds terrified, almost as if you were torturing him or holding a gun to his head."

"I just threatened to report him to his grandfather and drag him down to the police station," Rudy said glibly, evading

Butcher's eyes. He'd taken the precaution of deleting the parts with him threatening Oscar. He hurriedly switched to the video clips of the burglar. He then showed Butcher the photos of Oscar wearing the jeans with the stitching on the pocket, and a series of computer screenshots, all of which Amin had stored on a USB flash drive, and he explained to Butcher the process involved in capturing the data. Butcher listened intently and interrupted a few times to ask for clarification. At the end of it all, he looked totally gobsmacked. Rudy was so taken aback by his reaction, he wasn't sure what to say. "You look surprised," was all he could muster.

Butcher peered broodingly at him. "Aren't we missing something?" he said softly.

"What?"

"Your Facebook page with the photo of Olive's body. Where's the screenshot of that?"

"Oh shit .... I don't have one."

"Why not?"

"This had me so rattled, all I could think of was getting rid of it."

"You didn't even save the photo?"

"No!"

"I thought you said you're a journalist."

"I told you man, in my shock I deleted it! I wasn't thinking straight," Rudy snapped. He felt embarrassed.

"I'm extremely disturbed by all this; for more reasons than you could possibly imagine," said Butcher, a bleak look on his face.

"What do you mean?"

"You've made some very serious allegations that are definitely worth looking into. With regards to tracing the hacker, was that your handiwork?"

"I did it with some coaching from a friend."

"Who is that friend?"

"He's in the UK," Rudy replied without hesitation. He'd prepared himself for that one. Butcher gave him a hard stare but said nothing. He scooped up the USB voice recorder and the flash drive with the video clips and screen shots and dropped them in his pocket. "I expect you to come down to the police station tomorrow morning bright and early to give a statement."

"Yes, of course. Where do we go from there?" Rudy leaned forward eagerly.

"My men and I will go through the evidence thoroughly and bring Oscar in for questioning. He will quite likely be detained."

"What about Larry Thompson?"

"What about him?"

"Aren't you going to bring him in for questioning too?"

"We'll consider that as well."

"Consider it? What do you mean consider it? The guy is tied up in Olive's murder. For all we know, he could be the killer!"

"Let's not jump the gun. At the moment, all we have is Oscar's word, which only implicates Thompson in the robbery of the necklaces. What if Thompson denies any involvement in it? Assuming he does, are there any witnesses to corroborate Oscar's allegations?"

"What about Thompson's hacking spree? The guy has been blatantly hacking into my computer, screwing around with my Facebook account, spying on my emails, and let's not forget the smart locks were also compromised! Are you going to ignore all that?"

"That's a different matter. In fact, let me be straight with you. I don't expect to make much headway with it."

"Why not?"

Butcher sighed like someone with a heavy weight on his shoulders. "You're assuming that Larry Thompson is the hacker but so far, all it appears that you have established is a connection between the hacker and Thompson's IP address. Nevertheless, let's assume he is the perpetrator. Any attempt on the part of the police to tackle cyber-crime in this part of the world is a lost cause as far as prosecution is concerned."

"I don't understand."

"You and I have one thing in common; we tend to forget that we're not in Britain. Neither the Royal St Lucia Police Force nor the government of Saint Lucia have the financial, technical or human resources required to combat cybercrime. I am putting this to you in your capacity as a journalist. Perhaps it's something you may wish to follow up. When it comes to dealing with cybercrime and cyber-security issues, Saint Lucia and the other English-speaking islands of the Caribbean are light years behind the UK and other parts of the developed world. They have no laws or legal framework to address it. The few people in the public service who would be charged with the responsibility of drafting appropriate legislation have virtually no expertise in this area and don't have a clue how to go about it. What this means is that, as far as Larry Thompson is concerned, any attempt on my part to investigate or prosecute him would be a waste of time – or as they say in the Caribbean, it's like 'spinning top in mud.'"

Rudy looked dumbfounded, as if he couldn't believe his ears. "Are you saying that everyone on this island is at the mercy of these criminals?"

"Insofar as investigating and prosecuting the bad guys, I'm afraid so. In fact, it's worse than that. We have received intelligence over the years from Europol and the FBI indicating that revenues generated from cyber-crime, now estimated at over one trillion US dollars, have superseded that generated from drug trafficking. The Caribbean is viewed as easy pickings and is currently being targeted by the criminals.

"We have reason to believe that on a daily basis there are thousands of cyber attacks and infiltrations being perpetrated against both the public and private sectors, and the bulk of them go undetected or they're covered up. Most of these attacks are being perpetrated by international organized criminal gangs. But here's the scariest part. Are you familiar with the term 'Advanced Persistent Threat or APT?"

"No."

"An APT is a network attack in which a hacker infiltrates a computer network and sits there for a lengthy period of time undetected, sometimes years. Usually the hacker's aim is to steal data rather than cause damage to the network. APT attacks usually target organizations with high-value or potentially lucrative information such as from banks and government institutions. This is the kind of dilemma that we're faced with yet there's not a damned thing that the police or the governments can do about it!"

"So the likes of Larry Thompson can simply walk away and continue violating and attacking other innocent people with impunity."

"Precisely."

"And it doesn't matter if the information gleaned from tracing his online activities links him to Olive's murder."

"As evidence, I don't believe it would hold up in court."

"Bloody hell! I can't believe this. What you're saying to me in effect, is that all the home and business owners on Elysian island are practically sitting ducks, completely vulnerable to cyber-criminals who quite likely view them as soft targets."

"Pretty much, unless they're able to protect themselves with the very best technical and security controls and systems, such as firewalls and antispyware but even the best systems are not impenetrable. God knows how much I have stressed this point to Bill Thompson and the other Elysian Island Company directors in the hope they would use their considerable influence to nudge the government into addressing the problem. But time and again the response is the same; they agree that there's an urgent need for appropriate legislation and the implementation of information security best practices and standards, and then they simply go on to blame government bureaucracy for the lack of action and wash their hands of the problem."

Rudy rolled his eyes and shook his head defeatedly. Butcher stood up. "I guess I'll be heading off. It's been a very enlightening evening."

Rudy got up and they shook hands. He walked Butcher to the door. "Just to be sure," said Butcher, holding up the USB flash drive. "Is everything stored on this?"

"Definitely," Rudy replied.

"Good. I look forward to seeing you tomorrow. Bon soir." Butcher headed towards his car.

Rudy shut the door and returned disconsolately to the living room. He began pacing agitatedly. He recalled his vitriolic exchange with Bridget at Blossom House, and her near hysterical reaction when she discovered that the ingrate on whom she had bestowed her favor and largesse had had the audacity to go probing into the circumstances of Olive's murder without consulting her.

He recalled how, from the outset, she had insisted that he keep the police out of it. She sought to discourage him even more when she realized that he had uncovered evidence that could potentially implicate the son of Bill Thompson, the all-powerful CEO of the Elysian Island Company and her trusted confidante and business partner; and, for all he knew, much more than that!

She was obviously being driven more by panic than concern. She had been just as rattled when she found out belatedly that one of the main reasons he had come to Elysian Island was to help Edward write his memoir.

In light of Leroy Butcher's startling revelations, Rudy was now beginning to wonder if there might be a lot more to Olive's murder and the mysterious circumstances surrounding it. What exactly were Bridget and Thompson trying so hard to cover up, aside from the evident vulnerability of the homeowners' high-priced security systems? For sure, if more of them were found to have been compromised, it could cause a colossal stink among the island's elites, folks who seemed to value their privacy more than life itself. It would also be a great embarrassment to Thompson and his cohorts.

Memories of romance-filled evenings with Bridget back in England and her sweet protestations of love for him, flooded into Rudy's mind. He recalled that glorious stolen moment when the two of them went sailing and how, like star-struck children, they had watched in fascination as dolphins swam and cavorted all around them; and then that moment when they made passionate love out in the open, under the stars.

Since then, Bridget became even more irresistible, to the point that he actually started believing that something good could come out of their precarious relationship, although the odds seemed to be stacked against it. *Who knows, maybe the two of us could end up getting married; after all, her marriage is clearly doomed*, he'd thought to himself. That was how ridiculously smitten he had become – like a fucking teenage schoolboy.

All of a sudden, everything seemed to have crumbled under the weight of Rudy's growing impatience with Bridget's entrepreneurial obsessions. For the life of him, he just couldn't figure out how she could be so driven by ambition that she would stoop to the level of helping to shield a criminal son-of-a-bitch like Larry Thompson; even at the risk of offending the man she claimed to adore, and destroying their relationship. Like a true mercenary, she had proved over and over again that she would not let anything or anyone get in her way, not even her own husband.

Now that Butcher had explained the obstacles he would have to confront if he tried to pursue an investigation of Larry Thompson, Rudy knew without a doubt what he had to do. Reaching for his cell phone, he called Aaron. When Aaron responded, he said, "What are your plans for the next few days?" He listened anxiously to Aaron's reply then exclaimed, "Damn!" Aaron was not on the island. He had gone on a sailing trip to nearby Martinique. At the moment he was actually out on the high seas. Aaron's voice began to fluctuate due to a deterioration of the call signal. Rudy switched on his phone's loudspeaker. "Can you hear me?" he said.

"Yes but barely ... What's wrong?" Aaron called out over the sound of flapping sails and raised voices.

"I'm heading off to Soufriere. I was wondering if you'd care to tag along for the adventure."

"What the devil are you going to do over there?" Aaron demanded.

"I'm going on the hunt for Larry Thompson."

"What! Have you lost your mind? Why would you want to do that?"

"We've got business to discuss. He's been fucking with me and I've had it! I'm going after him."

"Easy mate, don't do anything rash. Hang on a bit and let's discuss this, shall we?"

"Meet me in Soufriere and then we'll talk."

"Wait ..." Aaron's voice trailed off and Rudy's phone suddenly went dead. The call dropped. He redialed Aaron's number but got no connection. He tried again twice, then gave up.

35

It was just past 2:00 p.m. when Rudy arrived at the foot of the hill leading to the five-star Anse Chastenet Resort in Soufriere, aboard a taxicab. The driver, a brittle-looking man named Ras Isley with copious dreadlocks bunched up in a woolly cap, and a craggy face that looked like it had been chiseled from granite, warned Rudy to brace himself as he began driving up the serpentine hill to the hotel. He negotiated the twists and turns with practiced ease, unperturbed by the prospect of plunging over the edge of the steep cliff. Glancing across, he saw Rudy gaping popeyed at the precipice. "That's a hell of a road, eh?" he said, grinning. Rudy felt safe with him, not just because of his judicious driving; Isley had served as his taxi driver once before. During his last visit to Saint Lucia four years ago, it was Ras Isley who had transported him from the airport to his hotel. Thereafter, Isley virtually became his chauffeur, taking him all over the island and introducing him to some great dining and entertainment spots, and the various historical sites, some of which he'd never had the opportunity to experience.

Rudy was pleasantly surprised to discover that Isley was still in the taxi business. They ran into each other purely by chance in the northern coastal town of Gros Islet, at the Rodney Bay Marina, Saint Lucia's largest privately owned anchorage. Isley normally operated from the airport but he had gone there to drop off a visitor.

Rudy had travelled to the mainland aboard the Elysian Island ferry soon after leaving the police station where he provided a written statement after patiently fielding almost half an hour of mostly inane questions from a bored-looking police officer. He left without informing anyone, including Bridget, and took the ferry without igniting anybody's curiosity. Initially he'd felt uneasy but at the dock no one took notice of him, not even the sole immigration officer who had been too busy chatting up two young, attractive American women to pay him much attention.

Ras Isley negotiated another sharp turn with a flourish. "We almost there," he said, reassuringly. A cheerful and loquacious character, despite his grizzled look, he paused his chatter to concentrate on the climb up to the hotel. All along he had been chatting away with gusto, partly because he was happy to see Rudy. From musing over the struggles of daily life on the island, he engaged Rudy in a vigorous debate about international politics. Then the conversation switched to Soufriere and Isley explained how the town was poised to become one of the hottest and most upscale touristic spots on the island. He rattled off the names of several A-list celebrities who had lately discovered Saint Lucia, including Morgan Freeman, Nicholas Cage, Stephen Segal, John Malkovich, the late Amy Winehouse, Eddie Murphy, and Oprah Winfrey who had assured the world, after visiting the island, that its twin mountain peaks, the Pitons in Soufriere 'are one of the top five places to see before you leave this great place called earth.'

At that point, as they came within sight of the town, Rudy began quizzing Isley about underground activities in the south of the island to see if he had inside knowledge of criminal gangs and the drugs scene in Soufriere. He gave the impression that he was asking purely out of journalistic curiosity. Isley said he wasn't familiar with the movements of the criminal underworld in the south, unlike the capital, Castries, his hometown. However, he offered to put Rudy in touch with a good friend of his who did; an ex-cop named Tyrone who used to work with the local police force. "I'll call him and tell him to expect you," he said. He gave Rudy the man's contact number, which Rudy immediately stored in his phone.

The taxi crested the top of the hill and came to a stop outside the resort. Rudy stepped out of the car and gazed in awe at the sprawling, multi-tiered structure perched on a ridge overlooking the island's western coast and the Caribbean Sea. From where he stood, the hotel seemed to sprout out of the lush-green womb of Soufriere, as if it was an offshoot of nature and part of the surrounding ocean of greenery. The rooms, many of them partially open to the elements included white gingerbread cottages and self-contained suites, all seeming to blend with the surroundings. Encompassing the property were several hundred acres teeming with dense forests, verdant foliage and flower-decked hillsides. On the west it was bordered by two separate bays blessed with black and golden-sand beaches. A long flight of concrete steps led from the hotel down to one of the beaches. Further away, overlooking the south-western coast, the Pitons stood guard over the approach to Soufriere like jealous gods. Towering over the town, they wore splendorous frondescent robes and crowns of swirling, cottony clouds.

Isley jumped out of the car and went to get Rudy's suitcase from the boot. Rudy handed him a hundred pound note and told him to keep the change. Isley gaped at the bill as if he couldn't believe his eyes. He beamed at Rudy. "Thank you, my brother," he gushed. "Jah bless!" They embraced each other warmly. Isley hopped back into the vehicle and drove off.

Rudy headed into the hotel lobby. A pretty young receptionist welcomed him with a sunny smile. Within fifteen minutes he was checked into one of the resort's Hillside Deluxe rooms. It was quite spacious with wood louver walls, an open-room dormer that allowed for natural airflow, and a balcony that afforded a panoramic view of the sea. Rudy went through the room, marveling at its luxurious features, including the exotic hardwood flooring, a plush king-size bed and an ensuite bathroom. He felt satisfied that he had made a good choice.

He had originally planned to put up at a small guest house he'd discovered after Googling hotel listings for Soufriere. He'd wanted somewhere easily accessible but away from the town centre, in beautiful natural surroundings. When he mentioned this to Isley, the Rastaman promptly suggested the Anse Chastenet. "If you're a man who believe in living in harmony with nature, that's the place for you," he said emphatically. He then went on to tell Rudy about the hotel's 'eco-friendly' design and open-air tree house restaurants offering 'whole-ton different menus' of every kind, including vegetarian fare. He sounded so much like a salesman Rudy couldn't help wondering what was in it for him if he took Isley's advice. He'd thought to ask him but then changed his mind. He didn't want to offend him. Along the way he did a Google search of the hotel on his iPhone and he was impressed with what he saw. He called to make a reservation, with Isley nodding his approval and grinning from ear to ear.

Rudy lifted his suitcase and tossed it unto the bed. As he began to unpack it, his phone rang. Bridget's office landline number appeared on the touchscreen. "What the hell are you doing in Soufriere?" she demanded as soon as Rudy responded. Her voice came through stridently, as if Rudy had put her on speakerphone. He knew that by sneaking off he would have pissed her off, and annoyed Edward as well, but he couldn't give a damn. The exasperation in her voice actually gave him pleasure, and because she was in no position to do anything about it, that made it even sweeter. Bridget lambasted him for several minutes after disclosing that she had learned of his whereabouts from Aaron. He listened to her quietly, with a dastardly grin. She demanded to know where he was staying and said she hoped he wasn't fooling around with any slut. He was deliberately noncommittal, further infuriating her.

When she was through haranguing him, Rudy reiterated his intention to uncover the mystery surrounding Olive's murder and bring her killer to justice, especially if it was Larry Thompson. There was a deafening silence at the other end of the line, then Bridget slammed the phone down, making Rudy wince. The abrupt end of the call had a disconcerting finality to it and it tempered Rudy's smugness.

Gazing around at the plushness of the room, he pondered the irony of the fact that it was Bridget herself who had made it possible for him to enjoy such luxury. He was paying for it with a credit card she had given him as a gift before he left for Elysian Island. It had a credit limit of three thousand US dollars. Up until now he had been reluctant to use it. Without it, there was no way he would have been able to afford such lavish accommodation.

What he planned to do next was hire a vehicle, since he would need one to move around Soufriere. He decided to try and contact the chap Isley had suggested. That way he could start off his manhunt first thing in the morning. His aim was to try and track down Larry Thompson as quickly and inconspicuously as possible. He had no illusions about the risks he was facing and the danger he could be putting himself into. However, his mind was made up. There could be no turning back now.

There was no question that he was nervous but inside him a vengeful spirit kept urging him to stay the course and not back off. It ruthlessly overrode any inclination on his part to think rationally. Off and on pragmatism reared its head and in its cold voice of logic it would goad him to reconsider; w*hy not do what any logical thinking man would do? You've given Butcher enough to work with, let the fucker battle it out and spare yourself further grief. Just walk away from this whole crazy affair.*

Maybe it was just his ego or perhaps the thrill of the chase and the adrenaline rush he got from it. On the other hand, maybe it was because deep inside he knew he would never be able to exorcise Olive's ghost, nor would he be able to deal with the pain of her death and the reality of being tied up in it unless he knew for sure that her killer had been found and brought to justice.

Perhaps too, it was personal – a burning desire for revenge and to get even with his tormentor.

Whatever the cause, Rudy knew that he had to go through with it. His soul demanded it.

36

A Hyundai Accent was in the hotel parking lot waiting for Rudy when he went down to the lobby at 9:00 a.m. The hotel had arranged for its delivery from a local rental car company. He collected the keys from the receptionist and took off for his rendezvous with the man Ras Isley had recommended. He'd managed to get hold of him and they agreed to meet at the Soufriere Waterfront Park, near the harbor

Along the way, Rudy stopped at a fuel station to fill up his gas tank then decided to take a slow ride through the town centre, for old times' sake. To his disappointment, not much had changed. It almost seemed like the town had been caught in a time warp. It still had the same narrow, maze-like streets and cramped sidewalks lined with Creole cottages and cinder-block houses, all squelched together, several of them rickety and aged. A few of them stood in the overbearing shadow of French Colonial townhouses, some of them feeble and decrepit and dating back to the mid-19th century. In the midst of this uneasy milieu, modern commercial buildings stuck out incongruously. Cars and trucks drove by within inches of each other, and pedestrians walked past and in between them, unperturbed. What struck Rudy the most was that the town seemed smaller than he remembered it, as if it had shrunk.

He soon came to the town square, a neat grassy space erected in the 18th century by Soufriere's original French inhabitants. As the traffic slowed to a crawl, Rudy caught sight of a stone monument inside the square denoting the notorious site of a guillotine where many lost their heads, including several aristocrats and planters, during the dark days of the French Revolution. It still made him feel squeamish.

A strong sulphuric odor filled the air, emanating from the Sulphur Springs high up in the mountains, the site of a volcanic crater with warm bubbling pools and hot springs spewing sulphur-laden steam. The smell stirred up more of Rudy's childhood memories, including bathing in the pools reputed for their soothing and curative properties.

He drove on towards the harbor, a jumble of jetties and berths where local fishing boats and canoes docked cheek-by-jowl with yachts, sailboats and tourist party-boats. Along the waterfront was a fish market and a roadside fruit and vegetable market, the latter spilling unto the nearby streets. It looked as if all of it had sprouted organically and haphazardly, rather than according to plan.

Further along was the Soufriere Waterfront Park, a public garden and promenade hemmed in by a seawall. It was cast with paving slabs and lined with street lamps and trees in concrete planters. The park afforded a spectacular view of the bay and sailboats cruising the waters, as well as boats heading in and out of the harbor. A small art-and-craft centre located right next to the park peddled a variety of handmade furniture, clay pots, wood carvings and straw items. Rudy saw a man standing next to it, waving at him. He drove closer to him and parked at the side of the road, behind a rundown cab pickup. Stepping out, he walked across to him.

"You're Rudy," the man said, extending his hand.

"Yes, I am," Rudy replied.

"Welcome," the man said, smiling. "I'm Tyrone but you can call me Trini. Most folks do." He spoke with a slight Trinidadian accent. He looked clean cut and well-proportioned with an athletic build and a ruggedly handsome face with a broad forehead and high cheekbones, and he had a personable air about him.

"Thanks for coming, I appreciate it," said Rudy. He noted the way Trini checked him out from head to toe, like a cop appraising a suspect.

"Let's go cool out over there," said Trini, pointing to a stone bench a few feet away. They went and sat down. "Isley pretty much twisted my arm to make sure I helped you out with information for some story he said you're working on. I'm a man of my word, plus I owe him one, so there was no way out for me," Trini said, grinning. "He seems to think highly of you."

"We're good buddies and he's a cool guy, that's for sure."

"So ... what is it you want to know?"

"First off, you're not a St. Lucian, are you? You don't sound like one."

"I was born in Trinidad but my father was St. Lucian. I moved over here about ten years ago."

"Isley tells me you're an ex-cop."

"I'm an ex-detective. I migrated to the US at the age of thirteen and on leaving college I worked with the US Drug Enforcement Agency for fifteen years before returning home to Trinidad. There I worked as a detective with the Trinidad & Tobago Police Service for ten years. I then moved to Saint Lucia and joined the police force and served as a superintendant up until four years ago. I decided I'd had enough and bought a ten-acre plot here in Soufriere and switched to farming. "

Trini's revelations about his background surprised Rudy. He reflected a while and said, "I've got to be straight with you. I'm not working on a story. I'm investigating a murder. Recently, a young woman was murdered next door on Elysian Island. I've been there for the past few weeks. The killer found a way to pin the murder on me and almost got away with it. I think I know who did it and I've been reliably informed that he's somewhere in Soufriere. I came here to search for him."

Trini gaped incredulously at Rudy. "Who the hell are you, James Bond? ... And did I hear you right - you've been staying on Elysian Island, playground of the rich and famous?"

"Yeah."

"The gods must have smiled on you. What happened, did you win the lottery?"

Rudy smiled. "No such luck, I'm afraid. Maybe I should back up a bit and tell you the whole story and a bit about myself."

"Good idea, I think you should."

Rudy told Trini about his life and background and explained why he'd gone to Elysian Island, carefully avoiding any allusion to his closeness with Bridget. He then gave him a quick rundown of the ordeal he'd been through since Olive's death.

Trini looked quite intrigued. "Vernon Allain, is he still out there?"

"Yeah, he's Edward Tennyson's personal assistant. Do you know him?"

"We're both ex-cops. He quit his job in protest while investigating a murder over there, some years ago. He felt certain people were trying to obstruct the investigation."

"Really!" Rudy recalled Vernon had refused to talk about this the last time he brought it up at the bar in the village, the same night he had the run-in with Oscar. "Are you serious? Is that really what happened?"

"Yep ... Now back to your story. First things first. What motive would this Larry Thompson kid have for killing the young lady – and for trying to pin it on you?"

"You sound like you and Leroy Butcher are reading from the same script. He asked me the same question. To be honest, I can't figure out what could be his motive, at least not yet. That's all the more reason why I need to locate this guy if he's here in Soufriere. He has a whole lot of explaining to do. When that happens I'll take it from there."

Trini shook his head and smirked. "Fighting words. Sounds like as far as you're concerned, he's guilty until proven innocent ... Why not let the cops handle it?"

"No offence but what I've seen of their performance so far doesn't give me much confidence."

"Act in haste, repent at leisure."

Rudy shrugged impatiently and said nothing.

"I know Leroy Butcher. He's a good investigator, one of the best on the force. I know all about Bill Thompson and the Elysian Island Company bigwigs. I can't say I know much about this son of his, though. As for the murder, I got wind of it through the police grapevine but, strangely, there wasn't much coverage of it in the local press, or at least not as much as one would expect. Seems like someone ensured it was kept under wraps ... The part about the hacking of your computer, are you sure about that?"

"Of course, I am. It happened exactly as I said and I have absolutely no doubt Larry Thompson was involved."

Trini gazed silently down at the sand. He looked perturbed.

"What's the matter?" said Rudy. Trini's expression had him concerned.

"Nothing ... Butcher will handle it somehow or other, I suppose," Trini replied evasively, not looking the least bit convinced by his own words.

"Do you think there's a chance Larry Thompson could be hanging out here in Soufriere?"

"If he's in Saint Lucia, he could be hanging out practically anywhere on the island ... I'd have to run it by some of my contacts in order to be sure. I must warn you though, if everything you've said about him and the sort of company he keeps is true, then you'd better watch your ass. You could be playing with fire!"

"What do you mean?"

"Take a look out there," said Trini, pointing toward the sea. Two speedboats sliced through the shimmery-green waters, heading north but keeping fairly close to the shore. "That's the Saint Lucia Marine Police patrolling the coast. They're part of a joint operation with Special Services ground units involved in patrolling the southern coastal areas and the surrounding hills for signs of drug trafficking and hidden marijuana fields. I pity those poor bastards, 'cause I know what it's like. There are so many secluded coves and bays all along Saint Lucia's coastline, trying to stem the flow of drugs is a fucking nightmare! As for policing the hills, it's even worse. Saint Lucia and most of the other islands in the Eastern Caribbean are pretty much in the clutches of the Columbian and Venezuelan drug cartels. They use them as transshipment points to dump drugs in the US and the UK and other parts of Europe.

"The police generally target areas in the north more frequently, including Castries, but lately they've stepped up patrols in Soufriere and other parts of the south. Evidently the drug lords are feeling the heat up north so some of them are hightailing it out of there and heading down south to set up shop. This part of the island is ideal because of its heavily forested terrain and so many secluded areas."

"Are you saying that Soufriere is becoming a base for drug trafficking?"

"The entire south is being infiltrated more and more. Real estate has always been an attractive proposition for money launderers and drug dealers. Soufriere and the nearby district of

Choiseul, as well as Vieux Fort have lots of attractive spots, including some of the island's most scenic areas." Gazing at the surrounding hills, Trini pointed to a couple of villas nestled against the forested slopes. "Most of these mansions are owned by foreigners and some of them are rented out as holiday villas. There's lots of good deals going for folks who have money to burn."

"Folks like my dear friend, Larry."

Trini shrugged. "Could be. If, like you say, he's the son of Bill Thompson, I imagine he's more likely to mingle with the social elites of Soufriere's expatriate community rather than the ordinary 'bad boys.'"

"I get the impression he's equally at home in both camps. He's had drug addiction problems. I've been reliably informed that he's been busted by the US police and he's clocked up a string of fines for speeding, driving while disqualified and assaulting a cop. I even discovered during an online search last night that on at least one occasion he was arrested for drug possession and was suspected of being tied up with a notorious drug dealer in Chicago."

"I guess that's how it is with Black Sheep Children from super-rich families. Getting hooked on coke and all the rest of it is the ultimate middle finger to the Establishment."

"Where do the rich folks around here hangout? Are there any spots for the younger crowd?"

Trini paused a moment to think. "People searching for a buzzing nightlife, especially tourists, typically head north to Gros Islet and Rodney Bay. The southern parts, like Soufriere, appeal more to those who enjoy the beaches and nature trails, and the quiet, gentle pace of Caribbean life ... That said, The Mirage nightclub, located in a place called Anse l'Ivrogne, just outside of the town, attracts some of the upper middle class and is also popular with tourists. It's a sort of lounge-cum-nightclub-cum-watering hole. It's a fairly new place, opened just six months ago. It's kind of under the radar and by design. People usually learn about it through word of mouth. It's a way of keeping it exclusive, I suppose, and free of the morality police. It allegedly belongs to a Venezuelan by the name of Carlos Rojas. It's the kind of place your man is likely to hangout, I imagine."

Someone called out to Trini from up on the seawall. He and Rudy glanced up at a young man waving cheerfully. "Ken! How you doing, little brother!" Trini shouted back at him. "Come on down here a minute, will you," he added. Turning to Rudy, he said, "He works for one of the local tour companies as a tour guide. He's familiar with all the nightspots in Soufriere. If you plan to go nosing around, which I suspect you are, you could probably tag along with him. He knows his way around. I'll run it by him. Just mind what you say to him, he's a bit of a loose talker. Most of all, be very careful how you go about this. Don't make it too obvious what you're up to."

The youth approached them all smiles. He looked to be in his early twenties. He and Trini greeted each other warmly and Trini introduced him to Rudy. "Rudy's looking for somewhere really irie and special to free up himself," Trini explained, adding, "The Mirage would suit him fine, what you think?"

Ken gaped at Trini in mock surprise. "You, of all people, biggin' up The Mirage? Wonders never cease!" Gazing at Rudy, he said, "If you looking for somewhere special, The Mirage is definitely the place for you, no doubt about it."

"He'll need a guardian angel to watch over him and help him find the place," Trini interjected. "What say you, can you help?"

"No prob, I'm on vacation. In fact, believe it or not, I've actually been using my free time to work at The Mirage and make a little extra dough. I work the nightshift five times a week. When you planning to go there?"

"How about this evening, if that's okay with you?" said Rudy.

"Yeh man, that's fine. You got wheels?"

"Definitely," Rudy pointed to the Hyundai.

"The action at The Mirage usually starts around 9:00 p.m. but my shift starts at eight."

"Great! I can pick you up, just say where."

"Let's meet here at the park around quarter past seven. I live just over there, across the road ... Oh shit!" Ken glanced at his watch. "I got to run now, there's a chick waiting for me up the road. See you guys!" He dashed off before Rudy and Trini could respond.

"I've got to hit the road too, unfortunately," said Trini.

"Thanks a million, bro, you've been a great help," said Rudy with feeling.

"No prob ,,, Incidentally, this shop over there belongs to me." Trini pointed to a small wooden shop about twenty yards away, opposite the park. "My girlfriend, Lydia runs it. We sell groceries and on weekends we do a little bar-b-que chicken and sell drinks. Most times, on afternoons, you'll find me there ... See you around and don't forget what I told you."

"What's that?"

"Watch your ass and don't push your luck. If I learn anything more about your man, I'll be in touch."

The two men shook hands and Trini made his way across to his shop. Rudy entered the car and drove off.

37

The Mirage turned out to be much further than Rudy had expected. The club was located outside of Soufriere in the adjacent district of Choiseul, one of St. Lucia's oldest parishes and also one of the most rugged and mountainous.

Rudy found the drive quite harrowing. He'd had to turn off the highway unto a narrow road with tight bends and steep inclines, and numerous potholes. The paltry illumination from the street lamps left the darkness unmoved. The pale, slivered light from a new moon wasn't much help either. There were no houses along the road, just vegetative blackness.

On the other hand, Rudy felt thankful that he'd sought Ken's help in getting to The Mirage. No sooner he mentioned Larry Thompson's name, Ken said he knew him and assured Rudy that Thompson was a regular at the club and popped in most nights. Rudy almost screamed with delight! Somehow he managed to control his emotions after recalling Trini's warning to be careful how much he let on to Ken.

"Is he a friend of yours?" Ken had asked, immediately curious.

"Yeah, an old friend and I just want to give him a surprise," Rudy replied with a straight face.

"Don't worry, I'll ask one of the waitresses to look out for him and I'll come and introduce you," said Ken.

Rudy agreed and told him it was a great idea.

As they came around a bend, they could see lights up ahead.

"We almost there," said Ken.

"How the hell do you and others without a vehicle get to and from this place?"

"The boss hires a minibus that carries me and the other workers back and forth every day. Nearly everybody else who come here own a car and have a whole ton a money. Is either that or they liming with rich people, or they screwing people who rolling in money. Here wasn't built for *malayway* (poor people)."

The club was built near the beach and within sight of the towering Gros Piton. Rudy eased into the parking lot, which already had ten cars. He and Ken strode through a dimly lit terrace towards the building. The sound of the surf rolling in and out could be heard nearby and there was a cold nip in the air. A doorman stood at the entrance, a tall, burly guy dressed in a white leather jacket, black T-shirt and slacks, and Ray Ban aviator sunglasses. His hair was styled neatly in corn-row braids.

"Gabriel, my brother, *ça ka fet* (how are you)?" Ken greeted him airily. The two of them exchanged friendly banter and then Ken introduced Rudy to the doorman. He looked impressed when Rudy said he was staying at the Anse Chastenet.

"Welcome to The Mirage," he said and, shaking Rudy's hand, he ushered him in. Ken took hold of Rudy's elbow and guided him inside. They walked through a translucent entranceway enveloped in burgundy-and-white curtains wreathed in white light. It led to a foyer which served as a dining lounge and reception area. The interior of the club was quite spacious with an exotic velvety decor, a sleek bar with fiber-optic acrylic counter-fixtures, a dance floor capable of holding about forty people and sensuous lighting. At one end of the floor was a dance platform with LED light tubes and two acrylic dance poles. A disco ball was suspended from the ceiling. Stately curtains were draped over Byzantine-painted glass windows with Romanesque arches and tables were set up close to the walls. Twelve people were seated in pairs or groups. Two young couples were on the dance floor shaking it up and showing off their hip-hop dance steps to Snoop Dog's 'Gin and Juice.' The setting was quite glamorous and it had a cozy, sensual feel. The music was not unduly loud, apparently because of the velvet-padded surface and pillars.

"Damn! This is cool. I'm impressed," said Rudy, glancing all around him. Ken grinned and said it was time for his shift. He patted Rudy on the back and excused himself. A young, fresh-faced woman with a slim, attractive body, walked up to Rudy. She looked slightly underweight. "Welcome to The Mirage, I'm Jacinta," she said and gave Rudy a beaming smile. She offered to escort him to his table. She obviously took her hospitality role to heart, and played it to the hilt. Rudy followed her to a table. She assured him a waiter would soon come over to assist him further and treated him to another warm, encouraging smile. Turning, she headed toward the bar. Within seconds a waiter came walking briskly across the floor towards Rudy. He was a superlative study in subservience and oily politeness, so much, Rudy felt smothered. He hurriedly ordered a beer to get rid of him.

He relaxed and focused on the dance floor where the two couples were kicking back their heels and prancing around. The waiter returned with his drink. Several more people had entered the nightclub and it was gradually filling up. The emcee's voice intruded on the muffled chatter pervading the room as he called for everyone's attention. The music stopped. He announced with exaggerated fanfare that the moment they'd all been waiting for was about to commence. The audience suffered through his fulsome introduction of two performers before he finally called them onto the stage. Multicolored light beams began flashing around the room, emanating from the rotating disco ball up in the ceiling. A loud burst of music erupted and two women, one brown-skinned, the other white, stepped gracefully into the spotlight, and unto the pole-dance platform to the Freemasons' stirring hit tune 'Uninvited,' featuring Bailey Tzuke. They wore black halter-style leather tops with shoulder straps and black booty shorts. Hooking their right legs around the poles and gripping them with both hands, they stretched their left legs outward and swung all the way around the poles in tandem, arching their backs gracefully. The crowd applauded and cheered.

The white dancer wrapped both legs around the pole and did a pole climb, pulling herself up artfully, all the way to the top before sliding back down. The other dancer stood with her back against the pole. Reaching behind her head, she grabbed the pole and began gyrating her hips as she slid down into a crouching position. Then, slowly, she caressed her breasts and run her hands down the front of her body. Loud cheers and feverish screams echoed through the nightclub and the crowd went wild.

Rudy's eyes were glued to them for several minutes when one in particular caught his attention. Due to their constant movement through the flickering lights and shadows, he hadn't been able to get a good look at her face. This time, as she spun around, a beam of light fell full on her face and Rudy's heart almost stopped.

It was Alina, the Ukrainian he had met at Kadija's home on Elysian Island. She continued to straddle the pole, slowly working her crotch up and down the smooth metal. Then gripping it, she bent forward at the waist and thrust her ass at the audience, and jiggled it tantalizingly. The audience screamed even louder, egging her on. Some of the men rose to their feet and cheered. Despite his shock, Rudy could feel his groin stirring.

"Be careful, mind you drool all over yourself," said a voice close to Rudy's ear. He glanced up. Ken stood staring at him and smiling.

Rudy grinned. "Can't help it, those two babes are bombshells!"

"You sure your blood pressure can stand it?" said Ken.

"I've just realized that I know this chick – the white one. She's Alina, a Ukrainian. What on earth is she doing here?"

"She's a striptease dancer and much more besides."

Rudy couldn't take his eyes off Alina. She and her partner clasped and stroked each other from opposite sides of the pole and engaged in an erotic dance simulating copulation. Rudy took a deep breath. He had to force himself to refocus on Ken. "How long has she been working here?"

"From the first day the nightclub opened several months ago."

"What about Larry? Any sign of him yet?"

"No, sorry. Nobody has seen him. It don't seem he'll be coming in. He hasn't been here for the past couple weeks."

Frowning, Rudy said, "I thought you said he's a regular here, and he comes in most nights."

"Yes, but not for the past few nights."

"Don't you have *any idea* where he could be?"

"No, not a clue."

A waitress popped out of the shadows and bent over Ken to whisper something in his ear and then quickly drew away. "Excuse me, I got to go," said Ken.

Rudy watched Ken disappear amongst the crowd. He found his abrupt departure odd, not to mention his sudden turnaround regarding Larry Thompson. He slumped back into his seat, disappointed. He gazed at the pole-dance platform just as the dancing ended to rousing applause. The two women headed backstage. The emcee stepped onto the stage, ablaze with excitement and urged the audience to give them another round of applause. They did, resoundingly. He then announced the next act, four go-go dancers dressed in miniskirts, bikini tops and knee-high boots. Rudy watched the performance distractedly. He was thinking of Alina and trying to comprehend the weird coincidence of running into her twice in radically different circumstances, in less than seventy-two hours. In the first place, what could she have been doing hanging out with a weirdo like Kadija, thousands of miles away from home? And now, to have ended up at a nightclub in Choiseul, doing pole dancing?

Rudy figured he should try and get hold of Alina before she slipped away. He checked his watch. It was ten-thirty. The go-go dancers were still going at it while the DJ fired them up with trap music. The audience screamed and cheered. Something told him Ken was not likely to return. He suddenly realized that he'd forgotten to ask Ken for his phone number. "Damn!" he muttered under his breath. He called out to a passing waitress and handing her his credit card, he asked for his bill.

Ten minutes later, there was still no sign of the waitress. Rudy rose impatiently and was about to head for the bar when he spotted her coming out from behind the counter. A woman cut her off and the two of them stood talking. Because they stood in the shadows, Rudy couldn't make out the other woman's face. He approached them irritably. At the same moment, the two women ended their conversation and the waitress commenced walking towards him, while the other woman headed towards the entrance of the nightclub. Light fell briefly over her face and Rudy saw it was Alina. She seemed to be heading out of the club. He rushed up to the waitress, snatched his credit card and receipt from her and ran after Alina. The waitress stared at him, mouth agape.

Outside, Rudy spotted Alina sitting alone on a bench on the terrace. She had changed into a blouse and skirt. She sat with her shoulders hunched and her head bowed, and she had a forlorn and defeated look about her. Walking up to her, he said, "Hello." Alina jerked back, startled. Although Rudy stood next to her, she hadn't perceived his presence. "Oh my, I'm terribly sorry, I didn't mean to startle you," he said apologetically.

Alina peered frowningly at him. Her face had turned chalk white and in the dim light, she resembled an apparition. She didn't seem to recognize Rudy. He found it hard to believe that this was the same woman who, minutes earlier, had set his hormones on fire with her dirty dancing. She seemed nothing like the Alina he'd met on Elysian Island. It was as if her personality had been effaced.

"Don't you remember me?" he said, "I'm Rudy. We last met at Kadija's place."

Alina stared woodenly at him. "What you want?" she demanded, her voice so low, it was barely audible.

"What's wrong? Is anything bothering you?"

Alina looked away and became even more withdrawn. Rudy noticed she kept clenching and unclenching her fists. The sound of footsteps and loud chattering behind him made him turn around. Two men and two women had just walked out of the nightclub. One of the women was Alina's pole-dancing partner.

"Hey Alina! Come on, let's go, it's getting late," one of the men shouted at Alina imperiously. Alina glanced up at him and remained seated. She watched him and his three companions as they climbed aboard a fourteen-seat minibus in the parking lot.

"You can travel with me if you don't feel like going with this lot," Rudy said to her softly.

"No," Alina replied quickly and glanced furtively at the minibus. "I must go with them. I have no choice." She looked very tense all of a sudden.

"Hey Alina! Come on, move it! Let's go," the man yelled at her again.

Alina got up and walked past Rudy towards the bus. Rudy followed her and paused next to his vehicle, which was parked a few feet away from the bus. Alina pulled open the side sliding door and climbed aboard the bus lethargically, as if she was weighed down by heavy shackles. The man who had shouted at her sat at the steering wheel chatting with one of the women who sat beside him in the passenger's seat. The other man and the woman sat directly behind them in the passenger cabin. Alina sat at the back, alone. The driver started the vehicle.

Rudy got into his car. As he watched the bus pull away, he decided to follow it. He gave them a three-minute head start and began tailing them. The bus travelled at a moderate speed. Knowing that there would be little to no traffic along the road, he tried to maintain a distance of about twenty-five yards from the bus and dimmed his lights so as not to attract the bus driver's attention. He felt a rush of excitement, and to his surprise he realized that he was actually enjoying the chase.

The highway intersection loomed ahead. The bus paused at the junction. Rudy slowed down and held his breath. Its right indicator light came on, indicating that the bus was heading to Soufriere. As it took off down the highway, Rudy eased out of the junction and continued tailing it all the way to the Soufriere town centre where it turned down a deserted street. The street had a row of tight-knit houses on either side and it was lit by a single streetlamp. Rudy slowed down and pulled over to the right side to avoid arousing the suspicion of the others in the bus. He waited till it turned into a lane and then he drove forward slowly, with his headlights off. Pausing close to the junction, he craned his neck to try and peer through the windshield to see where the bus was heading. It had stopped and someone was stepping out. It was Alina. She slammed the door shut and the bus drove away, leaving her standing alone in the middle of the deserted street. It took a left turn and disappeared from view.

The street had only one streetlamp and there were mostly vacant lots on either side, all overgrown with brush and weeds. In addition to four small wooden houses, there was an old, two-storied, French Creole townhouse with a pitched roof, several arcades and upper and lower balconies. It looked vacant and was clearly not being maintained. Like many of Soufriere's old French Colonial townhouses, it stood as a sad and sobering symbol of a bygone age of privilege and pedigreed living. Rudy tooted his horn and drove towards Alina. She moved quickly onto the sidewalk. He stopped abreast of her. Popping his head out of the window, he said, "Hello again."

Alina froze. Gaping at him, she said, "You! What you doing here?" She looked shocked.

"Watching over you," Rudy replied, smiling. Alina turned and walked away. "Wait!" Rudy turned off the ignition and got out of the car. Rushing towards Alina, he grabbed hold of her arm and forced her to stop. She gave him an exasperated stare. Rudy released her arm. "I was worried about you ... Seriously! I didn't like hearing the way this guy was barking at you. I could have kicked his ass."

Alina stared suspiciously at Rudy and then gave a wan smile. "Why should you care about me?" she asked.

"Why shouldn't I? This is the second time I've run into someone who's been picking on you and I don't like it."

Alina gave what was meant to pass for a smile, although it looked more like a grimace. In the dim light, her face resembled a death mask.

"Don't worry about me," she said half heartedly and walked away. Rudy sidestepped her and planted himself directly in her path. She continued walking, intent on ignoring him. Taking a few steps backwards, he said, "Can I at least walk you home?" The words were barely out of his mouth when he stumbled and fell on his butt in a puddle of muddy water. He had backpedalled into a pothole at the side of the road.

Alina put her hand over her mouth and began laughing. Rudy hurriedly rose to his feet. "If I'd known, I would've cheered you up much sooner," he said, gazing at the pothole. "Shall I do it again? I like the sound of your laugh." Alina laughed even harder. Rudy stared at his wet, mud-stained trousers with a grimace. Alina managed to pull herself together. Still giggling, she said, "You need to clean up. You have mud all over you."

"You bet." Gazing around him facetiously, Rudy said, "No sign of any standpipes around. You got any suggestions?"

"Do you want to come to my place for a while to clean up?"

Rudy sighed. "I was afraid you'd never ask. I most certainly would."

"Follow me." Alina walked past him. Rudy followed her. He found it puzzling that she was living in such a run-down area. He was about to voice his feelings when she turned unto a narrow concrete footpath between two vacant lots.

"Are you sure we're in the right neighbourhood?" said Rudy.

"Yes."

"Is this place safe – for you that is, considering that you're a woman and a foreigner?"

"I have no choice." Opening her handbag, Alina fumbled around in it and took out a torchlight. She turned it on and illuminated a secondary path to her right, leading straight to a house. In was a modest-sized structure with a high-pitched roof, a veranda, jalousie windows and filigreed trim. Rudy's curiosity peaked. He followed Alina up a flight of steps into the veranda. Quietly, she unlocked the door and turned a light on. "Wait here for me," she said and shut the door. A few minutes later the door opened and Alina asked him to come in. Rudy stepped into a modest living room with a sofa and two armchairs, a coffee table, a rocking chair, a TV set and a thick-pile rug on the floor. Alina stood holding a rag, and on the floor next to her was a nylon pail half filled with soapy water. Dipping the rag into the water, she began wiping away the mud from Rudy's pants.

"That's pretty nice of you," he said as he watched her working away at his trousers with maternal thoroughness. "Do you live alone?"

"No, there are three of us."

"The other two ... are they women?"

Alina nodded.

"Are they your roommates?"

Alina rubbed away the last mud stain, tossed the rag into the pail and carried them into the kitchen. She returned to the living room and stood near the door, as if to give Rudy a hint. "Yes, the other two are my roommates. I'm sorry, you can't stay, they will soon be here. Besides, it's very late."

"Do all of you work at the nightclub?"

"Only two of us ... Please, it's late."

Rudy noticed that Alina had become tense once again. It was as if she was willing him to leave.

He stayed put stubbornly.

"What, are you under a curfew or something?"

"I told you it's late, it's after midnight." Alina began to fidget. She exuded an air of quiet desperation.

"Are you in some kind of trouble?' Rudy asked.

Alina glanced sharply at him. "What you mean?"

"I hate to say this but you seem a bit paranoid."

"What?"

"Are you being controlled by someone?"

Fear returned to Alina's eyes. Pulling open the door, she said, "Please go. I beg you. I shouldn't have let you in."

A phone rang. The sound came from Alina's handbag on the couch. She dashed across and picked it up. Pulling out the phone, she said, "Allo." She listened a while and then burst into a flurry of what sounded, to Rudy, like Ukranian or Russian. He wasn't sure which. He could see that she was extremely distressed. She suddenly rushed out of the room and down the hallway. Rudy heard a door open and slam shut. He closed the front door and stared thoughtfully at Alina's handbag.

Moving across to the couch, he opened the bag and rummaged through it. It contained an assortment of items, including a compact mirror, a tube of facial moisturizer, several lipsticks, antimigraine and anti-gas tablets and several odds and ends that women normally carry around in their purses. He'd hoped to find a passport or driver's license or some other ID document but there was none. It didn't even have a wallet. He could still hear Alina talking on the phone. Reluctantly, he zipped the bag shut and tossed it back on the couch. He was about to walk away when a tiny metallic object caught his eye at the base of the bag. Out of curiosity, he picked it up again and peering at the object, he realized it was a zipper. On closer examination he noticed that there was a hard-shell compartment at the bottom of the bag. He opened it and saw it had two pockets, one of which contained something bulky. The other was empty. It was obviously a secret compartment integrated neatly and unobtrusively into the body of the purse for storing bulky items like eyeglass cases. He opened the pouch. Inside of it was a mobile phone. He took it out and stared at it.

An arctic chill swept through him. He was so frozen with shock, he could barely breathe. In his hand was a Google Nexus 5 smartphone. It had a faceplate with faux rhinestones attached to the bottom. It looked identical to Olive's phone. Rudy recalled she'd had her initials engraved at the back of it. He turned it over slowly, his hand trembling. There it was! The letters 'O' and 'H' etched neatly into the metal. He took a whiff of Ambergris, very faint but distinct. Olive used to be crazy about Ambergris, he recalled. He held the phone up close to his nose. There was no doubt the scent was emanating from it. Glancing up, he saw Alina standing a few feet away, a look of horror on her face.

"What you doing!" she screamed at him. "Chī vī bozhevil'ni? (Are you crazy?) How dare you interfere in my things!"

"This phone ... Where did you get it?" Rudy surprised himself by the steadiness of his voice. Alina rushed at him and tried to snatch the phone from his hand but he evaded her. "Answer me, damn it! Where did you get that phone?" he snapped.

"It's mine, I bought it!"

"No you didn't ... Come on, tell me the truth."

"I told you, it's mine! Give it to me and get out!"

"I won't go until you tell me the truth. I mean it."

"Then I will call the police."

"Be my guest. In fact, allow me to help you. I will call them myself." Rudy took out his phone and began dialing.

"No!"

"What's the matter? I thought you wanted to call the cops."

"Bastard! You treat me this way although I was kind to you."

"I just want to know where you got the phone from. Tell me the truth and I promise you I'll leave and I won't bother you anymore."

Alina turned away and went to sit on the couch. She run her hands agitatedly through her hair, leaving it all disheveled and hanging over her face like tendrils. She looked demented.

"I stole it," she said softly.

"From whom?"

"Kadija."

"What?"

"Is Kadija's phone. I stole it from her." Alina began sobbing. Rudy stooped down in front of her and placing his hand under her chin, he lifted her head gently. She looked badly shaken.

"What do you mean Kadija's phone? This is not Kadija's phone."

"I told you, it's Kadija's phone ... The day she came and found us together in her house, you remember?"

"Yeah."

"After you left, she treat me bad. Very bad. Before I left, I decided to steal the phone. It was the only way I could get my revenge." Alina uttered the last sentence with a malevolent gleam in her eyes. "I didn't think she would miss it anyway, and even if she had, I was not the only person coming to her home. She put it away and never used it. Is like she forgot all about it. I was searching through her things and I found it inside one of her drawers. Are you going to tell her I took it?"

"Alina ... Listen to me. This phone doesn't belong to Kadija. It belonged to Olive ... Did you know her?"

"Who?"

"Olive Henry. She was murdered a few weeks ago on Elysian Island."

Alina frowned. She looked confused. "Olive? ... The girl they killed. Yes, I remember."

Rudy held up the phone. "This belonged to her, it even has her initials on it." Rudy turned the phone over and showed Alina the initials. She looked petrified. He went on to tell her about the events surrounding Olive's death but before he could finish, Alina shot up out of the chair and covered her ears with her hands. She couldn't bear to hear anymore. She went and stood by a window overlooking the side of the house. Rudy watched her, a ponderous look on his face. He didn't doubt what she said about Kadija for one minute. He could tell instinctively that she was speaking the truth.

He pulled out the back cover of the phone to look for the SIM card. It had none. "Where's the SIM card?" he asked frowning. Walking up to Alina, he held her by the elbow. She yanked her arm away and recoiled from him.

"Did you find a SIM card in the phone?" he repeated.

"I don't know. When I took it there was nothing in it."

"She must have removed Olive's SIM. What do you think she did with it?"

"Leave me alone, I don't know! I don't know!"

"Alina, you've got to turn this phone over to the police."

"No!"

"You've got to, Alina. You can't keep it. Don't you understand? You're walking around with a phone that belonged to a woman who was murdered. If you found it in Kadija's possession, do you realize what this means? It means she is tied up in some way with Olive's murder. For all we know, she could even be the killer! If you don't turn it in and explain to the cops how you got it, you could be in deep shit."

"No, I will not .... Go away!"

"Come on, don't be silly. You've got to! Tell you what, you don't have to go alone. I'm willing to go with you and I'll speak to the cops on your behalf."

"I said no! Get out!"

Take it easy, stay calm, Rudy told himself. All along he had been trying to contain his exasperation but Alina was now seriously beginning to piss him off. He called to mind every cliché he could think of about the virtue of patience, to no avail. *Fuck it.* He rounded on her.

"Who are you and what are you doing in this country? What's more, how did you end up dancing at The Mirage?" he demanded.

"Stop asking me questions!"

"Another thing, how did you end up on Elysian Island and what's going on between you and Kadija?"

"Zalīshte mene! Leave me alone! Go away!" Alina flew at him, her fingernails bared like claws, and took a swipe at his face as if to rip his eyes out. Rudy dropped the phone and grabbed her arms in the nick of time. They careened across the room and crashed into the wall. Alina's body pressed delectably into his and the warmth of her flesh took his mind off the pain in his back crushed against the wall. He struggled to restrain her. Gripping her wrists, Rudy swung his body around and managed to pin her against the wall. Alina kept on struggling, refusing to give up. Rudy was amazed at her strength. Pressing her arms up against the wall, he pushed hard against her until he heard her grunt in pain. He savored the feel of her breasts rubbing against him in tandem with her labored breathing. Gradually, her body slackened and she went limp.

Seeing her weaken, Rudy became acutely conscious of his superior strength and the fact that they were alone in the house. Alina's skirt had ridden up to her waist, exposing her nicely rounded butt and well-formed thighs. Rudy breathed in the musky odor of her body and touched her ass, gently squeezing the soft, supple cheeks. Suddenly he jerked his hand away and stepped back. Alina slid down the wall and sat on the floor in a woebegone, sodden heap, her head bowed. Quietly, Rudy opened the door and stood gazing unseeingly into the darkness.

Alina lifted her head and said sneeringly, "What's the matter, don't you have balls? Don't you want to screw me? Go on, rape me – use me like all the rest of them!"

Rudy came close to apologizing but didn't. It would not only be a de facto admission of guilt, it would validate Alina's contempt for him. He couldn't bring himself to do it. His ego wouldn't allow it. "Goodnight," he said quietly, without looking at her. She didn't respond. He thought of Olive's phone and wondered if he should insist on taking it from Alina to hand it over to the cops, just to play it safe since he had a feeling she would not take his advice and turn it in. By the same token, if he took it and turned it in himself, how could he be sure that she wouldn't deny ever having it in the first place? Where would that leave him?

Rudy shut the door and climbed down the steps. He heard two vehicle doors slam shut and the sound of female voices. They seemed to be coming from the road. His instinct told him they were heading his way. He was halfway down the pathway when two women came walking towards him. He couldn't make out their faces in the dark. They halted on seeing him. "Good evening, ladies," he said cheerily and, sidestepping them, he continued walking. He could feel their eyes burning into his back. He didn't hear any sound of footsteps behind him, which suggested they hadn't budged.

Out on the road he saw the same minibus that had transported Alina parked a few yards behind the Hyundai. He entered the car and sat for a few minutes watching the bus through the rear-view mirror to see if it would drive off. It stayed put. No one came out of it.

Parking so close to the gap leading to Alina's house had been a mistake. It had obviously aroused the bus driver's suspicion, judging by the way he hung around after dropping off the two women, no doubt to see who was driving the Hyundai. Rudy had no doubt now that Alina was mixed up in some kind of shady business. He had to find a way to get the cops to move quickly and take possession of Olive's phone. He was afraid Alina would dispose of it. What this would ultimately mean for her, he couldn't tell, and he figured he shouldn't worry about that either, after all it wasn't his business what she did with her life. He would call Leroy Butcher as soon as he got to the hotel.

38

The sun was already disappearing below the horizon when Trini pulled up outside his shop opposite the Soufriere waterfront. He was surprised to find it still open and wondered why his partner, Lydia hadn't closed up yet. It wasn't like her to knock off late, especially being the sort who kept insisting, sometimes to the point of driving him up the wall, that they needed to spend more quality time together with the two children, neither of whom he had fathered. The shop was her baby, and she normally kept it open till five, except on Fridays and Saturdays when the prospect of more business from late-night strollers caught up in the TGIF spirit, induced her to keep it open till midnight and forget about family togetherness. Going to church still mattered to her, so they took Sundays off.

Trini had just returned from the southern town of Vieux Fort where Lydia had dispatched him to buy drinks and groceries to replenish the shop's dwindling stocks. Stepping out of the cab pickup, he called out to someone at the back. "Hey Morgan, move it! Let's get everything out and stack them up, otherwise you'll have to come and rescue my ass from the dog house."

"Okay boss," Morgan replied and hurriedly jumped down from the vehicle and began moving cases of canned juices from the cab into the shop. He was Trini's occasional handyman. A tall guy, he had a rough-hewn face that was fast being drained of its youthfulness, by the looks of him because of growing up rough and fast,. Trini usually hired him when Lydia needed an extra hand to help out in the shop or if he needed help transporting and stacking groceries on the shelves.

Lydia came out of the shop. Slim yet curvy, she had a cute oval face, come-hither eyes, tantalizing lips and a neat buzz cut. She looked middle-aged. She had a worried frown on her face.

"Thank God you here," she said. "For a while I was afraid I would have to lock up and leave your friend alone out in the balcony."

Trini frowned. "What friend, who you talking about?"

"The Rasta from England. He came here over two hours ago looking for you. He just sit there in the balcony drinking all by himself until he pass out. Something wrong with him, you better go and check on him."

"Rudy?' Trini gaped wide-eyed at Lydia. Morgan was about to lift a case of beers from the back of the pickup. He paused and sharpened his ears. Lydia said she had to go pick up the children and rushed across to a Mini Cooper parked near the shop, which looked overworked. "Your friend's bill is on the counter!" she yelled at Trini. Trini ignored her and entered the balcony. It had three makeshift wooden bar tables and chairs and barely enough space to move between them. Rudy sat slumped over a table with his head resting in the crook of his elbow and his locks covering his face. He emitted a dull snore. Grabbing hold of his shoulder, Trini gave him a solid shake. Rudy didn't budge. Trini shook him again, harder. Slowly, Rudy lifted his head and squinted up at him.

"Cone on bro, rise and shine," Trini said firmly. Rudy shook his head as if to clear it and sat up. He peered at Trini and squeezed his eyes shut as if hoping that Trini would have vanished by the time he reopened them.

"Looks like you had one too many," said Trini. "Don't get me wrong, I appreciate the business, but hell man, you look like shit! What happened?"

"They killed her," Rudy moaned, in a wobbly voice.

"Who? What're you talking about?"

"Alina ... The bastards killed her!"

Trini pulled a chair and sat down. "Take a deep breath and relax," he said gently. "Now let's talk about this. Who's Alina?"

Rudy took several deep breaths before he could pull himself together. He wished Trini hadn't woken him up. He felt a bit resentful. Willing his mind to pay attention, he urged his mouth to speak. He heard it telling Trini about Alina and his experience at The Mirage and later at Alina's house. Mercifully, Trini didn't draw it out by interrupting him with questions. He then told Trini about his phone conversation with Leroy Butcher after he returned to the hotel.

"Butcher was pretty pissed when I told him I'd been following up on some leads and he chewed my ass off. I begged him to move quickly to try and get hold of Olive's phone, but it turns out he has no jurisdiction over Soufriere. He referred me to Inspector Errol Miller who heads the Soufriere Police Station and promised to alert him and suggest that they get to Alina first thing in the morning to bring her in for questioning. He said he'd follow up with Miller afterwards and consider bringing Kadija in for questioning too. The next day I went to check out Errol Miller. According to him, his men visited Alina's house and met two women there. They said Alina had left the night before with a man with dreadlocks and the description they gave of the man resembles me. It's a bloody lie! I left the house at around midnight, *alone*. I did run into two women on the way out but I doubt they were able to see my face. A few minutes later, Miller get's a phone call. They'd just gotten a tip off. Someone discovered a woman's body near a ravine somewhere in Riviere Doree, in Choiseul. She's a white woman." Rudy shuddered. He tried to compose himself. He then recounted what, for him, had been the worst part; Inspector Miller calling him back to the police station a few hours later for questioning and giving him a thorough grilling that left him feeling broken and humiliated, to the extent that he couldn't even muster the strength to feel angry. The very thought that the Soufriere cops viewed him with suspicion was just too much.

Watching him closely, Trini asked, "Did they say how she died?"

"They suspect she was strangled."

"Looks like everywhere you go a dead body turns up."

If Trini had stuck a dagger in Rudy's gut, he wouldn't have looked so mortified. He gave Trini a reproachful stare.

Trini didn't bat an eyelid. "In the next few days they should be able to determine the precise cause of death through an autopsy," he said, adding, "I got to be frank with you. If I was in Miller's place, I would also be looking at you as a possible suspect."

"What are you insinuating?"

"Nothing. I'm just wising you up to the way the mind of a detective works and what to expect. In other words, you 'd better be sure you have a damned good alibi when the crunch comes."

"I had nothing to do with Alina's death!" Rudy snapped, his face livid.

"Fine ... If you say so."

"Thanks a lot for the vote of confidence!"

"If, like you said, you left this woman at the house where she lived, why do you think those two other women are fingering you and giving the cops the impression that the two of you went out together?"

"That's just it! There can be only one explanation for that, they're trying to frame me ... *again.* This is the second time somebody is trying to set me up *within the past month.* Talk about a recurring nightmare! It's crazy! What the hell is going on in this place? Whoever is behind it, why are they picking on me?"

"What about this Google Nexus phone you found in the woman's possession? What became of it?"

"The cops didn't find it. Miller said they later searched the house and her handbag, which they found in her room, but it wasn't there; which, to my mind, could be another reason why they bumped her off. Remember, I found the phone in a secret compartment of her handbag. She obviously hid it there hoping no one would discover it. In our struggle, it dropped to the floor. It was still there when I left. What if the two women came upon it when they entered the house and told their handlers? Somehow or other they must have found it and someone was smart enough to realize the danger it posed. *Someone like Olive's killer.*"

"And who do you think the killer is?"

"It could be Larry Thompson, it could be Kadija, it could be both of them or it could be somebody closely connected to the two of them, I don't know! .... All I know is that the fucker – whoever it is – keeps trying to make me the fall guy. Thompson's been hacking my computer, remember? Maybe the son-of-a-bitch is even sneakier than I thought and has been keeping track of my movements in ways I'm not aware of."

"Now you see why I warned you to be careful. It seems like you did everything you possibly could to make sure the whole world is unto you. Tailing the woman like you're James Bond and parking your car where no one could miss it, and in a spot where a blind man would know exactly where you had gone."

"Okay, okay! No need to rub it in."

"What about Ken? Was he any help?"

"Nah, he was a bloody waste of time." Rudy told Trini about Ken's odd behavior at the club. "Some woman came and whispered something to him and then he took off and never returned. He probably went to tip off Thompson and warn him that I was unto him. Come to think of it, he could be tied up in this whole thing. Maybe even the cops too, for all I know. Who's to say one of them didn't betray Alina by alerting her killer to what was coming down? Right now, I don't know who the fuck to trust."

"Maybe I'm part of the gang too, who knows? ... Or maybe you're just paranoid."

"Okay, so what's your hunch then?'

"I'm an ex-detective. I've learned to rely on facts and evidence, not hunches. What I will say though is that if your Ukranian friend's murder was a conspiracy, then someone screwed up badly."

"In what way?"

"Her death puts the spotlight on The Mirage. If half the things I've been hearing about this place are true, then the last thing they need is to be mixed up in such a murder, which is going to draw attention to the club as never before. The Ukrainian woman – she may well have been a victim of human trafficking. This is becoming a serious problem here. Some of our nightclubs and underground brothels and strip clubs, and also local pimps, are drawing women from the unlikeliest of places, like moths to a flame, and local girls too. Incidentally, a couple of months ago, the US State Department put Saint Lucia on a Tier 2 human trafficking watch list and issued s report stating unequivocally that the island is, to quote them, a 'destination country for persons subjected to forced prostitution and forced labor.' Many of the victims come from places like Haiti, Jamaica, the Dominican Republic, Guyana, and South Asia, including children under eighteen and they're being forced into commercial sex, including child sex tourism and adult prostitution. I wouldn't be surprised if this Alina woman got caught up in the dragnet."

"Good God! ... What the hell do I do now? At the moment, I feel completely lost."

"If I were you, I'd pack up and get the hell out of Soufriere. Return to the land flowing with milk and honey from whence you came."

"What for? Regardless of whether I stay here or return to Elysian Island, either way I'm screwed."

"Don't be such a pessimist. Call Leroy Butcher and find out if he's made any headway with his investigation of this Kadija woman you spoke of. Most of all, return to the loving arms of your protector – Lady Tennyson."

Rudy glanced sharply at Trini. Trini gazed pointedly back at him. Rudy glanced away. "What about Larry Thompson?" hc said.

"You've given the cops lots of useful information to work with. Back off and let them do their work."

Rudy groaned and let his forehead drop unto the table.

"Why don't you go back to the hotel and get some sleep? You need a rest." said Trini.

Slowly, Rudy lifted his head. "What time is it?" he murmured.

"Seven fifteen."

Rudy passed his hands wearily over his face. "How much do I owe you?"

Trini called out to Morgan and asked him to bring the bill Lydia had left on the counter. Morgan came out into the balcony and handed it to him. Trini glanced at it and said, "Your bill is forty dollars."

Fishing in his pocket, Rudy pulled out a fifty dollar bill and handed it to him. "Please keep the change," he said.

Peering at Rudy and frowning, Trini said, "What did you have to drink that put you in such a state? It couldn't have been that much."

"Six beers and two shots of white rum. It's the white rum that did me in. I hardly ever drink this shit ... which should tell you a lot." Pushing back his chair, he struggled to his feet.

"Maybe you should let me drop you off. Morgan can drive the car up to the hotel for you."

"No thanks, I'll be fine," Rudy replied and walked with leaden feet through the shop and out the front door.

39

"Boss man, excuse me," said Morgan from behind the counter. Trini turned to stare at him. "Don't say I minding y'all business but I heard you saying something about somebody looking for Larry. Which Larry? The reason I ask is because some time ago I make friends with a white American guy name Larry. Is it the same guy you talkin' about?"

"I don't know. Could be. Tell me more about him."

"He's a young guy, in his late twenties although he could be younger. He look real mash-up. He been here a few weeks now but is not the first time. He been here twice before and he does always come to cool out in Soufriere. The first time he and I meet was on his second trip here. It look like he well off and he have money to burn."

"How did you get to know him?"

"We met one day at the Malgretout beach. He was travelling on one of dem big *mapipi* (extremely huge) yachts – how you call dem?"

"A mega yacht."

"That's it! It park a good distance outside de bay and he and some other people on board come ashore on a shuttle boat. In dem days, I used to be pushing my little bead necklaces and coconut bracelets to the tourists on the beach. That was the day he and me get to know each other and after that we become good friends. I hear he rolling in money and is his father who run things on Elysian Island."

"You sure about this, Morgan?"

"Yeh man! Is true."

"When was the last time you met with him?"

"About a week ago. We even take out pictures together."

"Can I have a look at them?"

"Is one of Larry friends that take out most of the pictures on his camera but I think I have a couple on my phone that he had snap for me." Morgan took a Samsung Galaxy S5 out of his pocket and searched through it for the photos.

Watching him, Trini reflected ruefully on the irony of a perennially unemployed, barely literate ex-con struggling from day to day to survive, yet the proud owner of a two-thousand dollar phone. He had taken Morgan on as a handyman a month ago, mostly because he needed the extra help but partly because he had known him as a youth constantly in and out of prison, mostly for petty theft and marijuana possession, and he wanted to help him mend his ways and turn his life around. Despite his criminal background, Trini saw a flicker of promise in him

Morgan handed Trini the phone. "Here boss, check it out," he said.

On the screen was a photo of Morgan standing next to a beach bar. Trini scrolled to another photo of Morgan and Larry Thompson, this one taken at a different location, on a hillside property with a sprawling villa in the background.

It was the house that really caught Trini's attention. As he gazed at it, a wily face with mocking eyes and a contemptuous grin loomed in his mind.

Lucas Manuel.

An intense rage swept through him. Old memories that he'd tried so hard to bury came flooding back to him. His thoughts flashed back to the day, four years ago, when his good friend and fellow officer, Assistant Superintendant Elijah Foucher got gunned down in cold blood by a two-bit thug and murder suspect, known to most people by the chilling nickname Scorpion. He was killed in one of the capital's inner-city ghettoes. Acting on a tipoff, he and Foucher had gone to try and apprehend Scorpion in a house where he'd been hiding out. A gun battle ensued and the youth caught Foucher by surprise and blasted him with a semiautomatic pistol, right between the eyes. Trini was forced to call for backup and after a blistering half-hour shootout Scorpion was eventually captured after being seriously injured.

Two weeks later at Foucher's funeral, Trini watched in anguish as his comrade's body was laid to rest while he and his police comrades, and Foucher's grieving relatives, looked on helplessly, many of them in tears.

The police had long suspected Scorpion of being the right-hand man and personal hit man of a local drug dealer by the name of Lucas Manuel. They also had reason to suspect that in addition to drug trafficking, Manuel was involved in money laundering and racketeering on a large scale. He was also a hugely successful businessman with a stake in numerous investments, including three auto parts dealerships, a construction-equipment business, several medium-sized supermarkets scattered around the island, two palatial homes in upscale communities in the north, a farm and several fishing boats,

It was also believed that he had strong ties with one of the South American drug cartels. Because of Trini's connections to the DEA, he had a better understanding of the nature of Manuel's affiliations with the South Americans and the intricacies of their drug transshipment operations than did the other investigators in the local police force. He had no illusions about the threat Manuel posed to the very security of the state. Not only was he one of the shrewdest bastards in the business, Manuel was by far the most powerful and charismatic of all the local drug dealers, and controlled one of the more notorious gangs in the city. He kept them loyal by bankrolling them and their friends and relatives, and lots of other 'ghetto youts,' dishing out free cash, free schoolbooks, free clothing, free electricity and water, even free mobile phones. Many of them looked upon him as the poor man's savior and gave him a level of respect that local politicians could only dream of. For years, Trini worked hard to try and bring Lucas Manuel down, to no avail. He realized that, to a large extent, it was because Manuel had friends in high places. Rumors abounded about his secret campaign contributions to certain political hopefuls during at least two previous general elections.

At the time of Assistant Superintendant Foucher's murder, some members of Manuel's gang and a rival gang had been embroiled in a series of vicious gun battles that engulfed the struggling working-class community of Morne Du Don on the outskirts of Castries. It was there Scorpion was ultimately captured. For several weeks, they had been terrorizing the residents. Three youths got shot and killed in the shootout, gangland style.

After Scorpion's arrest, Manuel kept his distance and pretty much left him to fend for himself. Scorpion couldn't afford a good lawyer, so the state had to provide him with counsel. He was convicted and sentenced to life in prison without parole.

While in prison, Scorpion became so bitter and resentful, he succumbed to police pressures and agreed to testify for the state against his former boss and expose Manuel's nefarious dealings if he was ever brought to trial. With a life sentence hanging like a millstone around his neck, he figured his life was completely fucked over and he had nothing to lose or to fear. It put him in a vengeful mood.

A few months later, Manuel got busted by the cops. They found him and two other men in a house believed to be owned by Manuel. The police found several kilograms of cocaine and wads of cash carefully hidden inside the walls. Manuel and his companions were subsequently charged with drug trafficking and money laundering.

After repeated adjournments, the case finally got underway more than a year later. Three months later it was over. Incredibly, the prosecution lost the case against Manuel, and lost it miserably. Manuel's hotshot legal team ran rings around them. They were unable to prove that Manuel owned the house or that he had even been a regular occupant. They also failed to establish that he'd been aware of the presence of drugs and cash in the building or had had any prior knowledge of it. The other two guys were not so lucky. Manuel let them take the fall. Despite that, neither of them could be persuaded to testify against him. To make matters worse, all the crucial witnesses whom the prosecutor had been relying on to testify against Manuel, refused to cooperate. Although they had promised solemnly to testify for the state, someone had apparently put the fear of the devil in them. A couple of them even fled the country.

As for Scorpion, Manuel's lawyers, while cross examining him, managed to cast doubt on his credibility due to his being a convicted cop killer. Ultimately, Manuel was acquitted and Trini was forced to watch him walk out of the courthouse a free man, and there wasn't a damn thing he could do about it.

Manuel was believed to be the owner of the villa in Morgan's photo.

He had not only succeeded in evading justice, he went on to thumb his nose at the system by investing even more conspicuously in new business ventures and buying properties all over the island, following his acquittal. The house in the photo was built high up on a cliff in the upper reaches of Soufriere, overlooking the sea, with a stunning view of the Pitons. Manuel had reportedly bought it a year ago. Trini had known the previous owner well and visited his home a couple of times; a vast eighteen-room mansion with a spacious salon, French doors opening onto a wide veranda, and a spectacular infinity pool. It was surrounded by flamboyant, bougainvillea and palm trees and a variety of fruit trees. The house could easily be transformed into a small hotel or a guesthouse. Not only was it one of the oldest and most historic edifices in that part of the island, it stood out for its unique French colonial architecture, as well as its distinctive appellation; Maison de Royaume.

Not long after the court case against Lucas Manuel collapsed, Trini quit his job in disgust. His exasperation with the slow and inefficient government bureaucracy and the hopelessly clogged-up and hamstrung legal system had finally reached its peak.

For too long he and his fellow officers had had to be putting their necks on the line in the so-called War on Drugs, chasing down petty gangsters in the pay of the drug lords while the drug lords themselves and their enablers – coldblooded reptilians slithering in the shadows, the real powers behind the narcotics trade - got off scotch free. In cahoots with them were the high-priced lawyers pretending to be financial and corporate brokers, and helping the barons set up phony offshore foundations to launder their blood-stained cash. Aiding and abetting them also were the so-called financial advisors on the take, but most of all the bankers who, as far as Trini was concerned, were just as culpable, despite all the supposed anti-money laundering rules and guidelines they were mandated to follow. And the cops - overstretched and undermanned, woefully lacking in resources and outgunned by the gangsters and drug dealers; out on the frontline working their asses off with one hand tied behind their backs - well and truly fucked – yet they couldn't do shit about it. Surely, it had to be a fucking conspiracy!

Trini's rage all but boiled over as he thought of the number of cops, not just locally but in America and other parts of the world, who had simply said 'fuck it' and sold out to the drug lords and money launderers. Over the years, there had been so many of them, he lost count.

After two decades of policing, he had grown sick and tired of it all; of watching hopelessly as societies, especially in vulnerable areas like the Caribbean, become consumed by the systemic corruption engendered by all the drug trafficking and money laundering; the venal veil of secrecy surrounding the region's offshore financial sector and the outrageously lenient slaps on the wrist being meted out to convicted money launderers on the rare occasions that they were successfully prosecuted.

As far as he was concerned, the likes of Lucas Manuel could not have become so powerful and entrenched without an enabling environment and the help of the banksters, whether provided wittingly or unwittingly. He considered their refusal to sever the umbilical cord tying them to the criminals as glaring proof that the so-called war on drugs was nothing but a charade. To him, murderous sons-of-bitches like Manuel were not just scum; he viewed them as living testimonials of the moral and social degeneration of the country, and the mere sight of the photo of Manuel's house made Trini feel like he wanted to kill somebody! It upset him even more to think that the Larry Thompson guy was mixed up with Manuel in some way or other.

"Boss! Wha' happen? You okay?" said Morgan, sounding alarmed. This was his second attempt to get Trini's attention. Trini had been so absorbed in his thoughts he didn't hear him the first time. He screwed up his eyes as if he had woken up from a deep sleep. "What's the matter, boss?" Morgan reiterated.

Trini faced him, eyes flaring. "The house in the photo, it belongs to Lucas Manuel, right?" He spoke softly but with the venom of an agitated cobra.

Sensing trouble, Morgan tried stalling. "House boss? Which house?"

"The one in the photo of you and Thompson."

"Oh, that house! Honestly boss, you know I never really pay attention to the house in that picture," Morgan said airily.

"Don't fuck with me, boy!" Trini hissed. "Isn't that Lucas Manuel's house?"

Morgan hesitated, his mind racing as he tried to figure out how to bluff his way out of the mess he'd gotten himself in. He knew better than anybody else that the worst thing anyone could do was bring up the name of Lucas Manuel or anything to do with him, in Trini's presence. He had slipped badly with the photo and he knew it.

"Boss, honestly I never pay attention to no house, I just stand up there to take out the picture. Is a long time after that I hear somebody say who the owner is, and I was so surprise."

Trini lunged at Morgan and grabbed him by the throat. "Don't play the ass with me, motherfucker!" he snarled. "The last time they jailed your ass, you got caught trying to smuggle weed into the prison for one of Manuel's boys. Prior to that you were convicted of assaulting one of Manuel's girlfriends when he discovered she was screwing someone else behind his back. No one bought your story that she was your woman, albeit you may have been secretly screwing her. I may no longer be a part of the police force but don't think, for one minute, that I've forgotten your links with Manuel in the past."

"*Me*, boss! Oh no, boss, that not true," cried Morgan, a pained look on his face.

"Don't try to deny it, you bastard! You know damn well I've got my sources. I believed you when you said you wanted to turn your life around and make something useful of yourself. In any case, you're a grown man, what you ultimately do with your life is your own fucking business. But one thing I won't tolerate is you playing me for a sucker. Why am I getting the feeling that you haven't broken ties with Manuel and his gang? What, do you think you can work for me and still tag along with him secretly, like some fucking whore screwing two men at the same time - and both men sworn enemies? Are you out of your mind?"

Morgan looked dumbfounded. Walking towards him, Trini pointed at him threateningly, his face contorted with rage. Morgan backed away fearfully. He collided with the wall and had nowhere to run.

"Where is this Larry Thompson guy?" Trini demanded.

"I don't know bossman, honest to God!"

"Let's try again. *Where is Larry Thompson*?"

"Boss, as God is my witness, I don't know! The day I take out the picture with him, was the last time I saw him. I swear!"

"How close are he and Manuel?"

"I don't know boss, honest! All I know is that the two of them come aboard the big yacht and it seem they and some of their pardeners was liming around together. It was the first time I ever meet the American."

"Your nose is growing, Morgan."

"What you mean?"

"You're lying through your teeth again, like Pinocchio. And like all habitual liars, you can't keep track of all your lies. Earlier you said that you and Thompson had met months before. For all I know, it's probably thanks to you that he and Lucas Manuel are now friends. You probably hooked them up."

Morgan went down on his knees and held his head with both hands, shaking it agonizingly. "Oh, Lord boss, I swear on my mother grave. Let God strike me dead if what I tellin' you is not the truth! Is not me hook up the white boy and Manuel. I swear! Me and Manuel don't have dealings no more. Believe me, boss. I would never lie to you."

"Do you think there's a chance Thompson could be hanging out at Manuel's place?"

Morgan got up off his knees warily and kept his eyes on Trini. "He could be but I don't know for sure."

"When did you snap the photo?"

"Two weeks ago."

"Have you been hanging around at Manuel's place?"

"Me, boss? Oh no, never! I never ever set foot inside that place."

"Yeah, I bet you haven't." Reaching into his pocket, Trini pulled out his wallet. He fished out a fifty dollar bill and handed it to Morgan. "Thanks for your help. See you around."

Morgan took the money reluctantly. Normally, he would hang around a bit and he and Trini would knock back a few beers after he finished putting away the groceries. No chance of it this time. "Thanks boss," he said glumly. Turning, he walked away with the air of a chastened schoolboy worried that the teacher he looked up to, no longer cared about him. Trini watched him disappear into the night. Heading behind the counter, he took a beer from the fridge, paid for it and went out into the balcony and stood gazing out at the sea.

40

Rudy felt pissed off with Aaron. Around 10:00 a.m., while he was trying to get some sleep after tossing and turning much of the night, Aaron called, claiming to have made some major discoveries. He said he was calling from a friend's house in Soufriere, not far from Rudy's hotel. He'd arrived the day before, around noon. This gave Rudy quite a shock since he hadn't been in touch with Aaron for a couple days and had assumed he was on Elysian Island. Aaron said he knew Larry Thompson's whereabouts. He also had news of the latest developments in the investigation of Olive's murder, he added. Then, in his typical nonchalant fashion, which Rudy found so bloody infuriating, he suggested that they meet in person rather than discuss such matters over the phone – *over their own fucking private cell phones.* Rudy had to fight hard to keep from swearing. Realizing that he wasn't going to get any further with Aaron, he grudgingly agreed to meet him at the Soufriere Waterfront Park at eleven.

He tried to control his anxiety but it was no use. He decided to call Leroy Butcher to try and get more information but he was unable to get through. Butcher's cell phone seemed to have been turned off. He tried calling his office but Butcher was not at his desk. He then tried calling Vernon Allain – twice - but each time the phone just rang out. In his rage, Rudy almost smashed his phone against the wall. He wondered irritably if the phone company was encountering network problems on Elysian Island. He had no choice; he would have to wait till his rendezvous with Aaron.

When he finally got to the park, there was no sign of Aaron. He waited almost ten minutes but still nothing doing. Just as he was about to phone him, he glanced in the direction of Trini's shop and saw Aaron and Trini step out of it. Rudy got into his car and drove towards them, seething yet at the same time puzzled to see the two men together. He parked near the shop, behind Trini's pickup truck, and flounced out of the vehicle, slamming the door.

"Ah! There you are," said Aaron cheerfully. "I bet you thought I'd given you the slip. Sorry about that, I couldn't resist popping in to have a chat with my old friend, Trini. Didn't get the opportunity to the last time I was here."

"Rudy! How you keeping, my friend?" said Trini, grinning on seeing the scowl on Rudy's face. "I guess you're wondering what's up, seeing the two of us here."

"I can't imagine what on earth would make you think such a thing," said Rudy sarcastically and glaring balefully at Aaron.

Aaron placed his hand consolingly on Rudy's shoulder and said, with a slightly condescending air, "You'd be interested to know that Trini and I have one thing in common; mountain climbing. We first met a few years ago when he and some of his colleagues from the local police sports club teamed up with a visiting group of British mountain climbers from the Alpine Club, of which I am a member, to climb Mount Gimie, the island's highest peak. It was all part of a fundraising drive to assist the sports club. He exhibited extraordinary mountaineering skills, far more than did any of his police colleagues, I dare say." Winking, he added, "And what a glorious example he has set by publicly demonstrating his appreciation for the great British Alpinist tradition of conquering the highest mountains. I think he ought to have been knighted for his valiant efforts. Since then, he and I have become fast friends."

Trini turned to Rudy and said, "Our aristocratic friend needs a history lesson. He should be reminded that long before the British Alpinist tradition, our African ancestors had already conquered the hills and mountains. That's why the runaway slaves here had no problem whipping the Redcoats' asses when they tried to recapture them in the hills."

Aaron snickered. "I say, that's crisp." He turned to Rudy. "Believe it or not, Trini and I have just discovered that we share a common destiny; babysitting and watching over you. Isn't that amazing? That must surely make you feel proud."

"Can we cut out the clowning, and could the two of you please explain to me what the hell is going on?"

"Earlier this morning, I journeyed into town and, lo and behold, Trini and I ran into each other. No sooner I told him what had brought me here, we got to speaking about you and your predicament. We then came to realize that we've arrived at the same conclusion regarding the probable whereabouts of your adversary, Larry."

Trini gave Rudy a dour look. "It was by mere chance I came down to the shop today after realizing that I had forgotten my phone there yesterday, thanks to you. After you left, I made a very disturbing discovery. Right at this very moment, I'm supposed to be delivering a truckload of fruits and vegetables from my farm to one of the hotels. I worked my arse off to secure that deal. Fortunately, the hotel agreed to allow me to deliver the stuff later today. That tells you how crucial it is to me that you and I have a talk. But having spoken to Aaron, I have no problem with him being present. Who knows, maybe his showing up here may be more than just a coincidence. Maybe it's an omen." Pointing to the seawall, he said, "Come on, let's go sit over there."

"First off," said Aaron as they settled down on the wall, "Clifford Allen, your solicitor, as well as Bridget and Edward, are all very cross with you. They didn't take kindly to the way you just upped and left without consulting them, especially Clifford. In any case, he has informed Edward that Leroy Butcher and his men are considering going on a manhunt for Larry. The information that you provided to Butcher seems to have fired him up. Additionally, they're trying to get a hold of Kadija. She too seems to have vanished. Butcher informed Clifford of your encounter with a Ukrainian woman and your discovery of Olive's phone in her possession. Clifford has demanded that a search warrant be obtained to search Kadija's property and that she be brought in for questioning. I'm not sure what the situation is as we speak. So, there you have it. Oh, incidentally..." Aaron gave Rudy a pointed stare. "It may interest you to know that Bridget plans to head out to Soufriere, along with Vernon; probably in the hope of persuading you to give up the chase. They should be arriving this evening."

Rudy looked like he could have been knocked over by a feather. It took a while for what Aaron said to sink in. Before he could recover, Trini chipped in. "I've got a strong suspicion where your man, Larry Thompson is holed up," he said. He told Rudy about Morgan and the photo he had seen of Morgan and Larry Thompson. He also told him, for the first time, what had caused him to leave the police force. His face hardening, he gave a riveting account of Manuel's criminal background and his suspected drug running and money laundering activities. He spoke in a strangled voice, as if each word had to be painfully forced out of his throat. All throughout, Rudy was watching his hands. Trini kept flexing his fingers like some maniac reveling in the prospect of his next kill.

"That house in the photo is about a twenty minute drive from here. It is rumored that Manuel bought it about a year ago. That said, trying to trace his assets is a challenge in and of itself. He uses all sorts of legal stunts to conceal proof of his acquisitions. When I heard about this latest one, I did everything I could to convince the cops and the Justice Ministry to put extra surveillance measures in place to keep an eye on the guy because I know all too well what he and his Columbian cohorts are capable of. The aim of these South American drug lords is to completely subvert what they regard as weak little kiss-me-ass islands, so they can more easily exploit them as transshipment points for drugs to North America and Europe. The last thing the people of Soufriere and the surrounding communities need right now, especially the youth, is for those drug cartels to establish a beachhead here in Soufriere. But no one seems to be taking me seriously.

"The villa in the photo was originally named Maison de Royaume. There is a network of underground tunnels running through parts of the property, including one nearly a mile long that stretches through the mountains all the way to the sea. It is believed that another one ends somewhere beneath the town. Very few people around here are aware of this and most of those who do don't know the full extent or nature of those tunnels, nor do they really care.

"They were built in the 18th century by runaway slaves known as Brigands with help from French Republican rebels in Martinique and Guadeloupe. The Martiniquans formed alliances with the Brigands and other slave collaborators and local Republicans who supported the Revolution. They banded together to form the *Armee Francaise dans les bois*, as they called themselves. The tunnels were used to furnish the Brigands with weapons and supplies to fight the British and the French Royalists on the island. Similar tunnels in other parts of the island were used for the same purpose. This was between 1794 and 1797."

Rudy looked stunned. "Are you saying that Manuel is using those tunnels for drug running?"

"Some time ago," said Trini, "I received reliable intelligence indicating that the property has now become the favoured rendezvous spot for certain shady wheeler-dealer types, mostly

Americans, including some Latinos, and occasionally South Americans. Even a couple of Russians have stopped by. I have my suspicions about the owner of The Mirage but so far I've not seen the smoking gun."

"What do you think Larry Thompson's connections are with these people?" said Rudy.

"Internet scams," Aaron interjected. Rudy and Trini stared at him. "It is my understanding that Leroy Butcher made some enquiries with Europol and the FBI based on the information that you provided him regarding the hacking of your computer. He was able to establish that the US law enforcement authorities recently linked Larry to a major internet hacking scam which they had been monitoring for some time. Chances are he may have gotten wind that they were onto him and he fled to Saint Lucia."

"So the question is," said Trini, "Have Thompson and his friends moved their operations to an area where there is practically no surveillance capabilities to deal with these sorts of scams? And the most burning question of all; what is Lucas Manuel's role in all of this? What exactly is going on behind closed doors at Maison de Royaume? ... Until now, I knew very little about this Larry guy but I had been aware of the presence of suspected cybercriminal elements on the island, through intelligence sources. Although I tried not to show it, I was actually very disturbed when Rudy told me about what happened to him and the incidents surrounding it."

Trini abruptly glanced at his watch. "Oh shit! Listen guys, I've got to run. I need to make my deliveries to the hotel. I suggest the three of us touch base again later this evening. I'm mulling over a game plan but I'm going to rope in Inspector Miller and feel him out a bit." Peering at Rudy, he added, "What's your take on it? Are you cool with my suggestion?"

"I'm still struggling to wrap my head around all of this but hell, let's meet and talk. It actually feels like something is about to give, and for me it's a whole new feeling. Frankly, I was on the verge of giving in to despair."

Trini said to Aaron, "I leave him in your care. Make sure you watch over him." With that, he stood up and ran towards his pickup, jumped in and started the engine. Sticking his head through the window, he shouted to Aaron, "I'll call you!" and drove off.

Aaron waited till he was out of sight and said, "You're not throwing your lot in with him and the likes of Miller, are you?"

"Sure, why not?" said Rudy, surprised.

"With all due respect to the Soufriere police, what if there are moles among them and they're being bribed to keep the bad guys informed about what's afoot? Not even Trini can deny that some elements among the local police have been corrupted. By the time he's had his little chat with the inspector, you may as well kiss Larry goodbye, and likewise your hopes of ever solving this case; assuming that he is indeed holed up at Lucas Manuel's place as we suspect."

"Trini's an ex-cop and he seems to have strong ties with the upper ranks of the police force. Surely, there are folks in there he can trust."

"Indeed, I agree. I would further suggest that it's more than likely that he still maintains links with the US Drug Enforcement Agency and the FBI. Between you, me and the mountains, I have reason to suspect that he also has secret affiliations with the CIA. Yet none of this has kept him from losing faith in the law enforcement system nor did it dissuade him from quitting the profession he has dedicated his life to."

"So what do you suggest I do?"

"There's no reason you and I can't handle this ourselves. I suggest we sneak over to Lucas Manuel's place and snoop around to ascertain that Larry is there and find out precisely what's going on up there. After that, we scram and get hold of Butcher and have him light a fire under his police colleagues so that we can get some action. I assure you, thereafter we will get results."

"What the f….! Now I know for sure you've lost your marbles. This is your dumbest idea yet! You want us to break into Manuel's house? In the first place, how on earth are you going to get even within an inch of the building? And even if you do, how do you plan on getting out without a bullet in your ass?"

"There's an alternative route to the house besides the main entrance. If we use it, we can get up close quite easily without being detected. I'm familiar with the place and the surrounding terrain. Trust me, it's a cinch."

"No Aaron! Forget it."

"If we allow Larry to give us the slip, it's all over for you. Do you know that?"

"No way, man! That's a crazy idea."

"So be it, I'll sneak up to the house myself."

"What! Why would you want to do that?"

"Because it needs to be done. You heard Trini. These people are destructive and corrupt and they need to be stopped. Someone needs to stand up to them. Being a foreigner, that ought not to be my responsibility. But then, if you lot are too squeamish, someone's got to do it for you."

"That's bullshit! You're crazy."

"Please yourself. I'll go it alone. Besides, for all I know, by then you may be safely in the arms of Lady Macbeth who's coming over to protect you." Aaron crossed the street and climbed onto a motorbike, which he had apparently turned up with. A crash helmet dangled from the handlebar. He put it on and gunned the engine.

"Hey, wait!" shouted Rudy as he began riding off. Aaron paused. "You're joking, right?" said Rudy.

"No sir, I'm not."

"Can we talk about this some more?"

"I'm afraid not," said Aaron firmly. "What's the verdict, are you coming with me or not?" Aaron revved the bike's engine.

Rudy rolled his eyes and grunted in exasperation. Aaron suppressed a grin. He could see Rudy's resolve weakening. "Come on, let's go," he said and rode off confidently. Rudy got into his car and followed him, swearing.

41

Rudy swore under his breath as the drizzling rain blew wetly into his face just as the dinghy rounded the promontory and began skimming over the waves towards the coast. A crescent moon shone pallidly through breaks in the clouds and the shoreline materialised ghostlike in the distance. Before they set off Rudy had warned Aaron it would rain, judging by the cluster of dark clouds lumbering across the sky but Aaron pooh-poohed it and ignored him. It was six-thirty and already dark when they cast off from the Soufriere harbor in a fiberglass dinghy with a four-stroke engine. Aaron had borrowed it from one of his British expat friends residing near the town. The alternative route to Maison de Royaume he had alluded to earlier turned out to be over a beachside cliff which, according to Aaron, would lead them to the rear of the property. Without indicating how, he said he'd ascertained that there were no dogs guarding the place, nor any security guards. Still seething, Rudy recalled how Aaron had subtly goaded him by poking fun at his fears, and his desire to 'play it safe.' He even wondered aloud how Rudy had been able to make it as a journalist, all the while playing on his emotions and wounding his ego. The son-of-a-bitch was smart! Eventually, out of exhaustion and against his better judgment, Rudy caved in and agreed to join Aaron on his wild caper.

"Hang on to your hat, we're almost there!" Aaron shouted over the groaning of the outboard engine. Driven by the wind, the rain kept spitting in their faces and drenching their clothes. Both men wore black trousers, dark-colored T-shirts and dark woolly hats. Aaron had insisted this garb was necessary to make it more difficult for them to be spotted. To Rudy, it merely underscored the craziness of their escapade and made him feel like a character in DC Comics.

As they drifted into the shallows, Aaron turned the motor off and tilted it to avoid damaging the propellers. They quickly stepped out of the dinghy and pulled it way above the high water mark, among some shrubs where, hopefully, it wouldn't be spotted. They returned for the anchor and carried it to the same spot. Aaron took a small pouch containing a flashlight from the dinghy.

"Are you sure they're safe here?" Rudy sounded skeptical.

"They're quite safe, never fear." Aaron assured him.

"Where to from here?" Rudy glanced around him doubtfully.

"Close by is a cave and next to it some steps cut into the side of the cliff. All we do is climb to the top of the cliff and follow a trail that will lead us to Maison de Royaume. Come on, off we go." Aaron took off at a quick pace with Rudy behind, scrambling to try and keep up with him.

"Do many people use this beach?" Rudy asked, embarrassed by his own ignorance.

"This area is usually deserted, even in the daytime. If anyone uses the beach, most likely it's the drug traffickers. Let's hope we don't run into any of them. It could be a tad discomforting for us."

They plodded along with Rudy cursing and muttering and wondering why the hell he'd allowed Aaron to talk him into getting involved in such madness. Mercifully, the rain stopped. The waves broke softly against the sand and kissed their feet. They soon came to a small cave awash with seawater as a result of high tide. Rudy stared sullenly at the water. Among his pet peeves was walking with wet shoes, ever since he was a kid.

"Now we head up the cliff," said Aaron, beaming the flashlight at a flight of earthen steps, which had clearly been cut into the slope. Rudy sighed with relief. They climbed the steps quietly, walking briskly.

When they reached the top, Aaron turned off the flashlight. In the gloom they could see the land had a slight elevation and it was overgrown with thick bush. "Stay close to me and keep your eyes peeled," said Aaron as they made their way slowly through the bushes. About five minutes later he called out to Rudy, "Trail ahead! We'll have to do without the torch, I'm afraid. Remember, keep alert and proceed with caution. It's not a very long trek from here to the house."

Aaron forged ahead, setting a slow and deliberate pace. The intermittent light from the moon barely penetrated the darkness. They came to what felt like a huge tuft of elephant grass, thick and tall. They waded through it, relying on their ears and their sense of touch. Although the climb was not very steep, they were treading on loose stones and it required concentration to avoid slipping or straining their ankles.

"There's a forest patch ahead," said Aaron. "Stick close to me, this will keep you from running into the trees or decapitating yourself. Besides, we don't want the gnomes and fairies running off with you."

"Now hold on a minute!" Rudy retorted. "If there's a forest, then there must be snakes. Are you out of your mind?"

"Other folks have used this trail and lived to tell the tale."

"Listen man, we're in fucking darkness! Snakes are endemic to Saint Lucia's forests. God knows what else is lurking out there!"

"In that case, here's what I suggest. You wait here and I'll continue on alone. Keep your fingers crossed and let's hope Lucas Manuel's business associates don't run into you. On the other hand, it probably doesn't matter since the snakes will get you anyway."

"Will you cut it out! This is serious."

"See here, mate. Why the Dickens do you think I'm putting myself through all of this other than to save your ass? Don't think for one minute that you're out of the woods yet with the police. I have never shrunk back from a challenge and I'm not about to do so now. But if I have deigned to go through all this bother to try and save your skin, then by God man, you could at the very least give me the pleasure of believing that it was worth it!" Aaron sounded peeved.

Rudy was taken aback by his reaction and the sting in his voice. Quietly, he resumed following Aaron, feeling his way among the trees like a blind man. Vines and creepers dangling from the trees occasionally brushed against his face, startling him. The night was filled with a pleasant yet eerie cacophony of nocturnal sounds, from buzzing crickets to the throaty 'gleep gleep' of tree frogs to the whistling 'cokee' of coqui lizards, to the chirping of birds yet to fall asleep. Rudy could feel the land gradually leveling out under his feet. They came abruptly to a break in the trees. "There it is!" said Aaron. Together, they stood gazing down at the Maison de Royaume a couple of hundred yards away. "Brace yourself, now the action begins," said Aaron.

42

The villa lay on top of a ridge overlooking the sea and the mountains and valleys to the north and east of Soufriere. The moon came out inquisitively from behind a cloud as if eager to see how Rudy and Aaron were progressing. It was quite a vast two-storied mansion with the customary high-pitched roof and traditional arches and columns. There were no outside lights on. There was a faint glow in one of the upper rooms but the rest of the building was in total darkness. "Looks like someone is home," said Rudy. "Could be," said Aaron, sounding unperturbed. "We'll be fine, as long as there are no more than one or two," he added. Pointing towards the rear of the house, he said, "It'll be a mite tricky but I suggest we head this way and approach from the rear. There doesn't seem to be any sign of activity down there but it never hurts to be cautious in situations like this."

"Just to be clear, what's the game plan?" said Rudy.

"We get as close to the house as possible, sneak in if needs be and see if we can determine for sure whether Larry is indeed holed up in there. If he is, we telephone Trini and Butcher who will in turn alert the police and they will pay Mr. Manuel a visit. Don't forget they wish to bring Larry in for questioning. Presumably, by now there should be a warrant out for his arrest, certainly if Trini has his way, although with the local police one can never be sure."

"What happens if we're caught trespassing?"

"It's up to us to ensure that we're not. In any case, I took the precaution of requesting of Geoff – the owner of the dinghy – that he call Trini and inform him of our whereabouts if he does not receive a call from me by 11:00 p.m. – two and a half hours from now. Remember, I'm staying at his place."

"Does he know that you're planning to break into a drug dealer's home?"

"He does indeed."

"What was his reaction?"

"'Be sure to do it on a full stomach,' he said because, according to him, dying on an empty stomach could be quite dreadful. Geoff knows that I have an adventuresome streak and he's become quite used to it."

"Another one like you. God help us all."

They continued on in the darkness towards the house, weaving their way through thick grass and shrubs.

Fifteen minutes later they stood on the edge of the villa's back courtyard. By then Rudy was sweating profusely and his arms and face itched badly, evidently an allergic reaction to the grass and tree vines brushing against his skin. Bent double, they edged closer to the house, trying their best to keep in the shadows. At the back of the house was a portico with French doors and a courtyard-style garden. Aaron whispered to Rudy, "I'm going to check the door locks. In the meantime, why don't you go around the side of the house and keep an eye on the front. We don't want to be caught by surprise. It would be a bloody nuisance." Aaron went to check the backdoors.

Rudy went around the side of the house, bending low to avoid being spotted through the windows. Peeping around the corner, he scanned the front of the property, looking for signs of movement on the grounds. A brief shower of moonlight exposed an open-air terrace with seating, a garden and an infinity pool surrounded by stone paver walkways, including one leading to the front door. Two SUVs were parked beside the courtyard. The sight of them jolted Rudy. On their way down to the house, neither of them had spotted the vehicles. He realized now it was because of the location and alignment of the parking lot. From their vantage point back up in the bushes they would have been virtually obscured by the trees in the garden and the darkness. There could be no doubt now that there were people in the house, perhaps several!

Rudy ran to the back of the house to look for Aaron. He saw him fiddling with the backdoor, trying to pick the lock with a lock pick. "Hey, watch it, there are people inside," he said in a hushed tone, adding, "There are two SUVs out there."

"Luck's on our side. This lock is fairly easy to pick. Hang on."

"Didn't you hear me? There are people inside the house – could be several of them!" Rudy hissed.

"So what?"

"What do you mean, 'so what'?"

"Surely, we're not going to go through this tussle all over again, are we?"

"You bet your ass we are!"

"You're wasting time, Rudy," Aaron retorted, an edge in his voice. "If there are people indoors, then we must move fast. Do you mind if we fight over this when it's all over?"

"Fuck you and your crazy ideas! Besides, I'm sick of you ordering me around. I'm outer here." Turning, Rudy began walking back towards the bushes. Aaron stamped his foot in a rage. Glancing apprehensively at the house, he ran after Rudy then stopped, as if he was in two minds. He took off again and caught up with Rudy as he was about to enter in amongst the trees. "Wait, stop!" he called out. Rudy turned around. Aaron hesitated a moment, then said, "There's something I haven't told you." His voice was taut with tension. "Before coming here, I gave Jacquie Thompson, Larry's stepmother, my word that I would try to get hold of him and talk some sense into him, hopefully get him to turn himself in to the police so that whatever charges they may have against him may be dealt with in a proper and civil manner, and according to the law. At the moment, Jacquie is in a terrible state worrying about him. She can't bear the thought of him living the life of a fugitive. I would hate to disappoint her. You may go if you wish and good luck finding your way back to the beach and piloting the dinghy. As for me, I'm heading back to the house." Turning, Aaron retraced his steps.

"You lying bastard!" Rudy exclaimed. Rushing up to Aaron, he grabbed his arm. "You didn't come here for my sake, you used me to try and save your friend!"

"Poppycock! I already had an idea where Larry might be before I contacted you. I could have gone along and left you out of the picture. There was no need to have you tagging along, being an utter nuisance, which quite frankly is all you've been. I involved you out of courtesy."

"You rich sons-of-bitches are all the same. When it suits you, you know how to make us commoners feel like we matter. But at the end of the day, it's all playacting. You couldn't give a shit about people you don't need."

"Farewell. I wish you Godspeed," said Aaron. Bending low, he hurried back to the house. No sooner he got there, he heard footsteps behind him. "Welcome back," he whispered, grinning. Rudy ignored him. Aaron resumed trying to pick the lock. "Got it!" Slowly and quietly, he pushed the door open and stepped inside. Rudy followed him. The ground floor was in darkness and deathly quiet. They moved stealthily through a spacious hallway and paused behind a huge pillar near what appeared to be a grand salon with French doors and walls lined with arched windows. A chandelier dangled from the ceiling. A winding staircase led to the upper floor. They heard a sound upstairs. Aaron sidled toward the staircase and paused at the bottom, listening. Rudy's heart skipped a beat when he saw him crouch and begin climbing the stairs, moving like a seasoned burglar. He soon disappeared from view.

"Take it easy," a voice said gruffly close to Rudy's ear, and he felt the cold touch of steel against his right temple. "Keep your ass shut and do what I tell you!" said the voice. "Turn around slow and go inside the room on your left. Make one wrong move and I'll blow your brains out."

The door on Rudy's left was ajar. It was shut when he and Aaron tiptoed past. He felt the press of metal again, in the small of his back. Slowly, he walked towards the door. A hand grabbed him by the back of the neck and shoved him hard, propelling him into the room. A shadow slid past him. "Stay close to the door and remember, keep your ass shut until I tell you to talk!" the voice growled menacingly. Rudy kept still. Seconds ticked by agonizingly. He heard the sound of footsteps out in the hallway followed by silence.

"Rudy, where are you?" said Aaron, trying to keep his voice down. He sounded close to the door. The voice whispered in Rudy's ear, "Answer!" A gun barrel pressed painfully into his back, making him wince. "Aaron, over here," he said, trying his best to stay calm. Aaron entered the room and the figure promptly slid out from behind Rudy, slammed the door shut and turned the light on.

Rudy and Aaron gaped in shock at the gun aimed at them; an Israeli-made semiautomatic Desert Eagle 50E, rated by gun aficionados as one of the most powerful pistols. The man aiming it at them, probably in his late teens or early twenties, was obviously reveling in how mean and deadly it made him look. He sidled across to the centre of the room, holding the gun sideways, and trying his damnedest to look as gangsterish as he could. He had a face that could have been handsome, except that it was now rough and battle-scarred, and practically shorn of its youthfulness, no doubt due to gangland living. His hostile eyes were bloodshot, as if he had been smoking weed heavily. He was slim and muscular, with a torso that looked disproportionate to the rest of him. He sported a Guns n' Roses T-shirt, baggy jeans, Kanye West Air Yeezy sneakers and a New York Yankees cap.

Rudy and Aaron gazed around the room, flabbergasted. It was actually a home theatre room and looked extremely plush and spacious. The walls and paneling were painted a warm camel to create a cozy look. Chairs and couches with plush throws were used for sectional seating to create an intimate family-friendly environment. It was equipped with a projector and a projection screen, and plush carpeting. It even had a mini kitchen for added convenience. The ambience was slightly marred by an antique wood desk and leather chair tucked away in a corner of the room. They looked out of place.

Gripping the gun with both hands, the gunman glared malevolently at Rudy and Aaron, and said, "Lie dong flat on the floor, both of you! And stretch out your hands. Do it now!"

Both men went down on their knees reluctantly. Rudy lay on his stomach with his arms stretched out. Aaron hesitated.

"Don't try nothing foolish, unless you want me to blow your freakin' brains out!" the gunman warned Aaron sinisterly. He sounded as if nothing would give him greater pleasure. Aaron lay down quietly next to Rudy. The gunman took a mobile phone out of his pocket and dialed a number. "Come down here quick! In the theatre room. Move it!" Keeping his eyes on the two men, he slipped the phone back into his pocket. A few minutes later, running feet stampeded down the stairs and pounded through the hallway. Two men and a woman barged into the room. The men wore dark hoodie zip-up T-shirts. All three of them gaped in shock at the two men lying on the floor.

"Who de fuck is dem guys? Where they come from?" cried one of the men.

"I catch dem sneakin' around," said the gunman. "Don't ask me where they come from, I ain't got a clue. Search them, see if they have weapons," he ordered the other two men. He seemed to be the ringleader, judging by the imperious way he spoke to them. They moved swiftly and began frisking Rudy and Aaron. One of them pulled the woolen caps from both men's heads. "It's okay. They clean," he said and drew away. He stuffed the caps into his back pocket.

Still pointing the gun at Rudy and Aaron, the gunman said, "Get your ass up from the floor, both of y'all!"

Slowly, they stood up.

"They can't be cops, this one have locks," the gunman said confidently.

"Wait a minute!" yelled the woman. "The Rasta guy, I know him. He's the one who was in the club looking for Larry. The same one who went after Alina."

Rudy gaped at the woman, shocked. Where had he seen her before? He was having trouble thinking straight. Suddenly it clicked. She was the woman who had been pole-dancing with Alina at The Mirage, and one of the three people who had later travelled with her on the minibus. The gunman walked up to Rudy. He was a full head shorter than him. Glowering at him and trying his utmost to look ferocious, he snarled, "So you de guy been playin' detective ... and who's the white boy, your deputy?"

"Ask him." Rudy held his gaze, refusing to be cowed.

"I'm askin' you."

Rudy said nothing.

The gunman walked to and fro in front of him, his bloodshot eyes focusing on him like a laser. "How de ass de two of you get here? Where you pass?" he demanded.

"We were hiding in the boot of your car," said Rudy.

The gunman laughed. "So you're a comedian too," he said and shook his head. He punched Rudy hard in the stomach. Rudy grunted and dropped to his knees, gripping his stomach and blinded by pain. The gunman kicked him savagely. Instinctively, Rudy twisted his body and managed to blunt the force of the blow with his arm. He collapsed and lay writhing on the floor. Aaron moved but before he knew it, he was staring straight down the barrel of a gun. The gunman grinned evilly at him. Turning to one of the other two men, he said, "Give Lucas a call, tell him to come fast!" The youth bolted from the room. The gunman said to the woman, "Go look in the top kitchen cabinet you'll see some rope. Bring it for me."

"Me!" she squealed. "How is me? I don't want to get involved. I just passing through."

"Then what you doing in here? Get de fuck out!"

She turned and dashed out of the room. The other man drew a gun and aimed it at Aaron, as if to try and make himself useful. "So what we doing with these two fellers?" he asked. The ringleader scratched his head and seemed to be trying hard to figure out what to do. Thinking seemed to be a strain for him.

Rudy struggled back up to his feet. The man who had left the room came rushing back in. "Hey Yamaha!" he shouted, and handed the ringleader a cell phone. "Lucas want to talk to you. He tell you put the phone on loudspeaker."

Yamaha put the volume on speakerphone. "Yes boss."

"Yamaha! What's going on over there?" said a voice curtly. It had a slightly high-pitched, honeyed tone that made the speaker sound a bit like Al Jarreau. It was the sort of voice that was crafted to enthrall women and wielded well, it could easily leave them swooning. Yamaha quickly explained how he had come upon two 'strange fellers' sneaking around in the house. "Why are these two men still alive?" the voice demanded. "They broke into my property. For all I know, they could have been sent to assassinate me. You're my chief bodyguard, your job is to guard my home and protect me. Who're these guys?"

"A Rasta and a white man."

"What! Who's the white man?"

"I don't know. I never see him before."

"What's their names?"

"I don't know."

"Shit man! You don't seem to know a damn thing. So what the fuck am I paying you for? Where's Jeremie?" By then the honey had oozed out of the voice and it was now hard as steel.

"Jeremie right here by me."

"Give him the phone."

Yamaha handed the phone to his comrade.

"Hey Jeremie!" said the voice.

"Yeh Lucas."

"Tell me something. You think I should let Yamaha keep his job? ... Come on, talk to me."

"Uhm ... well ...." Jeremie stammered. He glanced uncomfortably at Yamaha who watched him apprehensively. Rudy and Aaron gaped from one to the other, captivated by the drama unfolding before them. A loud, cackling laugh came through the phone. Jeremie gazed at it, puzzled. "Okay guys, relax," said the voice. "Where y'all have these two guys?"

"In the theatre room," Jeremie replied.

"Okay, keep them there. I was already on my way up to the house when you called. I'll soon be there." The line went dead.

"He always playing dem old jokes," Jeremie muttered, still staring uncomfortably at Yamaha. Yamaha glared balefully at Rudy and Aaron. "Keep your eyes on them, I coming just now," he barked at Jeremie and stormed out of the room. Jeremie kept his gun trained on the two men.

Five minutes later, Yamaha returned with several long strips of polypropylene fiber and a roll of duct tape. "Turn around," he snapped at Rudy. He found Rudy reacted too slowly so he grabbed his arm and spun him around and began tying his wrists.

"Is this really necessary? We aren't misbehaving," Aaron protested.

"Keep your mouth shut, Englishman unless you want me to shut it up for you!" Yamaha growled.

Rudy grimaced as the cord bit into his wrists. "Hey, cool it!" he yelled. Yamaha ignored him and moved across to Aaron. He gave him the same treatment. Behind his back, Rudy jiggled his wrists to try and loosen the cord but it was no use, it was tied too tightly. "In case you guys are thinking of eliminating us," he said, "I must warn you that would be a bad idea. There are friends who would be able to figure where we've gone."

"Is that so?" Yamaha sneered. "You going to need their help to bury your ass or to bail y'all if the boss decide to call police and make them jail you for breaking and enter and trespassing."

The sound of a car engine drifted in from outside. "That's Lucas!" said Jeremie. Yamaha rushed out to go meet his boss.

43

Two vehicle doors slammed and voices could be heard outside. A few minutes later, the door of the theatre room flew open and Lucas Manuel walked in with Yamaha slavishly on his heels. Manuel had the self assured, well-fed look of a man for whom prosperity had become as trite as breathing. He was of average height and stout with broad shoulders and his complexion was on the lighter side of brown. His rugged face was not particularly good-looking yet, in some strange way, it was captivating. He was dressed simply but stylishly in a black Rocawear track jacket, a white, high-collar, button-down shirt along with a thick gold chain, dark denim jeans and black-and-grey lace-up shoes. He sported a sleek crew cut. He studied Rudy and Aaron, eyeing them from head to toe. He didn't seem perturbed by their intrusion into his home. Turning to Yamaha, he grinned and said mischievously, "But how you could treat the guys so bad, even though they're unwanted pests?" Approaching Rudy and Aaron, he said, "Gentlemen, how you doing?"

"Fine, thank you," said Aaron, adding, "We'd be doing much better with our hands untied, however. Rather uncalled for, I dare say."

Manuel laughed. "I dare say, you must find it even more disagreeable not to have been invited to stay for tea and crumpets," he replied, aping Aaron's British accent.

"Quite civil of you to suggest that."

Manuel gaped at Aaron in mock surprise. He turned to Yamaha and Jeremie. "What do you know, an Englishman with a sense of humor," he said, dripping sarcasm. Gazing at Rudy, he said, "What about you, what you got to say for yourself?"

"What do you want me to say?"

"Why don't you start by explaining what the fuck you and this clown doing in my house?"

"We're looking for Larry Thompson."

Rudy's directness threw Manuel. He hesitated a moment and then frowned. "Why are you looking for him?"

Glancing at Yamaha and Jeremie, Rudy said, "Why don't we discuss this in private?"

"With our hands untied, if you don't mind," Aaron added.

Manuel shrugged. "No problem." Turning, he said, "Guys, you heard the man. Give us some space for a minute, will you."

As they were about to walk out the door, Manuel shouted, "Yamaha!"

"Yeah?"

"Untie them."

Yamaha hesitated. He had a disapproving look on his face. "Boss, you sure about that?" he asked.

"Yep, go ahead. Don't worry."

Yamaha narrowed his eyes and pouted. He untied Rudy and Aaron's hands and left the room looking peeved. He shut the door quietly. Manuel grabbed two chairs and placed them in front of the desk in the corner, and went around and sat on the other side. Reaching into his jacket he pulled out a Beretta 92 SB handgun and placed it on the desk. "Please, have a seat," he said.

The two men sat down, staring at the gun. Manuel focused intently on Rudy, as if he was trying to unravel a mystery. Rudy shifted uncomfortably and tried not to show weakness by looking away.

"Why do I get the feeling I know you?" said Manuel.

"Search me. I don't know you."

"If there's one thing I don't forget it's a face. You remind me of someone I used to know back in primary school ... the Choiseul Primary school."

Rudy stiffened. Now it was his turn to peer quizzically at Manuel.

"Really? ... I did attend the Choiseul Primary," he said cautiously.

"Luke the Pussy Boy ... remember?"

Rudy sat erect. He looked stunned. "You! .... Pussy Boy?"

Manual nodded.

Rudy recalled the scrawny, slightly effeminate little runt who used to be the butt of non-stop jokes and wise cracks back in his stage-four class at primary school in Choiseul. They were both eight at the time. An only child of a single mother, Manuel used to be painfully shy and extremely sensitive, and very easily offended. The worst part was that he would burst into tears for the slightest imagined wrong against him. This was why Rudy and their other classmates had nicknamed him Pussy Boy. It was Rudy who suggested the name. He couldn't help despising Manuel, although to this day he wasn't sure why. Because of that, he had teased and bullied him relentlessly, more than any of the other kids, and he did so with relish. He would dare Manuel to report him to the teacher or his mother, but he'd never had the guts to. Perhaps he treated him this way because Manuel's weakness had stirred up a primal predatory instinct in him. Or maybe Manuel had wronged in him a past life and this time he'd been fated to take his revenge. Whatever it was, he'd just felt an intense and inexplicable loathing for him. And the very fact that he hadn't even made the connection when Trini mentioned the name Lucas Manuel, said a lot about how insignificant Manuel had been to him – like he had never ever existed. Pondering over it actually made Rudy resentful on realizing that the one-time sniveling little worm who had since metamorphosed into a big-time, drug-dealing businessman, had ended up supremely well off while he who had walked the straight and narrow, was financially struggling. He'd been sure that Manuel would never amount to anything in life. Even staring at him now, he still couldn't believe this was the same Lucas Manuel of two and a half decades ago. Surely, there must be some mistake. For what it was worth, he could still feel justified in feeling contempt for him because of his criminality. "I don't suppose you made it further than primary school," he said, drily.

"Wrong. I got as far as Cornel University. Got there on a government scholarship. Midway, I decided to quit."

"Why? Your few brain cells couldn't cope?"

Manuel smiled. "Wrong again. Two fellow students and I got introduced to a new and exciting business opportunity on campus. Unfortunately, the two of them got careless and they got busted by the cops. I was in the clear but I figured it was a good time to move on. I hung around in the States for about ten more years getting some more business experience before returning home. That decision, as I'm sure you can tell, has completely transformed my life."

There was a poignant silence.

The two men continued to stare defiantly at each other. In that moment of mutual recognition, there was no display of amity or warmth, no nostalgic reconnection; just a cold indifference towards each other and an emotional deadness that surpassed the aloofness between strangers.

"It truly is a small world ..." Manuel mused, looking and sounding even more detached. "It's amazing how the structure of your face hasn't changed much over the years. I recall you just upped and left and no one ever saw or heard from you again. Years later we heard you had gone to England. It may disappoint you to know that Pussy Boy didn't even shed a tear."

There was another uncomfortable moment of silence.

"And I promise you," said Manuel gently. "I won't cry for every little thing like I used to. I'm a big boy now."

Rudy glanced away and said nothing.

"So now you back from the Motherland, transformed into a little Englishman and sporting your gold-plated British accent. What's with the locks – you're a Rastaman too?"

"Not really." Rudy suddenly felt irritated at having to respond to Manuel.

Aaron cleared his throat. "If you two don't mind, could we get back to trying to solve our little impasse," he suggested patiently.

Manuel pointedly ignored him, as if to say, stay the fuck out of it. Gazing fixedly at Rudy, he said, "How did you two get here? I saw no sign of any strange car outside."

"I'm not at liberty to say," Rudy replied woodenly.

"You not at liberty to say? Who you think you are, some fucking CIA agent?" Rage disfigured Manuel's face and his eyes flared like burning embers. Then his wrath blew over like a passing rainstorm, as if he'd suddenly checked himself.

At that very moment, it struck Rudy that Manuel kept switching between precise English and the local twang, depending on his mood and who he was addressing, sometimes switching in midsentence. He did it so subtly, it was almost imperceptible. He seemed to be trying to bridge the gap between two different personas. It was like a form of camouflage and, Rudy suspected, a sign of his deceptive, chameleonic nature, rather than him just adapting to a given situation. It made Rudy feel very uneasy.

"Let's cut to the chase," Manuel said softly and with a composed demeanor that made him look almost fatherly. He toyed with the gun, spinning it round and round on the desk. "Since you and I were born here, we both know how hard it is to keep secrets on a small island like Saint Lucia, not to mention in a tiny community like Soufriere. In addition to that – regardless of what anyone may have told you about me – I'm a man who is well grounded in the communities. People love and appreciate me, unlike you. And because of these strong connections, I have my sources. I know exactly what you and your comrade sitting next to you – and the people you're working with – are up to. The woman who was murdered on Elysian Island, and the one they found dead here in Soufriere a few days ago, I know all about that too. You see that friend of yours sitting next to you? He's a foreigner, an outsider. I don't give a shit about him. He's not important. You and I, on the other hand, are fellow Saint Lucians and we're both black men, so let's be frank with each other and not bullshit one another. For now, let's forget the past. Whatever your reason is for coming here, whatever problem you have that's bothering you, tell me all about it and let's see what I can do to make it go away."

"Be careful Rudy," said Aaron.

Once again, Manuel ignored him and focused on Rudy. "Come on, talk to me," he urged him.

Eyeing Manuel's gun, Rudy pondered a while then said, "What about Larry Thompson, do you know him?"

"Of course, he's my friend."

"Is he here in this house?"

"Yes.'

Silence.

Rudy glanced at Aaron. Aaron gave him a warning stare. "Watch your mouth," he said.

Staring eye-to-eye at Manuel, Rudy said, "Are you aware that the cops are looking for him?"

"So I hear ... what, is that why you guys broke in here? What are you, bounty hunters?"

"No, we just wanted to be sure he's here."

Manuel laughed. "You guys are nuts!"

"If you know as much about me as you imply, then you should also know that my neck is on the line and I'm facing a possible murder charge, all because of a man – a foreigner, an outsider, to use your words - whom you're protecting. Chances are my ass could be grass all because the one who should be answering to the law is being protected by a fellow Saint Lucian, a fellow black man. Explain that to me."

Manuel bowed his head and resumed toying with the gun, passing his fingers lightly over the polished steel.

"Okay, I get you," he said, glancing up. "So tell me, what do you want me to do?"

"Turn him in to the police."

"Just tell me one more thing. Why exactly do you want me to turn him over to the cops? What has he done? And I want you to be straight with me."

"He's involved in the murder of Olive Henry on Elysian Island."

"What proof do the cops have of that?"

"He's fishing for information, Rudy. You may be walking into a trap," Aaron interjected.

Manuel snapped the gun up and aimed at Aaron's head. "If you interrupt one more time, I'll shoot you. Don't fuck with me!" The deadly glint in his eyes was chilling.

Placing the gun back on the desk, he turned to Rudy. "What proof is there that Larry is involved in the woman's murder? How can I be sure you not just slandering the man?"

"I can't speak for the cops but there is evidence pointing to his involvement in the murder – the brutal slaying of a young black, Saint Lucian by a white foreigner," said Rudy in a strangled tone as if he'd had to force the words out. It was an indication of the self-loathing he felt at having to resort to the xenophobic and twisted logic of an opportunistic drug dealer to try and sway him. More and more his contempt for Manuel was growing, to the point that it almost felt like back in their primary school days. This made him despise Manuel even more.

"I hear you," said Manuel. "But here's the problem. Larry is a grown man. I can't force him to do what he don't want to do. And besides, *you* say the police want him for questioning but I don't know that to be true. He's been here in Soufriere, in plain sight, for the past few weeks. Why haven't they gone after him? Why isn't there a warrant out for his arrest? ... You see my problem? I want to help you but ..." Manuel shrugged.

"I tried to warn you that it was a waste of time," said Aaron.

Manuel slammed his fist down on the desk. Grabbing the gun, he stood up, kicked over the chair and unleashed a barrage of expletives that resounded in the room. Rudy and Aaron froze. Manuel went around the side of the desk and paced back and forth, clearly agitated. Aaron and Rudy glanced apprehensively at each other. Slowly, they turned around. Manuel stopped pacing and gazed at them.

"Growing up as a kid, my mother would often say to me, if you want people to accept you, then the best way to achieve this is by being nice to everybody, give them what they ask for and share your belongings with them if they ask for help. So I listened to her and tried to do this all the time. But eventually, you know what I realized? I was putting other people's needs and desires ahead of mine.

"Most times I ended up agreeing with people's views rather than offering my own opinions. All because I wanted to be liked and accepted. And if I didn't feel loved and accepted, I would begin to sulk and get depressed. And yes, sometimes I'd cry. I used to bend over backwards just to help people who really didn't give a shit about me and would never do the same for me. But things have changed now. Reality has forced me to see the light. But you know how it is with us humans. Off and on you slip up and go back to doing the same old things all over again. You feel that need to be liked and admired – to be accepted. Then it fucking blows up in your face!

"That's what happened with me and Larry Thompson. You meet a guy, you get to like him and the two of you get along like a house on fire. You even consider teaming up and doing things together, maybe collaborating on business ventures. Before long you realize that it's probably not going to work out the way you had thought and, lo and behold, the dude causes you some grief. But for some reason you keep being nice to him and helping him out, although every day you have reason to be cursing his arse! The worst part is when you know deep down inside that, despite everything you do for that person, you're not really accepted by him, whether for racial reasons or feelings of nationalistic superiority or because of class. You're tolerated, even endured but not accepted." Manuel paused and stared at Rudy. "You grew up in England and you've been around folks like your friend there, so you should know what I'm talking about.

"Because of trying to be nice to a fellow human being, now I've got two assholes breaking into my house and trying to cause trouble for me; getting me so pissed off that all I want to do is *shoot them dead*! Now, if I was to do so, what would happen? More trouble and worries for me, all because of trying to be nice."

Manuel righted the chair and sat back down behind the desk. He placed the gun down conspicuously on top of it once more. Gazing at it, he said, as if speaking to himself. "The problem with this Thompson guy is the type of company he keeps, especially the females." Glancing up, he said, "I can do one of three things; call the cops and have them come and arrest both of you for breaking and entering; take advantage of the law that gives me the right to protect myself from a perceived threat from intruders breaking into my home, by shooting them if necessary, or I can allow you to meet and talk with Larry once you can guarantee me that afterwards you will leave and I'll never see nor hear from the two of you again. What do you say? Which will it be?"

Once again, Rudy and Aaron glanced at each other. Aaron said, "Can we have a word with Larry?"

Reaching into his pocket, Manuel pulled out an iPhone 6s and called one of his men. "Come up here, I need you to do something for me down in the cellar. Make it snappy!" He ended the call and tucked the phone back into his pocket. The three men sat quietly waiting, all of them tense, each wrapped up in his own thoughts.

44

There was a sharp knock at the door.

"Who's that!" Manuel bellowed.

"Yamaha!"

"Come in!"

Yamaha rushed into the room, looking all flustered. "Garcia and Jose just reach! They askin' for you."

"Shit!" Manuel hesitated, frowning. He tucked the gun back into his jacket pocket. "Send them in."

Yamaha slinked out of the room and two burley-looking Latino men wandered in.

"Hola, amigo! Looks like we caught you at a bad time," said one of the men. He had a strong Californian accent.

"Nah, it's okay," Manuel replied and switched to Spanish, speaking with a fluency that surprised Aaron and Rudy. The three men continued conversing in Spanish. Off and on, the two Latinos glanced warily at Rudy and Aaron, making it obvious that Manuel was talking about them. After a few minutes, Manuel smoothly shepherded the two men out of the room, then with a toss of his head he said to Rudy and Aaron, "Come on, let's go."

Yamaha was waiting out in the hallway, his gun drawn. He directed Rudy and Aaron through the hallway to the back door and out of the house. "Turn left and continue walking." He herded them towards a wooded area at the back of the building. He lit their way with the flashlight in his cell phone, all the while keeping a safe distance behind them. A couple hundred yards away they came to a single-storey wall structure resembling an old agricultural outbuilding built in a domestic yard or work area. Close to it was a privy with a shed roof. "Go to the back of that building!" Yamaha said curtly. The two men walked silently down the side of the building. Yamaha strode past them and paused near what looked like steps leading down into a basement. "Continue walking down dem steps!" he barked. Rudy and Aaron walked reluctantly down a long flight of stone steps. Yamaha lit their way with the cell phone flashlight. It was a long descent lasting several minutes. At the bottom of the steps, Yamaha flicked a switch and a light from a fluorescent bulb came on high up on a wall. It illuminated a medieval-looking passageway in what looked like a large underground chamber or cellar. It extended beyond the light and faded into blackness. The rugged walls looked quite ancient and the passageway had a dank, musty odor. Aaron began sneezing.

"Stop there!" said Yamaha. Easing past the two men, he pushed open a door to his right, one of four in the enclosure. He pressed a switch and a light came on in the room. "Get inside!" he barked and moved aside to let Aaron and Rudy enter. It was a cavernous space with rough-hewn, unpainted walls. It contained several splintered wooden crates stacked up in a corner. There were also a table and three splat-backed chairs, two wooden stools, an empty bookshelf and a bed with a mattress and no bed sheet in a corner against the wall. On top of the bookshelf were two bottles of brandy, a couple of glasses and a flat, book-sized gadget that resembled a Wi-Fi router. Opposite the bed was a rectangular wooden frame with a roller on both ends and a narrow plank in the middle. Yamaha kept his gun trained on Rudy and Aaron.

"Please gentlemen, make yourselves at home," said Manuel as he breezed into the room, sounding like a monarch showing magnanimity to his subjects. He caught Aaron staring pop-eyed at the wooden contraption with the rollers. "You find it interesting?" he said with a dastardly grin.

"A rack ... How did this get here?" said Aaron, looking quite astounded.

Edging closer to him, Manuel said, "I see you're familiar with it ... What about you, Rudy? In case you didn't know, in medieval times this was used to torture prisoners to extract confessions from them. They made the victim lie down on top of the frame and his wrists and ankles would be fastened to the rollers. The interrogator would use this handle near the top roller and stretch his limbs away from his body very slowly. Can you imagine how excruciatingly painful this must be? Shit! If the victim refused to cooperate, they'd stretch him some more until his arms, legs and joints got dislocated and snapped. Sometimes, to get a confession, all they had to do was force a prisoner to watch someone being ripped apart on the rack. This would've been enough to make the motherfucker squeal! Back then, so many people were given the treatment, it is said that the limbs had to be collected and emptied by the hundreds. Can you believe this shit!"

Manuel had a sadistic glint in his eyes that made Rudy shudder. The mere sight of the rack and Manuel's words echoing in his head, filled him with revulsion. "What is this thing doing here?" he cried, echoing Aaron.

"Your guess is as good as mine," said Manuel. "We found it here. I guess it came with the house. Who knows, if we explore further, we might even find a guillotine. It probably dates back to the old slavery days." Staring coldly at Aaron, he said, "I wonder who could have brought it here? ... Maybe your ancestors? Imagine how many limbs must have gotten ripped out here. Poor suckers. I bet hardly any of them looked like you."

Manuel pulled a stool and sat down with his arms folded and his legs stretched out. He looked quite relaxed. "Here's what I'm going to do," he said. "You want to know who's responsible for killing the woman on Elysian island, right? You came all this way to find the man you're convinced is the murderer. Well, guess what – you're in luck. I'm going to give you the chance to meet Larry face to face so you can ask him man to man whether or not he did it." There was a commotion out in the passageway. The door burst open and three men entered the room, including two locals - thuggish-looking youths, seemingly in their late teens. One of them was nicknamed Ice Pick. Slim and bony-looking, he resembled his name. The other was called Gaeboo. The third man was white. He was wearing a dirty white T-shirt, jeans and slippers. His skin looked blotchy and there were scabs all over his arms and face. It looked like he'd been scratching and picking at them. They resembled the sort of self-inflicted scars typical of drug addicts going through withdrawal symptoms or hallucinations. His eyes looked like pits in his skull and his cheeks were slightly sunken. The other two youths had to hold on to his twiggy arms and walk him across to the bed. They allowed him to sit and both of them remained in the room.

"Larry!" Aaron looked horrified. He rushed forward but the two youths cut him off. They had to restrain him. "Dear God, Larry, what the devil happened to you?" he cried.

Larry screwed up his face and squinted at Aaron. He didn't seem to recognize him.

"It's me, Larry! Aaron ... Aaron Ashdown."

Larry screwed up his face some more and peered thoughtfully at Aaron. He made the act of pondering seem like one of the most punishing tasks a human could ever have to go through.

"Aaron," he said at last, speaking softly and listlessly.

"So you two know each other," said Manuel as he took in the emotional exchange between the two men.

"Yes. I know his family. They are quite worried about him. That's why I'm here," said Aaron somberly, his eyes fixated on Larry. He spotted some red spots on one of Larry's arms. Peering closely, he realized they were needle marks. There were more on the other arm and they were scattered all over the skin in clusters.

"Is he back on heroin?"

"I tried to get him to stop using this shit but it's no use. He's been like that for the past couple weeks."

"Bloody hell man! Why are you giving it to him? Besides, you can't keep him penned up here like a flaming animal. Why haven't you tried to contact his family? He needs help!"

"He wants to have nothing to do with them. He's a big man, I can't force him to do what he doesn't want to do."

"Please don't worry about me, Aaron ... I'm fine," Larry's voice intruded feebly. As if to prove his words, he got up and walked slowly towards Aaron and hugged him. Aaron returned the gesture, his nose twitching at Larry's foul body odor. He reeked of urine and stale sweat.

Leaning forward, Manuel gave Larry a pained look. "See all the problems you're causing me, Larry?" he said. "You have these two jokers breaking into my home like fucking commandos. One wants to save you, the other one is trying to fuck you up!" Pointing at Rudy, he said, "You know this guy?"

"No. Who's he?"

"You recall the woman who was murdered on Elysian Island?"

"Uh huh," Larry said warily, avoiding Manuel's eyes.

Manuel pointed to Rudy. "That's her avenging angel over there. He believes you murdered her and he's come to get you."

"I don't know what you're talking about," Larry said cagily.

"Don't tell me, tell him."

"Don't you bloody pretend like you're innocent," Rudy snorted. He took two steps forward threateningly. "I've spoken to Oscar. Remember him? He confessed to the police that you asked him to break into the house at Albion Bay and steal my necklaces, which mysteriously turned up at the scene of the murder. You tried to frame me. Why?"

"If Oscar said that, he's a liar! I don't know what you're talking about."

Aaron stepped in between the two men as Rudy took two more steps toward Larry. He gave Rudy a stern look and shook his head warningly.

Rudy glowered at Larry. He was seething. He said, "I suppose it wasn't you who hacked into my computer." He told the others in the room about his ordeal after discovering a photo of Olive's body on his Facebook page. "And guess what," he added. "I was able to trace the hacker to Larry Thompson's IP address. I've already turned in the evidence to Leroy Butcher, the inspector in charge of Olive's murder investigation. You fucked up, Larry. They're on to you!"

Manuel looked startled. He shot up off the stool and glared hard at Larry and Rudy. "That bit about the cops, you serious about that?"

"You bet," said Rudy.

"Oh ... Larry, Larry, Larry," Manuel said despairingly, shaking his head. "That's what happens when you deal with fucking amateurs and spoilt rich brats! Now what am I going to tell Jose and Garcia? They were here just a short while ago and they're going to be back tomorrow to talk business. You screwing up our plans, Larry. You're a cool guy but you're out of control. You're allowing yourself to be led, and you're fucking me up in the process." Manuel scratched his head and began pacing. Suddenly he stopped.

"Wait a minute!" Glancing thoughtfully at Rudy and then at Larry, he shouted, "Ice Pick!"

"Yeh boss!" The bonier of the two men who had walked in with Larry, came forward. Manuel towered over him. "You remember the black bag I placed in the security safe?"

"Uh huh."

"Do me a favor, go tell Jeremie to get it and bring it to me."

Ice Pick slipped out of the room and returned five minutes later with a small storage bag and handed it to Manuel. Manuel plucked a handkerchief out his pocket and draping it over his hand, he unzipped the bag and pulled out a mobile phone. A Google Nexus 5. He placed it on the table. All eyes were glued to the phone.

Rudy turned to stone. "Where did you get this?" he blurted out.

"What's the matter, you recognize this phone?" said Manuel, eyeing him closely.

"It belonged to Olive - the woman who was murdered! Where did you get it?"

"That's funny, someone whispered to me that you and a pretty little Ukrainian girl were arguing and fighting over this phone, and guess what; that same pretty little Ukrainian, the one you were drooling over at The Mirage, so much you even went stalking her after she left the club – at least that's what I was told – she ends up dead!"

"You're a liar! I had nothing to do with this woman's death."

"Don't tell me, I'm not accusing you of anything. Tell it to the cops ... By the way, you wouldn't have left your fingerprints all over this phone, would you?"

Silence.

"You bastard! You're involved in this whole conspiracy!" Rudy cried out bitterly.

"Oh no, please don't say that. You got me all wrong." Manuel made a sad face and looked all hurt and innocent. "The house where the Ukrainian lived belonged to a friend of mine. You know how it is, you rent your house to people and, God forbid they die, they leave all sorts of things behind. My friend couldn't decide what to do with this phone, which the young lady left behind, not knowing her family, and wasn't aware that the phone was linked to a murder. But now my friend will be relieved to know he can hand it over to the cops and let them deal with it. Unless maybe you and him can work this out between y'all somehow ... I don't know."

"He's playing with you, like a cat toys with a mouse," said Aaron. "It makes you feel quite macho, doesn't it Mr. Manuel," he added, giving Manuel a pitiful stare.

Manuel snickered. "Why do you two keep blackening my good name?" He quipped. Then, in the blink of an eye, he changed skins and metamorphosed into a scowling, beast-faced alien. The transformation was astounding. Everyone in the room froze.

"Ice Pick!" he barked.

Ice Pick came running. "Yeh boss."

"Go get Kadija! Bring her here!"

Manuel returned to sit on the stool. For the next few minutes, an epic silence descended on the room. Rudy leaned on the table, trying to recover from the shock of discovering that Kadija was in the house. Aaron shifted from one leg to the other agitatedly, and every now and again he gave Larry a concerned look. Manuel sat scowling at the door. Then they heard the sound of footsteps out in the passageway. Everyone waited, quiet and tense.

45

The door opened and Kadija walked into the room. She looked quite drab in an oversized, white T-shirt, jeans and sneakers and her hair was covered with a head wrap that looked slightly askew.

"Kadija, the gentleman over there wants to know who killed the lady on Elysian Island. Can you help him?" said Manuel softly, staring coldly at Kadija.

"Fuck you! Screw all of you. Just get me out of this damned place! You have no right imprisoning me here." Kadija's contempt for Manual was obvious and she didn't seem cowed by him in the least.

"We've been keeping you here for your own good baby, show some gratitude," said Manuel consolingly.

"Go fuck yourself!"

Manuel's face darkened. "You wouldn't be here in the first place if you hadn't fucked up, and if Larry hadn't come crying to me for help on your behalf, so quit jerking around!"

Ignoring him, Kadija went and sat on the bed away from Larry.

Manuel stood up. "Come on, baby you and Larry have caused me enough trouble already. I welcomed you two into my home, treated you well. But having the two of you here is becoming a pain in the ass ... Now, the gentleman is waiting. Who killed the young lady on Elysian Island?"

"I don't know what you're talking about."

Turning to Rudy, Manuel said, "You know why she's here? All because Larry came crying to me that she's in trouble and needed to lie low for a while. The police on Elysian Island were about to go pick her up. I agreed to help, as usual. I arranged to have her spirited away from the island. It was only after she got here I got to realize the full extent of the trouble she's gotten her ass into, through my police contacts. I still wanted to help her but she's a real dumbass uppity bitch, with no fucking gratitude! Plus, she's a nut case.

"To make matters worse, I discovered that you and Tyrone D'Arcy, alias Trini – my fucking worst enemy – have teamed up and, lo and behold, you and Mr. Bean over there come sniffing around my house. Obviously, this whole thing has now gotten out of hand. You, Larry and Mr. Bean, and that bitch over there have no idea what you've started. It would be better for me if all four of you were fucking dead! ... Now Kadija, I ask you for the last time – *who killed the woman on Elysian Island?*"

Rudy stepped in. "Kadija, please ... Tell me the truth. Did you kill Olive?"

Kadija laughed. "Ask her. Bring her back from the dead if you can and ask her," she sneered.

"I'm begging you ... please. Tell me the truth. Did you do it?" Rudy pleaded.

Kadija walked across to Rudy and slapped him hard and spat in his face. "Kiss my ass!"

Manuel signaled to Ice Pick who immediately went to him. Manuel whispered something in his ear and he nodded. He grabbed hold of Kadija and bundled her out of the room. Out in the passageway Kadija vented her rage on him, yelling shrilly and screaming.

"Don't worry," Manuel said to Rudy, grinning, a cold gleam in his eyes. "She'll soon have a change of heart."

A blood-curdling scream echoed in the building. Rudy and Aaron were immobilized by the shock. Even Larry froze. Kadija screamed again hysterically, and this time it was drawn-out and escalated into an ear-splitting shriek.

"What the hell's going on? What're they doing to her?" Rudy yelled.

Manuel just stood there sniggering, as if he found the screams entertaining.

Aaron's indignation flared. He planted himself in front of Manuel, his face livid. "I demand that you put a stop to this. Now!" he thundered, glaring at Manuel.

Manuel's grin slid off his face like water draining out of a sink. He glared at Aaron in disbelief and opened his mouth to curse him but restrained himself. Turning to Rudy, he said, "Nobody's doing anything to her. Come, see for yourself." Rudy followed him out of the room with Aaron in tow, followed by Gaeboo, the other bodyguard. Yamaha remained in the room with Larry. The passageway was bursting at the seams with Kadija's screams. Ice Pick stood a few yards away in front of a door.

"Open the door!" Manuel yelled. A key clanked in the lock and the door swung open. There was a dim ghostly light in the room coming from a makeshift hanging light bulb. All five men stood staring at Kadija cowering in a corner on top of an old wooden desk, screaming and trembling and staring down at the floor in horror. Long black centipedes were crawling all over the floor and scurrying in the shadowy corners of the dingy, foul-smelling room. Aaron and Rudy recoiled from the shocking sight and drew away from the door.

"I think they call it Chilopodophobia – an uncontrollable fear of centipedes. I learned of this weakness of hers thanks to Larry," Manuel said, grinning. "You ready to talk now? Come on Kadija, don't waste my time or you'll spend the rest of the week in here."

Kadija began pulling at her hair and weeping. She looked demented.

"Bring her out!" Manuel ordered Ice Pick. Ice Pick calmly walked across the room and stood in front of Kadija with his back towards her. Bending forward, he said, "Hop on baby, let's go." Kadija leaped unto his back and wrapped her limbs around him like tentacles. She clung on for dear life. The force of the impact threw Ice Pick off balance, causing him to stumble. Somehow he managed to hold on to Kadija without falling flat on his face. He strode out of the room with Kadija screeching in his ears. He winced in pain. She refused to let go of him.

"Bring her back to the other room," said Manuel. Still trembling, Kadija stayed put and refused to get off Ice Pick's back.

"That's it baby, ride the donkey!" said Gaeboo, laughing. Ice Pick cursed him and carried Kadija back to the room. By then, he'd had enough. He straightened up and shook her off like a sack of potatoes.

Manuel walked in and waited for Rudy and Aaron. He ordered Ice Pick and Gaeboo to wait outside and slammed the door. Kadija sat on the floor hugging herself and whimpering. Manuel took down a bottle of brandy and a glass from the bookshelf. He poured a stiff shot and handed it to Kadija. "Come on, drink this." She hesitated, staring at the glass. "Drink it!" said Manuel, impatiently. Kadija took a sip. She downed the rest in one go. Manuel poured her another shot. Once more, it went down the hatch. She sat for several minutes with her head bowed and looked as if she had dozed off. Then she raised her head abruptly. She and Rudy glared at each other.

"Who did it, Kadija? Who murdered Olive, was it you or Larry?" said Rudy.

"Go on Kadija, tell him it wasn't me!" Larry shouted.

"Shut up!" Kadija bawled at him.

"And the necklaces they found near Olive's body, I had nothing to do with it – or with the Facebook photo. You've got my laptop. It's been with you for months. Go on, tell them!"

"I said shut the fuck up!"

"But you did help Oscar to steal my necklaces!" Rudy interjected, glaring at Larry. "He said so."

"It was meant as a prank! She wanted to spook you for not coming to her party. She said so."

Kadija scowled contemptuously at Larry. "You're pathetic."

"It's all over, Kadija," said Aaron. "The police will soon have the results of the forensic tests, if they haven't got them by now, and much more besides. They believe they have a good idea who the killer is."

Rudy edged closer to Kadija. Manuel stood aside watching them and didn't intervene.

"It was you! You murdered Olive," cried Rudy. "Why did you do it?"

Kadija gazed at the empty glass and tipped it to her mouth. She had a glazed look in her eyes.

"Answer me, damn it!" Rudy grabbed her arm and shook her roughly. Kadija pulled her arm free and flew at him. She punched him viciously. Aaron quickly moved between them and shoved them apart. "Cut it out you two! Let's not forget that we're in danger here."

Kadija drew away, glaring hatefully at Rudy. She said, "What's wrong? Is her soul hankering after you? Do you see her at nights?

You should have screwed her when you had the chance – like on the day you found her body."

Rudy lunged at Kadija. Aaron had been anticipating it. He cut him off before he could reach her.

"You bitch! You're a fucking psycho!" Rudy yelled.

Kadija laughed at him. "For mortals vanished from the day's sweet light, I shed no tear; rather I mourn for those who day and night live in death's fear," she said mockingly.

Manuel called out to Ice Pick and Gaeboo and they immediately came rushing in. "Get her out of here. Take her back upstairs. Take Larry with you - and him too," said Manuel, pointing at Aaron. "Leave the keys with me," he added.

Ice Pick tossed him a bunch of keys. He signaled to Gaeboo and together, with guns drawn, they herded Kadija and Aaron roughly out of the room. Manuel helped Larry up and escorted him out the door. He returned to the room and shut the door, and plodded to and fro agitatedly. Yamaha remained in the room. Manuel turned to him and said, "Give me a minute please, bro. Wait out in the corridor." Yamaha left and closed the door.

"Where were you guys this morning?" Manuel demanded, scowling at Rudy.

"What?"

"Where the fuck were you this morning? Both of you."

"Visiting a friend."

"Was it Trini?"

Rudy felt a chill crawl up his spine. Manuel watched him closely. "Why you look surprised?" he asked. "I told you, I've got eyes everywhere. Trini's up to something and you guys are in it with him. That's why you're here, am I right?"

"Trini has no idea that we're here," said Rudy.

"Bullshit! You expect me to believe that? That son-of-a-bitch has had it in for me for a long time. He's been sticking his nose in my business and trying to screw me for years. Although he's no longer a cop, the asshole is still at it. He refuses to give up. Still, I'm surprised he would stoop to using amateurs like you as his stool pigeons. This must be a sign of his desperation."

Manuel continued pacing. He was clearly flustered. He had Rudy on tenterhooks. Everything about him suggested that he was highly unpredictable, emotionally unstable and a potential powder keg. Off and on he projected an air of reasonableness when it suited him but Rudy wasn't fooled in the least. He was willing to trust Manuel as he would a rattlesnake.

Manuel gazed at him with furrowed brow. "Earlier, while we were upstairs, I got word that a bench warrant is going to be issued for the arrest of Larry and Kadija. That means by tomorrow the cops might come crawling all over my place. It's all your fault! If you hadn't come to Soufriere snooping around, all this shit wouldn't have happened. You have no idea how much I'm longing to shoot you, motherfucker! ... If the cops show up, I'll have to hand over Larry and Kadija. I don't need this kind of headache. It's bad for business."

"That's funny, I always thought that in the drugs business, that sort of headache comes with the territory."

Manuel smiled, unfazed. "You think you know me but you don't know shit! You're like all the rest of them."

"Alina, the Ukrainian girl who worked at the Mirage, you and your guys killed her, didn't you?"

"Don't have a clue what you're talking about. I can't even imagine why you would think such a thing."

"Do you take me for a fool? Why else would you have the Google Nexus phone in your possession?"

"I've already explained that to you. I don't like repeating myself."

"Yeah, right! ... So what happens to me and Aaron? You going to bump us off too?"

"Nah! Do I look like the violent type? Come on. In any case, I definitely don't want you guys around here. You're not welcome. I don't appreciate people breaking into my house and violating my privacy. The problem is you two are going to have to go out the same route you came in. I'll provide you with escorts since I don't have the heart to let you go out there alone in the dark. Unfortunately, I can't guarantee that you'll make it through safely. Those cliffs are so treacherous. I'll urge the guys to be careful. Don't want your bodies being fished out of the sea."

"You love playing mind games, don't you?"

Manuel smiled. "Off and on. But trust me, this isn't one of them. There's a ninety-nine-point-nine percent chance your bodies will be fished out of the bay tomorrow; hopefully at least, for the sake of your families. I hate to say it but I won't shed a tear."

"Why don't you just kill us now and be done with it?"

"Do I look like a murderer to you? I feel really hurt. But it doesn't have to be this way. You and your friend can return home safe and sound within the next hour. I'm even willing to loan you guys a vehicle or have one of my men drop you off. But that's providing you're willing to do a deal. I've got a package to deliver to one Tyrone D'Arcy, alias Trini. It's a surprise gift. He has a farm not far away, with a nice little farmhouse." Manuel glanced at his watch. "Eleven-thirty. I doubt anyone will be in but it doesn't matter. I'd be really grateful if you could drop the package off for me at the farmhouse. One of my boys will take you there and show you where to put it. Simple."

"What the f---! Are you planning to set the guy up?"

"No, my friend. *You* going to set him up. Are you familiar with the term 'poetic justice'? That motherfucker tried to use you to destroy me. Now I'm going to turn the tables on his ass! I'm going to use you to wipe out the son-of-a-bitch."

"Fuck you! No way!"

"Are you defying me?"

"I won't do it. I'd rather die!"

'Would you also rather your friend die?"

"What're you driving at?

"Listen man, I ain't got time to fool around with you. You going to do what I tell you or your friend will pay the price!"

"What're you gonna do?" Rudy shot back defiantly.

Manuel pulled out his phone and dialed a number. He waited then redialed and dialed again a third time. Suddenly, he began swearing. He'd gotten a dropped call each time due to an interruption of the signal. It had happened before because of the depth they were underground. He stormed out of the room and locked the door.

Despite his bravado, the pounding of Manuel's footsteps in the passageway filled Rudy with dread. He sensed the situation was about to get much worse for him and Aaron and something terrible was about to happen. It made him feel ill. He was extremely worried for Aaron. More than ever now, he wished, to God, he had followed his instinct and not allowed himself to be swayed by Aaron.

Although Manuel's coldblooded and megalomaniacal nature were now obvious, Rudy still couldn't believe he would be so reckless as to try and plant drugs on Trini's property and use him to do it; frame an innocent man and a former career police officer. A man who, despite being a stranger, had treated him like a brother. The thought was so despicable, pondering over it made him want to puke.

Yet how, in God's name, could he get out of this horrific mess – and get out of it alive? He didn't think Manuel was bluffing about their bodies being fished out of the bay. Rudy believed deep in his heart that time was running out for him and Aaron. Once

Manuel's mind was made up, he wouldn't think twice about rubbing them out. The odd thing about it was that he didn't think Manuel's attitude towards them was simply because they had broken into his house. Rudy suspected it was also about exacting revenge for all the hurt he had suffered back in his childhood. He believed Manuel still nourished ill feelings towards him, after all those years.

Time crawled by excruciatingly, yet there was still no sign of Manuel. Rudy moved about restlessly. The suspenseful wait was killing him. *Where the fuck is Manuel and what is he up to?*

There was pandemonium out in the passageway. Angry shouts erupted followed by a voice raised in protest. The protester sounded like Aaron. A key jangled in the lock and the door swung open. Manuel and his three henchmen piled into the room, hauling Aaron along with them.

46

"Now, back to the business of our Trinidadian friend," said Manuel, staring daggers at Rudy. "What say you? You ready to do the deal?"

"I don't do deals with drug pushers."

"I'm a businessman and very successful, so don't talk shit!"

"You're just scum with a whole lot of blood on your hands trying to play God! For as long as you live, that blood could never be washed off." Rudy caught the look of alarm on Aaron's face. He knew he was playing with fire and probably sealing their fate but that didn't deter him, for some reason. He was in a fighting mood.

"Who the hell are you to judge me?" Manuel retorted. "How many people less fortunate than you have you helped in your life? Like helping poor mothers with their children's education and health care, financing projects in low-income communities, helping young boys buy their sports gear and contributing to sports clubs. I do all those things and more. Do you?"

Rudy laughed. “That’s all well and good but guess what; at the end of the day you’re still a drug dealer and a money launderer!”

Manuel’s lips tightened. He began flexing his fingers. “You’re an asshole!” he exploded, murder in his eyes. “You want to talk about drug dealing and money laundering, then let me educate you.” He yanked his iPhone out of his pocket and tried connecting to the internet. “Yamaha!” he bellowed.

“Yeh, Lucas.” .

“Shift the router.”

Yamaha went across and moved the Wi-Fi router around on top of the bookshelf.

“Okay, that’s better,” said Manuel. Glaring at Rudy, he said, “Now, let me educate you ... In 2007 US Senator Carl Levin reveals to the US House of Congress that American and European banks launder between *500 billion and one trillion dollars* in so-called ‘dirty money’ every year. US Congressional Investigators and international banking experts agreed with him. Approximately half of that money flows to the US. Bear in mind these are 2007 estimates, so just imagine what it must be like now. But here’s the best part – and all of you listen up! Several international economics and financial experts have said that if all this so-called ‘dirty money’ stopped flowing into the US economy, the dollar would weaken, the living standards of Americans would drop drastically, access to investment and loan capital would shrink and Washington would be in deep shit!

“If that’s true of the US, do you think the situation is any different here on this insignificant little rock? The bottom line is businessmen like me are helping to keep the local economy afloat. We’re part of the economic fabric of this nation. Never mind all the chest-beating and moralizing by the politicians and the bureaucrats; they don’t want to bring the house down. If they do, the economy is fucked and they know it! Besides, the *real* powers that be, those who have a stake in maintaining the status quo and who are calling the shots, wouldn’t allow it. They’re just bullshitting you. You call yourself a journalist? Then fucking do your job. Get up off your ass and go do your research. Tell the people the truth. Stop helping the politicians bamboozle them!"

All three of Manuel's henchmen cheered. "Yeh man, Lucas, tell them!" Yamaha shouted, applauding. Ice Pick walked up to Manuel and they bumped fists. "True ting, boss!" he said admiringly. Manuel grinned and raised his arms in a victor's salute. "Okay boys, our friend Mr. Rudy has a job to do for us. Right, Mr. Rudy? You ready?"

"Like I said, I don't do deals with drug dealers," Rudy shot back stubbornly.

Pointing to Aaron, Manuel said, "Let's give him the treatment. Put him on the rack!"

Yamaha and Ice Pick pounced on Aaron, overpowering him. Aaron fought them off. Gaeboo joined in and they rained down punches on Aaron viciously. Rudy made to intervene but Manuel cut him off and pushed him back. Whipping out his gun, he aimed it at Rudy's head. "Move and I'll blow your brains out!" he said ominously. Aaron was down on one knee and weakening, still punches and kicks rained down on him. He caught a glancing blow to the side of his head that stunned him. Ice Pick got behind him and managed to put him in a headlock. Yamaha unleashed two solid punches to his stomach. Aaron crumpled and deflated like a balloon. The three men dragged him unto the rack. Yamaha dashed across to the table, grabbed two cords and hurried back. They fastened Aaron's legs and arms to the rollers.

When Manuel was satisfied that Aaron was securely tied, he said to Rudy, with a Machiavellian grin, "This one is for our ancestors." He signaled Yamaha who promptly turned a handle attached to the top roller. Slowly, it began stretching Aaron's limbs away from his body. Aaron felt himself being torn asunder. His body became a throbbing mass of excruciating pain. He let out an ear-splitting squeal.

"No! Please stop!" Rudy yelled.

"Let's hear the magic words, come on!" said Manuel' unmoved. Aaron's screams ricocheted through the room, threatening to crack the walls.

"Stop! You're killing him!" Rudy pleaded.

"Then say the magic words, 'Yes, I will frame Trini!" He signaled Yamaha to apply more pressure. Yamaha turned the lever some more, sniggering. An eerie howling filled the room and it felt like it could be heard all over the world. Spread-eagled on the rack, Aaron bore a striking resemblance to the crucifixion. His chest heaved up and down, as he struggled to breathe.

"Okay! Okay! I'll do it!" Rudy screamed frantically.

"Do what?"

"Frame Trini!"

"Not good enough. Get down on your knees and say, 'Please, let me frame Trini!'"

"Oh God, Lucas, stop this shit! Come on, man!"

Manuel gave Yamaha the signal. Aaron's screams made even him and Yamaha wince.

"Oh God!" Rudy moaned and dropped down to his knees. Tears streamed down his face.

"Let's hear it, come on," said Manuel, tauntingly.

More screams.

Rudy shook his head and said whimperingly, "Please let me frame Trini,"

Manuel told Yamaha to stop. Watching Rudy kneeling like a dog at his feet, he said, mockingly, "Go on, cry like a baby. Now you know what it feels like." Turning to Yamaha, he said, "Go get the package ready. We mustn't keep Mr. Rudy waiting. You heard him pleading with me to let him go do the job." Yamaha,Ice Pick and Gaeboo all laughed.

There was loud and frantic pounding at the door.

"Who the fuck is that?" said Manuel irritably.

"Who's that!" Yamaha yelled.

"Me! Open the door quick!" said a female voice.

"It's Mellissa," said Yamaha, frowning. He opened the door. It was the woman who had been upstairs with them.

"Come quick! A police jeep coming up the road. They still some distance away but I could see them at the bottom of the hill from upstairs." Turning, she ran back down the passageway.

"What she getting so excited about?" said Manuel, trying to sound unfazed, even as he rushed for the door ahead of the other three men. Pausing in the doorway, he shouted, "Yamaha!" Yamaha ground to a halt. "Yeh, boss." Staring at Aaron, Manuel said, "Leave his ass on the rack and you and Ice Pick tie up that other joker. Hurry up!" He took off down the passageway and Gaeboo followed him.

Yamaha covered Rudy with his gun and ordered Ice Pick to tie him. Within five minutes, Ice Pick had Rudy's wrists and legs bound up. They were clearly anxious to get upstairs to find out what was going on. As soon as Ice Pick tied the last knot, Yamaha was out the door. Ice Pick rushed out after him, slamming the door shut.

47

It started as a moan and then escalated into an eerie groan that broadcast Aaron's horrendous agony. It galvanized Rudy. "Aaron, are you alright? ... Answer me!" he cried out fretfully. He lay on his left side with his ankles bound and his wrists tied behind his back. He jerked and twisted his body to try and sit up so he could see Aaron. Aaron's screams were still ringing in his ears. The brutality of the torture inflicted on him still had Rudy shaken.

Rudy eventually managed to swivel his torso and force himself up into a sitting position. He glanced anxiously at the rack. Aaron had stopped moaning. He kept moving his arms and legs to try and free them but they were fastened tightly to the rollers. "Rudy," he called out feebly, wincing in pain.

"Yes, I'm here," said Rudy. "God, am I happy to hear you! For a moment, I was afraid you had kicked the bucket."

"The pain is unbelievable. I was pretty certain those two oafs would have done me in if it had lasted a minute longer ... Did I hear someone say something about the police?"

"Yeah. Looks like they came calling. Not sure if they're still out there."

"We've got to try and get out of here before that lot get back."

"How? We're both tied up."

"Keep jerking your wrists to try and loosen the cord. Then I want you to try and get a hold of the heel of my right sneaker. It's movable and it has a secret compartment. Just press it forward and it opens. There's a small penknife hidden inside. Use it to try and cut the cord around your wrists. Don't waste time, hurry!"

"What the hell will you think of next?"

"Mountain climbing has taught me to always be prepared for all possible eventualities."

Rudy tried loosening the cord around his wrists. Fortunately, the material was polypropylene fiber and fairly pliant. As he focused on it and flexed the muscles in his wrists, he could feel a bit of slack. "Believe it or not, the assholes forgot to lock the door," he said, still struggling with the rope.

"God bless them," said Aaron.

"Okay, I can feel it loosening."

"Attaboy! Now shift your bum around and try reaching my right heel."

Using his feet, Rudy was able to topple one of the stools and drag it closer to him. Pivoting on his ass, he grabbed it from behind and using it as a support, he dragged his bottom towards the rack.

"Hurry!" Aaron urged him. He eventually edged closer to the rack and managed to push up off the floor and sit on the legs of the stool with his hands almost parallel with the rack. Aaron's foot extended over the roller. After a few failed attempts, Rudy succeeded in getting a grip on Aaron's shoe. The pain in his wrists was unbearable. He gritted his teeth and pressed on. He felt the shoe heel move. Shutting his eyes, he tried to ignore the pain and concentrate. Something dropped into his hand. He barely held on to it. "Got it!" he said exultantly.

"Press the button and the blade will eject."

Rudy did, and the blade shot out of the handle. After struggling for about five minutes he was able to make a small incision in the cord around his wrists. Gradually the cut widened, and the cord split. He shook off the remaining strip and hurriedly cut the one around his ankles. Jumping to his feet, he freed Aaron from the rack and helped him to sit up. "Can you stand?"

"Don't worry, I think the old hooves will hold up." Leaning on Rudy, Aaron rose to his feet. "God only knows what's going on up there. This cellar is so deep underground you can't hear a bloody thing. All the same, we've got to try and escape before they return." Rudy opened the door slowly and stuck his head out. "Oh shit! The bastards turned the light off in the passage. It's pitch black out there."

"It doesn't matter, we'll find our way out." Aaron hobbled out of the room and Rudy closed the door. The darkness devoured them. Slowly, they made their way through its innards, running their hands along the walls to try and keep their bearings. They tried to stay close to each other.

A light flashed and blinded them.

"Stop right there or I'll shoot!" said a voice sibilantly. Aaron and Rudy froze. There was a torturous moment of silence.

"It's Rudy and Aaron!" said Trini.

"Damn, you were right!" said another voice.

"It's Trini and Vernon!" said Rudy excitedly. "Where did you guys come from? How did you get here?"

"Shh, keep your voices down," said Aaron testily. "Even though the walls are almost sound proof, let's not tempt fate."

"Yeah, you're right," Rudy concurred.

"I got a call from Aaron's friend, Geoff around ten o'clock," said Trini. He was wearing dark jeans, a leather jacket and a black woolen cap. "He told me where you guys had gone and said he'd promised to contact me if he hadn't heard from Aaron. You fuckers are mad. What the hell got into to you to make you try such a crazy stunt?"

"If you hang around Aaron long enough, you'd probably end up doing worse," said Rudy.

"Anyway, earlier I'd already been in contact with Vernon, so I called him and we agreed to come looking for you guys. We took a short cut from my farm which runs near the old farm building at the back of the villa. From there, we spotted a police jeep in front of the house but they were about to leave. We saw Manuel talking to them but we couldn't figure out what was going on. They left and drove off before we could get close. At that point we became really worried about you two, not knowing what had happened to you. Then we spotted two black woolen caps on the ground near the basement steps of the old farm building. I got a shiver up my spine for some reason, when I saw them. I followed my instincts and we came down here."

"The caps!" said Rudy. "They must be ours. They probably dropped out of one of Manuel's goon's pockets. He snatched them when we first ran into them at the house. Well mate, I sure am glad to see you." Briefly, Rudy told Trini and Vernon about Larry and Kadija.

"Lord have mercy! How the hell did she end up here?" said Vernon, sounding shocked.

"We can't stay here, we've got to go," said Rudy urgently.

"Wait, hold on," said Trini. He directed the beam of the flashlight deeper into the passage and ran off in the dark. He was gone for several minutes. He then rushed back to join the three men. "Come over here, quick!" he said, sounding excited but trying to keep his voice down. They followed him with Rudy and Vernon muttering in protest. The passage turned out to be much longer than it had initially seemed, extending approximately a further three-hundred and fifty yards.

"Look here," said Trini, flashing the torchlight on a wall that prevented them from going further.

"It's just a wall, big deal," said Rudy.

"Come on, lean against it on the right side - all of you - and push hard."

"Are you nuts? These guys could walk in on us any minute." Rudy had to restrain himself from cursing Trini.

"Come on, Trini," said Vernon, concurring with Rudy.

"Just help me push, damn it!" Trini turned the torchlight off as a precaution.

Together they pushed against the right side of the wall. Aaron grunted, clearly in pain. Nothing happened. "Keep pushing ... *hard*." Trini commanded them. Rudy cursed. Aaron groaned. The wall suddenly shifted, with a loud scraping sound. "Push! Push!" Trini sounded like he was trying to squeeze every ounce of strength out of the three men. Slowly the wall swung inward. Trini beamed the light on the opening. It was just wide enough for him to squeeze through. He did and shone the light all around him. One by one, the others slipped through. The darkness was so opaque, it overpowered the light, subduing and constricting it. Trini switched it off. "Come on, let's push the wall back," he said, now just a voice. "Hurry!" All of them groped unseeingly at the wall and began to push. Gradually, it moved back into its original position.

Trini turned the flashlight back on. The others gathered around him and gaped all around them in shock. It was now clear that the passageway was part of a hidden tunnel that stretched way beyond them, by the looks of it for several hundred yards, if not more. Incredibly, it was equipped with fluorescent lighting and ventilation shafts. It even had what appeared to be a small rail system, about three feet wide. Across to their left was a long flight of steps leading upwards to the ceiling. It seemed to be an alternative entrance to the tunnel via the interior of the house. Trini shifted the light and focused it on a spot several yards from where they stood. Moving closer, he saw a hidden staircase leading down into a hole in the ground. Across from it was a metal platform covered with a flat slab of dried mud. Trini immediately realized that it was movable and meant to conceal the opening. He climbed down the steps and the other three men followed him. They stood gazing at a large room with three separate compartments, each with a door. Trini turned the doorknob closest to him and, to his surprise, the door swung open. They all stood gaping inside the room in amazement. It was packed with dried bales of marijuana. Stacked away in a corner were several red, translucent zip lock bags. Trini suspected they were filled with cocaine. He tried the doors to the two other compartments but they were locked.

"This guy ain't fooling around. He's big time!" said Vernon, an apoplectic look on his face.

"The son-of-a-bitch has turned this tunnel into a frigging' drugs warehouse and transshipment centre. God only knows where he's moving this stuff to," said Trini.

"Could be to somewhere along the coast," said Vernon.

"It could be anywhere in Soufriere, including where you would least expect. Even beyond the town ... But here's the kicker. Any of you familiar with Joaquin 'El Chapo' Guzman?"

"Wasn't he one of Mexico's most wanted drug lords?" said Vernon.

"That's the man! One-time leader of Mexico's Sinaloa drug cartel. A few years ago he was busted by the DEA after they discovered a secret underground tunnel El Chapo and his boys had dug from Tijuana in Mexico to an industrial district in San Diego, California. They were using it as a warehouse and for the transshipment of drugs into the U.S. This tunnel is almost a replica of it. Now, what does that tell you?"

"That Lucas Manuel is bloody resourceful. For what it's worth, he does his homework and he's all heart," said Aaron.

"I bet there's a whole lot more than drug dealing going on down here," said Rudy. "The guy has a fucking rack in his basement – you know the contraption that was used to torture people back in the Middle Ages? Ask Aaron, they just used it on him."

"What!" Trini looked horrified. Vernon swore, shocking Rudy. Until now, he had never heard a swear word cross Vernon's lips.

Pushing past them, Trini said, "Let's not get carried away, guys. We need to get out of here."

They climbed the steps. A light flashed and suddenly the tunnel became engulfed in fluorescent brightness that resembled daylight. Up in the ceiling were three sixty-inch fluorescent light bulbs, all lit.

"Freeze! Not a man move!" shouted Yamaha threateningly. He stood halfway down the steps leading up to the house, aiming a semi-automatic at the four men. Poised behind him was his comrade-in-arms, Jeremie. He too wielded a gun. Trini stepped away from the other men. "One more step and I'll blast your fuckin' ass!" Yamaha warned him ominously. He took a cell phone from his pocket. Trini reached into his jacket, whipped out a gun and fired a shot, then threw himself to the ground and rolled over, all in one fluid motion. Yamaha's torso jerked and his legs buckled. He fell down the stairs, head first. A gun exploded behind him. The bullet hit the ground, missing Trini by a couple of inches. Another gunshot rang out. Vernon was down on one knee, gripping a Glock 19 pistol in both hands. He had just fired at Yamaha's sidekick. Jeremie grunted and leaned against the stair railing, clutching his left hip. His grip on the gun slackened and his hand dropped. Trini moved swiftly up the steps and gripped Jeremie's wrist in a joint lock, forcing him to drop the weapon. Grabbing him by the throat, he squeezed hard, making his eyes pop out of his head. Jeremie's mouth became a gaping hole, and he was gasping for air. The look on his face was one of abject terror. Loosening his grip, Trini whispered, "Who's upstairs with Manuel? ... Talk you bastard!" He stuck the barrel of his gun in Jeremie's mouth. Jeremie stared at him wild-eyed, fear secreting out of his every orifice. Tears streamed down his cheeks.

"In two seconds I'm going to pull the trigger. Who's up there with Manuel?" Trini reiterated.

"Ice Pick! ... Only Ice Pick," Jeremie gasped. Trini gave him a hard stare and released him. Jeremie collapsed against the steps, blood oozing out of his left side. Trini walked across to Vernon who was examining Yamaha. Aaron and Rudy watched him, their faces grim. Glancing up, Vernon said, "I think he's dead." Yamaha lay on his back. Blood leaked out of a bullet hole in his stomach. Rudy and Aaron just stood there in stunned silence.

"What about his partner," said Vernon, gazing at Trini.

"He took it in the hip. He's still alive," Trini replied.

"What're we going to do? He'll need medical help."

"Fuck him! Tie the wound with a piece of cloth if you like, to stop the bleeding. I'm going upstairs after Manuel."

"What! Have you fallen on your head?"

"You, Aaron and Rudy, get out of here before you get caught." Trini turned and ran up the steps before Vernon could respond. They watched until he disappeared from view.

Vernon shook his head. He turned his attention to Jeremie. Lifting his T-shirt, he stared at the wound. It didn't seem to be as bad as he had thought. The bullet had pierced clean through the flesh and grazed his hip bone. The bastard is lucky, Vernon thought to himself. Jeremie's face was contorted with pain. He avoided looking at Vernon and maintained a sullen silence.

"Is it bad?" said Rudy.

"Could have been worse. It looks more like a flesh wound."

"Here, let me handle it," said Aaron. He took hold of Jeremie's T-shirt. "Sorry old chap, I'm going to have to use this to stop the bleeding." Jeremie offered no resistance as Aaron pulled the shirt off him. He ripped it with his teeth and tore it in two separate pieces. He then tore both pieces and tied the bits together to form a single strip. He tied it around Jeremie's hip and over the wound in a bid to stem the bleeding.

"Okay, let's move," said Vernon urgently. "We'll have to leave him here for the time being. Come on!" he dashed across to the wall through which they had entered. "Let's hope the three of us can move this thing," he said as Rudy and Aaron caught up with him. The three of them began pushing.

"What about Trini?" said Rudy in between grunts as he struggled to push.

"Damn him! He's obsessed with this Manuel guy," said Vernon, sounding very annoyed. The wall began moving. They mustered their remaining strength and pushed harder. The opening widened a few more inches. Vernon managed to force his way through but not without some pain because of the tight squeeze. Rudy tried and succeeded with just as much discomfort. Aaron got stuck and they had to literally pull him free.

"It's a miracle no one seems to have come down to check on you guys," said Vernon as he strained his eyes to see through the darkened passageway.

"Put yourself in their shoes. Would you if the police came calling?" said Aaron.

"Shh, keep it down," said Vernon as they pressed on towards the steps leading out of the cellar. They made it without incident and bounded up the steps, occasionally losing their footing in their haste. Vernon and Aaron made it to the top and had to wait for Rudy who had stumbled and fell. He dragged himself up the few remaining steps and limped off after them, and into the bushes. Vernon led them back to the route he and Trini had used as a short cut, in amongst some trees, just to play it safe.

"The two of you stay here and lie low," said Vernon. "I'm going off to check on Trini. Don't come out until the coast is clear. If you hear a loud whistle, just know it's me. That'll be the all clear signal." With that, he crouched low and made his way back towards the house.

48

Trini felt a rush of adrenaline as he moved stealthily, gun in hand, towards the inner staircase inside the villa that led to the upper floor. Except for the grand salon, which was dimly lit, the rest of the ground floor was in darkness. The house was not unfamiliar to him since he had visited the previous owner. What had amazed him was the plan Lucas Manuel had devised to access the tunnel from within the building. The long flight of steps in the tunnel led directly up into a room set up as a library with nearly all the walls lined with bookshelves, most of them packed with books. One of the bookshelves was a secret door which opened into an adjacent storage room located beneath the inner staircase. It was designed so neatly, once it was pushed back into place, there was nothing to indicate that the opening even existed. The door of the storage room opened into the hallway.

Trini remembered thinking to himself that the secret doorway was concealed so perfectly, it could easily elude the most trained FBI agent or CIA sleuth. Fortunately, Manuel's two blockheads had left it open, making it easy for him.

His instinct and training as a detective had enabled him to determine very quickly that there was no one on the ground floor. He confirmed this when he heard the sound of talking upstairs. He made out Manuel's voice. Moving slowly up the stairs, he trained his ears to try and get a sense of Manuel's approximate position vis-à-vis the stairs. He wasn't able to. He edged closer to the top of the staircase, glancing behind him off and on to make sure he didn't get any surprises. The upper floor was an open space comprising of a hallway, a vast sitting room and bar, stately twelve-foot arches and a veranda overlooking the pool and gardens. It was similar to the ground floor, except that the other rooms were mainly en-suite bedrooms. There was no one in the sitting room, just as he had suspected. It sounded like Manuel and whoever was with him were out on the veranda.

Trini scurried across to the bar and hid behind the counter. The room looked different and far more plush than he remembered it, boasting a silvery-white, six-piece living room set, a loveseat and chair, a coffee table and two end-tables, crystal chandeliers and antique Victorian tiles. Manuel sounded like he was talking to someone on the phone. Trini kept still, listening.

"Don't you worry my brother," said Manuel. "Like I said, the cops can grill him from now till doomsday, they ain't going to get shit from him! Larry can take it, he's been there before. Besides, he knows all too well they have nothing on him, plus his folks can afford the best lawyers, if push comes to shove." Manuel paused a while, evidently listening to the response. "Oh no, he had nothing to do with this woman's murder on Elysian Island. I'm convinced of that," he said firmly. "Besides, you know how it is with our local cops and prosecutors – they're nothing but a clueless bunch of pussies who couldn't find their way out of a paper bag, much less crack a case of such complexity." Another pause, this time longer. Manuel let out a roaring laugh. "Gabriel's full of shit! My prices are unbeatable - anywhere in the region, so tell him to go fuck himself! I got a shipment scheduled for 3:00 a.m. – a couple of hours from now. Gaeboo and Valence will be coordinating things. The two of them went to take a pretty young lady for a moonlight walk in the woods but they'll be back soon." Again, he laughed. "Irie, my brother, stay cool and let's keep in touch." There was another pause followed by the scraping sound of chairs being moved.

"What the fuck is holding Yamaha and Jeremie back in the tunnel!" said Manuel, sounding pissed. "Listen Ice Pick, you better go check on Rudy and the Englishman in the basement." They entered the living room.

"You still want to use the Rasta to drop the weed off by Trini's place?" said Ice Pick.

"Of course, how you mean. Bring his ass out. Leave the Englishman on the rack, we'll deal with him later. Yamaha should be back with the weed by the time you get back. In fact, let me give him a call."

Manuel and Ice Pick were heading for the stairway when Trini emerged from behind the bar counter. "Stop right there! Both of you," he said, his gun drawn.

The two men froze. Slowly, Manuel turned around, and then Ice Pick. The shock on their faces was like nothing Trini had ever seen. "Put your hands up! ... Fucking do it!" he barked. Both men complied, Manuel seemingly out of shock.

"Did I hear right, Lucas? You got some weed for me?" Trini said gently. "Then you must be really happy to see me. Ain't that right?" Clutching his gun with a two-handed grip, Trini positioned himself so that he had a clear view of the two men and the veranda.

"What the fuck you doing in my house?" Manuel said furiously. He had recovered from the shock.

"I want you to walk towards me slowly," Trini said softly. "If you fail to do so before the count of three or you make one wrong move, you're going to end up in a wheelchair for the rest of your life. One ... Two ..." Manuel began walking towards him slowly. "Stop and turn around and lie on the floor."

"What're you up to?' said Manuel.

"Just do it!'

Manuel turned around and went down on his knees. He lay on his stomach reluctantly. All the while, Trini kept his eye on Ice Pick. He took two quick steps towards him and floored him with a karate kick straight to his face. Ice Pick's head jerked back and he dropped to the floor like a felled tree. Blood trickled out of his nose. Trini knew he wouldn't have to worry about him since he would be out for a while. "Stay on the floor!" he told Manuel warningly. He frisked Ice Pick. He found a gun in a holster strapped around his waist. It was concealed by his oversized, baggy shirt. He also found a penknife and a cell phone in his trouser pockets. Moving like a shadow, he did the same to Manuel. He found an iPhone 6s and his Bereta handgun. He quickly emptied the bullets from both guns and dropped them into his pocket. He tossed the guns unto the sofa. Stepping away from Manuel, he said, "Okay, you can stand up now."

Manuel pushed up off the floor and sprang to his feet, his face livid. "I'll make you pay for this!" he screamed.

"It's all over, my friend. You know it is. I can see it in your eyes," said Trini, gazing pitifully at him.

"First, these two maniacs break into my house – then you! What kind of madness is this? Who the hell do you think you are? You're not even a fucking cop anymore."

"I warned you that judgment day would come. It's here. And this time I'll make damned sure you don't slip away, *you dirty piece of shit*!"

Manuel began pacing back and forth and looked extremely agitated. "I blame Scorpion for this," he said in a strangled voice. "He should have nailed your ass, just like he shot that asshole superintendant, whatever the fuck his name was!"

Trini's face began twitching. He lifted the gun and aimed it at Manuel's head, focusing on a spot right between his eyes. "Just imagine, I could save this country a lot of grief with just one shot – here and now. You know how tempting that is?"

Manuel smiled. He went over and sat on a chair. He folded his arms and stretched out his legs and gave Trini a contemptuous stare. "You want to shoot me? Is that it? You've graduated from a chief inspector and ex-DEA agent to a petty housebreaker threatening to murder people; how the mighty have fallen. Every day hypocrites like you preach and moralize about justice and 'upholding the law.' Yet here you are, breaking into my house like the fucking Joker in Batman, and threatening to shoot me between the eyes. But despite that, you want to put people away for breaking the law. Now tell me, who's a greater threat to this country, me or you?"

Trini gave him a wily grin. "Nice speech. Why didn't you become a pastor instead? ... I've just been visiting your warehouse downstairs. A massive undertaking. Someone should nominate you for the Chamber of Commerce 'Entrepreneur of the Year' award."

Manuel shot out of the chair as if it had suddenly burst into flames. The expression on his face was a hideous blend of rage, shock and utter disbelief. He looked as if he was about to suffocate. He unleashed a barrage of expletives that almost winded Trini. "*Motherfucker*! I promise you, you're going to pay for this! Just remember – I've got lots of influence and powerful friends in high places," he yelled.

Trini laughed. "Dream on ... By the way, don't count on the cavalcade. They're missing in action – permanently ... Where's the Kadija girl? Where are you goons taking her?"

"Go fuck yourself!"

Someone gasped in the hallway. Trini turned and saw a woman standing there gaping at him in shock. Manuel lunged at him with the aggressive force of a rugby tackle. Trini saw him coming out of the corner of his eye but he reacted too late. The impact knocked him off his feet and sent him crashing to the floor. The back of his head struck a chair and the gun flew out of his hand. Manuel rained down punches on him, pummeling him with brute force, left, right and centre. Although slightly dazed, Trini managed to curl his body and cover up, and deflected most of the punches which were aimed at his head and upper torso. The few that were on target landed solidly and made him wince. Manuel's strength amazed him. Trini bore the pain and waited for an opening that he knew would come because of Manuel's desperation and highly emotional state. He could feel him breathing hard. Manuel eased off on the punching. Trini struck, hitting him in the solar plexus. Manuel groaned and rolled off him.

Both men rose to their feet. Manuel charged at Trini but Trini counterattacked with a martial arts foot sweep and knocked him off balance. Manuel spotted Trini's gun on the floor, about a foot away from him. He pounced on it and straightened up. Trini had anticipated it and was waiting. He flew in with a jumping front kick that caught Manuel square in the groin. He let out a squeal and buckled, then collapsed to the floor, writhing in pain. He lost his grip on the gun. Trini coolly walked over and picked it up. He pressed the barrel against Manuel's forehead.

"I believe earlier you were saying something about my buddy, the late Assistant Superintendant Foucher," he said quietly.

Manuel took a minute to get his wind back. Glaring at Trini, he said, sneeringly, "Screw you! And screw Foucher too. He deserves to be where he is – six feet deep and rotting in hell!"

Trini's hand began trembling. His finger was still on the trigger. His lips twitched grotesquely.

"This one's for Foucher," he said softly.

"No!"

Both Trini and Manuel froze. They turned at the same time to gape at Vernon. "No," Vernon repeated. "Don't do it! Don't let him bring you down this way."

Trini squeezed his eyes shut and reopened them. He stood still. He felt someone take the gun from his hand. Vernon stepped away from him. "Call the police. Go on, *do it*!" Vernon snapped.

Trini spotted Manuel's phone on the sofa where he had tossed it earlier. He went over and took it, dialed a number and waited.

"Hey, Errol," he said to the person on the other end of the line. "I have Lucas Manuel here and he's dying to see you. I'm calling you from his home and with his phone ... No questions, just get out of bed and get your guys and come up to Maison de Royaume ...*now*." He cut the call.

"You cops never learn! You're all assholes!" Manuel stormed. "You can't touch me. I'm too powerful for you."

"Yeah, right," said Trini.

Ice Pick stirred.

"Keep your eye on that worm." Trini said to Vernon. He went and sat down on the sofa to wait for Inspector Miller and his men.

49

The Soufriere waterfront was completely deserted when a rented SUV pulled up at 3:30 a.m. near a street light and behind a Hyundai car, the only other vehicle parked in the area. Seated at the wheel of the SUV was Vernon Allain. Rudy was fast asleep in the passenger seat beside him. Left to Vernon, he would have driven straight to the guest house where he had checked in the day before, and the two of them could have cooled out there till later in the morning. However, Rudy would have none of it. He insisted on returning to his own hotel room to sleep off the rest of the morning. He also said he didn't fancy leaving the Hyundai on the waterfront where he'd parked it before sailing off with Aaron on the dinghy.

When they left Maison de Royaume half an hour ago, the place was still crawling with cops. By now, Manuel and Ice Pick would already have been in custody. An ambulance had been summoned to transport Jeremie to the Soufriere Hospital. Vernon drove off after it left the villa, while Aaron went down to the police station, hoping to get a chance to speak to Larry. Vernon knew there was no chance of that happening and he'd tried telling that to Aaron but he wouldn't hear of it. He figured Aaron had probably been thinking that his aristocratic credentials and white skin would be enough to sway Miller and his men at the station.

Vernon thought about Larry for a moment. Personally, he couldn't see the cops keeping him in custody for more than seventy-two hours in a bid to put him under pressure and see what they could pin on him. Not even Trini believed that they could legitimately hold him longer than that. Their investigation of the two murders, including that of the Ukranian, was their primary focus at the moment. The evidence linking Larry to either of them was flimsy at best.

It was a slightly different matter with Kadija. Thinking of her made Vernon feel quite despondent. Notwithstanding all the shocking details that had been revealed to him about her over the past few hours, he still found it hard to believe any of it, especially recalling the gruesome and barbaric nature of Olive Henry's murder. That Kadija could have been capable of such insanity just didn't seem possible. This was a young woman whom he knew from since she was a baby. He and Kadija's mother, Emma, were first cousins. He recalled that he and his wife, now deceased, would encourage Emma to send Kadija over to spend time with them and their daughter, Cecelia. The two kids were in infant school at the time and were around the same age. Often, he would have Kadija perched on his lap while he read kiddie stories to her, or he'd just fool around with her and Cecelia. Those were the years just prior to him being transferred from the mainland to head the police station on Elysian Island. As a toddler, Kadija used to be a very sprightly and endearing child. Her mother used to work for Edward as a nanny to his two children. She was married and had had no other children.

Some years later, she left Elysian Island and moved to Jamaica with Kadija who was ten at the time. Back then, Vernon had wished he could have prevented the move. Emma and her husband had been having a stormy relationship for much of their marriage. Often it would be over Kadija. Her husband was convinced that Kadija was not his child. On several occasions he would subject both of them to mental and emotional abuse. Even Edward was forced to intervene at one point and he threatened to have Emma's husband arrested.

Soon after that, the couple broke up and Emma's husband migrated to Jamaica where he'd gotten a job at one of the Sandals hotels. He had previously worked at the Halcyon Beach Bar on Elysian Island. Kadija was seven at the time. Three years later, Emma and her husband came to some sort of rapprochement and she was seduced into joining him in Jamaica.

Vernon recalled how he and his wife had pleaded with her to leave Kadija in their care but she refused to go without the child. One year after they settled in Jamaica, Emma was dead, murdered by her husband during an altercation which turned violent. He was arrested and convicted and sentenced to twenty years in prison. Kadija was subsequently adopted by his sister who had also been residing in Jamaica.

As a former police inspector with two decades of experience in policing, Vernon had had to contend with scores of hardened thugs and suspects in violent crimes, many of whom were later proven to have been victims of emotional, physical and sexual abuse as children. But even then, none of them, as far as he could recall, had ever resorted to acts of such vicious and coldblooded barbarity as the one that had been perpetrated on Olive. On that basis alone, the idea that Kadija, whom he had once looked upon as his daughter, could be capable of such a heinous level of evil was, to him, unthinkable.

When he found out, a few days ago, that she had suddenly vanished from the island following the alleged discovery of Olive's phone and other related incidents leading up to it, he'd had to concede that her departure had seemed rather convenient, and for a while his faith was shaken.

But despite that, the revelation of her abduction by two of Manuel's gangsters had sent him into a murderous rage. Fortunately for Manuel, the police were present when he learnt of it from Trini. At that point, he regretted preventing Trini from killing him.

The cops later went in search of the two well-known ruffians, Gaeboo and Valence, but so far he hadn't received word from them whether or not Kadija had been found alive.

Vernon sighed and his head dropped slowly onto the steering wheel. He felt drained.

Rudy stirred. He opened his eyes and sat up. "What time is it?" he said.

"Three forty-five," Vernon replied, gazing at his watch.

"Damn! I went out like a light. God knows, I'm bushed ... Any word yet on Kadija?"

"Not yet?"

"She killed Olive. I have no doubt about it."

Vernon's face tightened. He said nothing.

"The only thing I can't understand," Rudy continued, "is why. What could have driven her to commit such a horrific act?"

"It's a good thing we're not living in the Dark Ages. By now you would be leading the charge to have her burnt at the stake!"

Rudy glanced sharply at Vernon. "I may be wrong but you sound a bit touchy and defensive. What's up?"

"Give the girl a break, for God's sake. She's innocent until proven guilty."

Rudy could feel Vernon's agitation and he found it baffling. The two men went quiet for a while.

"She hated Edward's guts. Do you know that?' said Rudy.

"What?"

"Kadija. She despised Edward. At least she made that plain to me. I couldn't figure out why."

"She probably had good reason to." Vernon spoke softly, as if to himself.

"What do you mean? What reason could she have to hate him, and so intensely?"

Vernon hesitated, a grim look on his face. "Edward is her father."

"What!"

"He all but admitted it to me some years ago when I confronted him about it. He had a brief fling with Kadija's mother. Her name was Emma. We were cousins. She's dead now. She used to work for Edward. He told me the two of them had a one-night stand. According to him, it happened while he was in a drunken state, after one of his late-night bacchanals. She was engaged to be married at the time. Two months later, by which time she had been married, she found out she was pregnant. Everyone looked upon her husband as Kadija's father, except the guy himself. He always insisted Kadija was not his child and he got criticized a lot for that. He treated her very badly.

"Emma eventually migrated to Jamaica, along with Kadija, to join her husband. He'd found a job over there. Just before she left, I cornered her and pressured her to tell me the truth about Kadija and whether or not Edward could have been her father. She eventually admitted to me that she believed he was, although a paternity test was never done to confirm it. She also said Edward had offered to provide the child with a trust fund after she brought up the subject of her pregnancy with him one day. She turned him down flat. She said they never really discussed Kadija's paternity at length but she took Edward's offer of a trust fund as proof that he too believed that he was the father. She left it at that because she felt that she wouldn't be able to cope with the fallout, not just with her husband but also with Edward's wife and children.

"A few years ago when Kadija returned to live on Elysian Island, I was tempted to bring up the topic with her but, for some reason, I decided against it. I guess I didn't have the nerve to. But then, like you, I did notice that she had developed an antipathy towards Edward, which was a radical departure from the way she had initially reacted towards him. At first they seemed to get on quite cordially, but then, gradually, things changed, at least where she was concerned."

"Were you ever able to figure out what caused the change?"

"I'm not sure."

"Didn't you ever think of asking her?"

Vernon shrugged. "Maybe I didn't really feel like dwelling on it. It's her business. She's a grown woman."

Both men sat in silence listening to the surf rolling in and out. Suddenly, Rudy sat upright and stared quizzically at Vernon. "Wait a minute!" he said. "Does Kadija know that Edward is her father?"

"I don't know."

"Olive ... how did Olive and Kadija get along?"

"They didn't. They hardly spoke to each other."

"You mean *Kadija* hardly ever spoke to Olive ... Right?'

"Put it however you want."

"I'm not putting it how I want, that's the way it was – wasn't it? Edward thought the world of Olive and made no bones about it. Chances are he didn't pay a fraction as much attention to Kadija. If she believed him to be her father, imagine how that would make her feel. And I'll tell you something else; that chick is extremely vindictive and she has a hell of an obsessive streak. I saw clear evidence of it and experienced it first-hand. Not forgetting, too, that she's a weirdo. As I recall, the first time I ended up on the wrong side of her was the day I declined her invitation to her party in favor of a date with Olive a couple days before the La Rose festival. Trust me brother, you don't want to get on the wrong side of this woman ... I believe Olive did, maybe without even realizing it."

"Quit speculating, it won't get you anywhere," Vernon said testily.

"And you know what else? ... That Larry Thompson guy seems cowed by her for some reason, like she has some kind of hold over him. How close are they?"

Vernon hesitated. Finally, he responded, almost grudgingly. "They get on well. They became friends while she was in America. Whenever he popped in to see his family, he always checked her out and they'd party and have fun together with mutual friends of their age group on the island." Vernon paused a while, thinking and then added, sounding defensive, "Bill and Jacqui Thompson like her very much and they admired her artwork. They thought the world of her."

"Are she and Larry lovers?"

"You'll have to ask them," said Vernon coldly.

"God help him if they are! She's a black widow in every sense of the word ... In any case someone wanted to punish me by pinning Olive's murder on me. That's how my necklaces ended up being stolen and turned up next to her body. This was a sick, evil and vindictive act – the product of a twisted mind! Kadija may be a brilliant artist and much more besides but take it from me, she has a very sick mind. She needs help."

Vernon turned on the ignition. "Are you leaving or not? I got to go. I need some rest," he said coldly.

Rudy looked quite taken aback. Reluctantly, he opened the door. As he was about to step out of the SUV, Vernon's cell phone rang. Vernon took it and glanced at the touchscreen. "It's Trini," he said. "Hi, what's up?" He paused a while listening. In the dim light of the lamp post, his face lit up. "Oh, thank you Jesus!" he exclaimed. He looked as if he was struggling to hold himself together. Eventually he hung up.

"What happened?" said Rudy anxiously.

"Kadija ... She's alive. She's safe. The police found her and the two guys."

"Where did they find her?"

"I don't know. Trini wasn't sure. Listen, I really have to go. I'll see you later." He reversed the vehicle and drove off.

Rudy gaped bemusedly at the SUV until it disappeared from view. He turned and headed for the Hyundai, shaking his head.

50

The three travel bags bunched together in the living room gave Bridget a jolt when she saw them. She really shouldn't have been surprised since Rudy had already made it clear he would be leaving. His mind was made up. She stood there staring at the bags without seeing them. She was thinking of her ex-fiancé, Clint. Early one morning as she sat in her living room sipping a cup of tea and watching 'CBS This Morning,' she saw him walk past all dressed up with his hold-all slung over his shoulder. He paused near the front door and said, without meeting her eyes, that he'd changed his mind about their engagement. It was over, and he was leaving – for good. He'd had enough of the constant tension and bickering in their relationship. His departure had been sudden and unexpected. The night before, they'd actually had a rare moment of flirtation and closeness and they'd made fantastic love.

As she recalled, what had touched her most was not so much the thought of Clint leaving but rather the tenuousness and fragility of human relationships; the suddenness with which they could collapse and disintegrate, notwithstanding the tremendous amount of time and emotional energy that may have gone into building them up in the first place. Like a building undergoing demolition, one minute the relationship was there, seemingly firm and holding up, the next minute it was gone.

At the very least, she'd known where she stood as she watched her ex standing before her, too coward to watch her in the eye, telling her it was over. And when he walked out and she heard the door shut, she had no doubt that it was done between them. Rather than allowing their relationship to languish in pain and uncertainty, he had at least had the guts to kill it and put them out of their misery.

Not so with Rudy. Physically, he was leaving but not really leaving. His words. It was so like Rudy, she thought. Still not able to make up his mind exactly what he wanted out of life, and even when he felt he knew, he still didn't seem to have the ability to clearly articulate it to himself nor the balls to go after it and claim it. Although initially she'd been hopeful, Bridget was now beginning to realize that this aspect of Rudy's nature would probably never change.

From her perspective, in terms of her hopes and expectations regarding their relationship, Rudy was a failed project.

She still loved him. That would never change. She had believed him when he said he loved her, and she still did. But he also felt threatened by her – or to be more precise, by her professional success and her wealth, and most of all, her spirit of independence.

The same as Edward. As for him, it was now almost a week since he returned to England, according to him for a brief sabbatical before he headed off to Tanzania to start life afresh at the age of sixty-seven, as he'd threatened to do. It was over between them and that was that. They had both agreed to a divorce. Bridget smiled ruefully. From having two men in her life, she was now at risk of losing both of them.

The truth of the matter was that neither Rudy nor Edward was willing to put up with her stubborn refusal to accept or validate their beliefs of what constituted womanhood. She was trying to be too equal, too empowered.

Increasingly, she was beginning to realize that whoever she chose to spend the rest of her life with, be it Rudy or some other man, she would have to suppress part of herself so that he could feel safe and secure, and masculine.

A door slammed. Rudy entered the living room, smiling.

"Hi baby, I didn't hear you come in ... What's the matter, are you okay?" he said.

"Yes, I'm fine," said Bridget. She gazed at the bags again, and then at him. "So this is it?'

Rudy nodded. "I need a break from here. Besides, I've got stuff back home I need to sort out – my job, my apartment and all the rest of it."

"Have you met with Clifford?"

"Oh yeah. He's the real deal. A top-notch legal mind. I know now, for sure, I'm in the clear and that's a huge load off my mind. I'll be returning to provide testimony at the trial, as needed."

"Aside from that, how long will you be gone?"

Rudy glanced away. "Not sure. We'll see."

"Should I keep my hopes up?"

Rudy took Bridget's hand, kissed it affectionately and squeezed it. "I love you baby, you know that. But I think Elysian Island has come between us. It's always going to be in the way."

Bridget smiled and gave him an earnest stare. "I want you to know that this island has been very good to me. It's like a pair of magic shoes that have taken me to new lands and greater heights than I could ever have imagined. In so many ways I feel grateful to everyone and everything here ... honestly. But I've realized – and at the risk of sounding cheesy, I'm going to wax poetic – to gain entry into your heart and claim your love, I would have to walk in without those magic shoes. I would have to leave part of me at the door."

Rudy glanced away and pretended to brush lint from a woolen cap on the handle of one of the bags. He changed the subject.

"How's Edward? Have you heard from him?"

"No, but I have received the divorce papers."

Rudy peered through narrowed eyes at Bridget. "Are you guys really going through with this?"

"Of course. A few weeks from now I'll be free and single again."

"What about Blossom House?"

"It's been put up for sale."

"I guess that's the least of your worries."

There was an awkward moment of silence. Rudy shoved his hands in his pockets and shifted from one leg to the other. He seemed uncomfortable all of a sudden. "I got an email from him last night," he said.

"From whom?"

"Edward."

"Really? What about?"

"The book. He said he'd be in England for a bit and wanted to know if we could meet to resume from where we left off."

Bridget shook her head and laughed. "What did you tell him?"

"I'll think about it."

Bridget gave Rudy a long, thoughtful stare. A wan smile flitted across her lips. "No matter what, I will always love you. You know that, don't you?"

"Of course I do … I love you too. Besides, I won't be gone forever."

Again, that feeble smile flitted across Bridget's face. "So long, Rudy. Please take care of yourself." She turned and walked out the door.

Shit! Rudy flung the cap across the room. He went and plonked himself down on the couch. This was not the sort of parting he had hoped for. Listening to the sound of Bridget's car driving off, his instinctive urge was to rush out and beg her to stop. His heart kept screaming at him to do it but for some reason he just sat there, paralyzed.

The odd thing about it was that all the while Bridget and Edward were together, he'd thought nothing of putting his life on hold and dropping everything to travel to the Caribbean just to be with her. The fact that she was married hadn't deterred him in the least. He'd felt a passionate longing for her and yearned to be with her. He truly believed with all his heart that he was in love with her. This, plus the fact that she was unhappy in her marriage, had made him feel justified in pursuing her. Now her marriage had finally come to an end. He knew without a doubt that she could be his for the taking. So why was he suddenly afraid to step into Edward's shoes? Why was he backing off? What was he afraid of?

Initially, could it have been just the allure of the forbidden fruit that made him so besotted with her? That coupled with the ineffable thrill of being sought after by an incredibly beautiful, rich white woman.

For now, he couldn't decide. He felt a bit confused.

As for Bridget's career ambitions, that was a whole different matter. The night before, in between puffs of weed, he'd sat musing over this, and the motivations of people like Edward and Bill Thompson, and all of Elysian Island's elites. It dawned on him that they all had one thing in common; they were fighting to protect what they treasured most. Like territorial animals urinating around their turf, they were prepared to do whatever it takes to guard and protect their lives of exclusivity and privilege. After all, this was what gave them a sense of self worth.

He couldn't say the same about himself. Prior to coming to Elysian Island his life had been an exercise of going round and round in circles, not making much headway and unable to find the centre. He was heading back for more of the same. But to some extent, his outlook on life had undergone a reboot and there were some things he needed to reconsider. Lots to think about.

His feelings for Bridget would not change. That he knew for sure. Maybe away from Elysian Island he'd be able to think more clearly and be more honest with himself about that.

It was hard to believe that he'd been on Elysian Island for only a month. It had felt more like thirty years rather than thirty days, so much had happened during that time.

He got up and went out unto the porch. It was an incredibly beautiful day. He glanced at his watch. Ten-thirty. His flight to the UK was scheduled for four. He had a lunch date with Amanda at one. She and her family were due to return home to the US the next day. Rudy smiled. He was looking forward to meeting her.

The End